MARGARET STORM JAMESON

was born in Whitby, Yorkshire, on 8 January 1891. Her forebears had lived in Whitby, then a small fishing and shipbuilding port, for uncounted generations: her grandfather was a shipowner, her father a sea-captain. She was educated at a private school, followed by one year at the Municipal School in Scarborough. Awarded one of the only three County Scholarships available in the North Riding of Yorkshire at that time, she took an honours degree in English Language and Literature at Leeds University in 1912 and was given a one-year research scholarship, to be held at University College, London: she found University College dull, and transferred herself to King's College. Her thesis, on Modern Drama in Europe, finally approved by Leeds University, was rewarded by the Degree of Master of Arts; it was published in 1920, by the firm of William Collins. In the meantime she had married and had a son.

In 1919 she returned to London, becoming for a year a copywriter in a large advertising agency. She published her first novel, and began a two-year editorship of an obscure weekly magazine, *New Commonwealth*. From 1923 to 1925 she acted as the English representative of the American publisher Alfred A. Knopf, and later, for two and a half years, was co-manager, with her second husband, Guy Patterson Chapman, of the short-lived publishing house of Alfred A. Knopf in London. She married Guy Chapman in 1925, a deeply happy marriage, broken in 1972 by his death, after a distinguished career beginning with the publication in 1933 of *A Passionate Prodigality*, his classic account of trench warfare in France, and ending in a study of the politics and history of the Third Republic of France.

Between the years of 1919 and 1979 Storm Jameson published a total of forty-five novels. She has also written short stories, literary essays, criticism, and a two-volume autobiography. In 1939 she became the first woman president of the British section of International PEN, where she was an outspoken liberal and anti-Nazi, and a friend and helper of refugee writers. In 1952 she was a delegate to the UNESCO Congress of the Arts, held in Venice. She was awarded a D.Litt. from Leeds University in 1943, and is a member of the American Academy and Institute of Arts and Letters. With her husband, she has been an inveterate traveller, mostly in Europe. She now lives in Cambridge.

Of her fiction Virago publish *Women Against Men, Company Parade, Love in Winter* and *None Turn Back*; they also publish her autobiography *Journey From the North*.

NONE TURN BACK

STORM JAMESON

With a New Introduction by Elaine Feinstein

Virago

Published by VIRAGO PRESS Limited 1984
41 William IV Street, London WC2N 4DB

First published in Great Britain by Cassell & Co. Ltd 1936

British Library Cataloguing in Publication Data

Jameson, Storm
 None turn back. – (Virago modern classics)
 I. Title
 823'.912[F]   PR6019.A67
 ISBN 0-86068-320-6

Printed in Finland by Werner Söderström Oy, a member of Finnprint

FOR

BEATRICE KEAN SEYMOUR

INTRODUCTION

By the early thirties, Storm Jameson had come to feel herself
enveloped by the great political issues of her age. The encroaching
brutalities of fascism threatened everything she most loved in
Europe. 'In 1933 this explained for me everything in sight . . . I
had the key . . . The Error—mine—was that I tried to open
everything with it, beginning with my novels.'

Her obsession was not an error; it led to her joining Anti-Fascist
Committees usefully, even while she observed, with remarkable
acumen, the several members who believed in the system of Russian
Communism with uncritical naiveté. But it was also one of the
factors that lead to her abandoning *The Mirror in Darkness* sequence
after this novel.

When she declared herself writing 'against the grain of my
talent', it was not because she felt herself inadequate to the broad
canvas of political events. She had a true gift for understanding the
temptations upper-class Englishmen felt for fascist principles. And
she is always right about the smell of poverty. Other socialist writers
might have to explore the houses of the poor to get their details right,
but Storm Jameson knew in her bones exactly what it meant to scrape
at dirty pans with a fingernail, sift out the ashes in the grate at six
a.m., or set a little cake in front of an ill-fed child as a treat. She is too
hard on herself when she declares; 'No single novel of the series had
a clear centre.' Certainly Nicholas and Hervey's difficult and yet
passionate need for one another forms a hard kernel in *Love in
Winter*. And *None Turn Back* vibrates with the same relationship,
terrifyingly precarious, in spite of marriage and the desperation
they share. All the intimate torments of the heart are recorded with a
nearly-miraculous sanity and hope.

Some of her reasons for rejecting the series seem to spring
naturally to the lips of Hervey Russell herself, through whose
consciousness we now mainly perceive the events of the book.

In the end I don't want money, I want to be alone, I want to think and
write a few words as sharp as bones, not write as I do, every day and all day,
thinking of money and debts.

Storm Jameson was learning to do precisely that; even though she brings little new to our apprehension of the General Strike. She is learning, even as she sets down the earliest quarrels with Nicholas which terrify them both; even as Hervey makes a gallant bid for a love she needs as much as life.

'I know,' she said painfully, 'you don't want me as you wanted your wife, Jenny—to possess all my mind and body. Yet I can't endure it when you make it so plain. It is like a knife in me. That's rather queer, isn't it?'

'No, I don't think so,' he said, 'It is natural you should want that from me. Only I can't. I don't want it.' He saw her face and said quickly: 'I know I hurt you, and I know I shall go on hurting you. I wish sometimes you had never come to me. But I need you—you know that.'

It is Hervey who understands how much she will have to see and accept without complaint if she is to keep Nicholas at her side. The whole novel turns on her recognition that she must continue to give all her energy and strength to a man exhausted emotionally before he fell into her hands. Her whole Yorkshire nature must have called upon her to save herself; but she stifled the impulse almost before it reached her consciousness. Well or ill, she is going to have only herself to depend upon.

Some of the best writing in the book rises from Storm Jameson's description of the surgery on Hervey's womb which proves to be necessary; and her subsequent gallant convalescence. In her autobiography, *Journey From the North*, Storm Jameson records the experience as her own; a dry account, with no self-pity, which frequently uses the very words of *None Turn Back*. (Even the sympathetic nurse who is not allowed to give her morphia calls her 'Poor Rabbit' in both accounts.) The awakening from anaesthetic into unbearable loneliness and pain is one of the finest passages in the book.

Of the characters who develop from the earlier novels, perhaps Julian Swan is the most remarkable, as he begins to take the centre of the plot into his hands. Unquestionably, he represents the greatest internal threat England has to face at that time. As Hervey observes him, she is struck . . .

as though this were the first time she had really seen him, by the strange blankness of his face. It was made of smooth, impenetrable planes of flesh, seeming shockingly dull, but the small full mouth looked cruel. He is training himself to be outside human feelings, she thought. He could now watch men being flogged without noticing that they were suffering. She was startled and saddened.

But he is drawn in depth. We enter below those terrifying planes of flesh. He, too, is possessed by love, maddened by desire for Nicholas' elegantly beautiful sister, Georgina. It is not a love that promises fruition; but Storm Jameson is accurate and honest enough to record Georgina's little flicker of excitement as she senses his longing for spilt blood and battle. True, as the novel proceeds, it is not only his political enemies, but sad and starved-looking Jews of either sex that he longs to see smashed. And we are not invited to sympathise with his growing neurosis.

The powers that decide the outcome of the 1926 General Strike are complex; and Storm Jameson barely attempts more than an etching of victors and vanquished. For Hervey, it is a battle fought through committees, letters, and signatures to be cajoled out of the famous. All this was something Storm Jameson was very concerned with at the time of writing *None Turn Back*, though in another cause.

One of the people Hervey approached was Ridley; and his refusal annoys her. But Storm Jameson herself must have had some sympathy for the reason he gave. 'When I want to do something for those poor brutes of miners, I'll write a good novel about them.' It was how he felt writers should help; and it may well have been how Storm Jameson was feeling as she put this novel aside. The defeat rankles in Hervey but, at the same time, she does not dismiss his refusal as self-seeking caution.

When Storm Jameson put *The Mirror in Darkness* to one side, many of her best novels remained to be written. I can only draw the reader's attention to *Cousin Honoré* and *Europe to Let*, and to her *Journey From the North*. But readers who have followed the central characters as they grow through the first two books of this series will not be disappointed in *None Turn Back*.

Elaine Feinstein, Cambridge, 1983

III

NONE TURN BACK

Thursday, May 6th
UNREAL CITY

CHAPTER I

HERVEY awoke very early, on the thought that she was alone in her house with her sleeping son. She lay quite still, in a room in a house far from the road, and quiet with trees. At this hour the light flowed into her room over and between leaves and branches, lightly changed by them. The sun was on the lower slopes of his climb, so low yet that his brightness was a thought of her own mind. She waited for sounds—the first bird notes, as cool as the air, the same sound a woman waking at this hour it might be ten centuries ago had heard. Listening and waiting Hervey heard then leaves sliding on leaves, the creak of a rafter above her head.

She felt an exquisite happiness. It sprang from a sense of being alone in a new world, alone in the house. For a moment other rooms in other houses came to life in this one, so that she felt herself living a score of lives, like a tree unfolding in every leaf. She was the child blessed with endless days, the young wife feeling her tireless strength before the day's tasks—and now that life, distant and too hard, yielded its sweetness into her surprised hand. But it had waited ten years, until this moment, to reveal itself.

She moved her arm to feel the coolness of the sheets. The watch at her side had moved less than two minutes past the half-hour—half-past five—since she awoke. The quietness of the house lay in front of her, smooth water in sunlight, now inviting her. She got up and went downstairs, listening first at the boy's door. The room beyond it, her husband's, stood empty and tidy—yet it seemed more lived-in than her own. Hervey made little mark on the places she lived in, as though she were always on the point of a journey, or had not been told she might stay.

The emptiness and stillness of the house closed over her. Even the movement of her arms gave her happiness. She opened the windows in the living-room and looked out, taking the light shock of the ripples of air on her body. These fields below her house were not the country, they were a crumb, a morsel of green dropped by accident between two claws of outer London, with this small house in the middle of them. It was not even a charming house, worth saving—it had been built of singularly ugly stone in the year of the Great Exhibition in Hyde Park, by a builder who wanted to live in it himself and would have liked a castle. It had six rooms and four turrets. But it was as solid as a cliff and from the mullioned windows no other house was visible, only trees and grass. A line of pear trees in blossom dazzled the sky above the farthest field.

Hervey made herself tea in the kitchen and sat drinking it and reading. There cannot possibly be a purer pleasure than to drink tea and read, at six o'clock of a fine spring morning, alone in your own house—better than alone, with your son safe and asleep upstairs. She turned the pages of the book, as delighted by it as by the first sharp taste of the tea. To read Giraudoux's *Bella* for the first time is as strange as a journey to Thibet. She had just reached the evening when Fontranges, ' this gentle, ignorant, good creature,' calls on my father and my uncles in their disgrace. No one else has been near them, he may be the last survivor of human kind; and to entertain him, these distinguished men bring out all their gifts, and Fontranges takes them with as much simplicity—he inquires about lighthouses; they promise to make and show him models. Although he is never able to come back, the models are made, and for some nights people in Paris can see the lights flashing from Marly—' it was my uncles signalling to the last man.'

With a smile of pleasure, Hervey shut the book: she sat

for a few moments listening to the words in her mind and to water dropping slowly into the stone sink, drip, drop, drop, drop. This sound seemed to have been going on a long time, all her life, in fact.

At last she stirred. Rinsing her cup she glanced at the calendar on the wall. Five days, she thought, and nodded to it.

Five weeks ago, while Nicholas waited in the next room, she listened with an air of calm to the surgeon who was telling her what would now have to be done. The surgeon, an older woman, did not know whether she was sensible or pretending to be. ' How old are you? ' ' Thirty-two.' ' Why didn't you come to me eight years ago? '

Hervey looked at her, not able to explain that women like herself and her mother do not run out to doctors with a mere pain. ' At first it was not unbearable.'

' Well,' the surgeon began. She smiled instead with much kindness. ' Shall we fix the day now? '

' If you like,' Hervey said, politely.

She was not surprised, although she had not expected anything of this when she came. It confirmed something her body had known for a long time, without ever finding the proper moment in which to speak about it to her mind. She had had dreams in which a knife was thrust without pain or sight into her womb, even a waking thought of it. She was afraid, but she was ashamed to let this woman see it.

' I shall be able to work shortly afterwards, shan't I? ' she asked cunningly.

' Of course not. Not for six months at least. Perhaps not for a year.'

By this and by that way, in the next weeks, Hervey learned all she could understand about this particular operation. Not to know would have vexed her beyond patience. Now there were only five days left, but she had made all her plans and no one except Nicholas knew how much she feared it.

She thought seldom about it, and it did not spoil the flavour of tea or of *Bella*.

As soon as she was dressed she went to her son's room to wake him. He lay with his face pressed into the pillow, little to see except the angle of a red-brown cheek. In sleep he was still her child; the instant in which he awoke and looked at her out of fierce blue eyes divided them. If he only talked more readily, she would think: are all ten-year-old boys as silent?

She touched him gently. 'Wake up, Richard. It's time.' He roused at once, and moved his long thin body so that it made a resistant knot inside the blankets. She reminded him that he was starting for Yorkshire within an hour, in the kind Waleys' car. At that he sat up, half asleep still, yawning and stretching. He was going to her mother in Danesacre, and he would not hear anything about the operation until it was over—but it was strange that she had no idea whether he would have minded it, she knew so little about him. Leaving him to dress, she went away to prepare their breakfast.

In a few minutes he came downstairs and came straight to her, holding out a letter. 'Look at this awful letter,' he said; 'whatever shall we do about it?'

Hervey read: '*Dear Sir, On the 3rd April, we had the pleasure of sending you a copy of our Catalogue giving full particulars of the various lenses and cameras we manufacture and supply, but up to the time of writing, do not appear to have been favoured with a further communication from you. . . .*'

Richard's eyes watched her face as she read. 'It came one day when you were out.'

'This doesn't mean anything,' Hervey said gently. 'They sent it because they had your address. It is—a sort of advertisement by post.' He has been carrying this about with him, she thought, for ten days.

'Are you quite sure? It reads to me like a summons.'

'It's not.' She explained the method. Nothing could

have made her so happy as these words—' like a summons '—
they were the proof that, for all his silences, he did trust her.

' Eat your breakfast,' she said joyously.

In his sharp relief Richard's spirits rose to the end of
his tongue: he talked comfortably to her on their way
through the field to the road and the Waleys' car, even
asking her, with an insistent smile, why she was not coming
to Danesacre, although this gave away the fact that he much
disliked travelling with strangers.

' I'll come up in July,' Hervey said. It did not occur
even to her body that there was a possibility of her not
coming at all. She felt unshakably strong and happy.

He took no more notice of her when he was in the car.
She tried to talk to him, but he was interested only in the
car, asking Mr. Waley about the engine and how fast it
could go. He seemed to know a little about engines.

' We must be starting,' Mrs. Waley whispered to her.

' Good-bye now, Richard,' she said.

' Good-bye,' he said, glancing at her. He did not smile
at her; he seemed indifferent.

When the car was out of sight she went back to the house
and prepared it for the woman who came in at ten. Then
she walked down the road again to the garage. The garage
man talked to her while she looked in her car. ' The traffic's
all over the roads to-day, Mrs. Roxby. You should look out
you don't think of something as you drive.'

This was a joke between them. Driving a car bored her
so much that she was apt to become sunk in her thoughts,
especially in the emptier roads where there was no fear of
hurting people. The car had suffered a number of minor
injuries in her absence of mind.

' You've been driving for the strikers, haven't you? '
he went on.

' Yes,' Hervey said.

' You left this card in on Tuesday. Well, don't get
shot. There'll be plenty more General Strikes, it would

be a pity, wouldn't it, if you missed the rest by overdoing this one.'

The first part of her journey was through narrow lanes. She drove carefully at first, but soon in spite of herself her mind slipped away. It was a relief that Richard was going to Yorkshire, out of any possible trouble—it would take more than a General Strike to shake Danesacre, which really had not much respect for the rest of England. But Nicholas, she thought, reckoning the time before she would see him. Did she care that he had lost every penny? Not in the least—money was nothing to her: but (she took a corner suddenly) the devil in it was the money he had not lost. Not lost, not touched, the income he gave to his first wife.

But at once she was vexed with herself that she had had such a thought. She drove more slowly. When the bills have been paid, there will be nothing. She shook her hair back and thought of Nicholas's faithful secretary, Mrs. Hughes, who in two years had robbed him of more than eight hundred pounds—by the simplest of methods, you could hardly imagine any simpler unless she had been able to take the money out of his pockets. It was known to accountants as ' teeming and lading '—she pocketed the money given her in payment of bills and left them in the ledger as unpaid; before she ran away she had destroyed Nicholas's bank books, the paid-up cheques, the cash book, and made a confusion of the ledgers. Nicholas was to blame for trusting her with everything—he had actually given her blank cheques to fill in. But I don't blame him, Hervey thought—I trusted the woman myself. I liked her.

She had a strange feeling of guilt towards Mrs. Hughes, as though she ought in decency to have gone to her. The creature has hidden herself, wondering whether or not we have set the police on her. She would dearly like to tell the wretched woman, whose friend she had been, that nothing, nothing at all was being done to her. The money she stole was gone, spent, and all the rest of the money Nicholas had put into his business was gone, too. It was an end, let it be the end. I am a fool, but I am yet sorry for her.

It was the grace of God that sent me to Marcel Cohen that morning.

Coming within sight of the highway into London she saw it overflowing with vehicles of all kinds. She had barely turned into it when she was hailed to give a lift to two people, a man and his daughter, clerks in the same firm. The father reminded her of the field plants she used to press in blotting-paper as a child—he sleeps at night, she thought, smiling under her hand, between sheets of it. The Strike had worked a faint animation in him and he looked out at things along the road with a bright gentle smile. His daughter was ruddier and less gentle. They sat silent at the back— she soon forgot them. Had Marcel Cohen known that she was making use of him? But he began it, she said, frowning blackly—when he told me (he boasts) that he had taken the business of an antique dealer in payment of debts; afterwards I had only to put my thoughts into his head until in the end he asked me, himself, whether Nicholas would manage it for him. I was careful, I pretended to consider, I wrote Nicholas's letters for him—did I seem to give myself away? One thing I will not do—I don't care to ask any person for favours.

The traffic became unmanageable. She edged her way closer and closer to the kerb until at last she had one wheel over it. At last crawling into Marylebone, she shook off her passengers and found a little space in a garage. 'Another second and you'd have been welcome to stow it on the mantelpiece,' the man said, grinning.

CHAPTER II

THE city on the third day of the General Strike was freer
and livelier than a Jubilee. But these crowds were themselves
the procession. They walked it along the pavements or rolled
past in lorries and private cars or pedalled it smiling like
circus riders on bicycles. It was all the difference between
a spectacle and one of those common holidays of which we
have lost the knack. Rules were being broken, and familiar
streets skipped like rams—old clerks, seeing for the first time
houses, gardens, and buildings under which they had burrowed
for years to reach an office in Threadneedle Street, fell
passionately in love with the city as perfect as Tyrus; the
young ones counted on an adventure a day. The girls wore
high heels on their shoes to be ready for it.

Hervey was caught up in this sudden release; she believed
she could run, and not be weary. Her body felt strong and
light. She had two people to see before she met Nicholas.
Walking quickly, she passed Kensington Gardens and reached
William Ridley's house at eleven o'clock. She was shown
into a room on the first floor to wait. It was a room with
three windows, filled with furniture from the eighteenth
century—only things unblemished by time had been allowed
in. Hervey approved this. There were three book-cases and
in one of them were placed in order of birth all William
Ridley's books, one out of each edition, with the translations,
and copies bound in parchment and intended for the British
Museum at his death. Hervey did not admire these novels,
in which there were no thoughts or feelings but had been
in every purse in the kingdom for years: reading them was
an experience already too familiar. Turning any page

the reader caught sight of the nose his aunt Mary had bequeathed to all her children; or he was in a party, or a hurry, or eating, marrying, or being born, or discovering one of those truths on which the race cut its teeth. In fact they were as fine novels as you could want, for persons who like a great deal of company of an easy sort.

She did not wish Ridley to catch her looking at his books, and moved to the window. There was a glass beside it and in that she saw him come into the room. He was heavier than he had been two years before, with the face of a farmer, stubborn, sly, greedy. It was a gross face, but not brutal. It was not mean—Ridley would spend money and give it away. You could not, or Hervey could not, dislike him simply because he was acquisitive, with the vitality of the strong flesh, and never satisfied. He came forward, smiling, his little shrewd eyes, now friendly, almost disappearing behind his cheeks.

' Now,' he said warmly, ' what do *you* want? Will y'have a glass of sherry or a cup of something? It won't take the servants a minute.'

Hervey declined. She was thirsty but she wanted to get away. ' I've come to ask you to do something—not for me,' she said quickly. ' A group of writers——' with a sharp smile, she told him the names at once; but Ridley did not respect writers without money, he was not yet confident enough of his own greatness to give them marks for only the truth or for insight or revelation. Noticing this, Hervey went on:

' It seems treacherous to us for writers to show no opinions or passions at this eleventh hour, hour of decision——'

' Come now, is it all that? ' Ridley said, looking at her ironically, with suspicion.

' Yes, I think it is,' Hervey said. She was not ready to say more to him about her beliefs, but she forced herself to add: ' You know what it says—*They helped everyone his neighbour; and everyone said to his brother, Be of good courage.*

So the carpenter encouraged the goldsmith, and he that smootheth with the hammer him that smote the anvil, saying, It is ready for the soldering: and he fastened it with nails, that it should not be moved. The new England is almost ready for the soldering, but it can just as well be broken—unless——'

She stopped short. 'I haven't come to make a speech,' she muttered, smiling. 'You are so widely known that you ought to be the first signer of the letter we intend to send to both their papers——'

'A letter!' jeered Ridley.

'What shall we do then? March? What ought writers to do except write?'

'Show me your letter.'

Hervey gave it to him. She did not watch him as he read it, since she knew already what he was going to say. She was unguarded. Her mind had played her a familiar trick and with its ear to his she could hear his thoughts before he let them out; but she was only able to listen, not to fight or argue. No one does both at once.

'This is all right,' Ridley said, 'but why don't you ask Bernard Shaw?'

Hervey grinned at him: 'One can't trust him not to be clever. We don't want to set a chair for him for the sake of seeing him kick it over—it has become too dull a joke.' She waited.

'Well, I shan't sign. When I want to do something for these poor brutes of miners I'll write a good novel about them. That's *my* work, not climbing on platforms. You should know that, my girl. Do you call yourself a writer——! Now look here—writers don't serve causes in this way, they serve them by persuasion and art, I know what I'm saying and I warn you now not to lose yourself in the wilderness, by God, you'll be sorry if you do——'

You serve yourself first, Hervey thought clearly. She listened to him, with a polite smile. His loud resolute voice, his contempt for her as a dreamer, silenced her against her will. For this moment she was again a trembling uncouth girl and his voice any of the harsh voices dominating her childhood. She was submissive, anxious to avoid being punished. On a jetty of her mind, reaching backwards, a child raised her arms, a thin curve of bone and flesh, to protect her shoulders against the Malacca cane. All this was as close as the room in which she sat looking at William Ridley—but she saw, too, a new certainty, with the gold links in his cuffs, and the flesh spreading downwards from his jawbone. He prospers, she thought, because he has accepted this world and his own loneliness: five years ago he was still (at times) afraid because he knew he was alone in a world that is becoming darker and colder as though in the hour before dawn. Now he remembers this less and less often. He is making himself secure. He has bought a house, his money is well placed, he chooses his friends shrewdly, meaning to use them. Only very seldom he feels the icy wind blow against his face from some country he has never visited, and he lifts his hand—William Ridley is not a coward—but he is alone, in prison.

She looked at her wrist-watch. ' I must go at once.'

' Forget all this nonsense about neighbours,' Ridley said warmly. ' *I'm* a more comfortable neighbour than he that smootheth with the hammer—do you see? '

' Yes, yes,' Hervey said, smiling, eagerly submissive.

Outside his house, walking towards the café where T. S. Heywood would be waiting, she thought coolly about Ridley's new novel. Her mind entered it as it lay spread out, and cut through layer after layer feeling for the nerves: which were missing. Now that she could not hear Ridley she was not afraid of him.

Entering the café she saw her friend at once, at the far end. He had his back to the door. He turned his head and saw her, and smiled. His eyes were the least human thing in his face, brown and very bright, and inquisitive. In the minute before she reached him Hervey fell ten years and an awkward girl of twenty-two moved anxiously towards a young man anonymous in a uniform. She sat down.

' You're tired, you ought not to try so much,' T. S. said in a warning voice.

' Didn't we come here once during the War?'

'Where didn't we go during the War?' he grinned. ' Every capital in Europe was full of us.'

He had ordered coffee for her. She drank it eagerly, scarcely noticing the sweet taste of rum he poured in it, and gave him the message from her writers' committee. Would he, a scientist well enough and not yet too well known, prepare a manifesto for his fellow-scientists and persuade some of them to sign it?

He shook his head slowly.

' But you're on our side,' Hervey said.

' Yes,' he said, ' yes.' He let his head drop forward and folded his hands, as though he meant sitting here for hours.

Hervey looked at him. He, too, is evading us, she thought. There is nothing to be done with him. Yet she waited. She had a little time and her thoughts were confused between her love for him and her cold unloving judgment. She would never write what she thought about him, as, when the Strike was over and her operation, she intended to write truthfully about William Ridley.

' I can't run about with a manifesto in my pocket, it's not my rôle. Ask Huxley to do it—but he won't. Do you know what? the miners are beaten—they were beaten before they came out of their holes. They lost their chance in nineteen-nineteen. That was the last moment for a general strike—why, if the army had been sent home by regiments instead of men from this company and that, scattered groups, strangers, they would have started it themselves. The men who rule this country are too clever for you. They'll outlive every-thing, even their time. What is in front of us is a slow crumbling, decay, barbarism. Drink your coffee—I had a drop of rum put in it, good for you. I'm not going to waste my energy, what remains, in protests. I've furnished my room in a tower and intend to sit there and work, making records and a chart, for the eyes of our successors—men or ants. Don't ask me to do anything for you.'

Hervey nodded. ' You'll do as you please '—as you are made, she thought. ' Thank you. I'm on my way to meet Nicholas. He stayed in London last night.'

' You're losing patience with me? '

' Never with you,' Hervey said.

She touched his arm for a moment, and went away. She had only to cross Trafalgar Square, but the traffic, undirected at this point, met in five currents in which cyclists, like minnows, darted from one to the other. She waited on the edge of the pavement. Her thoughts were still busy with her defeat. Some other person should have gone to see Ridley, she thought: I can't argue. It occurred to her at once that it is never possible both to understand human beings and to conquer them. At the time of seeing through Ridley she lost her identity and her voice: and always would. She saw a space between two lorries and made her way across quickly.

Her husband had seated himself on the stone parapet of the pool to wait for her. She was late, and an anxiety he would not look at seized him. When he caught sight of her his great relief set him hurrying towards her. For a moment, as they touched hands, he felt a familiar thin edge of strangeness between them—then it was gone and the sense of ease and confidence came back. ' How do you feel? ' he said.

' Very well,' Hervey said instantly.

' Where shall we go? When are you seeing Cohen? '

' At half-past one—at the Carlton. Let's sit here.'

Seated on the parapet with him, Hervey thought that her house and the time with Richard were a hemisphere away. She was here another woman, less anxious, safer. Both lives were actual; in one she was Richard Vane's mother, in this Nicholas Roxby's wife, and in neither was Hervey Russell entirely welcome.   But here I am well and happy, she thought, folding her hands.   ' We have twenty minutes.'

' Shall I come with you to see Cohen?' Nicholas said in a clear voice.

' Oh no.   Better that I see him first alone, to make sure. It is arranged, too.   You're expected at a quarter to three, for coffee.   There's nothing more to settle and you might only——'

She broke off, with a teasing smile.   Nicholas felt a twinge of resentment.   Yet he was relieved to be forced to see as little of Cohen as possible.

' Think, Nicholas, you must, must, not say too much to Cohen about selling only perfect things, he doesn't understand your attitude, he can't.   Leave him to find it out. He won't interfere very often in the business.   With his newspapers and the rest he can hardly have time for what is an incident to him.'

Her husband looked at her directly.   ' I don't believe I'm going to be able to work for this damned fellow.   I'd almost rather clear out at once.'

' Clear out to what?' Hervey said calmly.   ' What could you do?'

He did not answer.   The very quietness with which she had taken his failure made it harder for him to speak.   Does she even know that I'm ashamed? he wondered.   In the most indirect ways possible she had let him know that she knew why he had failed.   Yet she had never said in as many words, You failed because of the vanity that makes you give your first wife the money we could have lived on, and because you are unbusinesslike and unmethodical and not interested in making money.   At times he thought that she understood even his feeling for Jenny—it was not only vanity, it was memory, pity, and memory of love.   To live with Hervey was like living with a mirror which gave back an image so clear that you could not be certain it was untrue.   It is true that I am a failure, he thought sharply.   But you haven't, she had said, the proper impudence and chicanery to make money; it takes both to-day. Then why have you succeeded? he asked silently, disliking her.

There was a shadow across her cheek, like a thumb moulding the flesh into a hollow below the bone. His mind became blank with terror. If she were to go, he thought.

'Hervey, are you sure you're not doing too much? All this driving. What did T. S. say to you?'

'He said I looked very well,' Hervey answered.

Their shoulders touched, as if by accident, but the sense of comfort was not an accident. It sprang between them more readily when they were threatened. Very simple and familiar things released it—a word spoken gently or a gesture known so well that it stood for a year of kindness. Hervey was silent for a minute, grateful for sun, for rest, for the shadow of Nicholas's hand on the stone, granite is it? between them. Her uneasy mind roused her. She wanted to be certain that he would please Cohen, and she was not in the least certain.

'Please think,' she said again. 'I am sure you ought not to tell him you have lost the whole of your money.'

'Doesn't he know it?'

'No. I've been very careful. At present he thinks only that you are willing to take over *his* firm, because it is better known and larger than yours. That doesn't seem strange to him at all, but quite natural.'

'God damn him,' Nicholas said with energy. 'As if I would have given up *Nicholas Roxby Ltd.* for his or any other man's business, if I were not compelled.'

'You could hardly expect him to think that,' Hervey said, smiling. 'But be very careful. He would be a great deal less anxious to have you if he knew that *Nicholas Roxby* was finished in any case—that you were giving up nothing to come to him.'

Her husband looked at her without smiling. He is impossible, she thought, impatient; he will spoil everything.

She felt the deepest respect for his integrity. He would not have deceived Cohen, not even if their living depended on it. She knew herself too well—it was not only to help Nicholas that she had worked to persuade Cohen, but she enjoyed handling people. It gave her pleasure to match her mind against the mind of the shrewd worldly Jew and be more Jewish than he was. Her life had taught her these tricks. But I was a ready pupil, she thought: no one could have taught Nicholas to be dishonest.

'After all, you wanted to go on dealing in old furniture, you know everything about it,' she said sharply. At this moment she was convinced that nothing she had ever done was worse judged than this. It can't work, she thought. She turned to Nicholas, meaning to cry, Let's run away now, clear out, live on tuppence in a village. She said nothing.

'You're perfectly right,' Nicholas said. 'I must have work, I can't live on you.' How the devil did I come to this place? he thought wryly. What's wrong with me? A lorry filled with soldiers was making its way through the traffic. Watching it out of sight he thought, A pity the War ever came to an end. During the past weeks his wish to write down what he remembered about the War, about his battalion, had revived, and so strongly that he could scarcely keep it to himself. He almost believed that if he had time now, and quiet, he could begin.

'I must go,' Hervey said.

'No, don't, I don't want you to.'

In the end he walked with her as far as the door of the Carlton, now reluctant to let her out of his sight. She, too, felt that they were wasting exquisite time.

CHAPTER III

ALTHOUGH she was late, ten minutes passed while she waited, seated in the hall, for Cohen. He came in at last with the young man Julian Swan. The two of them stood talking in front of her, Swan taller by a head than the elderly Jew but beside him seeming less. 'Trust me,' Swan said, laughing. 'I know what to write and how to write it. The miners' leaders will smell to heaven when I finish with them.' He went off, not troubling to look at her.

'That's a clever boy,' Marcel Cohen said, turning to her. 'He's going to write a fine series of articles for one of my papers as soon as this tomfool business is over. You know he runs the Economic Council?—you know what that is?— I tell you he's a brilliant boy, he'll do well for himself.'

Hervey kept silent. She disliked and distrusted Julian Swan with a serious bitterness. He was at every turn her enemy and the enemy of her beliefs. So also was Cohen, but of the two she feared only the young man. He was a newer enemy, he would outlive the other. Beside that the old wealthy Jew had a generous root in him. There was nothing generous in Swan, but all green bitter wood.

'How did you come here?' Cohen said genially. 'Well, the comrades have overreached themselves with this Strike. This finally finishes socialism in our time, eh, Hervey?'

She looked at him, at his thick yellow hands and neck, at the womanish bullying mouth. She had not the courage to tell him she was on the side of the strikers and so end it. 'I don't like your Julian Swan, he's vain and ridiculous,' she exclaimed.

'He has something to feel vain about,' Cohen said, with

27

a flash of rage. Actually he did not like Swan, but he liked less to hear himself contradicted, and gentleness was not his way. His good humour returned as soon as he saw that she was blushing and at a loss.

'Now, we're going to make a great business of this firm, Hervey. Yes? I don't know yet so much about selling old furniture, but I'm a sharp scholar. Do you know what— I've tried many things in my life——' he paused suddenly, staring without pity at the child, the ghost, scrabbling towards the light—'I never did this yet. Maybe you think it's not important to me—just something I own by accident, a bad debt. Put that clean out of your mind. When I touch anything it's important—see?—if I can sell newspapers I can sell chairs and tables. Why not?'

'You own newspapers, you don't sell them at street ends,' Hervey said.

'Ha, I've done that, too,' Cohen answered. His upper lip stretched, unsmiling, to display the strong yellow teeth. 'You never did that, eh?'

'No,' Hervey said.

'You were never hungry?'

'Yes. Many times.'

Cohen stared at her, suspicious without cause, reflecting. 'Your husband, now, Nicholas Roxby, he's had a level easy life. You think he can do what I want? I never touched one single business that was a failure, Hervey—not one. His own firm, now, it's a small affair, isn't it? You think he can learn to steer a large business? I don't take any interest in miniatures. I like growth, a quick growth.'

Hervey looked down. I can smile, I can listen, she thought, but I don't accept. She roused herself to seem very attentive. A faint excitement sprang in her mind beneath repugnance. It was the thought that she could by this become notably secure as she had never been—this thought, an image of brass, grinned in the back of her mind.

'This operation,' Cohen said suddenly. 'You're quite

certain you need it? How long is it going to lay you by?
Not long?'

'About three months,' she answered in a low hurried voice.

'Three months, eh?' He stared again. 'Hm, well we
haven't yet discussed salary.'

Hervey opened her mouth, then shut it quickly. She
waited.

'Now listen, Hervey. I'm taking your husband into this
because he knows a great deal about it, he's the expert. But
I'm relying on you to do better than your share. Unless you
can promise me to give half your time to it, half of every day,
it's no use—you know that?'

Why did he believe he could make use of her? He saw
something in her, some energy, greed, hunger, the other
face of his own.

'How much do you make a year by writing?'

'A thousand,' Hervey said, persuaded he would believe
her. For half my time he must pay, she thought, the half
of that sum.

'I'll tell you what,' Cohen exclaimed. 'You'll do less
and less writing, yes, after this. You'll be so interested in
the business your writing will become a side line. That's
what I prophesy. The day you come to me and say you
want to work whole days I'll pay you double the money.
You don't want only to be a writer. You want money,
of course you want money. You're a clever woman.'

A time will come when I have nothing to write, Hervey
thought. She could feel already in her mind the burden
of words, of adding words to words, words replacing things,
imitating the form of life. But it was not *yet* time and while
she seemed to agree with him, she repeated secretly, Never-
theless I *shall* write.

'I'm going to pay you and your husband a thousand pounds
between you, between two of you, for one year. At the
end of the year, if things have gone well, we'll make a new
agreement, with a share in profits for you both. But mark

you, Hervey, I'm paying it for two of you—a thousand
pounds for two—not five hundred pounds each.   Do you
promise me to give at least half your time to it? '

'Yes,' Hervey said gravely.   She meant it and did not
mean it.   As well as he did, and more nearly, she knew that
she could not divide herself into two persons, a writer of
books and a seller of old chairs.   She would not yet face
what the choice implied.   She began with an instinctive
cunning to praise Nicholas.

'It was his idea to use the whole house as a showroom,
furnished as a house.   In this way sometimes '—it had
happened once—' he sold everything in a room, the whole
roomful, as it stood.'

'What rent is he paying? ' Cohen asked in a sharpened
voice.

'For the Chelsea house?   A hundred pounds a year.'

'We'll take a larger house, maybe we can rent one in
Berkeley Street, or two, maybe, opening a door.   Now
listen——'

She listened with her two minds, the one that answered
and the one that denied him.

When she saw Nicholas coming towards them she felt,
with relief and happiness, that he shared the burden of Cohen
with her.   But she could not relax.   She must listen the more
carefully, fearing that in his blundering honesty he would
say the wrong things.   He had none of her quickening sense
of another's mind.   He gave honest answers, not apt ones.

'What was your notion in taking a whole house? ' Cohen
questioned him.

'That was the way I wanted to work,' said Nicholas slowly.

'You said it showed the things better,' Hervey warned him.

Smiling, Cohen kept his eyes on Nicholas's face.   'I bought
a dozen old chairs last year,' he said.   'Maybe eight of them
were untouched, real, and the other four were patched up
from old wood.   I knew it when I bought them, there was
no lying about it, I——'

Instead of listening to him Nicholas interrupted brusquely with a venomous tirade against the fakers of old chairs. He made too much of it. It is not after all important, in a world so troubled as ours, whether old furniture is genuine or not—a few fakes more or less do not matter. But Nicholas spoke as though the whole social order were involved—and as she listened, nervously, and anxious about the effect of it on Cohen, Hervey realized all at once that it was for his own sake he was making it important, and because he had to create a world in which everything was at least honest. While she watched Cohen's face closely, ready to make good any shocking error Nicholas made, she was on Nicholas's side with her whole heart. She respected no one as she respected him.

' Yes, yes,' Cohen said, with good humour, ' of course. But now let me tell you, Nicholas '—it was the first time he had used the young man's Christian name—' I believe in walking the world with my eyes open. I don't waste my strength trying to form opinion. I give way to it, I use it. Don't you read either of my newspapers? When there's cynicism in the world, and more cynicism than hope, I'm at hand to provide it—I'll provide honest sentiment if it's wanted—only what's wanted—served up sizzling. I don't care for this anatomical steel furniture, it's inhuman, but it's going to be bought because it belongs with aeroplanes and oil turbines. Maybe we'll sell it alongside your old furniture, maybe not. I own a glass works now in Czecho-slovakia, it turns out, yes, the loveliest glass in the world, and the process is so slow it just can't compete. So what do you say, I'm putting in machinery that makes something rather like it? Isn't that the right thing, Hervey? '

Without evil intentions he corrupts the whole world, Nicholas thought. He saw that Hervey was very anxious about him, and he bit back his words. All he said was: ' So long as you don't expect me to deal in faked chairs and tables, sir.'

Cohen could respect honesty, although he would not allow it to interfere with him in any way. He was not sorry either, to know that here he had to deal with an honest and scrupulous man, since this saved him one care. He had the lowest opinion of Nicholas as a man of business. At this turn he expected Hervey to do all that would be needed. With reason he expected it from her. She had every instinct and quality of a sound business man: it never entered his head that she might be thinking of something else.

'We'll have a formal conference as soon as the Strike ends,' he exclaimed. 'You, Nicholas, can start at once and Hervey here in three months, sooner if she's fit. But for these damned humbugging miners we'd march right ahead——'

A look of anger came over Nicholas's face. He was about to retort sharply when Hervey stood up, laughed, and said in a light merry voice:

'You won't need to wait three months for me. I'm so strong I shall surprise everyone.'

CHAPTER IV

WHEN Hervey and Nicholas were alone, hurrying together through the streets, she took his arm. 'Tired?' asked Nicholas.

'No. Glad to be here with you. I wish I lived with you in some place where there was no one else.'

'My God, how I wish it,' he answered.

Now Hervey felt only dejected by the thought of giving the half even of her spirit to this business. She did not say so aloud.

'I daresay we shall enjoy it,' she said.

Nicholas frowned nervously. 'Well I hope so.' He hesitated. 'I don't think I'm the right person,' he said. 'I shall quarrel with Cohen if he wants to sell anything and everything: his whole attitude is false and rotten, he's worse than dishonest, since he knows what good is and falsifies it so that he can sell more of it. Am I talking like a fool, Hervey?' He pressed her arm against his side.

'No, my dear, dear Nicholas. But don't have so many doubts. We'll try it. That we can work in it together is a God's mercy.' She said this, feeling doubt in her deepest heart. In these depths she knew that she was undertaking what she would not, not ever, fulfil. Yet she hoped for a miracle. She thought in vague images of worldly success, she was sharp set for it, and if she had not been born with a double mind might have achieved it early. In the end she achieved—but when is a life ended? When the spirit knows itself? or at the grave? when? when?

Nicholas looked at her with a smile. 'Very well—no

33

more doubts, and I'll try my damnedest. But you're not going to be fit to work in three months. Why on earth did you say so?'

'Why did you look at Cohen as if you couldn't endure him?'

'And I can't endure him when he talks brutal nonsense about the miners. I could have strangled him with his silk scarf.'

'We shall never have any money or any peace if you go about the world strangling rich newspaper proprietors,' Hervey sighed. 'It can't even help the miners. And this operation will cost a fortune.' Nicholas was silent. She glanced at him. 'Are you angry?'

'Yes, with myself,' he said. 'Hervey, I promise you I won't run the risk of another failure. If only you'll get well, and strong, I can do anything. Without you nothing is any good.' He held her arm and frowned. The certainty that he was making another wrong start remained, but he would not examine it deeply. Unlike her, he felt no respect for Cohen, not a trace, but he would give his whole mind to Cohen's business where Hervey grudged every stroke and hand's turn she lent it. The trouble was that he had no mind for business.

The tide which had set citywards earlier in the day was turning back. As Nicholas and Hervey walked east along Fleet Street it flowed past them in the afternoon sun. The city was emptying itself along every channel. Walkers scurried like light corks at the edge of a swirling stream of carts, lorries, even a wheelbarrow stuffed with papers and pushed along by a civil servant holding a rolled umbrella under one arm. Here a boy with a merry face strutted under the wall, with a mouth organ on which he played *Marching Through Georgia*. These people felt no grudge against the miners who were making them walk, nor sympathy for them either. They walked. It was a new feast of the Passover.

'One of these years,' Nicholas said, 'we'll leave London for ever and live alone in the country. There's so much I want to learn, and no time to learn it.'

Hervey did not answer, but she felt her mind move towards his as though they were really alone together. Whatever happens, she thought, and so long as I live, I shall never be happier than I have been these two years. The pleasure of this thought quickened her steps, and she felt strong for a time.

They reached the Middle Temple. Here she left Nicholas and went in alone to the rooms, borrowed from their owner, where Nicholas's sister had expected her for an hour past. Climbing the stairs took her a long time.

Georgina Roxby was lying at full length on a couch, a cigarette burning out between her fingers and a small molehill of ends in a bowl. She looked extraordinarily lax, as though she were incapable of sustained movement. Her long, very beautiful throat was pressed back against the hard end of the couch and one thin leg, muscled like a dancer's, hung down over the edge. She was now thirty-one, and two deep lines running past the corners of her mouth gave her face the look of a mask but it was an exquisite mask. It would be hard to say what made her beautiful, now that her fine skin was dulled and her cheeks fallen a little. Her bones seemed wonderfully put together, as if to show what a good sculptor can do only with the skeleton. There was a curious quality in her face, which had appeared there only lately—indefinite, almost an invitation, sensual. Hervey noticed it as little as she would have noticed any other physical mark in her friend.

When she came in Georgina sat up and said warmly: 'Where have you been in these crowds? Nicholas must be mad to let you walk about now. It's five days, isn't it?'

'Because of that, one can't behave as if the world

were coming to an end,' Hervey said, laughing. She sat
down.

'You're not nervous about it, are you?'

'No.'

That's a lie, Georgina thought. She looked up at the
ceiling and said quietly: 'Do you know what to do? I
can tell you. Before they come to fetch you, you should
sink in yourself, down as far as you can go—that leaves
room between you and what is happening, and you'll find
you don't mind it nearly so much.'

Hervey listened to this with interest. It seemed to mean
nothing, however, and she preferred not to talk about her
fears. They would discredit her if she gave them the least
chance. She closed her eyes. It was comforting to be with
Georgina, who knew her so well that she had no need to
explain anything.

After a time she fell asleep and dreamed that she and
Georgina were making their way underground through the
galleries of a mine. But the walls of the gallery were
hollowed into small rooms, in each of which was only a
bed and a lamp, and Georgina, who had died, was to
lie in one of these beds and the door be sealed up for ever.
Hervey cried, many tears, because she was leaving her
there and because Georgina had not wanted it. When she
awoke, for a moment she still saw the walls of heavy earth
and the many rooms. Georgina had left her couch.
She was preparing tea in the kitchen, and she brought
it in and gave her full cup to Hervey and watched her
drink it.

'You were smiling when you were asleep,' she observed.

Hervey was startled. 'Smiling!'

To forget her dream as soon as possible, she began speaking to Nicholas's sister about him. They were curiously
alike in looks, but where Georgina had grown sensual he
took less and less interest in his body, as though it scarcely
existed for him. Hervey tried willingly to acquiesce in

this without giving trouble, and except for one or two humiliating failures she went on easily and pretty well. Like any vagabond of the spirit she could live merrily on crusts.

'You know,' she said, 'the responsibility for this new firm is mine. *I* put the idea into Marcel Cohen's head to ask Nicholas to manage it for him, and it was I encouraged Nicholas to accept. I ought to cure myself of this habit of arranging other people's lives for them. This time I may have made a complete mistake. Certainly Nicholas knows everything, all there is to know, about old furniture, but he knows nothing about business, he isn't even willing to answer letters promptly.'

'You can do that,' her friend said, with a little malice. 'If you can persuade a man like Cohen to do what you want you must be very adroit.'

'But do I want to be adroit in business? Very often I believe that the only thing I want, the only thing, is to live alone, as barely as you like, and to write. But, you know, Georgina, fewer and fewer words are fit to use. The others are being corrupted by the life they live nowadays. If I were a great writer I should be able to create out of the rags and old bones, but I'm only honest. I——'

Georgina laughed and lay down, her legs crossed at the round knee. 'You know very little about yourself,' she said merrily, 'you should live more and think much less. I suppose that living with an idealist like Nicholas you serve up the bones of your mind at every meal. In another ten years there will be nothing left—unless in the meantime you notice that you have, after all, the usual load of senses. But you won't notice it. Tell me, are you happy?'

'If I had a hundred pounds a year I didn't earn I should be the happiest creature living,' Hervey said. 'Everything else I need I have.' She stood up and went over to her friend and laid a hand on Georgina's shoulder. The warmth this light touch communicated was finer and gentler than her words, which had been spoken in a curt voice. 'Now I must go,' she said, and walked out.

'Take care,' Georgina called after her, adding under her breath—'yes, take care of yourself, since no other person will do it.'

CHAPTER V

Towards six o'clock Georgina rose, changed her dress, and went out to meet Julian Swan: she was dining with him this evening as she had done every evening for close on a month.

The offices of the Economic Council were as much like a Staff Headquarters as Swan could manage, without uniforms to sound a martial air. Georgina was taken straight through to his room, the inmost of three; the walls of all of them were covered with maps on which Swan himself eagerly traced lines and moved flags. He was busy at one when she came in, and she sat down to watch him. His fine close-cropped red hair and quick body moved her to a familiar excitement. In a few moments he finished his work and came towards her: she felt a quiver of pleasure when he laid his hands on her, and yielded to it smiling, her thinly-clothed body on his. He began blindly to run his hands over her, but she drew back and walked to the window. She leaned her back to it and looked at him with a smile which invited him, openly. She knew he would not follow her because to cross so much of the room gave away that he was lame in a foot. Even desire, or desire at this stage, could not free him from the thought of it.

' My poor Julian,' she said softly, ' what do you want me to do ? '

He looked at her with as much calmness as possible.

' I should like us to marry,' he said.

She thought in the same moment of his lameness, his appetite for her, her own inner defeat. An impulse seized her to say, But you fool, I'm in love now, here, with a man

39

who can't take me; I've had others. Then she felt almost sorry for him.

'Should I help you at all if we married?' she asked him. This, which she meant seriously, made her smile.

'If you liked,' Swan said.

'You didn't intend us to marry when this started,' she went on in a half derisive voice. 'I shan't do it.'

He did not answer. It was true, and he was scarcely certain that he would forgive her for becoming necessary to him. He began to walk slowly to her, taking pains not to drag his foot, and aware as he came nearer that she was warm and roused. Excited vanity and love made him, not knowing, smile.

Georgina looked at the door. 'I think someone is coming,' she said quietly.

The man who came in was Swan's second in command. She knew him a little, and had he shown an interest in her she would readily have responded. She took him to be near forty—he was actually fifty-five—and she found attractive his air of arrogance and power, the gross violence covered by a youthful and charming smile. For the first time, as he came forward, he looked at her closely. Her arms and shoulders were uncovered and white, she was laughing and very lively. From the first he had supposed that she was Swan's mistress, but now he doubted it.

He turned to Swan and said: 'I've ordered a review of the Special Service Corps for Monday morning, is that right?'

'We decided Tuesday,' Swan said.

'Yes. I thought Monday better,' said Hunt easily. He knew exactly how near he could go in pressing the younger man—to the breath in which Swan's hysterical temper caught fire and he called Hunt down in front of anyone who happened to be within hearing. He was like an emotional woman in his demands, he must have loyalty and obedience and devotion, and when he was assured of receiving these he would allow liberties to be taken with him—just so far as they fed his self-confidence. Hunt knew in this instance that the pleasure of reviewing his ' troops ' would outweigh everything else.

' If they'd give us rifles,' Swan said. ' They'll have to in the end—another fortnight of this and the Reds will be in the open, and then——' a curiously rapt expression came into his face, the gaze of a mystic. ' A little blood-letting will do good, the only way with rats is to shoot them.'

Georgina felt another tremor of excitement and happiness; she wished Hunt out of the room. But when she glanced at him his look of cold mischievous cruelty struck her. This look is so rare on human faces that she did not recognise it. She thought vaguely, He will enjoy the shooting. He turned his head when he felt her looking at him, and their looks met for a moment, during which the woman felt herself become weak. She moved to a chair and sat in it with shaking knees.

' You know that fellow David Renn,' Swan began.

' Renn,' Georgina echoed. He was not speaking to her, but she needed to hear her own voice.

Swan went on: ' An out and out Bolshevik, a really dangerous fellow. We——'

At this moment the telephone rang on his desk. He went to it and stood listening. ' Mr. Harben is coming up here now, to see me,' he said, in a quickened voice. ' Georgina, you must wait for me in the other room. I'm sorry. You can go, too, Hunt.'

Georgina stood up, letting the ash from her cigarette fall over the floor. ' Is he so important? ' she said, with a smile.

' You know what he is—a colossus—ships, mines, tanks, steel works. Far more important to me at the moment, he's the chairman of the Economic Council. I'm reponsible to him, not to any of the others.'

She went out, marking her impatience and mockery of

his state by walking slowly; she had hardly seated herself
in the outer room when Thomas James Harben walked past
and turned his large vulture-like head towards her for a
second because she was out of place. The door shut.

Harben placed his gloves and stick on Swan's desk and sat
stiffly and unsmiling. He had conceived a distrust of Swan,
but nothing in his manner marked it except a rudeness
which, since he behaved to any inferior in much the same
way, Swan could think was natural. He suffered from it
no less.

'You can drop all the talk about Moscow and revolution,'
Harben said. He thrust out his lower lip in contempt of
both these objects. 'The fact is it serves no purpose at
the moment, when the immediate enemy is at home and
the immediate crisis is wages. I want you now, without
waiting for the Strike to end, to prepare meetings and
pamphlets drawing the moral of the Strike—that Trade
Unions are a menace and the larger they are the larger the
menace—interference with my mines is a piece of damned
impudence—my property is my property, to manage in
my own way. Make it clear even to fools. But there
are more fools than anything else. Say it's no longer a
question of this industry and that, the basis of society is
being attacked and this is where we shall stand. Don't
become high-flown.'

He allowed the young man in front of him to talk
for five minutes, then cut him short in the middle of a
word. It seemed he had not listened to anything. He had
wanted to rest before going away. He stood a moment,
looking round the room, from the desk to the maps, but
what thoughts he had he kept to himself, not by any movement of his heavy face expressing the profound contempt he
felt for this display of enthusiasm. If he had said, Mine is
the power, the kingdom, and the glory, it would not have
sounded ridiculous, but it would have made Swan's maps
with their flags ridiculous.

CHAPTER VI

WHEN Thomas Harben came into his wife's sitting-room he saw, but not in time, that she was talking to another woman. The other woman was her ally—it was an alliance and not a friendship—Evelyn Lamb, the wife of T. S. Heywood, a scientist whom he employed. The figures of the two women were outlined against a gold curtain, their faces indistinct in the shadow. Harben stood still in vexation, with his hand on the door feeling for the edge. Two women together, of the class of well-bred cultured women, appeared to him as his enemies. He could not have given his impression words, nor would have troubled. Beside that he disliked and despised Evelyn Lamb, and was the only person who persisted in calling her by her married name—Mrs. Heywood. He did it to mark his contempt for her reputation as critic and writer, but it was not a wilful contempt—he was seriously unable to think that any but idle people busied themselves with the arts. Thus the trouble Evelyn Lamb took, to preach and persuade that a world created by Thomas Harben is the only world in which the arts can live, was wasted, for simply he did not care whether she lived or died.

Fortunately she had a large unearned income and could afford a generous passion.

Lucy Harben turned her head as her husband came slowly into the room. By some trick of the light it was a younger man who came forward, and she stood up in involuntary panic, pulling at the curtain to let in more light. Light filled the room, revealing the pains Evelyn Lamb took to give an air of youth to what was ageing, the pinched contour, and the

43

tendons of her neck. Her beauty was becoming desperate. As for Harben, even in the strong light he looked a great deal younger than his sixty-two years, but it set his wife's heart at rest, she who (but it was a long time ago) had forced herself to endure being a wife for three detested years.

'Is there any fresh news?' she asked. It was seldom he came into this room.

'Of the Strike?' Harben said. 'None. I give them another week.'

'But it would be fatal to make terms too soon,' Evelyn Lamb cried. 'The one thing to be feared now is an inconclusive peace.' She was little disturbed by an echo. These words had been often in her mouth during the War and by an easy trick men and women speaking English took now in her mind the place of the enemy.

'After all, we went into this to protect our liberties against revolution. I don't trust Baldwin—we should have a much stronger man, a leader who won't be afraid to shoot if the time comes. Sometimes I believe Baldwin dislikes fighting!'

Harben looked at her with a cold fury. He had no softness, having no imagination, and he could endure bloodshed as well as any general or politician. But he disapproved of women who were admired for their cleverness, and he thought of Evelyn as unstable, a restless source. She was —but how did this gross-minded man know it? He was now vexed by having to argue with her.

'That is completely unimportant,' he said curtly. 'There had to be a show-down—we were ready for it, we've been ready since January, and the other side weren't. In fact they were bluffing. They'd bluffed once before and it came off, but you can't take two tricks with the same bluff. That's all. Nothing else. Nothing.'

'Oh, but Mr. Harben,' said Evelyn, 'more, far more, is involved. Either the State is supreme or it is not. There must be authority. If *we* don't govern, some other class will. Think of Ireland. Think of Russia. One knows—how one knows!—what happens in a country where the natural order is inverted. There must be discipline, there must be authority, there must be obedience.'

Lucy Harben was made uneasy by her guest's violence. Lying back, her heavy white arms on the arms of her chair, she considered Evelyn. She felt again that Evelyn Lamb was at the mercy of her mind. Nothing held her steady. She had no land that had belonged to her family for generations, no tenants. She did not know that the bond between a good landlord and his tenants is more than the money that passes between them. Now I, thought Lucy, alone, am responsible for the happiness and prosperity of four hundred souls. Not one of these has found me unjust or without a good understanding. In four years I have given back part of their rent to the farmers, I mend roofs and walls, I gave a hall, a new wing to the hospital. When a child is hurt in an accident, my motor-car takes him to the town. The women know me, I sit talking to them in their kitchens, that year I paid his fees for a boy to study at the university, I helped another to emigrate, and another.

She looked calmly at Evelyn. 'You have forgotten the country,' she said. 'In Northumberland my farmers and their labourers are all hard-working and satisfied. An incident like this Strike is nothing. They will hardly notice it—what has it to do with real things, the seasons, the weather, bad years, good years? It would be a mistake to punish anyone. When it is all over let us shut the book on it and begin again. Perhaps something can be done for the miners without ruining ourselves and them. Even if there is nothing that can be done, they must not be allowed to feel injured and neglected. That would be against our traditions.' But what do you know about traditions, she thought, looking at the other woman with pity. To you they only mean good or bad writing. What poverty! In me they go down three hundred years into the earth, with the roots of trees planted to shelter the house from the winds tearing from the north-east.

Her husband listened to her without comment. He had let his head sink forward, and his long fleshy nose shadowed the lower part of his face. If he found Evelyn a nuisance, his wife made him deeply uncomfortable. He could have reminded her that his money, money he drew out of mines, steel works, and ships, and the money that fell from his mouth every time he spoke, flowed into her land and watered it, cleansing and fertilising, yet he said nothing. Not because he would not speak of it in front of the other chattering woman. But he thought his wife had condemned him, not at this moment, but years ago when she married him. He had never been at ease with her, but from the first uneasy and frustrated. She had married him and she allowed him to approach her; taking his money she gave it to her fields. He waited a year, two, three years, expecting she would have a child. This never happened and before long he found it hard, then inconceivable to come to her. She would not refuse him, but he, insensitive, greedy, turned from her out of a sort of shame. Perhaps he thought it his fault that she was sterile.

He stood up. ' If you'll take my advice,' he addressed Evelyn, ' you'll keep out of the way now. There are far too many of you women with nothing more urgent to do than imagine yourselves Joan of Arc. There's no need for women in this. The police have it in hand. There are soldiers. The men's leaders are defeated in any case—no call for women to offer themselves as strike-breakers. If what you want is excitement——' But he did not tell her how she could find excitement without becoming a nuisance to him—in fact he neither knew nor cared.

He shut the door on them, wishing suddenly that he could turn the key, and went downstairs. His car had been waiting. He went off in it through streets growing cooler and emptier to see the only man toward whom he had ever felt as a friend. He had not even had an ally until now. As yet he had not noticed that the warmth was only on his side. He was still too puzzled and surprised at finding himself moved, although so timidly, by an emotion which had nothing to give him beyond itself.

William Gary was nearly thirty years his junior. The two so separate in age were not unlike in build and in a certain heavy immobility of feature. But if time is a spiral indelibly drawn in space the younger man's feet were already on Harben's shoulders. They seemed to see the same country, the slag heaps, the wheels, ships lying at wharves, the thin shafts of factories, broad turbines. In fact there was nothing they saw with a like vision. Harben was content so long as his money flowed out and in by tidal journeys he understood. Left to himself he would have fastened children of five years to his wheels, just as and with the best will in the world his grandfather did. He had been born without a conscience and without love. And perhaps nothing very much can be done to make the world a tolerable place, until surgeons can detect and destroy spiritual monsters at birth. Why is a boy who will later blind and torture helpless prisoners in a jail or a prison camp allowed to be born? Why are Thomas Harbens nourished? Why did not the womb reject him?

Certainly Harben did not know, when he gave an order, that because of it one woman would die of hunger and a young man hang himself from despair, but if he had known he would not have acted otherwise. He did not *know* how to act in any other way.

William Gary thought that he knew. He thought he could change the world without changing his place in it. He believed that most men ask only to be well fed. Humble and kindly meaning, they are content with as little as children or private soldiers. He forgot that children are innocent and that soldiers have had a vision. But perhaps it is not important.

He spoke to Harben with his quick curiously sweet smile, hiding the surprise he felt at seeing him here in the half hour before dinner.

' My friend in the Labour Party—Louis Earlham—was here until one minute ago,' he said smiling. ' He is a great deal more alarmed by this Strike than you are.'

' They are all compromised and they know it,' Harben said. ' Your friend Earlham is a fool.'

' No, he is a good decent creature,' Gary said. ' When he understands what at most he can do he'll be helpful. He lives in an unreal world still. But I like him.'

' My wife sees him,' Harben said.

' Will you have dinner with me ? '

Harben moved brusquely. ' No. I——'

' I'm dining alone,' Gary said.

The obscure disturbance which began in Harben's mind made as little mark on the surface as the fall of earth in a mine. It would have been the simplest thing in the world to accept, and now that he had said No he could only regret it, with an energy out of all reason. ' The Strike will collapse next week,' he said angrily. ' What with naiveté and bungling—and your friend's fears—I think another week, by which time everyone will be deathly tired of walking and glad to be shut of the miners and their folly— is Master A. J. Cook a friend of yours, too ? '

Gary glanced at him under nervously twitching lids. This was the first moment in which he realised that he was as strong as Harben. He knew already everything Harben could teach him, and it was not an accident that this moment had come at a time when they were perfectly agreed. Together they had foreseen the need for the Strike, they knew how to use it for the best, to cripple and discredit the men's unions at the opening of a campaign in known country. The Strike was an incident in the campaign. They believed, both believed, that England was becoming weaker in the world. To whip her up to first, yes to second place meant—but here, without Harben's knowing it, he was as alone as he had been all his life. His new friend was not his friend. Harben thought only of persons—those he could use and those who ought, if he had the excuse, to be killed or put away. He was learning to speak of the cloud of his old enemies as Reds and this was as near as he ever came to dreaming what the younger man knew. What was flesh is dying again into the word: and things are becoming larger and more menacing than men, even man the creator. William Gary moved knowingly in a world of things. When he thought of men he saw them in their places among things, ruled by things, humbly standing only to serve them.

And the things were his! Ships, aeroplanes, coal, oil, ore, all were his, all to be served. He hated waste, of oil or men. In his vision he saw the race of men whittled and parted into companies of obedient happy servants. He had once commanded a battalion and he believed that men enjoy obedience and hate starving. He with his memories was a generation wiser than Harben—Harben who believed that the simplest way with men is to drive them. Had he but eyes to lift up, he had seen them with their vacant mouths, pleading to be led. Ah, pleading.

'These figures are a great deal more important than the Strike,' Harben said. He pulled out of his pocket a single sheet of paper and handed it to Gary. 'Something must be decided before the meeting—shall we pay a dividend from reserves or pass it up—for the first time?'

The room in which they stood had become darker: Gary turned on lights.

This paper he held had to do with the great shipping and shipbuilding firm of Garton's. With all its owned and allied firms—they included coal mines, iron works, steel mills, chemical works, heaven alone knows what lying under it they did not touch—it was still his symbol for power.

It had been that in his youth, when it was owned by Mary Hervey; on his table at this moment lay a letter from Mary Hervey's grandson and his friend, Nicholas Roxby, asking him whether the rumour was true that Garton's was going to pass its dividend.

An amazing exhilaration seized him. He reached across for Nicholas's letter, tore it, and dropped the halves on the floor, astounding Harben with a loud burst of laughter. But then Harben had never heard him laugh, never squatted beside him in a shell-hole, or ducked him, by a fortunate accident, in the young Thames once.

CHAPTER VII

HARBEN went and another visitor was announced. This is my day for seeing old men, Gary thought. But George Ling, a year younger than Harben, was bowed to the ground under his one-and-sixty years. He came in leaning on the malacca cane which had belonged to his father and before him to Mark Henry Garton, and took the chair farthest from the windows. He expected the revolution to begin at any moment. This room was on the ninth floor, but he was anxious not to run any chance of being killed by a shot fired on the barricades of St. James's Street. It was with the heaviest foreboding and only after he had rung up acquaintances at the Foreign Office and Scotland Yard to ascertain what his chances were of making the journey from Grosvenor Crescent to Piccadilly in safety that he had ventured out in a car with all the blinds drawn. So that he did not actually know whether Hyde Park had fallen into the hands of the revolutionaries or not.

During these days he thought a great deal about his son, who had been killed in the War, and for some reason he could not help feeling angry with the dead boy. He remembered that in the last four or five years of his short life Robert had often disobeyed him. On one occasion indeed he had looked at his father with open dislike, yet in the same moment and with the same gestures and slow way of speaking he reminded Ling of the timid docile little boy to whom every word his father said seemed delightful and perfectly right. His death was a last act of defiance and disobedience: it was a long time before the father forgave him. Now once again it seemed to him that Robert wanted his father to

51

be threatened and humiliated, and his money taken away
from him. Wherever he turned he thought that the boy's
mild blue eyes followed him, and in the car on his way here
he broke into bitter complaints, entreating Robert to tell him
what he had against him and why he was behaving unkindly
towards the father who loved him, and had only reproved him
because it was his duty to warn his only son that everyone
in the world is wicked, lustful, and a liar.

He was thinking of this when the first words he said, after
he had seated himself and groaned a little, were: ' I shouldn't
be here if my son were alive to defend me.'

Gary looked at him with curiosity. He remembered
Robert Ling distinctly, too distinctly for his comfort now
that the boy had come into the room and silently taken his
place against the wall. Run away, Rabbit, do, Gary said to
him; and with all the diffidence he had shown in life, and
his anxiety not to outstay a welcome, Robert Ling, nick-
named Rabbit, smiled and moved obediently out of sight.
His trench coat was too large for him. It flapped against
his thin knees.

' What can I do for you? ' Gary said politely.

' Tell me what's going to happen,' old Ling said in an
exhausted voice. ' Ought I to go abroad? Then there's
my daughter, your friend Roxby's wife, that is his first
wife, I know nothing about the second, I——' he became
confused and stopped. ' I've transferred some money to
France,' he said desperately, ' not much, just enough to
keep me alive for a year, but how do I know whether things
will be safer there? '

' England's safe enough,' Gary said.

' Not with these Labour men allowed to plot murder and
ruin—plotting under our noses—I've always said we were
fools. It ought to have been stopped, someone should stop
them. Do you know, they say mining is dangerous work—
as if that were an excuse, as if we could do without coal
for that, as if they didn't burn coal themselves. It's un-

democratic. This is civil war. Ramsay MacDonald ought certainly to hang for it!'

'Heaven forbid,' Gary laughed. 'He's less anxious for civil war than you and I are, sir. That's true, I assure you. I have every confidence in him and his party.'

George Ling looked at him with suspicion and growing horror. 'No, no,' he exclaimed. 'Think what you're saying. These scoundrels, these traitors—why they're trying to blow us up. They want to take away our freedom and our money. Think what will happen if they succeed, think of the women '—his chin trembled at visions he conjured up, of rapine, outrage, and the mad lusts of Labour leaders—'it's our duty as Englishmen to oppose these murderers. Yes, to the last—and let this be the last.'

Robert had come back—to whisper slyly in Gary's ear: The last penny and the last drop of blood. Surely you haven't forgotten that? His smile was faintly reproachful, and faintly—though Gary could scarcely believe this of so gentle and willing a creature—mocking. He turned brusquely away, avoiding Robert's blue eyes.

'And that isn't all,' Ling went on, trembling. 'What's happening to my shares in Garton's and Harben Ling? Tell me that, tell me now, tell me. You can't deceive me any longer, you and that fellow Harben. I knew I was being robbed. I knew it. Just think what a fine safe snug business I had, safer than when my father bought it from Mary Hervey—why, I knew who held all the shares, and a man would speak to me in the street, he'd say: "That was a sensible speech you made at the shareholders' meeting, Ling, all my money is invested in Ling's, every farthing of it in your hands, Mr. Ling." And now what? Where is Ling's Steel Works? Don't tell me it has simply taken the name of Harben Ling—that's a lie! Everything has changed. Who and what is Harben Ling? Who persuaded me to change, who borrows the money—a million pounds pounds, borrowed borrowed borrowed from the bank? Oh, it's madness.' He started up in alarm. ' Don't turn on any more lights! Think what a target these large windows make.'

Gary had moved to the window to conceal his yawns. Dropping his arm, he turned round. ' But your shares in Harben Ling are all preference shares, they pay you interest,' he said coldly. ' Why are you afraid ? '

' My shares in Garton's are not preference shares,' said Ling. ' They're ordinary, they used to pay me thirty per cent——'

' That was during the War.'

' It was during the time Mary Hervey controlled Garton's,' Ling retorted. Only to speak of the stubborn old woman—of whom in her lifetime he had been mortally afraid—gave him spirit. ' She would never have bought and bought and borrowed and landed us in such a mess. In her day Garton's built ships, it didn't borrow money. I don't understand anything. My God, when I think what men used to say of Garton's—that it was safer than the Bank of England—when I think it I think that nothing is safe. Nothing, none born will be safe again. What will become of me before it's over ? '

Fear overcame him again; and now he thought that nine stories or one, a room facing the Green Park is terribly unsafe. He had become aware, too, of Gary's boredom. I had no right to come here, he thought; no one has the least respect for me, I should be better dead. He was afraid of death, however, and when Robert died (of a bullet in the forehead) he had found comfort in thinking that the older Lings were invariably stronger than their children. To turn his mind from unpleasant images, he decided to go home and send for his daughter to come and stay with him. Although he knew she would refuse to come this kept him quiet during his drive home. He even dared to lift one of the blinds.

CHAPTER VIII

In the minute before Ling left, Gary heard his servant opening the front door of the flat: steps crossed the hall to his library. He remembered what he was going to do.

The door of the library had been left open. Facing the doorway, the man who had been his personal secretary for two years stood as though he were in the orderly room. This window faced north, and the coldness of the light emphasised the curious quality of David Renn's face, its delicacy of a skull, the absence of colour even in the lips. From a short distance he seemed to have no eyebrows, but a little closer the fine wavering arch traced the eyebone. The eyes beneath had the depth without colour of night windows.

He as well as Gary had the image of the orderly room in his mind. As Gary came forward, opening his cigarette case, another image took the place of the first, without shock, since they were on the same level of time and it was easy to walk out of the orderly room into the shadows of a trench at night, and from the tiny flicker of a match, the face above the cupped hands, the wall of earth felt in the darkness, cold, heavy, recreate a world, an age, and save oh God the murdered men. Hollebeke, August, '17.

Renn blew the match out, and so standing, with the cigarette alight between his fingers, he said:

' I have to resign my job.'

As soon as he had said it he knew, what had lain in his mind as uncertainly as a fear, that Gary had meant to dismiss him this evening. Gary said only: ' Yes. Why ? '

'I'm working on a Strike committee.'

'You go there in the evenings.'

'The position isn't possible,' said Renn. 'I can't decently go on living in it. I'm sorry'—the point of his tongue moved rapidly across his upper lip—'I don't like appearing as an idealist, and I'm very grateful to you for kindness.'

'What sort of a socialist are you?' Gary said.

'Oh, an unlikeable sort—not liked by any side. I distrust the State, I dislike violence and appeals to emotion, and I want to enjoy a world without rich and poor men.'

Gary had watched him closely. 'You have never found your work for me'—his mouth twitched—'let us say *useful*, in your other—your crusade?'

Renn put his hand out to feel the desk at his side. His heart moved painfully. It came to him that all this time he had been hoping for a miracle. Against reason the reasonable man hoped that he would be allowed to serve two masters without being ashamed.

'I have not made any use of what I learned here,' he said. Now spare me.

After a moment Gary said: 'That's impossible.' He looked as though he were yawning. He was perhaps only hungry. 'I accept your resignation, of course, and I shan't give you a reference. In the circumstances you won't ask for it.'

You have a right to act in this way, Renn thought. He went out, and out of the flat into the lighted corridor. There was a window at the end. He stood here and looked over London. This city is perfect only in May and June. Then the air is clear yet soft, the sky limpid, and the trees glow with strength. The light seems within the trees, the sky, bricks, and spreading from them, not, as in the rest of the year, only revealing them. Renn looked from the green line of the trees nearly below him in a garden to the exquisite feathering of grey walls in the distance. He pulled an envelope from his pocket and began reckoning his money. If I eat carefully, I can last out for a longish time, he thought. There was his mother to consider. He sent her two pounds a week: on that and a pound a week she had of her own she kept herself and her husband—he had been lying in his bed without speaking for so long that Renn had given him up as a father. She must not know that he had lost his job. This was easy to arrange—it was not the first time he had played this trick on her.

He turned to walk downstairs. From the ninth floor this took some time. The stairs were wide, the right-hand wall panelled in waxed oak. On every landing there was a window and the corridors branched away from it with concealed lights and carpets of astounding thickness.

Half-way between the fourth and third landings he reminded himself that he could not avoid telling Hannah. He stood still, trying to breathe easily. I'll tell her this very night, he thought.

He began to walk to Deptford. A lorry, returning empty into Kent, took him part of the way. When he was within a short space of the Committee rooms he saw his friend Smith walking towards him from a by-street. He waited.

Since he had become an organiser for the Independent Labour Party Smith lived in Deptford, in one dark room. Yet he looks, Renn thought, as though he slept in the fields. His fresh reddened cheeks, broad shoulders, mouth smiling in repose, were of the country, and, yes, the lazy country. He fell in beside Renn, shortening his steps to fit Renn's, and they went together to the Committee room.

After the brightness of the street the room was dark, over-warm, and crowded with faces. These turned toward the opening door, and a shout of welcome broke out. You could think a party was going on here.

There were actually four strike committees in two rooms, but no one had thought of separating them. It was a help and saved time when four separate and contradictory orders arrived from the General Council, to be able to puzzle over them together, discover any thread of meaning they concealed, and pass it to a Council of Action sitting irregularly in the scullery.

Renn went into the second smaller room. The door, marked Propaganda, Permits and Defence, stood open. He had invited Hervey Russell to help him with his local Bulletin, and she was at work on it here. Her cheeks were burning and very red from excitement and weariness. Renn did not see it—he himself worked and he expected everyone else to work until they dropped. An order had come through from Headquarters forbidding them to print the Bulletin, but he decided to go on. Very likely another message would allow it. A man had set off to Eccleston Square an hour since to ask permission.

'I've been out to the kitchen,' Hervey said. 'By to-morrow we can give the children a meal at one, and we're buying food. That old Mrs. Fisher was born a quarter-master sergeant. She ought to be managing this Strike.'

Renn left her, to cover herself afresh with ink—her device should have been an ink-stained bone—and went into the outer room. A man shouted to him from the corner allotted to the representative of the Trades Council. He had lighted the gas jet above his desk, so that his face, streaked with sweat, stood against the wall like a gargoyle—a large face, inquisitive and conceited, and little shrewd eyes, gleaming with Yorkshire malice. Joe Bradford despised politicians; he was delighted not only to be working with more ease than he had ever worked in his life, but to have good stories to tell against them.

'Here,' he said to Renn, in his quiet voice, 'have you heard what happened on Sunday night? They was all at

Downing Street, all our great men, promising everything, begging, pleading, striving, as Thomas says, *we 'ave striven, we 'ave pleaded, we 'ave begged,* and the Prime Minister sends for them downstairs and, I'm sorry gentlemen, but this here is the end, he says, a certain newspaper is having trouble with its men, our efforts for peace, he says, are unavailing, so gentlemen, he says, and Mr. Thomas, you can kiss your-selves good night. So Thomas and the others run upstairs, repudiating everything, and run downstairs to the Prime Minister's room, and when they come there all the lights have been switched off, and a servant steps up to inform them that the gentlemen have gone to bed and Mr. Thomas and friends are not welcome, he says, to stay to breakfast.' Joe struck the desk with his open hand. His face was shining with the cruel ironic laughter which Renn hated, and Hervey, because she was a Yorkshireman, knew to be part shyness and part distrust. 'I'd give a year of m' life to have been hid there and seen them gaping into th' empty room,' he cried.

'They've stopped the Bulletin,' Renn said.

'That's to keep th' Communists out,' Joe smiled. 'Eh, Grassart.'

Grassart turned his lean yellow face towards them. It caught the light like a fish turning over on its belly in the water. Dear knows what he lived on, to be that colour he was—his party paid him a small wage to starve for it.

'Say the word and I'll go out and leave you to do your own work.'

He was the Finance and Demonstration committees—he had had less than eight hours' sleep in three days. None the less he went on working, and Joe did not provoke him again.

In truth Joe Bradford was too happy to quarrel even with an old enemy. To-day his fingers puzzled him by feeling about his stomach for the buckle of a belt he had left off in 1918, with the rest of his uniform. His excitement was

the deeper for being repressed out of shame. Doors
opened and shut, men came in with news and to hear
the orders, and if one came Joe did not know by sight, he
tried to guess which Union he was of by looking first at
his hands.

Nicholas Roxby came in with a few copies of the Council's
own newspaper, the *British Worker*. He was driving the
car Henry Smith had bought for four pounds to carry
him about his district. It was not so much a car as a
miracle. Called up for Strike duty it panted between
Deptford and the Headquarters in Eccleston Square without
breaking down under its load of indecision, orders, and
counter-orders.

Through the open door Hervey saw him come in, warm
and smiling, his face younger and lively. Among these
men he was happy and at home. She watched him
speaking to Henry Smith and Renn, standing in the circle
of light below the gas bracket, and it was as though they
were in another country and she looking at them through
a glass.

She stood up to go out to him, but the pain caught her
across her body and she fell into her chair, her hand at
her mouth. No one had noticed it except Henry Smith.
He came straight away to her and whispered:

'What can I do?'

'Nothing, it's over,' Hervey said. She was pleased by his
kindness. It was as though he had praised her.

'You must either find me a paper-worker or a paper-
worker's card,' Nicholas said laughing. 'Without one or
the other on board they won't give me the *British Worker*—
I managed to wangle these copies from a regular. And,
you, don't sign any more letters for the Council of Action.
Headquarters don't like it, and they wouldn't answer the
letter. Very touchy they were about it, too.'

A man came in, propping his bicycle in the passage, and
handed Renn a letter. Nicholas was struck by his face.

There was nothing extraordinary in slightly hollowed cheeks and a patient rather puzzled stare, but Nicholas had seen this face so many times, above a uniform, shoulders thrust forward under the weight of a pack and rifle, in rain, in sun on long roads, in light and darkness, that his heart stood still with a feeling between grief and the most intense pleasure. In the same moment he thought, I know you as little now as I did then.

'What do you make of this?' Renn said in a quiet voice, reading aloud. '*No permission given to print local Bulletin unless and with full permission in writing.*' He dropped the letter, open, on Joe Bradford's desk. 'The place downstairs is short of paper—unless you want to cherish this in your files.'

Joe laughed. At this moment the gas jets in both rooms flickered and went out, leaving them in darkness. They were without a shilling for the meter. Frank Rigden, the cyclist, went out to change Renn's florin, and they heard him stumble in the passage. There was a moment's silence after he had gone, then a sudden voice, Grassart's, said:

'Why don't they call out the light and power workers? To sit in darkness would put the fear of God into them in Park Lane.'

A calm jeering voice, Joe Bradford's, answered him.

'You want too much all at once. You and your penny plain revolutions!'

An anonymous voice rising and falling said: 'They should call out the sanit'ry men. I'd —— well like to see they volunteers in plush fours mucking out t' dust bins.'

'You want too much all at once,' Grassart mocked.

'You want to hold your tongue,' Joe said to him, with light warmth. 'I'll tell you, this Strike—as no one wanted——'

Someone laughed, and very free it sounded in the dark.

'The mine owners certainly wanted it,' Henry Smith called out, 'and the Government has been preparing for months while our people looked the other road and said their prayers.'

'Who prayed?'

'Mr. Louis Earlham was praying last Sunday in this very room for someone to save him from General Strikes and Bolshevism, Lord God MacDonald deliver us.'

'A friend of mine on the *British Worker*,' said Nicholas, 'is kept so busy respecting King and Constitution he writes his column kneeling.'

The laughter—how quick the English are to laugh—was broken short by Joe Bradford's voice—you could hear his contempt in it.

'This is a General Strike that has been called,' he said 'and a strike isn't civil war and revolution's not something you, bring on of a wet day.' He spoke slowly, giving every word its rights. 'We're out to win this for the miners and to prove as none of us can be bullied—and when it's over, we'll——'

'On the contrary you're going to lose this for everybody,' said Grassart. They could hear him strike his left hand on the table. It made a curious light sound, having only two fingers—he lost the others in a machine in the days when he was an honest workman.

Renn said with bitterness and energy: 'The truth is that if we succeed we shall have brought off a revolution against the wish and under the noses of the leaders. And if we fail it means ruin,' he said quietly, 'oh not of any obvious kind, but the most complete moral ruin in history. More than one here thinks Earlham was speaking for his betters in the Party—and your Trade Union betters, too, Joe—when he said that General Strikes left him cold and un-believing and he only wished it had never happened. They're all cold unbelievers at Headquarters. They make me think of a man who's been boasting for years what a fine horseman he is, and one day they bring the horse round and say to him "Ride!" He daren't say he never wanted to ride or meant to ride, and to save his face he gets on the beast's back and he feels damned uncomfortable—all he thinks about is how soon he can get down without injuring himself.'

Hervey had come up beside Nicholas. She put a warning hand on his arm. She was always fearing he would give himself away. He had joined the Labour Party to satisfy her, and he had no more understanding of its wordless loyalties than a foreigner. Each time its spokesmen let out that they were more bewildered, timid, and foolish than other leaders, he lost patience, because he could not see that the Party was a world deeper and wider than its leaders.

A young voice said slowly: 'They've getten us out. They're bound to see us right now, aren't they?'

'They'll see you right, my lad,' Joe said.

'If they don't,' Nicholas said—he was so moved by the young man's words coming after Renn's that he stammered—'they ought to be shot. Unless they know exactly what they're doing, I mean unless the whole thing has been worked out ahead—if it's another hoax——'

'We shan't let it be,' Renn said.

'Now that's better,' Joe said. He smacked his desk and laughed. Joe's laughter always shook him as though it were alive and living in his body. 'Th' orders are work and say nowt. Here comes th' light.'

Frank Rigden came in running, with the coins. The strife in darkness of the voices ended suddenly as it had begun. Henry Smith, with three men to keep order, went off to speak at his meeting. Hervey moved to go back to her room, but Nicholas held her. 'You're overdoing it,' he said anxiously. 'We'll go home.'

His fingers moved on her wrist. This caress unseen by anyone gave her so much happiness that she felt able to do anything. But she was tired.

As they went out of the room together a man brushed past them and went up to Joe's desk. They saw Joe look at his hands. He growled out a word.

' Yes,' the man said quickly. ' I was t' ask how late you'd be here.'

' How late? ' Joe said. He looked at the man with his sarcastic smile. ' I s'll be here all night. I'm permanent, by God! '

CHAPTER IX

FRANK RIGDEN took his bicycle to go home. He walked with it—in the crowd outside Headquarters his lamp had been broken. As he walked he noticed small things which usually he passed unseeing: the blackened stones of old houses, a geranium plant withering on a step; the sky itself appeared to him, as angels appeared to ordinary men and women in the past, with a surprised familiarity. It was not that he was less tired than at the end of his day's work driving a lorry, but a skin had been peeled from his eyes. He was wide awake.

As he neared the dock gates he saw the crowd gathered outside them to hear Henry Smith. He stood at one side by the wall. He was not listening, but he felt restless. If Mr. Earlham was to show himself now and say, Frank Rigden, he would answer, Here I am, Mr. Earlham, what have I to do? Do he would anything for Mr. Earlham.

There was a lamp lifted over the big gates. In its light he saw two men wearing picket badges and at the other side the soldiers in tin hats, with packs and rifles. He counted them—half a platoon. They were standing anyhow, listening to the speech. Behind the dock gates he saw the tops of cranes. The silence of the dock began to worry him. In the dark he touched the wall with his hands. It was the feeling of a trench at night and himself watching into the darkness. He looked quickly round him. There a few yards from him he saw a man in the crowd with his head sunk on his chest. It was the man he mucked in with in his first weeks in France and he had not see him since. It must be him. Whoever else stood like that? The trouble of wheeling

65

his bicycle through the crowd took time, and when he reached the place the man had gone, nowhere seen. He felt empty. I'll go home, he thought.

The crowd had thinned. Now he caught sight of Sally standing by herself, her shawl folded over her head and face. She must have slipped out of the house in search of news. He was surprised and glad to see her there.

Hurrying to her, he found that it was an older heavier woman than Sally, in a shawl like hers. He turned away. There was something uncomfortable and queer about a crowd at night, the white faces lifted to the speaker, the arms hanging. At night these streets of small houses looked narrower, and at one turn he caught a glimpse of the marsh that was like No-man's-land again. He thought he would be glad to get home. The excitement and strange turns of the day were nothing to him now but another reason to hurry. I'll tell her what it was like taking the messages, he thought, and that woman in the car she'll laugh what she said and the men coming in from th' country and what cheer have you heard the news and Mr. Earlham was there knew me.

Here at the end of the street he saw a light in his kitchen.

CHAPTER X

Renn left the Committee rooms at eleven. After walking a short way he stopped a lorry taking food to one of the large hotels. It took him as far as the Embankment. This was half darkened as in war time. He stood a moment looking at the river, at the furrows of black and brown light. His room was half an hour's walk away and when he moved to go on he felt the scars of his wound beginning to burn and throb. He stood under one of the street lamps to light a cigarette. A man hurrying in the opposite direction—in spite of a dragging foot he walked quickly—glanced at him, checked, moved to walk on, then turned and stepped in front of him. Renn looked up.

' Oh it's you, is it? ' he said.

' I tried to speak to you this morning,' Julian Swan said, ' but you weren't in your office.'

' I was there. I told them to get rid of you.'

Swan looked at him as though he would gladly hurt him. ' You don't imagine I had anything to say to you, yourself. Why should I? '

' If it was Mr. Gary's secretary you wanted,' said Renn, ' you should have asked for one of the others. After to-day: I'm not one.' He noticed that Swan was holding an unlighted cigarette. ' Do you want a match? '

Swan took it without thanks: he seemed vexed that he had taken it; stooped over the tiny flame his face was angry and thoughtful. The light touched the fine reddish hairs below his cheek bones. Suddenly he said: ' Look here, why do you do it? '

' What? ' Renn asked him, with his slight smile. He

believed that his smile irritated the other man, who thought
it insolent and spiteful, where it was only the reflection
outward of Renn's profound scepticism, touching his own
as nearly as other men's deeds and hopes.

'You're an educated man—why have you gone with this
rabble, socialists, all that swinishness and nonsense?'

'Why do you want to know?'

'Because I've never understood it,' Swan said. 'Not
because I mind what happens to you, I dislike you.'

'I don't know why I should talk to you,' Renn said.
'But if it helps you—not that you want to understand
anything, you're only feeding your vanity—for instance,
why did you say I am educated? You know you don't
look on any person as educated unless he was at one of
three, or is it two schools. It's true I'm better informed
than you are. I know more, oh a great deal more, than
you do, of the same things you write about, economics,
the relations between finance and industry, the form of
society——'

'Are you about to ask me for a job?' Swan said.

'No. I'll try to answer your questions if you're ready to
answer one of mine. Why do you dislike me? I was not
in your way, not, let us say, after your job.'

'That's the kind of tradesman's reason you would imagine,
you,' Swan said. He had no hat, and in the light from the
street lamp his head looked naked, the hair close cropped and
very fine, and the white bones showing through the skin—
it was a curiously-made head, flattened at the sides, and
broad, with the tops of the ears set forward. 'I disliked
you because you'd scuttle the ship you're living in—damn
you, can't you see you'll drown? You don't really believe
that working men, fat Trade Union secretaries, Labour
members, Earlhams, could govern. What's wrong with
you? It simply is that I don't know what people like
you think of.'

Renn moved to walk on. He looked into Julian Swan's

face smiling. This is absurd, he thought, two men, not friends, standing in the middle of London, the middle of the world, to ask questions.

'Don't imagine I want to govern—I'm too thin-skinned. I can't stand the sight of poverty, poor children, women in shabby coats turning over the cheap meat on stalls, defeated men, men touching their hats to me. I don't mind having superiors but I can't endure inferiors. I don't want anyone to touch his hat to me or feel worse educated or less free in soul.'

Swan looked at him in surprise and contempt. 'Men *are* inferior, the many to a few.'

'Each has a right to be himself, I mean to possess his soul. You can't tell, by looking at a child in his cradle, that he will have no soul, but if he is poor you behave to him as if he will not, you starve him of knowledge and of life. You make a slave of him.'

'We'll see which of us he listens to,' Swan laughed. 'You or me. I wouldn't give much for your chances. Unemployed men don't want freedom. Common men and women want common things, work, bread, and easy orders. And of their leaders eleven out of twelve want to be respected. One of these years your friend Earlham will be in the list of Birthday Honours.'

'He is fitted for it in every way,' Renn said lightly.

He walked off. A wind was blowing grit and scraps of paper along the embankment. The air was cool with a faint breath not of the sea but, yes, of ships in it, the smell of tarred ropes and iron.

Renn walked quickly, but it was almost one o'clock when he reached his room. Hannah had covered herself with a rug on the couch and was asleep. Her short dark hair fell across one cheek. He touched it. She awoke at once and sat up. On her other cheek was a round mark made by her ear-ring—her ears had been pierced when she was a few months old and the small hoop of thin gold inserted.

She was proud of them and they went with her brown skin
and lively narrow face.

'I thought you were never coming,' she said sleepily.

'I walked part of the way,' Renn said.

He made coffee on the stove and brought her a cup with
the bread and butter and apples his landlady had left out
for him.   She yawned over it and laughed at him, then
told him everything that had happened to her in the day
from the moment she set off to walk to the shop that
morning—it was a long walk from her rooms to Madame
Baring's, in Wigmore Street, and she hated walking: of
course a car had stopped for her, a kind man, too kind—
'I let him talk, David, and when he drew up in Oxford
Street to set me down I thanked him for the drive.   But
it wasn't necessary to ask me to supper, I said.   The
people passing looked at him and smiled and he drove off so
hurriedly you never saw, and with a red face.   It served him
right,' she cried.

Renn smiled, thinking of her loud merry voice, as sweet
as a bird's and more piercing.   It was fortunate that his
landlady was deaf.   She did not mind the girl's coming here
but she would certainly mind if she were wakened by
Hannah's voice.

'Tell me what happened to you to-day,' Hannah said.

'In a moment.'

He lay beside her and looked closely at her, with love
and grief.   He could deny the grief.   'How old are you—
twenty? twenty-one?' he asked.   She looked five years
younger.   Her gestures, like her voice, were childish.   Her
unformed body was brown, thin, smooth—he knew its
least line and that she was not a child in ways or thoughts.
She was ambitious and pleased with herself, and more than
anything she wanted, as she said, to know she was alive.
She was insatiable.

He knew her so well.   He knew about her everything that
was fine, simple, and gay, and everything, too, that was only

rough and greedy. Her delight in living was all these. He had seen her father and mother, and there was nothing in them to explain how they had given birth to a girl who cared only for sensations and yet was intelligent and quick-witted. She was not mercenary. And how kind she could be, soft and loving. She was ten years younger then he was, he ought to feel ashamed of making love to her. If not I, then some other, and very soon, he thought. Only her body was innocent and inquisitive: her mind knew too well what she wanted—no fear of her missing it through blindness or weak pity.

' I've kept the best to the end,' Hannah said. ' After all, they're giving me my holiday in June—the same fortnight when you have your leave. Look pleased, Davy.' She laughed herself for pure joy. ' Think of us together in France, my dearest! '

Renn thought of it. To save himself he drew her close to him and kissed her mouth and slender jutting nose and her narrow pierced ears. Never in his life had he expected this happiness, this love, which pierced his heart, for which there are no words—and he had never felt this intolerable anguish. What must I do? he thought. What can I do?

' To-day I lost my job,' he said, smiling at her. ' That is, I resigned—I was just in time, another day and I should have been sacked. In fact we can't go away. Have you noticed many unemployed—I mean of course unemployed without incomes—on the French boats? And even if I find work at once '—he could not tell her now that he had been dismissed without a character—' they will hardly give me leave in June.'

Hannah looked into his face for a moment. She brushed her finger gently below his eyes. ' You're crying. Good heavens, what a baby.' Smiling, she drew his head down and held it rocking him against her thin breast. ' Never mind, never mind, my dear.' She lowered her voice. ' Everything is all right, bless you—you know we can be ridiculously happy in London. If you're still unemployed we'll buy apples and eat them riding on the tops of buses.' Still radiant and smiling, she let herself fall gently on her back, taking him with her in her arms.

CHAPTER XI

LEAVING the main road Nicholas drove more quickly than was safe through the narrow lanes. He was anxious about Hervey. 'This is your last day in town,' he said, frowning and too emphatic, because he felt he had neglected her.

'Until Monday when you take me in to the Home,' she answered. From the darkness the scent of young leaves came into the car. She held her hand out to feel the air on it and the coldness dropping from the trees. She was too tired to fall asleep. When they reached the gate where the path went to her house there was a shabby car drawn against the hedge, and T. S. Heywood seated on the running board. He stood up and came forward slowly.

'I had to drive a man, a German chemist, to Harrow, and I came back this way,' he said, with an air of doubt: 'I wondered how Hervey was. She shouldn't run about London.'

'She's not going to,' Nicholas said curtly.

'You can help me down to the house while Nicholas takes our car to the garage,' Hervey said, speaking—to console him for Nicholas's roughness—as if he were the only person she cared to see.

'I won't stay ten minutes,' T. S. said.

'Stay the night. You can have Richard's bed.' The very thought of a third person in the house, and having to think of him and spread sheets on his bed, made her tired to her death. But, except her family, only he and Georgina were dear to her, and she knew the dryness of his life. He helped her along the path awkwardly, with love.

'I shan't stay the night.'

When Nicholas came in he had repented of his bad humour.

73

He made T. S. sit down, drew the curtains, put a match to the stove and gave himself all the airs of a friendly man. He tried to send Hervey to bed, but she had made herself tea and she moved about the room slowly with her cup, drinking and looking into cupboards and behind shelves filled with books.

' A cup of tea is the first thing I shall ask for in the other world,' she said, making a joke of herself.

All the time Nicholas was talking to the other man, one at either side of the stove with the whisky between them, he was aware sharply of his wife moving about the room. After a time he knew what she was doing—preparing this room for when she went away from it on Monday and if she should not come back. Now as he listened to T. S., and answered with an acute mind, a part of his mind went from him and stood beside her as she touched first one and then the other of her possessions.

' I've thought about Hervey's manifesto,' T. S. said.

' Not mine,' Hervey murmured, straightening wearily her back, as women do after long stooping. This is the oldest gesture in the world, older than falling on knees or holding out arms.

' Well, I dislike manifestoes. The miners have been shabbily treated, but I shan't side with them, because I'm tired of war. And *this* war will end in all our deaths. Hervey and her friends are arranging their own executions '—(Here Hervey took out a letter from a drawer, read it, looked queer, and tore it into the smallest scraps. Silently Nicholas asked her, What is it? Thinking him absorbed in his talk she did not even look at him)—' but they don't know it. The simple truth is—there is no way in which the miners can become well off without ruining the mine owners. And do you suppose the mine owners will allow that? Why should they? Why should the class—no, it's more than one—which has enjoyed power and property now lamely give it up? Of course they won't give it up, they're not fools or saints.

They'll keep it, they'll fight if necessary, if by any miracle the people who have no power and no property worth hoarding should turn revolutionary and want to fight. What fools you all are!'

T. S. was speaking quietly, with so much bitterness that his listener started, and even Hervey turned her head for less than a moment. She had emptied a shelf of its papers and was dividing and tearing up.

'But the miners' quarrel is with the owners, not with society,' Nicholas said, frowning.

'We're not talking about the miners,' T. S. said roughly and quickly. 'We're talking about civilisation. Can't you understand yet that the only way things can go on is for a great many people to spend their lives slaving, under and on the earth, on the sea. They *are* slaves, they must be always. Why not say it? They're not beaten, no one starves—and the intelligent ones escape. Look at me! My father was a small shopkeeper who died bankrupt, from incompetence, my mother kept me and herself alive by mending and washing for eight families——' He had become confused now with anger or excitement or a memory, and he stopped abruptly.

'If you think it was right that Nicholas should be sent to Eton and Christ Church while you and I——' Hervey began gently.

'I don't say it's right, I say it was necessary,' T. S. said. 'To change it you must pull down society, you must destroy—I hate destruction, I hate violence, I hate cruelty. And do you think you can have a revolution without violence? You, you, Nicholas, who have had everything out of it—what do you think of the death of society?'

Nicholas had listened to him with growing bewilderment. He could not imagine why the other man was so moved. 'You've thought about it more carefully than I have,' he said at last. 'To be honest with you, I don't know yet where I stand.'

He noticed that Hervey had turned back to her labours. Oh my dear, he thought, what do I care about anything more than you? He wished devoutly that T. S. would leave them.

But T. S. went on anatomising the corpse of society with as much pleasure as if he hated it. Half listening, Hervey on her knees heard him say: 'And then the Dark Ages again.' At once she had the strange sense she had had perhaps a score of times in her life, of living in the life of another woman, as easily as if Then and Now are one moment. Kneeling, she felt a kinship, half knowledge, half pity, with some woman living in the simpler not crueller time caught between the words Dark Ages. Clearly, as in the moment before dusk, and when dark clouds have covered the zenith so that all below them the light is strengthened and sharp, she saw a field, a may tree in blossom, a house, and all beyond these darkness, but a darkness without certainty. This poor scene, as if it were all, filled her with longing and sickness for her own youth. She moved books and glasses, and taking up a stocking from her mending shelf looked at it carefully before putting it on one side, and so came back to the room and her body: which was heavy with its own fears.

She stood up slowly and went over to Nicholas's chair. She put her hand on his shoulder. So joined they were alone together. T. S. felt this and he felt that he was in their way and must go. He imagined them turning to each other when they had locked the door at his back, and sighing with thankfulness.

' Well,' he said, standing up. He touched Hervey's hand. ' Good night, Hervey.'

Why do I care for her? he thought. She is unscrupulous, devious, cold to all but a few people—of whom I am not one. Her kindness is only want of heart. Suddenly he kissed her, which he had not done in the eighteen years he had known her. She was too much surprised to move, but she looked at him with her fine intimate smile and blushed.

'Come to see me—after—I mean in the Home,' she said in a low voice.

The door closed on him and on the night, and Nicholas turned to her with impatience. 'Why did you bring him in?' he said angrily. 'I thought he was going to be here all night.'

She was hurt and secretly pleased with his anger. With self-pity she thought, He ought not to lose patience with me now. And in the same moment she was filled with happiness because he was scolding her, because they were here together, alone, in the small shabby house, truly because they were alive and had married and were fond of each other. This, she thought, is real—as though reality were not in all things but descended by grace into only a few of them. Words, looks, gestures, events, slid between the fingers like shelling peas into a bowl, full pods coming among those dry and spoiled by the frost. She looked at Nicholas and said:

'Perhaps I shan't see him again.'

Nicholas's looks changed at once. He put his arms round her, in bitter self-reproach. 'I'm a careless beast, please forgive me,' he said.

Hervey could feel that he was trembling. She was ashamed of the trick she had played on him, but not too deeply ashamed—she could not help feeling a little pleasure in its success. To forget it and to make Nicholas forget it, she said:

'Did you see William Gary to-day?'

'No,' he said. He moved away from her and sat down, anxious and preoccupied at once, as soon as she spoke of Gary.

He thinks more of William Gary than of me, she thought, watching him narrowly. It was not true, but there was more than a grain of truth in it, since the love between Gary and Nicholas involved as many trivial, awkward, and serious events as a marriage, without the effort.

'But you are going to see him?'

'On Tuesday evening.'

'Talk to him about the Strike.'

'Of course I shall,' Nicholas said, with a smile. 'But don't get it into your head that I can move him. Since he began making money instead of merely spending it, his notions about life and how one should live have changed. Mine have changed too.'

'That was my fault,' Hervey laughed. She went to the writing-table and began turning over the papers. 'Do you know we shall need money when this is over? How soon do you suppose I can begin to write again? I wish I had been more firm and insisted on finishing my novel before the operation. I should have finished in three months.'

'Then you'd have died,' Nicholas said.

'Nonsense. Every doctor talks in that way—it is nothing but ju-ju and I was a fool to be taken in by it.'

She waited a moment, to know whether he would speak of the money, but he said nothing, as if her words had had no meaning for him and half sighing she went on: 'I shall recover quickly, months before they expect it. They have no idea how strong I am. I was always strong, I can't think of myself as dying or even wanting to die. No matter what happens I should want to live simply to be alive. Think of not being able to see the trees, why, it's not thinkable at all, unthinkable, unbearable, and in fact I don't believe it. I feel quite certain I shall live to be a thousand. Could we have some music—now—before I go to bed?'

'It's close on one o'clock,' Nicholas said, but he went to the gramophone and chose a German record. Hervey listened to it with less than half her mind—she was thinking of the money, of her unfinished book, and at last of Richard, her real and everlasting care and vital business of her mind. If I could see farther ahead, she thought; if I were sure that next year I shall have Richard, Nicholas, and peace to write in—it is all I want: ever—shall I have it? Suddenly the music, quickening to its close in an astonishing splendour of the violins, hurried her on a strong current into the thought of infinite space. For a time she listened to it deliberately, then

failed and allowed it to wash over her without understanding.
When the record ended Nicholas took out another.

'No more,' Hervey said, standing up.

'Just one more. There's time.'

'On your last day you'll be saying, Just one more minute,'
Hervey laughed. 'You're helpless, unpractical, you have no
head for figures—and neither have I and so I love you.'

'What was the paper you tore into such small pieces?'
he asked her suddenly.

'Shall I tell you? It was a letter from your lawyers
about the divorce—my divorce from Penn, not yours from
your wife. I've kept it these two years and now I've torn it
up and to-morrow I shall destroy everything belonging to
those days. Listen, if anything goes wrong—it won't, of
course—but if it should, or in any circumstances you will
never let Penn take Richard, will you?'

'No. Never,' Nicholas said. He came over to her and
touched her gently. 'My only love, if anything happened
to you I certainly shouldn't want to live. But now you
must go to bed. I'm going to help you to undress, and put
you into bed.' He stroked her cheeks and lifting both her
hands he laid them against his face. 'My love, my lovely
Hervey.'

She felt so surprised, joyous, and grateful that she did not
move. Thinking of her first husband, of Penn, had reminded
her too nearly of days without any certainty of kindness.
Indeed so long as she lived she would not feel certain of it.
The lesson had been too sharp. Gentleness would always
surprise her freshly.

Friday, May 7th
THE LION AND THE UNICORN

CHAPTER XII

IF William Gary had not been castrated by a shell bursting close to him in October 1918 he would have married, spent his money, had children. As things were, he had nothing to do less deathly than make money breed. He inherited his mines in Scotland in the same year he was wounded. He joined them to other mines, north-east to Stirling and Fife, east to the Lothians, south and south-west to Lanarkshire and Ayrshire; burrowing under the shires like a mole he saw the sun again in south Yorkshire. If you travel to the north, look out for trucks painted with the names Harben and Gary (names covering the ranks of back-to-back houses marching crazily from Field Bottom to Steep Row, covering burning heaps of ash eating into the soil, covering wheels and hoists, the pithead anatomy, covering cage, galleries, roads for men and ghosts in the heavy earth).

And now, since his coal fuelled blast-furnaces everywhere, it was an easy passage for him to owning the furnaces. There are cool shining streams near the coalfields and sometimes a boy working in the pit remembers one and he looks up queerly at the roof of earth as though he expected to see through it upwards to the stream running clear in sunlight between its banks. Clyde, Tyne, Tees, Aire, and Don are fed by such remembered bright trickles—five rivers that are straddled by William Gary, who had something, some drop of profit, from eighteen works making or using steel on their banks.

His miners carried all these on their stooped shoulders. You could say that if there were no miners, if no man had ever been found as needy and desperate as daily to face death underground (trapped, my God, under the earth, under his own floor, under the feet of his wife) by suffocation, flame, falling rock, there would have been no Age of Enlightenment, no discoverer of radium and electricity, no Fokker planes, no Bristol Fighters, no newspapers for journalising priests to wipe onto, no Hollywood, no Garbo, no democracy. The architects of the modern city of the world buried a living man under the first stone. It is an old custom.

Gary was long-sighted. Leaders of the common men, the careful Citrines, bold Bevins, haggle with him for wages, busy as beavers, ascetics in a cause which, time was, had other martyrs. He gives them a third of a shilling to their pockets and at once dismisses a thousand men, bringing in their room a machine. He knows that his quarrel is not with these men's leaders. He has a more hideous quarrel with time. How long before Clyde, Tyne, Tees, Aire, and Don flow between stony rubbish? How long before America and Russia, to say nothing of the rare East, catch up and overshoot this country? How long before he can tell careful Citrine, bold etc., etc., to eat grass, because the kingdom is departed from them and the answer to everything left doubtful in the past is a lemon? And by that time will his issues, his dear children, maggots every one of them, be naturalised in another country?

With him on Friday morning in the room were two men, Harben and the Jew Cohen. Swan was cooling his heels in the outer room, having been ordered to come at ten and it was now a few minutes off eleven. For some time Gary had said nothing. He watched Harben. The sun falling on the older man's face glazed it, like fresh varnish filling up the cracks in a painting, so that it looked nearly smooth. How much longer will he live? Gary wondered. He intended to keep certain of his undertakings separate from Thomas Harben's until he felt himself to be clearly and undeniably the stronger. Until then he was Harben's ally, but there was no allied command.

Harben was talking for his benefit. Lately he had been astonished to find himself being assailed and knocked down by ideas which had nothing directly to do with ships, steel, oil, or banking houses. They came into his head when he was alone or when he lay in bed at night, and sometimes kept him awake. He was so unused to accidents of this kind that he was at first uneasy and disturbed, but it soon came to him that he could make presents of them. He did not give them either to his wife or his mistress—he saved them to bestow on Gary. He felt a strange pleasure, almost the shyness of an awkward lover, in speaking about them to him. None of his ideas were fresh or living, but he was not a judge of that. He had a high opinion of all of them.

'Why,' he said—for some reason he looked fixedly at Cohen—'did we form the Economic Council? Not simply to tread on this snake or that, but to crack up the general need for authority. Do you know authority's the thing, the one important thing? That came to me the other night. I say that even common and stupid people know in their hearts you can't have freedom—freedom for what? For scavengers and miners to refuse to work? But all these have been so choked with butter by socialists, tub-thumpers and rogues, that they go on talking and scribbling about their freedom, and you get strikes and conscientious objectors and the communist rabble and so forth. Well, isn't this Strike our God-given chance? Swan—or if he's not the man we'll dismiss him and bring on someone else—must mobilise opinion to praise authority, authority, authority. D'you see?'

He leaned across and with pretence of seeking a paper touched all four edges of his desk. Gary noticed it. That gesture of yours, my friend, is a habit, he thought. The image of Harben's skeleton, leaning backward sightlessly fingering corners, came to him and made him smile.

'We have the authority—isn't it better to say as little about it as possible?' he said softly.

Harben's gift was left on his hands.

'A nearer business,' Gary went on, 'is the need of subsidies for steel and shipping. We want newer plant. We need to squeeze the water out of Garton's.'

'And why should we pay for it ourselves?' Cohen said smiling. 'Time was when a man whose business was not prospering borrowed or went bankrupt. Lately he goes off to the Exchequer to save himself. I intend to begin in the *Daily Post*, and later in the *Evening Post*, a campaign on the lines of, It can't go on like this—the Government must do something.' His eyes, protrusive and too full, were almost merry. 'Something must be done. The oftener you say it the better. Something must be. Somingmustbe. Subbimusby. Subsidy.' He smiled sharply at his little joke.

Gary looked at him with intense curiosity. The most astonishing of your virtues is that you are not cynical, he thought. On the other side, you are very unpleasant —sentimental, inquisitive, destructive. If you can't manage to be less clever you'll destroy yourself in the end. The feminine softness and mobility of Cohen's mouth surprised him again—in the face of the fifty-seven-year-old Jew it was strange and provoking.

Harben looked down his long nose at the joke. He distrusted Cohen without troubling to know why. Hoping to disconcert him he drawled:

'You know best how to sell your papers.' He looked at Gary. 'And now let's have Swan in and tell him that this leaflet won't do. It's merely ridiculous to set up Citrines, Thomases, and MacDonalds as leaders of revolutions. It will make the Economic Council look ridiculous—even in the eyes of your readers, my dear Cohen.'

'It's certainly difficult,' Gary said with a smile, 'to make a horrifying figure out of the man who said, *At one minute to twelve I would have grovelled for peace*. I'd feel more inclined to reward him. But in the meantime what has been done to arrange an armistice? Has what's-his-name come on the scene yet, with his unofficial overtures? My prophecy is that he'll find these leaders of revolutions waiting to lick his hands with relief and joy. I know what I'm saying!'

He laughed.

When Swan came in he glanced at him in silence, with an air of irony. He knew that the young man looked on him as a friend and while this had once been true it was true no longer. He had not liked him, he had been sorry for him. For a time, the thought of Swan's crippled foot, and the pain, the least part of it physical, it gave him, had overruled his dislike of Swan's vanity and arrogance. But he had been told tales about the young man which displeased him. He had heard that Evelyn Lamb, when she was Swan's mistress, had given him large sums of money, and that he had humiliated her by bringing gross ridicule on her before her friends. Thinking of this, he listened with a cold smile to Harben's rating the young man for his silly leaflet. He believed that Swan could be useful to them.

Swan stood stiffly at the side of the desk. He blushed all the way down his neck and his eyes became glazed with anger. He looked suddenly at Gary, and believing that he paid no attention to what Harben was saying he tried to appeal to him in his reply.

'I imagined that what the Council needs most now is funds,' he said in a firm voice. 'The leaflet you don't like was meant for private circulation among smaller firms, to convince them that they ought to become members.'

Gary glanced at him for the first time.

'You meant to play on their fears,' he said.

'Exactly,' Swan said. He wanted to say a great deal more, to speak to Gary as though, if not friends, they were equals. Gary was indeed only six years older and of his class. It seemed to Swan that Gary must certainly feel more sympathy for him than for two much older men, one of whom had the ill-luck to be also a Jew. Swan's dislike of Jews had so many roots that he would have been puzzled to count them. It grew stronger the whole time. He had begun to feel an impulse of violence towards certain Jews and at unexpected times. Only a day or two before, leaving the room where he had gone with a woman late at night, he met on the staircase a young starved-looking Jew in a shabby coat and at once he felt such loathing for this poor and inoffensive creature that he would have enjoyed beating him about the head.

He looked at Gary with an expectant and candid air. For all he felt, he had not the confidence to speak to the other as his equal. He waited and suffered. But Gary did not speak a second time, or look up when Swan left the room.

'That young man imagines himself a hero—or worse still, Mussolini—or the Messiah,' said Cohen, when he had gone.

Harben considered this remark another senseless joke. He stood up to go away and turned his back on Cohen.

Cohen watched him walk the length of the room: with his hand on the door he spoke to Gary, lowering his voice so that it was inaudible at the other end. Cohen knew that both men mistrusted him. They think of me that I am too clever to be trusted, they think I am not English, not of sound bone, a man whom they use because no one else has taken my place.

He was surprised, when he had thought this, to feel that he knew more about England than either of them. He who had grown to childhood in a slum in the East End had felt under the filthy paving-stones the soil of the country. He had taken it for his country then, with knowledge. It says in the Scriptures—*He shall cause them of Jacob to take root.* But this '*bitter and hasty nation*'—that, too, is in the Scriptures—contemned him. Why?

Gary closed the door on Harben and came back to the desk. He wanted something from Cohen and disliked asking for it. At last he said abruptly:

' I notice that your newspapers have fallen into the habit of attacking Louis Earlham—I can't imagine on what grounds, he's not dangerous. In fact I like him, and find him a very decent reasonable fellow. Need these sneers and scoldings go on any longer ? '

' Certainly not, not in the least,' Cohen said, laughing. He looked at Gary sharply, his face warm and alert with his unsleeping curiosity. He always wanted to understand motives. If he cherished any hope that Gary would satisfy him he was disappointed, for in the shortest time Gary very civilly got rid of him by going with him to the door.

' I'm much obliged to you,' he said smiling. He added: ' I assure you Earlham is worth sparing.'

CHAPTER XIII

It happened that Earlham dined with Gary that evening. It happened: because for a year, since they became intimate, they dined every Friday in Gary's flat. A pity if the accident of a General Strike, in which one of them was a mine-owner and the other taking the part of the miners, should spoil a pleasant custom.

Gary gave him a light meal and a little wine. His instinct (for friendship) warned him that the plainer and scantier the food the better this week his friend would enjoy it. Earlham was tired out, his skin stretched across his bones. He had thought on his way here that he could neither talk nor sit in his chair, but insensibly, as the food restored him—and then one glass of a thin hock—he felt relaxed. The strange part was that he felt easier in this room, windows looking towards the Park, ebony and walnut table, Chinese rugs, light hidden in the cornice—than he felt now in his room in his own house. Here he was easy.

With the coffee Gary said: 'It would be awkward and foolish not to talk about what is in both our minds. Do you agree? And if I say anything that offends you—as we arranged at first you can rap hard on the table,' he said, smiling.

Earlham smiled. 'Why do you suppose we never made a rule against my sometimes offensive remarks?'

'Because you can never offend me,' Gary said gently.

'God knows I'm sceptical and cold at heart about the whole business,' Earlham said wearily. 'I don't like General Strikes. I don't believe we shall achieve anything by it—

and if it drags on many more days there'll be trouble in
certain districts, and nothing for it but violent repression. Is
that a more cheerful prospect to us than to the Government?
It's plain hell.'

'But you have your people in hand?' Gary said. 'I
thought the Labour Party's speeches in the House very
reasonable . . . I'm going to give you a very small *fine*.
The rum ration. It tastes no better this way.' He held
the glass to the light for a moment.

'Oh it's not a question of the Party in Parliament or of
the Council,' said Earlham—'at any time common sense
and experience would keep us straight. But what can you
do with the ignorant mass of the Party in the country?
So long as it does as it's told—well. But one hothead forming
a ridiculous Council of Action could begin mischief.'

'Yes, I see,' Gary mused. 'And do you—would you
say that the miners are less reasonable than other Unions?
If you remember, I showed you the figures of my own mines
a month ago.'

'I remember them.'

'This is difficult for you,' his friend said. 'And I give
you my word, not only for you. If you, if anyone, the
devil or Mr. Cook, could tell me how to reorganise my
mines without shortening wages, I'd give him a mine or
two for himself. This has kept me awake.'

'I haven't had three hours' sleep a night since the
twenty-eighth of April.'

'My poor Louis,' Gary said.

'And why in the name of God are your people
mulish and impossible?' Earlham cried. 'The whole of
Saturday, and until two in the morning, Pugh, Thomas, and
Citrine, with the Prime Minister, the Minister of Labour,
and two others '—as he said them, the names were like any
names coming at the end of an old document, the event
now dust—'worked out a formula. Allowed cuts in
wages—certain wages. And next day one of them said: *Never*

mind what the miners or anyone else says, we accept it.
We had worked our heads off for weeks to avoid this,
imploring action. Your side deliberately forced this thing
on us. The palpable farce of Sunday night!' He leaned
back in his chair, gripping the arm. 'You really should
rap the table,' he said, forcing a smile.

'I'm not a politician,' Gary said. '*You* know,' he said
quietly, 'this is a larger struggle than anyone is likely to
explain to the poor bloody infantry on either side. Between
your would-be dictators and ours what is there to choose?
Both of them will get men hung up on the wire, to no
good.' His eyelids twitched. 'Given time I could get the
job done without fuss,' he said. 'Come here, Louis.' He
was at the window, and Earlham walked across to him.
'Do you know any hour in any month when London looks
as well as it does now?'

From the clear air of the foreground, the light choosing
out certain walls and steeples as if at random, so that they
seemed made of a more fluid matter than brick, all that
multitude of buildings melted at a great distance into the
mist.

'You don't imagine what it's like to live in some of
those streets,' Earlham answered.

'When you were living in one room and half starved,
were you unhappy?'

'Not more often than I am now.'

Gary stood against the window. He was heavier in body
than he had been twelve months since, in spite of the
exercise in the gymnasium, and fencing. Louis noticed it.
He lives too well, he thought, bitterly.

'You can't *think* when you're hungry,' he said loudly.
'That's a lie—I've proved it. Living in one room, and
the smells, and rotting your end off—trying to fill yourself
up with bread and scrape and to think you're not
half dead—what's surprising is not that there are four
thousand communists, but that there aren't a million of

them.' He put his hand to his head. ' I shall have to go. First to Eccleston Square, and I must show up in my constituency. If I were not so unbelievably sleepy—And when I go to bed I *can't* sleep.'

' Your constituency,' Gary repeated. ' Yes. We'll have some fresh coffee first. That's South London, isn't it ? I think there's no trouble of any sort there.'

' Not yet.'

' Not likely to be.'

' The truth is,' Earlham said, and he yawned. ' With only reasonable luck we shall avoid trouble everywhere. The bulk of the men are ignorant, but they're not bloody fools. There's a man in the Deptford branch of the Party, Rigden, employed as carter at the Stokes Chemical Works, ex-soldier—very often I can't remember his name—patient, obedient. I'm sure he was a willing, clean soldier. I can't imagine what treatment would make that man violent. But of course it's the numbers, a crowd of five hundred reasonable decent men can become one mad dog. What do you expect from a fellow like Cook, irresponsible, an actor ? '

He sat down. The man came into the room with the fresh coffee and placed it near Gary on the table. He was going to draw the curtains, but Gary said: ' Leave them.' He pushed the tray across. ' Help yourself, Louis,' he said, smiling.

' Aren't you drinking it ? '

' No, this lot is for you, to help you to keep awake.'

He watched Earlham's other hand, not holding the cup, gripped on his knees, with at first the bone pressing against the skin as if it would burst through, and then relaxed and the fingers lying apart open. He had long, well-formed fingers. Looking at them, Gary felt a serious liking for him; it was sharpened by the scarcely noticed drop in it of contempt.

CHAPTER XIV

When Earlham had pushed his way through the men waiting, talking, silent, standing beside motor-cycles, patient, impatient, he was stopped by a man who knew him and said:

'Louis, the guv'nor was telephoning half an hour ago to find you.'

'Where is he?' asked Earlham. As soon as he had the answer he turned and made his way out impatiently, and went as quickly as he could for having to walk the whole way, to the House of Commons. He could not imagine why he was wanted—the more so that when he entered the room he got nothing except a wave of the hand and a smile. He sat down to wait.

At last the other man began talking, and from his first words Earlham drew a sudden excitement. Not that he heard what was new or secret, but that he for some reason was trusted with this man's soul. (The reason, as it turned out, was a small one, smaller than a man's vanity—'My dear Earlham, I want someone to know my prog-nos-ti-cation of events.') So now, being very tired, Earlham had the sensation of following an endless corridor to the one window, as treacherous as smoke, at the end. End of the endless—that is or equals a vain man cured of his vanity.

'I have never concealed my belief that the way out of this mess, this awful diabolical mess, must be found immediately—any way must be better than none. . . . Talks have been set on foot—and I think—I may say to you—now a matter, yes, of time. But let us be perfectly absolutely clear. We have been within sight of a revolution. For one party in the nation to try to terrorise the government of

94

the nation, what—if it could succeed—is that if it is not revolution, civil war, the rape no less of the constitution ? '

He was struck by this metaphor and repeated it several times, varying ' rape ' to ' outrage ' and once to ' defilement ' —' defile the virginity of the constitution,' he said—' this defilement. . . . The elected government of this country must govern. Defied by one body of men it must oppose that body: except an irrevocable suicide, no other way is open to it. Now I want you to observe my profound, my unalterable refusal of Bolshevism and general strikes, in short, revolution. In sober fact there is no such thing— there is the everlasting possibility of disobedience, civil disorder, destruction, yes, yes—but the mere whisper or cloud no larger than a man's hand of revolution in this country is madness. If it were attempted it would lead only to repression, and once repression begins it goes on, my dear Earlham, and on, until at a certain moment in the fixed course of society it threatens even your freedom and mine. . . .'

Here followed a discourse on freedom, and extremely fine it was, in short eloquent. Earlham was moved, too, by the other's fiery earnestness. He saw that the man was as tired as a dog—wearier than I am, thought Earlham— over-wrought and in a bad temper. And yet he talked— my God, how he talks, Earlham groaned—and fixed the younger man with a stare that went through his head as if it were a nail nailing it to the wall behind him.

It was impossible to discredit this man's emotion. He was not always the same man. When he had finished with freedom even his looks changed. His expression became almost spiteful.

' If I am asked to listen to any more balderdash,' he said, ' about the historic mission of the proletariat, I shall very probably be sick.'

Earlham could not help smiling, but he nodded and said: ' I rather agree with you, sir.'

'There is nothing historic about the proletariat, nor heroic nor fruitful—not even in our great country—and any man who says there is is a fool or a rogue. Do you know, when I was a child my father used to tell us that the carver had to choose between being a fool or a knave— if he gave away the best slices he was a fool, and a knave if he kept them. . . .'

He laughed as merrily as a child. Earlham felt only relief that the time for confidences was over. It was not the first time he had been favoured in this way. A friendly squeeze of his shoulder, a deep sigh, and he was free to go.

CHAPTER XV

HE went back to Eccleston Square, found a despatch rider
with a side-car going into Sussex, and asked him to go
through Deptford. He fell rather than stepped into the seat.
The driver, a precise taciturn young man, did not talk to
him. Earlham shut his eyes. He thought irritably that
David Renn, to whom he was going, would still be full of
enthusiasm for the Strike—and hard at work—with his
ridiculous Finance and Propaganda committees, Defence
corps, Food, Permit and Transport committees and all the
clatter of busyness—while I, he thought, and held his head.
And fools like Grassart, he cried. He recalled that Grassart
had talked to him one night about the tactics of street fighting.
It would be ludicrous if it were not barely conceivable.
How can I know whether there won't be fighting in Deptford
next week? In his exhaustion even this short journey in a
side-car began to smack of civil war.

He remembered another thing—an Englishman who
was involved in the fighting in St Petersburg had told him:
he was in charge of a district and one morning—it was
still dark and the roofs grey, wet with the mist—he gave
a wrong order by mistake, it was a misjudgment, he had to
decide at once and to give the order and his mistake cost the
lives of seven or eight good men, one of them his nineteen-
year-old brother. It could happen to anyone, thought
Earlham. And much worse—could I order an Englishman
to shoot down Englishmen?

' How's it going? ' the driver asked suddenly.

' What? '

' Why, the Strike, I meant. Are we winning, or not? '

97

' Bound to win,' Earlham muttered.

' *They* all seem in a doodah there,' the man said. He jerked his head back.

' If you were responsible for a show that could turn to civil war in a week—men being shot, killed—you wouldn't feel about it that it was a picnic,' Earlham said sternly.

The other did not answer. Outside the Committee rooms he lifted his hand when Earlham thanked him and clattered away suddenly into the darkness. Earlham looked after him with proper envy. To have no responsibility, to be under orders, he thought, must be heaven on earth.

He was thinking this when he walked into the inner room searching for David Renn. He went first to him because he would as gladly as not forget him. The uneasy liking he felt for him—it had been love when they were in the same company of a battalion, and afterwards for at least five of their years in London—gave him no pleasure. Yet he felt bound to Renn, as he certainly was not to Gary or to another man. He felt too that Renn had not ceased to be his friend, in spite of arguments and bitterness.

Renn was alone in the room, writing. He looked up from it and smiled.

' Why, Louis, we'd given you up long since—we didn't expect you at this time.'

' I couldn't get here earlier,' Earlham said. He sat down. ' What is that you're writing? Shall I go away? '

' My to-morrow's Bulletin. Give me a sentence or a message to put into it, Louis. They'll expect one from you.'

' Tell them to keep quiet and to cultivate their gardens,' Earlham said.

' I've done that already,' Renn said softly. ' Is it all you can think of, Louis? '

' My God, I am dog tired,' Earlham said.

' You look it. If you'd leave the House to amuse itself

in its own way and work here for a few days you'd feel livelier. I'm very serious, Louis. Those swine at Headquarters will be the death of you. Can you tell me what's happening? Is it true that peace talks are going on behind the curtain?'

Earlham drew down the edges of his mouth. 'Don't you want peace, David?'

'Not peace at any price. Not this time. We're in this together, not some to be saved and the others left to rot.'

'Are you prepared for trouble?'

'There won't be any trouble. We have only to wait— like stones.' He took up his pen. 'That's useful, I can use it. If the whole body of English workers lies across the path like a stone the owners can't get at any of the men to ruin them.'

'And if the Government were to use force?'

'You mean the army? Order soldiers to fire on unarmed men? They wouldn't dare.' Renn was actually gay. 'They've put the wind up you in Parliament, Louis. You had better stay here!'

'Don't think I'm not heart and soul for the miners,' Earlham exclaimed. The affection in Renn's voice did not help him—he knew too well that Renn watched him and, in spite of his love, had judged and found him wanting. He resented it. 'I happen to be in a more responsible position than you are——'

'I'm in no position at all,' Renn said easily. 'Yesterday I lost my job. I resigned it, but I should have been sacked if I had not.'

Earlham was at a loss. He could not think what to say. After a moment he said with a smile: 'We shall have to find something for you to do.'

Renn was looking at him. 'Don't trouble, Louis,' he said quietly. 'I shall find something for myself. I always do in the end.' There and then he decided not to tell his friend he had been sent off without a reference, that indispensable part of a civilised man's goods, more necessary to him than a passport or the means to beget children.

' I was hearing last week of a man who wants a tutor for his son—to go abroad with him. You have how many languages? '

' Four,' Renn said. ' Where did you hear it? The company you keep nowadays, Louis! Did you by any chance hear it from Mrs. Thomas Harben? I don't think I should be an acceptable tutor to a friend of hers.'

Earlham felt a throb of rage in his body. It gave him the energy to get up and walk out of the house as far as the marsh. The meeting at which he had promised to speak had dribbled to nothing, but at sight of him it rallied. He climbed on to the cart and with the first words he felt happier and nearly alert. In no time he had the men shouting and cheering.

Renn was alone for a few minutes. He sat at the table holding his pen, and thought with an extraordinary bitterness, I have written thousands of words during my life and not one will survive me. He was disappointed in the face Earlham had shown to his news. But what had he hoped?

Henry Smith came in and offered to help him with the Bulletin: it was all but finished and Renn pushed the page over to him without looking at it. He felt unable to squeeze out another word.

' I hear Louis has been in,' Smith said, writing.

' He went away ten minutes since.'

' So far as I'm concerned he can fall into the dock and break his neck,' Smith said. He looked up to see how his friend took this.

' He means well,' Renn said.

' The old men at the Base have fairly eaten his heart out. It must always have been weak. And, mark, that's not the whole of it. . . . He has too many wealthy friends. What excuse does he give for being friendly with Thomas Harben's wife? If it was her food——' Smith chuckled.

'I like a damned good meal m'self,' he said, smiling, 'but I'm damned if I don't think Earlham has a soul beneath eating.'

'If the old men—and they're not all old, but they all wear chest protectors—were honest socialists, their young men would be,' Renn said. 'The Party is sound—the rot begins at the top, in the will. And what did we expect? We've been trying to make the best of a society of jackals— is it surprising if some of us begin to think jackals not so nasty? Or at least to prefer them, because they're familiar, to the naked icy darkness of a new world, and the way to it dark, and no safe jobs, no birthday honours, no sitting in conference with permanent officials, no compliments from the honourable gentlemen on the other side? Louis is not a scoundrel—he's a victim.'

Henry Smith struck his hand on the table. He looked older, and though he smiled he was severe.

'No one likes eating and drinking better than I do,' he said. He had a warm lilting voice, not truly Welsh, since he was fully six years old when his mother took him to live in a room in Swansea, but with something of that strangeness overlapping the original, which may have been north country—Yorkshire, he had told Hervey, to please her. He liked to please women, and he was fonder of Hervey than he chose to know.

'If I could live as I pleased, Davy, I'd spend all my days travelling about the world, with a library, a kitchen with a first-rate chef, and a motor-car. That's what I'd like. And, by God, if you offered it to me to-morrow for the rest of a long life—I know I shall live to be ninety—on condition that I came out of my class and wore a claw-hammer coat and sometimes consorted with sin in the shape of court breeches and gave up working with bloody sweat to turn honest workers into revolutionaries—I'd shoot m'self if I gave it one look.' Suddenly he laughed, his eyes half closed and every line of his face turning up into a broad mask of mirth. 'Oh, Davy, Davy,' he exclaimed, 'to think I sat up until four this morning to finish writing a pamphlet when I could have been warm and snug in bed with a girl.

> *Du fragst mich Kind was Liebe ist ?*
> *Ein Stern in einem Haufen Mist.*

If a poet says love is a star dropped on a dunghill, who am I to contradict him? Eh, m'dear?'

Renn watched him with a smile. There was some dryness in his affection for the younger man. He still thought of himself as being responsible for Smith, because he had once saved him from jail or the workhouse.

'So you think Earlham is leaving us?'

'No, I didn't say that,' Smith answered gravely. 'All I said was that you can't become very friendly with well-placed people on the other side without losing your primitive desire to ruin them, and once you cease wanting to ruin your everlasting enemy you're well on the way to wanting to preserve him, and you talk about making terms with him and then of working with him for the common good. On the day you persuade yourself that there is good in common between William Gary and locked-out desperate miners you cease to be a socialist. It's the end of you so far as socialism is concerned, though no doubt you will still do excellent work embarrassing the enemy, taunting him with not wanting to do things you're afraid to do yourself, although you promised them and he didn't.'

He turned sharply round as a man came into the room. 'Ach, Roxby,' he cried, 'I was just warning Davy here that you can't trust the upper classes, they'll always let you down in the end and in you come. Well, m'dear, how is Hervey?'

'She says she's well,' Nicholas said, smiling. 'Am I in the way?'

'You're never in the way,' Smith said, warmly and swiftly, before Renn could speak.

Nicholas stretched his legs and yawned. He was reluctant to go home. The small airless room, the conversation of these two men, whom he thought he had known a long time, though he had known neither of them longer than the twelvemonth, satisfied in him a need left unsatisfied by his life with Hervey. To a point he preferred the society of men. When he had spent two, three, five hours among men, talking a great deal and listening when he was not bored, he became impatient and abruptly left. As soon as he was at home he would tell Hervey, rousing her if she were asleep, that he had wasted his evening, and so vehemently that he believed it as he said it.

He was entirely innocent that although Smith and Renn liked him neither was wholly at ease with him. He was not, as Hervey was, their friend. For worse or better his up-bringing had made an alien of him, in ways he did not suspect, or if he had suspected them he would have thought them unimportant. It was not his fault that when he asked questions his voice became peremptory, or that he had never been starving or hungry, and did not know what poverty smells like.

He had scarcely finished stretching when Louis Earlham returned. He was still flushed with the effort of speaking, and his excitement. Slow as Nicholas was to catch other men's thoughts, he felt the air of restraint that came in with him. He knew little of Earlham, and did not like him, but he would have been put to it to say why.

'Two men—they were either the whole of the Communist Party in Deptford or two young friends of yours,' Earlham said to Henry Smith, 'tried to ruin the meeting. Tell Grassart to make his fellows behave themselves—if they were his and not yours.'

'Grassart has been working here till all hours,' said Renn. 'We're not afraid of him, we're too busy.'

'Grassart lives next door to 98 Smith Lane,' Smith said with an air of solemnity. 'You know the house I

mean. I told you about it almost two years ago, a house
so filthy and rat and bug ridden that it scarcely bears thinking
of, but there are children still living in it, and I am working
still to get it closed. I told you it would survive a Labour
Government—oh you reformers!—and another and another.
The dear heaven knows how many times your backs will
bend sweetly to office while my house is still lived in.'

'Where is this house?' Nicholas asked. The thought of
children being tortured by bugs made him feel sick.

'Not ten minutes from this room. I can take you to it.'

Renn had been watching Earlham during these minutes.
Now he felt an impulse to help him.

'What luck did you have with the Anglo-Catholic priest,
Harry? One that works here,' he told Nicholas. 'I
told Smith to go and see him. I thought he could do more
than any of us, as a priest and no politician, to get the
house shut.'

'He's drawing out a genealogy of the place for me,'
Smith said. 'But the ground belongs to the Church and
the house itself to a company, to which a number of very
respectable and some noble persons have lent their money
at interest. The house at 98 Smith Lane—*lane*, mark
you—and the other almost as disgusting houses on either
side of it have roots twisted in the foundations of
cathedrals, bishops' palaces, and fine well-built houses about
England. When I try to drag up these old filthy roots to
burn them out of the soil, I find I'm disturbing the stately
homes and what not. All honest comfortable people are
alarmed—even Louis Earlham, Labour Member for South
London, that is also for 98 Smith Lane.'

Earlham's smile had been hard to arrange and was not
worth the trouble. 'Why don't you join the Communist
Party and have done?' he asked Smith. 'You could pass
the rest of a logically pure life drawing the plans for your
slave state.'

'But *is* communism slavery?' Nicholas blurted. 'Surely

what's wrong with us all is that we have too little communism. That's the danger. Too much isn't a danger yet.' He stammered, frowning, in the effort to make clear a thought struggling obscurely in the womb of his brain. 'We're too much individuals, the devil take the hindmost, and not enough human. *Nothing that is human is alien to me* is what I mean. Do you know, I've always felt that an ordinary serving soldier—I was one of them for four and a half years—is the only free man? He is not forced to make profits, he obeys the same orders as everyone else, he has no responsibility except that if he is an officer—I speak of any man up to the colonel of a battalion, beyond that they're out of their depth—if he's an officer, I say, he is responsible for his men's comfort and so on and so forth. But in himself he is free. Bound yet free.'

He stopped—not because he had nothing to say; he had too much and not the words for it. He felt foolish. Smith looked at him quickly, with a smile of surprise and affection.

'Nick's right,' he laughed. 'We're not living in a society. We're living in two camps, and some we thought were friends have turned up in the other camp, the swine!'

That is not what I meant, Nicholas thought.

Earlham went out quickly. He went into the other room and spoke to Joe Bradford, whom he did not trust. He believed that the trade union secretary had not much respect for him. This unfortunately was true. Vexed at being hindered in his work Joe gaped for a moment, and in answer to a sensible remark of Earlham's he growled: 'So you've come, have you?' and returned to his desk.

Earlham looked round and caught sight of Frank Rigden. The man was watching him with a look on his face which Earlham did not give himself the trouble to name. It was enough that Frank admired him and believed in him with his heart. He went over to him and spoke.

'You hard at it, Rigden?' Thank God he had remembered.

' I'm the one that goes to Eccleston Square for th' orders,' Frank Rigden said softly. ' Y'see, I've m'bike.'

' Good.   Good work.'

Feeling warmed to his stomach Earlham moved away, to speak to the others.   Rigden's eyes followed him with the unseeing gaze of a lover.   He then went out into the passage to repair the puncture in his tyre to the glory of Louis Earlham.

A man whose face he knew passed him.   He was the coal merchant in the High Street and he had come to ask permission to move a little of his coal from here to there.   He was directed to Joe Bradford.   Bradford questioned him curtly and at last refused the permit and the man had to go disappointed away.   He was muttering to himself when he passed Rigden for the second time.   Without any feeling of triumph but only a warm certainty Rigden thought: Mr. Earlham has his eye on you, you as charged Sally price and a quarter for one bag of cheap coal last fortnight and made a favour of it, you, now it's your turn.

Joe Bradford, too, had the feeling of a column of men at his back and himself marching with them, the level sun touching one side of his face and body.   He was filled with a strong tearing gaiety and as confident as ever he was in his life.   He thought he was lifted on a hill and saw the whole country.

He caught sight of Earlham and at once he was alone, not knowing what was in this man's mind.   The orders Frank brought from the centre were often contradictory or impossible to obey.   God knows what is happening in Newcastle or Glasgow or Plymouth, he thought queerly. He was possessed by a frenzied thirst for news, any news, of what men were doing in other towns.   They may be fighting, he thought, or the Strike may have collapsed already.   He was a man cut off in a shell-hole.

A man walked in stiffly and stood in front of him. ' Thought you'd like to see this,' he mumbled.   He was as thick with fatigue as dust. ' Anyone of you got a drop of oil for th' pip emma?' he asked, coughing. His eyes, bloodshot and red-rimmed, stared round the room. He smiled. ' Snug here.'

Joe Bradford unfolded the paper. ' MAIDSTONE. N.U.R. All still solid here. Success seems certain,' he read to himself. He handed it back to the despatch rider, who was drinking water in noisy gulps. ' Off with you,' he said quietly. The man went out, swaying, his leather coat slapping his knees. In the delicate web of Joe's mind he was reflected unnumbered times, now in the half-lighted street of a market town, now pelting in the darkness down the everlasting road between the witches' walls in Northumberland, now passing the night-paled walls of cottages, now on the high-level bridge at Newcastle, now in Gloucestershire between a stone wall and a hill round and smooth as a bare shoulder, and Joe was in every one of these riders and he was in the sleeping multitudes and he was in some part of the minds even of his enemies, in his sly shrewd conceited way.

Saturday, May 8th
HENRY SMITH

CHAPTER XVI

At eight o'clock the next morning Smith drove his car along the West Road towards London, as fast as the traffic and the natural infirmities of the car allowed. He was sleepy and stiff, having had less than two hours cat-nap in the back seat, after speaking at four meetings and deliberating with five strike committees between Southall and Reading, the last at three that morning. But he was as happy as a boy to be jolting along in the first sunlight, excited, and filled with an exultant joy that was taking the place of food in his stomach. He felt himself lifted on a wave rushing over the country from Cornwall to London, where it met others sweeping in from the north, the east and the south, a torrent to drown all the enemies of the people like straws. He sang to himself loudly as he drove, and as always when he was happiest the song was a sad one. He was singing *Early one morning*.

He had learned it at school in Swansea, and his mind was soon loose in the warren where he had lived as a child, streets stranger and grimmer than a nightmare, filled as he remembered them with yellow Chinamen, dark-skinned lascars, and men black with grease and coal-dust. His mother —she and he lived alone—went in terror of her life and his. She was always afraid that someone would murder them or kidnap him on his way from school. One evening he stayed to watch a fight with knives between a negro and a donkeyman from one of the ships, and the negro's little finger, sliced off as neatly as a piece of wood, flew into his hand. He dropped it, picked it up again, and ran holding it to the house of another boy where both of them hid it

III

under a pile of kindling. Then he cleansed his hands and ran home, but in the night he awoke trembling with the finger sticking its nail into him back and front. That was a terrible night. In the morning he sought and buried the finger in the most Christian way he knew, and thereafter it did not trouble him.

Thinking of the finger reminded him that a friend of his, a workman from a town near Barcelona, had all his toe- and finger-joints broken in the prison of Montjuich, one a day, to teach him not to be discontented with his lot. The sunlight of Barcelona quivered behind his eyes, blinding him, thrown back from the whiteness of the walls. His friend held out one of his maimed hands in the most curious way, as though it did not belong to him.

He came back to the tepid light and air of the West Road. A modern factory, as white as the house near the harbour in Barcelona in which he had lived then, but less dazzling, was on his right hand. Another near it was half built. They were both hideous, like a white leprosy on the once green fields of this part, just what you would expect a rich firm to put up in 1926, with no organ of taste and no instincts. By the side of the road, between two walls of earth, a man was resting, with a woman, a baby in a perambulator, and a small bundle of their goods. Henry Smith stopped the car to speak to them. They were from Durham, the man told him. He had a thin face, twisted, with bright grey eyes, the real face of a north-country peasant, a touch of the light-hearted rogue. He took to tramping a year ago, after he had been out of work for two years and could not fetch it, he said, any longer. His wife parted the rags of two jackets and an old vest to let her baby find her breast. The baby itself was wrapped in the pieces of many garments, too many for the time of year, but it lay as still in them as if it were indifferent.

' Are you happier on the move ? ' Smith asked.

The woman laughed suddenly. ' There was nothing for

us on any road, as long as we lived,' she murmured. 'We might as well see a bit of the world.'

As Henry Smith drove on he had a vision of the roads of Europe, flat roads across plains, the steep stony roads of hills, cart-tracks between vineyards and through forests, all of them with their light burden of foot-loose men. In America too. They were ruined peasants and farmers, broken off from the land, men driven out of the towns by machines—too restless to die quietly where they had lived. These outcasts, able to eat, sleep, and get their children in ditches, might survive the next war and carry over the seeds of civilisation. Perhaps these seeds would contain a Dante and a Michael Angelo, as well as machines and dictators.

Or they might give birth to the Messiah—the curiously still child might be the one expected—who would break open the prison doors of the human race so that every man saw his likeness in other men and knew that all men are born *by promise*, not some free and some bond. The machines have enslaved man because he first enslaved his neighbour. In his strength he forgot what he had known in his weakness, the comfort and peace of being one in a multitude of his fellows: he said, I am only I, and hardened his heart against the rest; so was born fear, guilt, and hatred. The places of kings, who oppressed the bodies of their slaves, and of priests who bound their minds, are being taken by dictators who bind and scourge both, so that it is inevitable a man shall be valued less than a machine. If he can crouch in a ditch, let him.

We expect the Messiah, who shall restore us. We need not be ashamed or surprised if he is got in a ditch between two outcasts with chapped hands and feet and stinking clothes.

In Chiswick, Smith passed a motor lorry; on the side of it was chalked in large letters: By Permission of the T.U.C. He burst out singing again. Now they know who's master, he thought; when the lights go out and the power fails and the sewers are choked they'll know whose hand has been removed——*ho-ow could you u-use a poor maiden so?*

The open part of Hammersmith was so choked by five torrents of vehicles that he was kept standing for ten minutes while an amateur pointsman strove to clear it. During this time he almost fell asleep. He opened his eyes to find that a young woman was standing close to the car, watching him with a smile. She had a slender merry face, a brown skin, dark hair, and thin gold rings in her ears. He smiled at her at once, and opened the door of the car.

' D'you want a lift, m'dear?'

She jumped in beside him as the traffic cleared a little ahead and he was able to move forward. The car moved with a jerk that sent the girl's head against the windscreen, hurting her sharply so that she began to cry. Smith drew up at the curb again and put his arm round her. She put her head on his shoulder and cried and then laughed, drying her eyes on the edge of a silk handkerchief she wore round the neck of her dress. Looking up into his face, she laughed again, loudly and merrily; he drew his arm closer.

' I think we go now more careful?' she said, slowly.

' I ought to have known you weren't English,' Smith said. ' What are you? French, eh?'

' No. I am German. From Berlin. But I think I speak English very well.'

' Like an Englishwoman, m'dear. What's your name? Mine is Smith. Is the poor head better?'

' My name is Anna. Shall we go already?'

He started the car carefully, and spoke to her in German. She gave him a startled glance, answered him shortly in German, then said she would rather speak English. And so they did, except when she used a German word inadvertently. She chattered away, precise and ungrammatical, and told him that she had been sent to England by her Berlin shop, to learn how to serve English visitors and to study the English clothes. She had a pocketful of sketches she had made, which she showed him. He was enchanted with her. She was alert, so gay, and intelligent, and without a trace of shyness. There was something fresh and sharp in her, like a fine bitter apple. He was drawn to her by a sudden ardent liking, he wanted to keep her with him to amuse him, above all he wanted to put his arms round her.

When he set her down in Wigmore Street he asked her when and where he could find her again. Women liked him, he was used to it, yet with that her willingness surprised him a little. She told him, smiling into his face with half-closed eyes, that she would be free at seven in the evening; if he liked she would have dinner with him. He arranged to meet her, and drove away, smiling with happiness. His body was wide awake and energetic, as though he had slept. He smiled, thumped the car in his excitement and hummed beneath his breath. *O don't deceive me, O never leave me.*

He drove on to David Renn's rooms in Marylebone, and found him lying on his bed, clothed, but unable to move because of the pain in his legs and back. The pains started from the scars of his wounds when he was tired, at their worst they were paralysing. Drops of sweat stood out on his forehead and the backs of his hands.

' I can't walk,' he said, smiling.

' You had better,' said Smith, ' take your shirt off and let me rub your back, if it's not too late to do any good. Why didn't you tell me last night—you must have known it was coming ? '

' I thought a night's sleep would ward it off,' Renn said.

' It didn't.'

' I didn't sleep.'

He lay face downwards on the bed, his hands grasping the sides of the mattress, while Smith rubbed his naked back in the way which sometimes gave him relief. Stooping over Renn's thin body, he seemed larger and stronger: the broad fingers of his hands, when the palms were resting on the shoulder bones, met half way down the spine.　He pressed in deeply over the tortured muscles and nerves, but so smoothly and gently that Renn was able to bear it without wincing.　After several minutes Smith had the satisfaction of feeling his body give way and relax.　He stooped lower, his face flushed with warmth and exertion. At last he took Renn between his hands and turned him gently over on the bed, and looked smilingly at him. ' Is that better ? ' he said gently.

' A great deal better,' Renn answered.

' Here.　Put your clothes on,' Smith said.　He gave Renn his shirt and jacket and went over to the washstand, where he stood noisily gulping water with his head held back, his throat a smooth red-brown column.　Putting the glass down, he stretched and shook himself, his face glowing. He came back smiling to the bed.　' You're not coming to the Strike Committee.'

Renn sat up and began putting together various papers scattered over the table.　He felt a sudden irritation with his friend's strength and self-confidence.　He determined against all reason and common sense to go to the Committee, although he knew that the pain had only withdrawn to prepared positions, as we used to say, during the War, of a forced retreat.

' Of course I'm coming,' he said curtly.　' You're going to drive me there in your wretched car.'

' Have sense, for once, do,' Smith began, with anxiety. He was interrupted by a knock on the door.　T. S. Heywood put his large head round it, and came in frowning and untidy.　He had had a postcard that morning from Renn abusing him for his indolence, and he had come round in a bad temper, to defend himself.

Renn greeted him with a smile as colourless as his lips. He could not account to himself for the impulse which made him write the card. It's not my business to disturb other people's consciences, he thought ironically. He liked Heywood, having guessed his secret at once, that he hungered and thirsted to be liked by everyone, but imagined that people laughed at his looks, his head was much too large for his short thick body, and his uncouth manner and contempt for the human race were his defence against being despised by them. He is too intelligent to join the side of repression, Renn thought, but since he believes that most men are either cruel or stupid he will give us away through despair: it will be surprising if he does not become a mystic, or at any rate a worshipper of something he will call pure science while he earns his living as a research chemist in poison gas. None the less, Renn liked him; he felt closer to him than to Smith, who shared every one of his beliefs, and what is more, loved him.

'What do you mean by writing me a silly spiteful post-card?' T. S. said at once. 'If you have time to do that sort of thing you don't need any help.'

'You've come to offer it, all the same,' Renn said in a calm voice. 'I need you, too. You can be a co-opted member of the Propaganda sub-committee in place of Hervey Russell, and get out the Bulletin. It has been banned by Headquarters, so don't think you're obeying orders: you remain an independent agent.'

Smith burst out laughing, and T. S. looked at him with loathing. He disliked and distrusted a man who enjoyed living so much as Smith did; he felt that he must be grossly stupid or grossly sensual, and he envied the younger man his assurance and peasant good looks. By a natural impulse he turned to Renn, who looked ill.

'Very well, I'll come with you,' he said, without enthusiasm.

They went downstairs and squeezed themselves into the car. It was a coupé, and the single seat was none too wide for Smith and one passenger: two made sitting in it a martyrdom, possibly a fatal one, since Smith was driving with his elbow on Renn's shoulder.

'I detest motor-cars,' T. S. said, with the energy of fear. 'They are like every other time-saving machine, inventions of the devil to make life shorter, nastier, and more uncertain. If an internal combustion engine had never been made we should still be living leisured reasonable lives, free of the fear of being blown to death from the sky or mangled on the ground.'

'You mean you would,' retorted Smith. 'You would be a comfortable short-tempered member of the Royal Society, quarrelling over your experiments with your friends, while the common men, like me, worked if they had work and starved or froze if they hadn't!'

'Even common men, as you call them, were freer until machines squeezed the life-blood out of society and covered England with foul stinking heaps of factories and slums,' T. S. said quietly. He added: 'Besides, I am a common man. My mother was a servant.'

'She would have been glad of a machine to do her work,' Smith exclaimed.

'She would have been glad of peace and quiet,' said T. S. to himself. For an instant his mind sank like a stone through darkened water, and he was a child in his mother's kitchen, watching her with mingled rage and pity, pity because she was tired, and rage because she was untidy and always in a muddle and smiled at him with such timid anxiety to please. To-day as usual she was late with his dinner, but she was later than usual and he would have to go back to school without it. With trembling hands she began to tie up for him a parcel of bread and dripping. The string slipped from her fingers with their swollen and shiny knuckles and the parcel fell to pieces. He turned and ran impatiently from the house without anything, pretending not to hear her voice calling him to come back, to wait.

It was from this moment that everything went wrong,

he told himself. To get away from that life I worked until I became the dry barren tree I now am. And what have I got for it? I married a rich woman who does not sleep with me, she sleeps with any man who is flattered enough by it not to notice that she is growing old; I have my research job in the chemical works owned by that world-leech, Thomas Harben. I am as helpless as my mother to bring order into living.

'We are all caught by the neck in the trap we have made,' he said, cheerful now that he had found a gloomy explanation of the world. 'Man has invented his own destruction. The terrifying efficiency of the machines has turned him back into an animal, a million times more destructive than the others. I am one of the inventors. Why? Because there is nothing in which I believe, except myself and my own mind. I know my own mind and there is nothing else I know. I am only and helplessly a scientist, as other men are only hands operating a loom or only bankers.'

'Do you remember what it was like when you were only a soldier?' said Renn. He was enduring tortures from his cramped position, and could not even make room to lift his arm and wipe the sweat from his face.

'But then I was not only one man, I was at least ten, sometimes a hundred,' T. S. answered. Other men are equally lonely, he thought; as afraid of me as I of them, sundered from me, hating me, ready to defend themselves against me. I want only to be left alone, and I am forced instead to help on the ghastly violence that will destroy my world. It will be destroyed from within by men like these two—does Renn know what he is doing?—or from outside in the new wars it breeds. From violence *nothing* comes except violence and death, never life.

'You are really a lot of fools,' he said, amiably, to Smith. 'What sort of society do you hope to evolve by choking out the middle classes, the only educated, intelligent and urbane people? However, you won't get far. After the gassing out of the cities, and typhus and famine, those who are left will be fairly brutish—on their way down, in fact. I don't think they can civilise themselves again. Upon my word I hope not—the results are not worth it.'

'I don't in the least mind the whole race being wiped out and disappearing,' said Renn. 'But in the meantime I can't bear the sight of one hungry child, or one more common soldier with his entrails hanging down over his legs.'

Henry Smith gave a shout of laughter. He dug his elbow into Renn's side. 'Look you at that!' he said. He waved his hand at an opulent limousine just passing them in the traffic. Its passengers were four well-nourished men and women, and it was labelled 'For Food.' 'They're going to offer themselves up,' he chuckled.

He had scarcely listened to the other two. He was feeling too well and happy to want to talk. When he was working he was able to concentrate the whole of his magnificent energy on to one end, and as soon as he released it it leaped a dozen ways through him, a fountain of delight and good-temper. At the moment, he felt he had in him the strength of the anonymous millions of strikers. He saw another lorry marked 'Permission of the T.U.C.'

'Did you see that?' he asked T. S. Heywood. 'We're tasting our strength. One day we shall use it to draw everything into our hands. In that day we shall set *you* to work to multiply machines for our purposes. Which are not those of your present employer.'

He braked the car suddenly to avoid a collision. T. S. was flung against the windscreen and groaned. Smith only laughed. The accident reminded him that he was going to see Anna again, and he began to imagine the romantic adventure it might turn to when he had time for it.

The first person he noticed in the Committee rooms was

Louis Earlham, looking ill and exhausted. He jumped when Smith spoke to him. His nerves are in a poor state, thought Smith: he despised the other man heartily for not enjoying the crisis. He's as weak as water, he thought; I always knew it.

'What's this about Herbert Samuel meeting the Council?' he demanded. 'Getting ready to sell us, eh?'

'I know nothing about it,' Earlham answered. He looked into Smith's smiling face with the dislike he felt. He had never known how much he disliked the man until now. His health, good looks, and carelessness, taken together, irritated Earlham beyond bearing.

'If you want my opinion,' he said, quietly, 'I think the Strike a hideous mistake. Why involve all of us in a dispute about wages—which in the end will have to be settled by ordinary methods? For that, all of us have been exposed to defeat and reprisals. You'll see we shall get them.'

'But, God damn you, this is not a wages dispute,' shouted Smith. 'It's the opening of a concerted attack. Upon my soul, I don't know what happens to you when you get into Parliament. You can't defeat the whole working class. Don't you know that Headquarters spends half its time telling men who aren't out yet to keep back? Bring them all out and you'll see.'

He broke off to ask Frank Rigden a question. Rigden was waiting there for orders, his blue eyes patient and empty. His hands hung useless. He had been wondering whether Sally would take the children to the relief kitchen this morning. He told her to, and she had not promised. Smith's sudden voice startled and confused him, he lost his head and stuttered: 'I dunno.'

'You'll talk to me next about seizing power,' Earlham said in a low voice. 'What would you do with it? Give it to *that*?' He looked with quiet contempt at the back of Rigden's bent head.

'It's not what we can do now, but what it's in your mind to do,' said Smith.

He turned away, afraid he would lose his temper here. In the next room he saw Joe Bradford at work and went in to him. Bradford greeted him with a watchful smile. He disapproved of the younger man, but they were cut out of the same cloth and he could never feel worse than anger with him.

'What's the matter with Earlham?' Smith said. 'Is he wriggling out? Is that what they're up to?'

'Ah, he wears his bottom out looking for a place to put it, he's a politician,' Bradford said calmly. 'He's fond of good society, too. You don't suppose he wants to talk to you and me.'

Smith laughed. 'I'm taking the evening off,' he said. 'It's the first for five weeks, and I have a girl.'

'You play about too much,' Joe growled. He turned back to his everlasting papers, and Smith went out. His business took him to Bermondsey, Erith, and Tilbury. For the past two months he had been an organiser in the Independent Labour Party but he was now also the Communications sub-committee in Deptford and himself a part of the communications for which he was responsible. Like the rest of them, he was doing four men's work. It suited him. On his way home, he was halted by a terrific procession. Nearly a hundred and fifty lorries of food were being convoyed from the docks to Hyde Park by mounted armed Guards in steel helmets, sixteen armoured cars, a large force of volunteers and mounted police. The street was lined by delighted and astonished crowds. A man standing beside Smith's car said: 'Coo, I haven't seen tin hats since I was in France.' Shawled women pushed their children to the front. 'Let Albert look, then. See, dearie, soldiers.'

Looking over the side of the car, Smith saw a man he knew in the procession. Julian Swan was on foot, walking

with a body of younger men in khaki drill shirts, part of
his own volunteer defence corps. He was limping badly,
the crippled foot dragging behind the other. Obeying a
mischievous impulse Smith shouted:

'Do you want a lift?'

Swan turned his head. His eyes were half-closed and
staring in his red face, the mask of the leader. It altered
for a second, becoming younger. He spoke to one of his
young men, setting him in his place outside the ranks, then
dragged himself quickly to the car.

'Did you mean that?' he asked, 'or is it your idea of
a joke?'

'No, get in, get in,' said Smith jovially. 'I'll drive you
where you're going. You won't get far on foot.' He did
not see Swan turn sullen at this reference to his lameness.
His feeling for Swan was free of any trace of the contempt
he felt for Louis Earlham. He would shoot him with
pleasure if they were on different sides in a civil war,
and in the meantime he did not dislike him. They were
alike in a devouring energy and a love of good food and
drink.

'Where are you going?'

'As far as Hyde Park,' said Swan.

The last mounted policeman passed, with the thin cheering
of a group of little dirty-faced boys. Smith started the car.
'What are *you* doing in the East End defending sacks of
flour?'

'Volunteers defend what they're told to defend,' Swan
said stiffly.

'I have the advantage of you there,' said Smith. 'I only
defend what I believe in. But then I'm not a Leader.
How is the Movement, by the way? Is it true that you're
drilling young men with dummy rifles and encouraging
them to salute you? I wonder what you're going to get
out of it.'

'I can tell you one thing,' Swan said, irritated, 'you and

your friends will fail, in the end, because you have no leader. You have only respectable politicians and discreet secretaries of trades unions. Why should young men follow them into danger? Not that they will put their necks in any danger, not they, but who can even believe in them, let alone obey them? I tell you,' he went on, thrown violently forward as the car caught the edge of the pavement, 'men and women are craving for a belief. For authority and obedience. You are blind if you can't see it, and something one day is going to rouse you with a great shock.'

'Someone, you mean,' Smith jeered. 'Julian Swan the great leader. I don't believe a word of it. If you want my opinion, men who whine for leaders to tell them what to believe are not men at all, and heaven forbid there are enough of them in England to fill a jerry. If there are, you can have them.'

'Ordinary men must obey someone,' cried Swan.

'Why?'

'To save them from the horror of loneliness and anarchy.'

'A slave is as lonely and fearful as a free man,' Smith retorted. 'Why not obey some thing—an ideal—the thought of your fellows? Leaders being inflamed egotists, become abominably cruel even to their slaves.'

'Oh, call it what you like,' said Swan irritably. 'In the end it comes to the same thing. The man who won't obey your ideal must be forced, and so the leader, the violent man, comes forward.'

'Ho, ho. Try to force us!' said Smith. He felt swollen with inward laughter.

Swan looked at him with half-puzzled friendliness. 'I ought to dislike you,' he said quietly. 'I wonder why I don't. You're destructive and a corrupter. Authority and obedience are the corner stones of the State, any State. Blind obedience. Absolute authority. You undermine them. You spread rottenness with your talk of equality and social justice, and all the time you know in your heart there is no equality and that social justice means nothing except that the strong govern and the weak are happy to obey.'

' I am strong but I can't govern this car,' Smith said. It had just slid forward on its worn tyres to within a nail's breadth of a large lorry. He turned to look at Swan with a sharp smile. The lines running outward and up from the corners of his mouth deepened: he looked an intelligent clown. His long nose seemed longer and his lower lip came forward, giving him an air of malevolent humour.

Swan had turned a brick-red with annoyance. ' Laugh if you like,' he said, with an air of indifference. ' But you'll see I'm right.'

' If I didn't make a joke of you I should have to throw you out of this car,' Smith answered. ' So you think I'm a corrupter? What I think of you is even less polite. If I believed, but I don't for a moment, that you and your employers know how to make Englishmen into good children, to do what they're told and come when they're called, I would really drive you under a lorry. But I don't think you're worth the trouble.' He felt a flash of murderous rage as he spoke. It surprised him.

' We'll see,' Swan repeated. He had recovered his temper now that he thought the other man was angry. ' I put my trust in leadership and discipline. You can put yours where you please. We'll see which of us wins this time. It will be an omen for the next! '

' Speaking of discipline,' said Smith, genially, ' the discreet respectable secretaries of trades unions have not done so badly this time. In another week there'll hardly be a man at work. How's that for discipline and obedience? What's your answer to that? '

The car was drawn up close to the kerb in Piccadilly, and Swan caught sight of a dozen of his khaki-shirted young men marching along the pavement towards the Park. He shouted and beckoned. They came up at the double, halted in front of the car, and saluted with eager arms.

'*We* are the answer,' Swan said in a loud curt voice. He opened the door of the car and stepped out. Smith roared with laughter.

On his way back to Deptford he realised that he was very hungry. It was now two o'clock. He went into the nearest cheap café and sat smiling and humming until the girl brought him the meal he had ordered. 'Thank you, m'dear,' he said, smiling into her face.

He ate quickly. He was going to visit 98 Smith Lane. This house, which for two years he had been trying to close, held a strange place in his mind. It had become a symbol of the society he was labouring to destroy. But it was more than that. It drew to itself all the unconscious fears of his childhood, the infection of his mother's terror in him. Its rat-infested cellars occupied the same level of his mind as his memories of negroes and dark narrow greasy streets. The child he had seen on his first visit, sitting on its bare bottom on the floor, playing with a knotted bundle of rags, was himself. The child's face was marked in a curious way with dark blotches, the skin inflamed where it had scratched away the bugs which tormented it in its sleep. He was determined to save it, though he could save only that one out of the many.

Smith Lane had once been a long narrow alley-way. Part of it had disappeared in the 'eighties and there were now only twelve houses, numbered from 87. Number 98 was the end house. He went into it, and walked about it like a man searching his own mind. The two basement rooms were in perpetual twilight. On one overcrowded crockery-laden dresser stood a geranium plant. It was withered because sunless, but the child always hoped for a flower. This was the living room for a man and woman and their three children; the children slept in it at night, but the rats frightened them awake many times during the night.

On the ground floor the walls dripped with water. One room, ten feet wide by nine long, was entirely filled by two beds, a single and a double bed, in which the mother and seven girls slept. Two boys slept in the adjoining room, the kitchen. One night the elder was so hungry that he crept out of bed and ate all the food they had: it was kept in a cupboard between the bed and the fireplace. This terrible theft was discovered at six o'clock in the morning when the father came in from work. He was deeply puzzled as well as furious, because he knew he was a good father to his children and a good husband to his wife; yet she tried to stand up for the boy. In his scanty daylight he had boarded in the tap and sink in the yard, where they washed, to make things more comfortable for them. The rooms were alive with vermin. In winter the wind came in and the rain and fogs soaked through the walls. In summer the young ones tried to drag their beds out into the street but the police drove them in again.

On the next floor lived a family of six, and the great sorrow of the mother of this family was the behaviour of the eldest boy with his sister: she knew about it but she could not punish them, and she felt that in some way it was her fault and the fault of her dead husband. There was a third room on this floor, and here lived a man and his wife and four children; two slept in their parents' bed, and two on the floor.

Another family lived in the attics of the house; these were regarded with pity by all except the family in the cellars. Father, mother, and son slept in one bed, two daughters slept in another, and the youngest boy on a chair with his feet on their bed. The lot of this family was indeed hard, since there was no room between roof and floor for any air to move about, and no windows. There was a skylight. The best air came through cracks in the roof. There was one water-tap in the house, and one dilapidated water-closet, in the yard. The wash-basins for each family were fitted outside the windows looking over the yard, so that anyone anxious to cleanse himself had to stretch the upper half of his body outside of the house. He could have no other reason to lean out of the window, for there was no view. That part was a tangle of dark narrow streets and ways between yards, cul-de-sacs, and little courts. On every side the light was cut off.

Henry Smith walked up the staircase, which was dark, narrow, the stairs deeply worn. The child he had been went with him. He turned back at the foot of the attic steps and went down to the very bottom, to the cellar. An oil lamp spilled its yellow light in the centre of the room. There was no gas in the house. The women in 98 Smith Lane were always afraid of fire as the children of rats.

Smith had to hold his breath because of the foul smell. Sewage water came into the room where the children slept, forced back from the choked sewers. The mother worked very hard to keep the rooms neat, but she could do nothing about the foul smell. She was alone in this room when he knocked. She turned with her hand on the dresser, and smiled at him. That to him, and to the child always within him, was the miracle of this place.

The strange thing was that the owner of the house set a value on it. Seventeen years ago an officer of health managed to get an order closing the whole house. The owner appealed twice: the first time he lost his case, but then in a higher court still he won it, by agreeing to close the cellars. For a year they were closed, except to the rats, who had this part all to themselves now and supposed it had been surrendered to them. After that year the boards were taken down and the man and his wife moved in. They had one child when they came, and two others had been born here since.

Yes, in this room.

None of the tenants knew the name of the owner of the house. Neither did Smith yet.

Leaving the house, he went to visit his new friend, the

Anglo-Catholic priest Ernest Cecil Hart, called Father Hart.
He was married, with two children, girls. His wife, whom
he had married shortly after he was ordained, against the wish
and advice of the man he revered under God, the head of
the theological college where he was taught, had become an
invalid at the birth of her second child, and she was now
helpless. His sister looked after her during the day, and
he slept beside her at night so that he could lift her round
when she needed relief from lying motionless on one side.
When she was first stricken he had been working in a country
parish; he had moved to Deptford in the third year of her
illness, bringing her with him because she refused to be left
behind, although the doctor warned him that a slum parish
would be the death of her. He loved her, but his wish to
punish her and himself was too strong to be crushed. He told
the doctor, his wife, himself, that his duty was plain before him.

They had now been in Deptford eight years and she was
still living. She was as obstinate as he was and would not
die. But she suffered, lying in the room from which she
saw nothing but the wall of a house, not even a feather
of the sky. When he came in and she said to him, ' Move
my right arm, please,' she smiled into his face as he stooped
over her. At times her mind was convulsed with an emotion
she did not recognise. The words, Kill me, kill me; finish
me off, rose in it; but before they reached her tongue they
had become, ' Please move my arm.'

Father Hart was a strong-looking man, now nearing fifty.
He had been a farmer's son, and his face was that of a
Cornish farmer, the strong shrewd peasant look over-lapping
another. The network of nerves under the ruddy-yellow
skin was almost visible. His eyes were quick, black, naked-
seeming. He worked like an over-driven servant. He
held the proper services during the day, though often he
was alone in the church except for an old woman; and
until late in the evening he went among his parishioners.
He cooked for bed-ridden women, comforted the dying,

washed babies, talked to the men over their meals, and was once found with his skirts tucked up to the waist scrubbing the floor in 98 Smith Lane attics, when the woman was in the hospital. He needed to be strong, because of his habit of coming in to a meal in his house and lifting it off the table to take it as it was to some house where food was short. His sister half admired and half hated and despised this way of his. In some secret corner of her mind she thought he did it from an overweening pride and vanity. More likely he did it because his nerves would not stand the sight of half-fed children.

One evening at nine o'clock a woman coming home from the offices she cleaned saw him leaning against the wall in Smith Lane. When she came up to him she saw that his face, turned upwards, was that of a man in the extreme of bodily pain. 'Oh, Father, what's the matter, are you ill?' she said to him in alarm.

'No, no,' he said. 'Nothing. Nothing is the matter, nothing to be done.' He moved away quickly, his legs thrusting against the black petticoats, as she called them.

He had been to see the woman on the first floor of Number 98, to speak to the boy and girl. 'I don't know what to say to them myself, Father,' she said. And when he saw them in front of him, the boy of seventeen with his dark bright eyes and fine lips, the girl a year younger, her half-formed body thrusting against the tight woollen jumper on to which she had pinned a lace collar, he, too, was filled with a silent agony like the mother's. He spoke to them about their sin; he saw their cheeks flush and their bodies wince, and he saw the instinctive movement the girl made towards her brother, for protection and comfort. It was almost unnoticeable, the slightest turn of her head and breast. It struck his mind like the threat of a blow. So it was comfort these children wanted, to be cherished and saved; in the hell of 98 Smith Lane they had sought it in each other: and he talked to them of sin.

The sin and the disgrace was as deep as the everlasting pit; its rottenness spread from the room where they stood into other rooms. None of us is untouched by it, he thought, in horror of himself and all men. The boy and girl were the least guilty, because their innocence was taken from them the day they were brought to live in this place.

He finished what he had to say, and went away. His soul had been tormented for many years, but now it *knew* that it was in hell. The knowledge was the last turn of the screw. He had a dream that night, in which he was alone in the gallery of a mine, in darkness. He knew in the dream that he had been led into the mine and left, he would never return, the passage in which he was crawling was closed at both ends. As he went on the walls on either hand narrowed. He could breathe only with difficulty. He was in mortal fear: then a slab of stone fell forward from the wall on to him, crushing him. But still he was not dead, though his body was mutilated in an indescribable fashion: he could think, and he could see through the earth, through the layers of coal and rock to the clay with small stones, worms, and the roots of grass fast in it. He saw the imprint of feet on the grass, pressing it, and when a man leading a cart passed above him he felt the wheels and the feet of man and beast in each nerve of his crushed yet sentient body. He believed that if it were not for him lying in the mine in his agony, the earth, the grass growing on it, and the man leading his cart would collapse and perish. When he awoke he was still afraid, stunned with fear. He scarcely knew that he was living until his wife murmured something beside him. He moved to lift her thin brittle body in the bed and lay it down in more ease.

The shrewd peasant side of his mind had taken to Henry Smith at sight. He saw that the young man was sensual and self-indulgent, but that this was the least part of him; the rest was his passion for change. He called it socialism or social justice, but it was a flame like the wall of fire in a mine, rearing up against the current of air. He was against the whole of society because it issued in Smith Lane. The anger, the black bitter anger, always in him, concealed by his smiling merry humorous face and talk, broke out of him when he was making a speech. Again it was like the explosion in a mine; it tore through him, shaking his big solid body, so that he swayed on his feet, his face red and sweating, a voice of mingled brass.

Smith was not conscious of liking Father Hart : he did not, he said, care for the black-skirted tribe. But there was a sympathy between them that fastened on their points of likeness ; a tough coarse strain in the priest as there was in Smith. In both of them it sprang from old roots : both had known poverty and cruelty in their childhood, both were incorruptible by any ordinary bribes.

Father Hart was writing at a table in his room when the young man came in. He was surprised to see him.

' I thought you were conspiring somewhere,' he said.

' So I am,' laughed Smith. ' But this is the day you told me to come for information about Smith Lane. We know who owns the ground, but who holds the lease, whose are the houses? Who owns number 98 ? '

' The land belongs to the Church,' Father Hart said.

' I knew that,' said Smith gently. He saw that the other man was in torment.

' The Ecclesiastical Commissioners,' Hart said distinctly, ' lease the ground. The lease is held by a body known as Liability Ltd.—it seems to be a recent amalgamation of various smaller bodies. I don't understand these things. The present chairman is Thomas Harben. Some of the shares are held by Lucy Harben, I suppose his wife, some by a Mrs. Groelles, some by Marcel Cohen, the newspaper proprietor, and a great many by another company. Here's a list.' Searching among the papers in a basket, he gave Smith a sheet covered with his small irregular writing. He wrote like an old man.

' Thank you,' said Smith.

' What are you going to do with it ? '

' Oh. Use it in speaking and writing. I shall get that house closed and pulled down if it takes me the rest of my days. Likely it will, too,' he laughed.

' It's only one house out of a million,' the priest said. His eyes looked at Smith with an almost triumphant bitterness. ' You can do nothing. There will be no change without a change of heart. You can make your speeches and write your books and articles, you can make a revolution and kill and be killed, but at the end of it nothing will have been changed, you will still be trusting to violence, still killing and being killed; still blaspheming the Holy Spirit, and you will still have missed the way. The road along which you have come is paved with living tortured bodies '— he remembered his dream for a second—' and so it is ahead. There is no forgiveness for having shed blood. Not God Himself can forgive it,' he said softly.

' Well, I'll try reasoning with Thomas Harben,' smiled Smith. ' If he surrenders peaceably I'll sentence him and his wife to no more than a month's residence in 98 Smith Lane. She'll be wishing she was dead at the end of a week of it.' He drew his thick eyebrows together, frowning, in sudden malicious disgust. ' By God, when I look at that basement room I could kill the Thomas and Lucy Harbens inch by inch.'

' One of you will kill the other before long,' Father Hart said shortly. ' And much good it will do the woman in that room and her children.'

' Well, I must go. Good-bye, and thanks,' said Smith.

The priest's hand was perfectly lax and cold when he shook it, and he dropped it quickly. He is a spiritless poor devil, he thought as he walked off. But he knew that was not true : he had seen a spirit in the other man's black eyes and it was one he felt thankful not to own himself.

He had an hour before he met Anna. He spent it looking at the outside of Thomas Harben's house in Davies

Street. When he had admired the teak and walnut door for some two or three minutes it opened, and was held open by a liveried servant, and a woman came out. She strolled in the direction of Bond Street. He followed her. She was a fine figure of a woman, very well dressed, but what he noticed were her shoes. They were black and white, with high heels made of ivory: he came close enough to them to be sure. For some reason this detail infuriated him more than anything else he could have learned about Mrs. Thomas Harben. His face grew red.

When she went into Asprey's, he swung round and walked to Bruton Street. This time it was Fanny Groelles's door he watched: he saw her two children, a boy and a tiny girl, being taken in by the nurses, one child, one nurse. The boy was handsome and dark-haired; the little girl had red curls and a face of strangest delicacy. Smith looked at them both and thought of the child seated on its bare dirty bottom, playing with a rag.

He reached the corner of Wigmore Street just as Anna came towards it. She looked at him with an open, smiling face. At the sight of her his anger turned into another feeling; he felt his body grown hard with desire. He was on the verge of leaving her for no other reason than that he could not take her, but his kinder self intervened. By the time they reached the restaurant in Oxford Street he had grown calm and could jeer at himself.

Anna was gay. She told him in her loud merry voice that a woman, one of their regular customers, coming in that morning had ordered them to make her a dozen frocks. She was leaving for France to escape the revolution. ' But do you know what,' cried Anna, ' we also have to make for her a nurse's uniform. She is half thinking of staying behind to nurse wounded officers when the fighting begins.'

' Aren't you afraid, too ? ' Smith teased her. He put his face close to hers, and she looked at him under her eyelashes, provoking and friendly. Her eyes glowed.

'I? No, never. I love things happening. I should like to see fighting in Wigmore Street.'

'I believe you would.' He looked at her, at her narrow face and long thin throat. He liked the way her small nose jutted, fine and very delicate, from her brown face, and the strong arch of her eyebrows. They were as black as pitch and so was her short hair. He did not believe she was a German. She is playing the part very well, he thought; it's all the same to me what she is.

'I want to see and enjoy everything when I am young— travel, adventures, life. So many old women come to us to be dressed up to travel. Why don't they stay at home? When I am old I shall choose a place I like to live in, and I shall live in it, until I die.'

'Perhaps they couldn't afford travelling when they were young.'

'I shall have everything,' Anna said. 'Money, excitement, strange places. I must live.'

'Don't you want to marry?'

'What? To live with one man the whole time, trying to remember what he likes, saying Yes dear, No dear, How clever you are dear.' She smiled like an anxious wife, and moved her hands. They were thin, very brown and fine, the fingers long and wide apart. 'Never!'

She made a good dinner, talking the whole time, asking him questions, laughing at him, making fun of the other diners, in a whisper almost as penetrating as her voice. He thought she was very beautiful and he wanted to take her out of this place, to be alone with her. He was not sure about her, but he was almost sure.

She said she had nothing to do that evening. 'I thought you would take me for a drive in your car,' she said, smiling.

'It's in Eccleston Square. Near Victoria.'

'We could go there and get it.'

'Very well.'

He drove her to his room in Deptford. She found the

street and the drab house very disgusting, but she liked his
room. It was clean and tidy—he kept it clean himself—
and the quantity of his books impressed her.

' Do you read only economics ? '

' Nothing else.'

' Why ? '

' It is part of my job.' He turned her round by the
shoulders and led her to the shelves of German books.
' There you are,' he said.

She looked at him and began laughing. ' I'm not a
German,' she laughed. ' I can speak German and read it.
Were you taken in ? '

' I was at first. Afterwards I guessed you were lying.'

' Well, never mind. You're not angry with me, are you ? '

' No.' He put his arms round her and drew her against
his body, feeling the small bones of her knees on his legs
and touching her breasts with his hand, gently. He wanted
her so much now that he was able to be gentle, to coax her.
But she came to him gladly at once, as if it were the simplest
thing in the world to lie down with him on his shabby bed.
She is a lively pretty animal, he thought; it is as natural
with her as that. He was grateful to her for her simplicity
and her generosity, making the moment perfect, as the
moment of physical passion seldom is. If she had seemed
doubtful or ashamed it would have been spoiled.

Afterwards he went out to the landing, where he had a
gas ring, to make tea for her. She was still lying on the
bed when he came back with the tea-pot and two cups on
a tray. He set the tray on the table and came over to her
and slapped her lightly on the thigh.

' Get up, lazybones,' he said.

' You ought not to do that,' she said, looking up at him.

' Why not ? You are lazy, lying there.' He pulled her
up, restraining his impulse to slap her again—she was very
tempting—and put his coat round her shoulders. He felt
extraordinarily well and light-hearted. Walking about the

room, he hummed *Early One Morning*, and sent a chair flying out of his way with his foot. At the same time he began to wish she would dress and go away. He had some writing to do before the morning, and he liked to sit up in bed to write.

' Come now, get dressed,' he said, kissing her.

' Don't you like me any more? ' she said confidently.

' I adore you.'

He brought her her clothes, smiling, and talking nonsense to her. She was in no hurry to leave, and it did not occur to her that Smith was becoming impatient. Radiant, she loitered over her dressing, smiling at herself in the glass. She was surprised he did not ask her to stay longer with him.

Sunday, May 9th
THE BRIGHT DAY

CHAPTER XVII

On Sunday Nicholas had to spend the day with Cohen in London, looking at a house in Berkeley Square, and discussing plans and the cost. Cohen had sent a car for him. He was angry and resentful because he had to leave Hervey. He made her promise to rest. She promised, and as soon as he had gone she went down to the garage and took out their own shabby car. She had left a note for him, supposing he returned before she did.

It had been in her mind all along that she would spend this last day before she went into the Home in the one place she loved, after Danesacre, more than any other. This was the Hampshire village where she had lived during the two last years of the War, with Richard—he was two years old—and her first husband. She scarcely thought of Penn now, and although she was driving into the past in which she had lived with him in a complete intimacy, she was able in some way to shut him out. Now at least.

When she had passed Andover, the country was familiar. She had travelled these roads so many times in the trap belonging to the farm where they lived. The farmer's big red-cheeked wife drove the trap and touched the fat pony with the ends of the reins. There would be their packages on the floor, and she held Richard on her knee. In winter her fingers holding him grew numb and she longed for the journey to be over.

She drove down a long hill, and followed the narrow country road beside the stream towards Broughton. The valley drowsed and the high line of the downs was faint with heat. The chalky hollows were dazzling where they came in the way of the sun. There was white dust on the leaves of the hedge, and dust thick over the road.

She crossed the stream and drove very slowly through the village. Eight years ago this was my life. Here I was one of a few men and women whom the War ravished from their usual lives and set down here. For me alone of them it was my real life. The past invaded her senses slowly, so that for a time she was caught between two moments, until the past opened and closed round her, like moving into deep water.

She felt the strange tense expectancy of that time, stirring along her nerves. One expected, consciously, more and sharper life, because unconsciously death was what was expected all this time. A young man, a boy, is burned alive in the wreckage of his aeroplane, here in this field, on the same day as there are killed in France twenty thousand of the best of young Englishmen—so many deaths, so much agony, must be balanced, somewhere, by an intenser life. And the fire rises from the blood, a bitter consuming flame, and sinks leaving a little dry bitter dust. In those days I had everything, she thought: I was young.

Passing the house in which the wife of another Air Force officer had lived, she smelled the lilacs. The feeling of those days was as close to her as this scent in her nostrils; and yet she was divided from it. She felt it altered by the present in which still she was less alive. The ecstasy, the humiliations, the mingled pain and confidence of those days glowed for her again in the heavy scent of the lilac; and it was only now when they were long past that she could savour them with this poignant surprise and joy. They were like the moment on the quay at Antwerp when she was a child, when she felt the utter strangeness of being in a foreign country as never since; it must feel a little in that sort to English bones to find themselves buried in the heavy Flanders clay or the dry crumbling earth of Greece: and like that other moment in the kitchen of her house in Liverpool, the first where she had lived as a married woman; she was standing there alone, wiping a dish at the sink, and the child in her body moved the first time and she was at once afraid and ashamed. You could say that these three moments were one and the same, since in each of them she had lived completely, so that there was neither past nor future but the whole of her life was present with her from the instant of birth to the instant of death, whole and complete, like a moment in eternity.

The War, when it had killed her brother, the ambitious silent boy of eighteen, when it had spoiled finally her first husband, changed her, too. The fumes of that acrid wavering excitement, the smoke rising from a blood sacrifice, filled her brain and possessed her senses. Every greedy ambitious instinct in her awoke and cried aloud to be satisfied. She could not go on in the old way, tending her child, writing a little when she had time, putting up with Penn's sordid infidelities; she could not. So began what would not end until she did.

She turned the car towards the downs and stopped it in the sunken lane, near the farm where she had lived. Beyond this the road became a chalk track, steep and slippery.

She looked round her at the sky drained of its colour by the sun, at the swelling line of the downs, pure, heart-lifting. I was here, she thought, when I fell in love with the American. Ah, here at last was something she could not feel again. She could erect the bones of the thing as it was; see herself, very young, unformed, confused by her needs, burned by her passion for a man she neither liked nor respected. She was possessed by him. By night and day she thought of him, imagined his look, his touch, his warm quick smile. She surrendered to him in her thoughts, her senses roused and heavy. A pain of joy filled her when she was with him. I stood here, she said, and watched the road along which he would come; when he came I spoke to him as I liked, there was no need to pretend for him that I am pleasant or friendly; I could be as rough and bitter as the mind took me, while my eyes looked after him and the roots of my tongue were thickened with love.

When the moment came that he would have taken her, she turned away from him. She escaped from him by a trick; by a sneer which stung him so deeply that he would as soon have slept with an adder. Why did I do that? she asked herself again. I have never felt like that for any other man, and never shall now. I was filled by him; my veins were like straw caught by the fire and my flesh ached. Never, never, shall I have that again. Then why? Why did I not take him, and once in my life know what it is to be satisfied in the body?

The answer, she thought, is myself. Since I don't yet know myself, it is no good asking questions. But she knew that she had been afraid of the American himself. He was a violent man, greedy, adventurous, sentimental, astonishingly alive.

She knew suddenly that the person she had feared was herself. When I am most like myself I am like him, she thought; I am violent, greedy, eager to live in the body, almost gross. I sneered at myself. I turned away from myself. Then what am I now—to what am I going?

Leaving the car hidden under the deep hedge, she turned to climb to the downs. The track became so narrow that she brushed the hedge on either side with her dress. The sickly sweet smell of decaying hawthorn filled it. She could see the downs on her left hand and on her right the wide valley with the clear glassy stream running through it.

Nicholas is seated now with Marcel Cohen, planning the new business. A violent revulsion against Cohen and all his works seized her. I can't do it, she thought; I can't go on, I can't live like that; we must get out, get away. I would rather live on bread and tea again, scrub my own floors, clean my own grate, than give my mind and my energy to selling to rich stupid useless women. In the end I don't want money, I want to be alone, I want to think and write a few words as sharp as bones, not write as I do, every day and all day, thinking of money and debts. I do know that peace is from within, but I want to live in my own place, with the people who knew me when I was free and innocent. London will be the death of me, she said angrily. To think that I have fastened myself to it for a year, years—I must be a senseless fool.

She felt confused, and did not know where to lay the blame for the pass things had come to. There was the failure of Nicholas's business. One evening they had quarrelled suddenly and bitterly about their future. It was before she had seen Cohen, and before the chance of working for him was offered. And before they knew that she was in danger of her life. Nicholas had just told her that when all was cleared up he would have fifty pounds in the bank. Nothing else except the income from the shares his grandmother had left him. And this—it was now four hundred pounds a year—went to his first wife, under a promise he had made her.

He was ashamed because of the completeness of his failure, and because he had no money except this which he could not bring himself to touch; and he spoke curtly and irritably. Hervey was offended by his manner. She thought that if you are poor it is no reason for behaving badly. She said coldly:

'What do you propose we should do?'

'I don't know,' he said, vexed by her.

'We could go to live at Danesacre. The money from my books would keep us there.'

'I don't like the place,' he replied. 'It's neither town nor country. I'd rather live in the real country than there.'

Any suggestion that Danesacre was less than the only perfect town in England infuriated Hervey. Her eyes started with contempt and anger; she was glad to have something to quarrel about, since she would not quarrel with him for giving all the money he had left to his first wife Jenny Roxby.

'I will *not* go to live in a house where there is neither gas nor water. If you had ever lived like that you would know there is nothing romantic about it. It is only drudgery for a woman. And I have my own work to do.'

'But you think I ought to be willing to live on you in Danesacre,' said Nicholas. His face had become stiff and sallow with pain: he was bewildered by the suddenness and fierceness of her resentment. He did not know what had happened to her or why, suddenly, she had turned on him. It had never happened to them before.

'No,' Hervey said.

'Then what?'

She half turned from him. Her breast was hard with grief because they were strangers, hating each other, and with pity for herself tied to a man who would always keep her from living close to her roots and yet did not cherish her to make up for the bitter loss.

'I don't know,' she muttered. 'I should like to be free.'

'Free!' Nicholas scoffed. 'What do you mean by it? There's no such thing as being free. There is always the burden of existence, and if you have any spirit in you, you would rather balance a heavy burden than a light one.'

But it is I who must balance it, she thought. 'Very well,' she said, foolishly. 'I will live where you like and as you like. But it is slowly killing me.'

Nicholas began to lose his head. He hated her for speaking in this exaggerated way. He felt the resentment in her mind against him, and he wanted to drive it out of her. His head was light with rage and fury.

'That is not true,' he said. 'You know it is a lie. Say now whether it is true or a lie. Say it.'

He looked at her with bright hard eyes, trying to force her to speak, to take back what she had said. But she would never do that. She would never admit that she was in the wrong: *he* must give way to her will, give in, ask her to forgive him, and then, then she would comfort him. She did not want to quarrel with him. Her heart relaxed and became quick with love for him again. But still she said nothing, only watched him with the heavy look which made her seem harsh and ugly.

He was horrified by his loss of self-control, and by the hatred he had felt. At all costs he must get back to her again. And he, too, wanted the comfort she could give him. He was defeated by the failure of his work. He had felt humiliated coming to her with the news; he had expected—he did not know what he had expected, but not to be accused and flayed by her. That was the last thing he had looked for. Why was she like this?

He came towards her and stood, not touching her, with his body close to hers. ' What is the matter? ' he said gently.

' Nothing,' she answered, in a hard voice.

' Yes, something is wrong,' he said, still gentle. ' Tell me.'

It is wrong that you do not touch me or kiss me, she thought heavily. Why don't you force me to be kind? Don't you see I can do nothing of myself? His calmness dazed her. She turned from him.

' Very well, I'll never speak to you again about getting away from this life.'

' You can talk to me about anything,' Nicholas said. ' You know that.'

' Do I? What do I know? ' she said, jeering at him.

He winced, hating the brutal jeering note which came into her voice when she was angry. It made him feel murderous, and he understood, although the act horrified him, how her first husband had been able to ill-treat her. She came of a family of domineering and intolerable women.

' Allow me to apologise for annoying you,' she said, in the same voice. You hate me, she said to herself, in a desolate anguish. In a moment she would begin to cry, tears from a grief without end. All the tears she had shed in her life were only a few drops of it.

'You are an ass,' Nicholas said. 'Worse than that, you are cruel.'

'Have you taken out a monopoly in cruelty?' she asked, smiling at him. 'I shall now go to my bed and you can sit here and think how superior you are to me.'

'I'm not thinking any such thing,' he said. 'You are an intolerable woman. I won't stay to be bullied by you. I'll go.'

'Where will you go?' she said. She felt a cold excitement.

'Away from here.'

'When? To-night?'

'To-morrow. Do you want me to go to-night?'

'I don't mind,' Hervey said, with a false calm.

Nicholas took hold of her by the arms and shook her, then pushed her away from him on to the couch. She sat there trembling. Now she was shocked out of her excitement, afraid of what she had done.

'I am sorry,' Nicholas said, slowly, lifelessly. 'I never did that to anyone before in my life.'

And you do it to me, she thought. As she stood up and hurried from the room, she found herself weeping, with some of the old helpless anguish of her youth. Nicholas followed her to her room; she made him stand aside for her. Her hands moved blindly, while the tears ran over her face. She could not see him, she was trying to check her tears before they were beyond her control. It was many years since she had wept in this uncontrolled bitter fashion.

'I'm not crying because I'm hurt,' she said to him. 'Nor because I like you.'

He put his hand on her arm, and she drew herself quickly away, without knowing that she did it. 'Do go,' she said. 'You bore me.'

He went away then, and she felt that everything was broken in her, her will, her strength, her life itself. Instinctively she put her hand over her womb, as if the pain there must begin again. Then she lay down on the bed: her grief seemed to tear her flesh as it made its way out in bitter cries. Nicholas came back. Stooping over the bed, he lifted her so that she was lying against him.

'Don't, Hervey—I can't bear you to cry,' he said, hurt beyond bearing by her grief. He had never seen her broken in this way and he was almost afraid to touch her. He was shocked by her blind face, as sunken and ugly as an old woman's. He thought she must hate him, and he wished he could die at once, to be rid of himself.

She still wept, with a long, shuddering, exhausted sound, becoming quieter as she held herself tense, then breaking into a shocked wail like a child.

'I never want you to be hurt,' he said. 'I want only happiness for you.'

'It's all spoiled,' she began. She caught her breath sharply, and stopped.

'No,' he said, in fear.

'You didn't hurt me in the least, but I wish it had not happened,' she said. The effort she had made in speaking checked her tears, and she began to dry her cheeks with her hands. Nicholas put them down gently and wiped her face with his handkerchief. She was ashamed to look up at him, feeling her eyes sightless with crying and her cheeks sore. 'I have made myself ugly,' she said.

'You know I don't care what you look like,' he answered. She said nothing, and he asked her at last: '*Is* it all spoiled then ?'

Now she looked at him for an instant. She was startled out of herself, and felt an agony of love and pity for him.

'Oh my love, my love,' she said, comforting him. 'I'll live in any place, do anything.'

'I don't care where I live,' Nicholas said. 'I'll live anywhere if it is with you.'

She drew him down to herself, making her body soft and humble: she made much of him and made herself weak so that he could be whole. Or he will be angry afterwards, she thought, because he asked forgiveness for turning on me when I provoked him.

When he was asleep beside her she lay with one arm lightly over him, afraid to burden him with the weight of it. This is the first time he has been angry enough with me to hate me, she thought: it must not happen like this again. I must—oh, I must—keep quieter in myself, then I shall not fail him.

After this she found the house near London, withdrawn in the middle of its field, and brought Richard from Yorkshire to live with them, because she thought that in this way, if she had her son with her again, she would be more at peace. And she was—but not for long. In no time the familiar nagging began in her soul. Why are you here, shut in a dull house, in dull unfriendly country, with a little boy and an absorbed tired man—writing, preparing meals, darning stockings, mending clothes, worrying over bills for things you never wanted, writing, writing, writing?

Her dreams at night were of places she had never seen, foreign cities, and landscapes in vivid unreal colours, a marsh covered with creeping rose-hued plants, cliffs flaming with trees in all the colours in the world. She returned again and again to these imagined cities, recognising a street or a house from an earlier dream, her body throbbing with joy when she found herself in a square of tall buildings and fantastic shops. She kept her house well ordered and saw to many things herself. She was a good if extravagant housewife. And hated a domestic life and everything that goes with it so much that she was sometimes half insane with impotent rage, which she had to keep to herself because it *was* insane. Who ever heard of a woman without the least instinct to make and live in a home? So she piled heavier earth on the body of her reckless, violent, disorderly self, and trod it down.

Richard did not like the school where he went daily. She thought he had inherited her dislike of communal life. It seemed odd to her that he did not want the society of other children, until she attended a garden-party at the school and saw for herself how unspeakably boring it is to be the youngest boy in a society ridden by conventions. She began to think he must go away to a very different sort of school. Here her conscience smote her. Am I thinking that I shall be more free when he goes?

The thought of sending him away was bitter to her. If she had not left him when he was little, because she wanted to go into the world to make her fortune, she might have been readier to let him go now. But the wound she had dealt herself then was still unhealed, and would be to the end of her life. If she could have felt certain she had not wronged him too—but of that she was never certain.

She stood a moment on the steep track to get her breath. Richard's calmness, when he went away from her four mornings since, came back into her mind with the sharpness and suddenness of a pain.

She remembered an evening four years ago, when she left him at Danesacre with her mother; he cried and said: ' I've been missing you so and now you're going.' The memory of that moment was unmitigable agony. And the funny unchildlike phrase he found to say, when she had comforted him, words he had picked up from listening to older people talking. ' Something tells me you'll have a happy time and come back safe.'

A blind movement of her thoughts tore the husk off an older memory. When she was a little girl, seven or eight years old, her mother went on a voyage with her husband, leaving her to board at a dame's school: the days were easily bearable, but she thought of her mother at night and cried over her, with an unwilled obstinacy, every night

for four months. The next time Mrs. Russell went on a
long voyage she was scarcely sorry at all and had hard work
to squeeze out a tear at parting.

It is the same thing, she thought, half smiling. But her
mother had fastened herself to her with a web of emotion as
intimate and dangerous as though they were joined at the
veins, and part of her life was always drained away in thinking
of and being sorry for her mother. I will not behave like
that with Richard, she thought: never. He is absolutely
free, I will never call on him.

The ache in her thoughts persisted. To be rid of it
she thought that he might at this moment be riding the
pony she had hired for him. That he was enjoying something she had given him filled her with the keenest bliss.
Her spirit soared and swooped like the bird which cut over
the edge of the downs and came to rest in the hedge.

She went on through the trees at the top, and came out
on the downs. A shelf of fine short smooth grass hung above
the valley, sheltered on three sides by the beech-trees. Here
was only the living quiet of this secure, brooding country.
This was the place she had been coming towards the whole
morning; and she stretched herself on the grass with a sense
of peace and joy such as she had long been unblessed with.
It is my last chance to think, before the operation.

But at first she was only aware of her body lying stretched
in the warm sun on the grass. She touched it lightly,
wondering a little at the thought of the knife working in
it, as if she were already free. Under her other hand she
felt the chalky ground, hard and smooth as a skeleton,
clothed with the living grass. Can one so seize the shape of
one's life as to feel the bone under the unessential flesh?

Under the calm of her marriage was always strife. An
endless, silent struggle between them—she wanting, above
everything, certainty, the complete possession of him, to
know herself master in his heart; he holding her off,
defending himself now in this way, now that, punishing her

because he was tired in body, ash-dry and impatient in mind. She knew so much about him now that it seemed she had known him all his life, before the War caught him young and used him too hard. She created a young Nicholas: and found herself denied by an older sceptical man, who loved her only as much as he was able, and at times hurt her to death.

One day she told him that he had tricked her. He was angry in an instant, turning on her with a contemptuous look. She was afraid, but stood up for herself; and told him that what she meant was that life had tricked her, using him.

'Then what did you want?' he said, gentle again.

'I know,' she said painfully, 'you don't want me as you wanted your wife, Jenny—to possess all my mind and body. Yet I can't endure it when you make it so plain. It is like a knife in me. That's rather queer, isn't it?'

'No, I don't think so,' he said. 'It is natural you should want that from me. Only I can't. I don't want it.' He saw her face and said quickly: 'I know I hurt you, and I know I shall go on hurting you. I wish sometimes you had never come to me. But I need you—you know that.'

'Then why?' she said, looking at him, determined to understand him, at any cost, 'why do you do it? Why do you push me away from you, so often, as you do?'

'I can't give myself to any one person. You mustn't mind—I can't give myself away. I want something that will never let me down—I haven't found it yet, but I shall one day.' He stopped. He wanted to tell her that he had sacrificed a great deal, all he believed in as between a man and a woman, in order to live with her. But he did not know how to say it without hurting her again, and in an unforgivable way.

'I don't want you to give up your work,' said Hervey. 'I only wanted you to be with me as I am with you. It's a

state of being, of soul, if you like,' she said, with difficulty.
' It has nothing to do with material circumstances.'

He looked at her with a slight smile and stroked her face
gently with his finger for a minute. ' You're very young.'

' I'm thirty-two,' Hervey said.

' But it is probably the first time you have been really in
love,' he said, with an an apologetic smile. ' You think it
ought to be all pleasant. But it's not.'

' You know a great deal about it,' she said, half mocking
him.

' I loved utterly twice,' he said, with an off-hand simplicity,
as if he were telling her something that had happened to
another man. ' A woman and a man. I can't give myself
away now.'

' But I want so little,' Hervey cried humbly.

' My love. What *do* you want? '

' I told you. Only for you to accept me, and want the
whole of me. As you wanted Jenny,' she added in a low
voice. She was ashamed to be comparing herself with the
other woman.

' It was Jenny who absorbed me—not I her,' he said
quickly. He wished she would give up probing him, with
her maddening insistence on knowing—always she must
know, she could never leave anything half hidden or secret.
There was even now something cold and impersonal in
her curiosity.

' I've lived thirty years in the last ten,' he said, tentatively.
' A concentrated growing-up. I'm too sunk in my way of
life to change for anyone.' He felt a sudden impatience.
'Nor do I see why I should change. After all, why did you
come to me, why did you marry me? I warned you.'

' I came—because I wanted it,' she said.

' That's not a reason worth touching,' he said. ' I want
you as an equal and a companion. The only love worth
having is in the mind.'

' Then why do you trouble with my body at all,' she said,

with a hostile triumph. It vanished quickly when she saw that he was silenced by her question. She had not meant to strike him.

After a minute he said: ' It's the normal thing between a man and woman, isn't it? I have a few sparks of my manhood left.'

' I am happier living with you than ever in my life since I was a girl,' she said. ' Better contented.' This was true, in so much as she respected him and need not feel, as she had felt always with Penn, that she was degraded by living with a man for whom it was not worth making any effort to live well: not any use, since he suspected everything she did and was.

' You're not really very happy,' he said, smiling. ' I know quite well that you're being held to a life you detest. I've known it a long time and I feel it's wrong.'

His face had the grey pallor that came in it too often, obliterating the traces of his youth. He was thirty-four, but he had grown rigid in a half-unwilling resistance to life; his life was drying up in him like a river cut off from its source. He stared at her without seeing her, his sight turned inward. ' My body's so tired, and I'm tired—dead. You'd better find someone else before it's too late.'

' But you don't want me to go,' Hervey said, with fear.

' Of course I don't! But if I don't give myself away to you I can't, and don't, expect you to give me anything lasting.'

' Now you're being perverse,' Hervey exclaimed. She came up to him and smiled into his face. ' Just to satisfy your poor Hervey, tell me how much you need me.'

' Very much,' he answered, with a quiver of energy. ' Without you I should be nothing—finished, *kaput*.'

' And still I come second to your work. Your work and your life come first.'

' Someone has to come first. In love one always absorbs the other, I found that out a long time ago.'

Insensibly, they had drawn together, their arms round each other's shoulders, their bodies resting each on the other, in search of comfort. They embraced without passion, with a strange anguish of love and pity, like refugees meeting in exile.

As Hervey rested there, she was thinking that Nicholas's new wife was less fortunate than the old: she had to see without complaint herself placed second to a lifeless ideal; to give freely and be glad of a little in return. To ask for nothing, for fear she should be asking too much, and vexing or wearying him. How wicked of you, my dear, she thought lovingly, to close your frontiers against my rich country. Her mind slid one thought over another, like an old woman spreading cards over a crimson tablecloth, and she saw first a grate full of unswept ashes, then herself as a child listening to her mother reading out of a book: *How cold it is, how very cold, said the little lamb, as she crept nearer to the shelter of the hedge.* The nonsense one remembers a lifetime, she thought dimly.

Another time Nicholas told her, when he came home in the evening, that a friend of his had been cited in a divorce case: he had only met the woman once, at a dance, and had taken her home afterwards; he had not seen her since.

'But why did he do that?' she said, with instant contempt.

Nicholas looked at her quickly, a curious smile in his eyes. 'But it could happen to any man. An attractive woman, sitting on his couch with him at night, openly putting out signals of distress—any man is likely to succumb.'

She was suddenly dissolved in fear. 'Not you.'

'But why not? Given the right ingredients, I might lie with an attractive woman and it would only be an affair of one hour of my life: there wouldn't be any question of my loving, or even liking her.'

Hervey was trembling. No matter what my reason said, she thought, I should not be able to endure the thought of his body lying in another woman's arms, even for a casual hour. I am too earthy.

'You told me once,' she said, stammering, 'that thinking of Jenny had kept you from the brothels in France.'

'Well, if I did!' he smiled. 'You had no right to deduce from it that I am a tower of strength against temptation. Perhaps the right ingredients were not present. Or perhaps my views have grown laxer in the past seven or eight years.'

She felt as panic-stricken as a child when it first realises it is lost. After a long silence she said quietly: 'I don't like knowing that the loyalty you gave her is withheld from me.'

'It is not withheld. You have no right to suppose it would be,' he said.

Her spirit was still shaken. 'If you had been discussing these things years ago' —she meant with Jenny—'would you have been so—judicial?'

'No,' he said.

It is like the way he counted the cost, and under my eyes, before we married. He did not count it when he married Jenny. I am a fool to surrender myself so completely; I had better keep something back, not to be too hurt. She wanted to save herself. But that, too, was bitter, because she had rejoiced secretly in the thought that she could safely give and give, he would not humiliate her, or poison her life with lies as her first husband had done. He wounded her when he told her she had no right to imagine herself safe. Even though it is true, she thought; and no one had the right to be safe or to feel confident.

She turned to go away. But as if he had just realised that she was hurt, she found him blocking her way: he held her closely, and said in a quick curt voice: 'Don't go away, don't leave me, will you?'

'You do want me with you?' she asked, shaken and uncertain of herself.

'Yes, yes, yes.' His face was younger and softer, as though

some tension had relaxed in him.   He kissed her lightly and
eagerly.   I shall never know you, she thought, sighing.   She
allowed her doubts and her pain to vanish, but something of
them remained.

So the strife continued between them—and part of her
effort was diverted against his first wife.   Jenny Roxby no
longer wrote to him every week, as at first, half-insane
letters.   They had almost ceased.   But one day Hervey
opening a drawer to put away Nicholas's mended socks,
found he had thrown into it a quantity of letters, fifty
or more.   With an impulse of rage, she took up the lot
and threw them into the stove.   When he asked where
they had gone she told him.   He looked at her with arched
brows, very angry.

' Did you want them? ' she asked.

' No.'

' Then what's the matter? '

' You have no right to destroy anything of mine.'

' I am sorry,' she said stiffly.

After this she went about more carefully and subtly,
seeking in him for traces of Jenny, trying to erase them, make
them weak and ridiculous.   The less Nicholas thought of
Jenny, the more sure she was of him herself, the fiercer
grew her jealousy of the other wife.   It was an old impulse
in her.   She wanted to put right what could never be put
right, to destroy the past, to make it as if Jenny had never
been, asking and receiving the whole of Nicholas's young
passion and turning it in him to a dry ash.   When she thought
about it, she was ashamed of her meanness, yet it went on in
her below thought, below even her clenched will.

There were days when Nicholas was so near her that
doubt vanished, and she lived and moved in a deep quiet
happiness.   Her look as unmoved as ever, she preened herself
secretly in joy.   He would come to her and lie in her arms
at night, touching her body as though it were precious,
placing his lips to it.   ' You are lovely,' he told her.   ' My

lovely Hervey.' The knowledge that he was afraid and uncertain in his ecstasy sharpened it for her. She could talk
to him now simply and merrily, making him laugh out and
kiss her for pure comedy.

' You are better and more delightful than anyone ever was,'
he said, ' and I love you more than I loved anyone.'

' Is that true ? ' she asked.

' I think I never loved anyone before,' he answered.
' The rest was stuff and moonshine.'

But moonshine can be intoxicating, she thought. Yet,
she was glad. She surrendered to him again completely,
delighting in his fineness and honesty, delighted above all
that she was able to coax him out of his mistrust of himself
and his dryness back to life. The tension in him broke for
a time and she could feel that she was winning a victory
against the past, against time.

Yet again she was hostile to him. It was after the failure
of his business. In one of their endless discussions about
the future he said in an impersonal voice, as if speaking to
himself:

' Well, thank God, Jenny is provided for at least.'

She was seized by a familiar resentment. No matter how
poor they might be it would be an agony to him to deprive
his first wife of the money he allowed her, though now it
was the whole of his income.

' It's wrong, I think, to give her all your money,' she said.

At once he turned on her, with a quick urgency, out of
all reason. ' You're going back on your word,' he said.
' You knew of the arrangement and agreed to it.'

' At the time, yes,' she said, calmly.

He was deeply offended, she knew. ' A woman would
not understand what I am doing with that money,' he said
with a sharp smile.

' Giving it away is a good gesture,' said Hervey.

' I won't have that said.' He was furious with her. He
went out, leaving her feeling humiliated and a little con-

temptuous. He apologised in the evening, but he was still resentful of her. Seeing herself treated in this way, she was filled by self-pity and wept as desolately as before—until he turned to her and was humbly kind again and gentle. They were reconciled; but she remembered it against him.

The strife between them was her truceless strife with time. When she was burning the heap of Jenny's letters, a page from one detached itself and fell, smouldering, on to the hearthstone: before lifting it back into the fire she read the sentence: 'I always see you as you were, kind, and very young.' She felt a prick of grief, because this she could not alter. She could think of a willing, smooth-skinned, and confident young man but she could not possess him. He was for ever out of her reach. Her flesh felt the bone below the skin, the hard unliving bone under her hand.

The hot sun, wheeling above the trees, now fell mercilessly upon her; she closed her eyes for a moment and felt it strike through her eyelids to the brain. She sat up. The wide back of the downs, with flexed muscles of hills and deep smooth soft-shaded hollows, quickened in sunlight. The valley was the gentle hollow between the breasts, and light poured over it from every quarter of the sky. A bird sang far, far up, like the voice of the heat that blazed between earth and sky.

She was caught out of herself into a moment's ecstasy. Her life turned about her as the earth to the sun, seeking and finding light. Everything is now mine, she thought. In the past week Nicholas had surrendered to her as never before: he no longer told her she came second to his work, he told her instead that he cared for nothing except herself, nothing else. She did not ask how much the change in him was due to her danger and his failure. She accepted it with a confident heart, having learned nothing from the past.

She was not thinking of him now. She felt a new life

quickening in her veins; her thoughts darted upward, mingled and yet distinct like the wings of a flight of swallows in the clear air: the American; her hard life in London after the War, when she was nothing, no one; Nicholas, the divorce, her books; one after another they flocked past her eyes and tumbled out of sight. I did everything myself, she cried; I had no money, and no man helped me: it was I, only I, who gave Hervey Russell a name, a reputation, a place.

Her limbs trembled with joy; her hands, awkward, with long awkward fingers and square palms, became the symbol of her success. She held them up against the sun and saw them bright and glowing. There is nothing waiting for me in life that I can't do with, she thought; she laughed to herself. A half memory of the lively young man Henry Smith came in her mind, with the thought that she would like to know him better. Surely the brilliant Miss Hervey Russell could make friends of whom she chose.

She laughed again and lifted her face to the light. This is Hervey Russell, the young Hervey that was; I created her from nothing; I lived, worked and endured to give her life. Nicholas my love. I wish everyone could know what I have done and that I am as clever as Marcel Cohen. Where are all my fears? Why was I afraid of ridicule and failure? There is nothing I cannot now do: from now on my mind will always do what I tell it to do. I shall learn, I shall press forward, I shall help and cherish Nicholas, and I shall get for my son everything he must have. I live, I shall live, my body is so strong with life that I cannot die; no matter what they do to me.

A cloud hid the sun for a few moments. She felt the grass shiver under her hands in a light breath. Lying back, she closed her eyes. She was a little abashed, but not ashamed of her ecstasy. Indeed I started with everything against me, she thought soberly. She saw the bedroom of the grey drabbled commercial hotel in the Midlands, Penn lying in bed and the shabby quilt folded at the foot. He was ill and she nursed him. She was never able to stifle her aversion to sick rooms and sick people, but she did all she had to do with unmoved face. They were poor, they quarrelled; and Penn tried to keep her in her place by the easy sarcasm of a schoolmaster. She wrote her first book.

The outskirts of Liverpool, a flat colourless country, fields and raw streets. The small flimsy house in a street of small houses. She ran from room to room, dusting, lifting clothes from the rinsing water and carrying them out to the bare untidy garden to dry. Her hands were red and roughened from the water. She folded the blanket over Richard and wheeled him in his cart to the shops, looking anxiously at the prices of things he must have. Moist from the bath, he lay across her knees and she dried him, her fingers, the strong clumsy fingers of a schoolgirl, moving over him with the lightness and softness of feathers.

One morning—she had been ill and was still weak and uncertain—Penn offered to help her with the work before he went out to his own. She gave him the long brush to sweep off the loose whitewash from a ceiling and a cap to cover over his hair. When he had finished it he put his hat on over the cap, and set off down the road carrying the leather despatch case and his stick, with the pink frill of the cap showing under the hat: she had to fly, breathless, half down the street behind him. He was vexed and tore the cap off and gave it to her without a word.

She felt herself smiling; her lip quivered. The extraordinary thing—but it was terrible, too—was her intimacy with Penn. In this moment she felt that he and he alone knew her, not only what she was but what she had been. He knew her in the lasting intimacy of marriage. Yet she could never bring herself to live with him again. Her body, and within her body her spirit, withered at the thought. From Nicholas she was, deeply, separated, except in a few rare moments; yet she lived with him. She was hurt, bewildered, exasperated by him, but nothing touched her contentment in him. Already she was settling herself beside him like a tree sinking on its roots.

With part of her mind she knew now that the sense of unwanted intimacy with her first husband, of knowing and being known by him, would shrivel with the years until it was nothing, a pinch of dust in an unvisited room. But she could not yet cease thinking of him. She forgot his cruel meanness and remembered that time, when she lived with him, had still something of the shining endlessness of time in her childhood. The sky stretched interminably over long glittering forenoons, and only slowly the twilight came and then dark. Especially now she remembered this, when she was weighed down by the knowledge that soon she would have to move to London and take up the burden of Cohen's work. London did not suit Richard; he would have to go away. Her heart sickened at the thought.

But more than this—she had the sense that she had betrayed in Penn a young lover. And a queer notion that she had striven ungenerously for herself, leaving him behind.

She was half dozing over this thought. Suddenly she started awake, crying: ' It was my fault. The whole blame was mine.' If I had loved him, he would not have gone to other women. From the beginning I failed him. I let people see that he lied, and bragged about himself, and treated me meanly. I have told Nicholas things about him I ought not to have told anyone. There is something cruel and treacherous in me too. Why do I do these things? Why did I show Nicholas the blustering letter he wrote asking me for money?

I believe, she thought, that in her heart of hearts a woman dislikes the first man who takes her—no matter how she loves him. He has destroyed her and made her as common to life as other women. My mother hated my father openly and made us all know it. When she was in one of her fixed awful rages she could not be satisfied unless her children hated and avoided him. I remember she left the house once, crying that she would never come back to it while he was in it. I trailed desperately after her, following miles into the country, afraid to let her out of my sight. I thought she meant it.

One of Hervey's earliest memories of her mother was of running in to her to ask if she might go on a picnic with other children. Her mother looked at her with a cold serious smile, and said: ' But if you go, I shall be alone this afternoon. Surely you don't want to leave me alone? '

The little girl was struck to the heart to think of her mother sitting in her house lonely for the whole afternoon. At the same time she wanted vividly to go with the others. Their voices came through the window from the road where they were waiting in an impatient little group. She hung back, uneasy and distressed.

' But you wouldn't be alone for long,' she urged. ' I should be back soon. You could go out to the shops.'

' By myself? Carrying the heavy bag, and no quick clever Hervey to run in first and put the kettle on the stove for me? '

Heavy-hearted, she went out and told them she could not come, her mother wanted her at home. They ran off without even a word that they were sorry, without a look, and she went back into the house and tried to pretend she was pleased to stay. It would never do to look as if she were disappointed; that would mean a long afternoon of disgrace until her mother softened towards her and she cried and was forgiven.

The scene came again and again through her childhood. The sense of responsibility and guilt—guilt for the rare times when she defied her mother and went off—remained, strengthened in her by time.

But why think of it now? she said, restless. It is past, forgotten. But just as she had felt guilty leaving her mother alone when she was a child running to play with other children, so, now, she felt herself guilty of leaving her first husband, and none of the wrongs he did her, darkening her youth, suspecting her, hurting her body in anger, teaching her to mistrust herself and all other men, seemed as worthy of punishment as her own act in leaving him at the last.

She turned from thinking of him to think of Richard. He was less than four years old when she left him, driven out by the fever of ambition in her that burned to set her about her own business. She saw herself dressing him that last morning, and half knew freshly the agony she had concealed then. Her cheeks burned, and she felt her throat hardening with tears.

I mustn't be a fool, she thought grimly; I came here to be quiet for to-morrow. The thought that she was very ill now gave her a singular satisfaction, as though in some way it balanced the sum of her mistakes and sins.

One night—a week before she called on the woman doctor, before she had made up her mind to ask anyone's advice on the pain that inhabited her body like a fox its hole, sometimes asleep, sometimes awake and tearing the earthen walls—she was lying in bed, her mind wandering in a half-dream. Without his usual warning the fox awoke, and drove his claws deep, deep into her flesh. She was taken by surprise and cried out: 'Oh, oh!'

The door of Nicholas's room was open. He heard her and ran across the landing to her room. She did not answer him at once. She was unsure of her voice. He switched the light on and saw her face. It shocked him and he ran across to the bed and took hold of her.

'What's the matter, Hervey? What can I do? *What is it?*'

'Don't touch me,' she said.

He was afraid. 'I won't touch you. But what's the matter? You're ill, I must get a doctor. Can I leave you alone?'

The thought of a strange doctor being brought in roused Hervey more quickly than anything else could have done.

'No, you can't,' she said. 'I can't bother with a doctor when I feel like this.' She bit her lip. 'It's coming again,' she said, looking at him with a smile.

'What? Tell me what it is,' Nicholas said.

'Please turn the light off.'

'But then I can't see you.'

'Turn it off. It hurts my eyes.'

He walked to the door and turned the light out. The light was on on the landing and he set the door widely open, so that the room was not quite dark. He came back to the bed. Hervey put her hand out and touched his.

'Don't mind,' she whispered. 'I can tell you I shall be all right in a minute.'

'Are you sure?' he asked.

'Quite sure. It comes now and then. I was asleep and didn't know. I'm sorry I made a fuss.'

Her hand and face were both wet. Nicholas was beside himself with fear. He had no knowledge of illness, and he thought she might be dying. 'Please let me go for a doctor,' he said, in mortal fear.

'No. I don't need one.' She turned her face into the pillow and made a short stifled sound. 'It would worry me. I don't like doctors.'

'Where is the pain?'

'Here.' She laid her hand lightly on the point of her body for an instant. 'Don't worry, Nicholas. I know all about it.'

'Have you had it before.'

'Yes, often.'

'My God, how often?'

'Every two or three months,' Hervey said. 'It comes oftener than it did, but it always goes away again in a few minutes.'

'How long has it been coming?'

'I don't know. Yes, I do. About eight or nine years, I think.'

Her voice sounded cheerful. She began to feel about with her hand under the pillow. 'My handkerchief.'

'I'll bring you a clean one.' He took it out of the drawer and came back to her. She smiled at him, moved herself gingerly, and gave a long sigh of relief.

'I don't mind anything when it goes,' she said.

'You must tell me about this,' said Nicholas. He made an effort to speak gently, although his anger with her for neglecting herself was almost as great as his fear. The bed was a wide one and her body took up little room in it. He looked at this rebellious stubborn flesh and wondered. What made her endure tortures rather than speak about them?

'What is it like?'

'Oh I don't know,' she said thoughtfully. 'Like a wild animal.'

'It comes and goes? Why haven't you spoken about it?'

'I don't care to speak about myself. Least said soonest mended. I expect it's nothing out of the way. If I asked a doctor he might laugh at me, then I should feel a fool.'

'But you don't know.'

'No.' She touched him again. 'Don't be angry, Nicholas.'

'Angry? I'm not angry,' he said, his body trembling with anger and love, so that he was scarcely conscious of her, the cause of it. 'I'm abominably afraid. I don't know what to do for you. Can't you understand? Suppose you are really ill.' He put his arms round her and lay with his face on her shoulder. 'Oh, my love, my love, tell me what will be of any use to you. You don't know what you were like when I came in—you looked as though you were being killed.'

'It hurt me,' said Hervey.

'I know, I know.'

'But you don't mind so much as that?' She was over-joyed, seeing him distracted on her account. The idea that she might be very ill did not alarm her. She did not believe it. She felt an exquisite happiness. Now I am loved, she thought.

'If anything happened to you I should be done for,' he said. 'I have nothing else in the world—nothing.'

'But I come second to—I don't know what,' she said slyly.

'I was an ass, a fool, a brute. I don't want anything except you. I talk like that out of vanity—and because I'm ashamed.'

'Why were you ashamed?' she asked.

'Because I'm nothing,' he said, in a steady dry voice. 'I've made only mistakes, and failures, too many failures. I'm no good as a husband. What else is there I can pride myself on?'

'You're all I want and more than I expected from life,' Hervey said.

Nicholas did not answer and she began to feel like sleep. She was exhausted. He lay across her heavily in silence, in the dark room, almost as though he had forgotten where he was. Can he be asleep already? she thought. Her head fell sideways in weariness. He moved and sat up slowly. 'I don't want to leave you.'

He left her for a moment, to turn the light off on the landing. He shut the door, came back to her, and getting into bed, put his arm under her head. 'Can you sleep?'

'Oh yes,' she sighed.

'Is the pain all gone?'

'Yes.'

'Do you feel anything?'

'It — yes — I feel apprehensive, that is, sore: no, apprehensive.'

'Here?'

'Yes.'

He laid his hand over her womb. 'Do you feel safer?'

'Yes,' she said. She was half asleep, and warmth was

coming back into her body after the cold of sweating. She felt a deep thankfulness and quiet.

'Then sleep, my love, sleep.'

But I must go, she thought. The sun had come about a stage or two, so that the beech threw its shadow over her. She moved her arm out to lie in the sun. Instantly, as though the gesture had recalled him, she saw the American as clearly and steadily as if he were beside her. He had sat there, and she here, and she had stretched her arm out to catch the last rays of the sun on this high place. When they rose to go home, she watched him. His vitality, splendid and inexhaustible, matched her own. He was tireless and stubborn; he had as much ambition as she had. In short, he was her worst and most violent self, less intelligent and more unscrupulous, more lax, but not more alive. He made other men seem insipid. Her mind and her life were thrown into a tumult—yet not by him, by the ambitions and desires she had been able to control until his set them off.

How much strength I had then, she thought. But I shall never now live as I meant. This thought shocked her.

'I am changing, I am growing old, or cold—or both!' she cried. The change was two-fold. She had become stricter towards herself as she was learning to ask less and less from Nicholas. And from her life. She expected very little now. She worked a hundred times harder at her writing, crossing out twenty words for one she wrote. She was profoundly dissatisfied with it, too. The zest went out of it when the strictness began.

She felt a curious sense of uneasiness, of revolt. She almost thought that she had willingly entered a trap. Again she felt the bone under the living flesh. Time pinched her. She was afraid, not of dying, but of living and being over-taken by dryness. Must I be *this* Hervey and no other? she cried. Do *this* and nothing else all my life.

She stood up quickly, brushed the dry grass from her skirt, and began to go down to the valley. When she reached her car she stood for a moment looking into the farm garden, still empty and asleep in the sun. She had the thought that if she waited long enough, or knew the right thing to do, she would see herself in the old dress embroidered with coloured wool crossing the garden to fetch Richard. He waited for her at the top of the steps, his fair hair standing out in soft gleaming curled flames, his blue eyes fierce with laughter. His hands were folded over the small cat.

I am tired, she thought. And because she was tired she seemed to be at the end of everything, even of her love for her husband. It was the same with Nicholas as with everything, and everyone else; she gave her whole self, to exhaustion, and then had to take enough back to go on living. That was what her friends disliked in her. Among each other they said she was not reliable: but when it came to the point they relied on her for more than they had the right to, and—whether to her credit or their own—usually received it.

She felt empty, tired, and vexed. She resented furiously the new Cohen adventure, and was ready to blame Nicholas for it. As if she had not begun it herself. Alone, Nicholas could never have imagined himself running a business for Marcel Cohen.

As she drew nearer to London, she thought: How did I ever come to this soft part of England? The luxurious trees, smooth fields, and polite handsome villages, said nothing to her heart. By contrast, her rebelling heart said, the grey hideous towns and villages straggling over the Yorkshire fells, and the *dark Satanic mills* below them, burst their stones with life. You climb up out of them, and in a cleft between moors a lane quivers in spring with the clear wavering light of wind-flowers and the sulky flame of the foxgloves in summer. And in Danesacre—she was in Danesacre at night, looking inland: the air and the sky were filled with a clear

watery light, like the bronze of water at dusk; on the edge
of the sky a line of spectral trees rode the earth.

She stopped the car for a minute and sat with her
hands pressing her cheeks. Everything will fall to pieces
if I am not careful, she thought; I will really be more
careful.

In the hedge near her was a green lolling board, on which
she could just see the half-obliterated word *TEA*. She went
up to the house and knocked at the door: when no notice
was taken of her she ventured into the passage and stood
there looking round. It was a small private house, with no
sign of being ready to feed wayfarers. She was about to
go away again, sighing—because she longed for a cup of
tea—when a door on the right opened and a middle-aged
woman came into the passage.

'I beg your pardon,' Hervey said nervously. 'Do you
serve tea? There is a notice.'

'Yes, I can get you tea,' the woman said. She seemed
surprised. Probably no one had ever read her timid sign
before, and she had long since given up expecting a customer.
She showed Hervey into the room behind her, a small sitting-
room with two tables, and disappeared along the passage to
the back of the house.

Hervey looked about her. There was a horsehair couch
with high carved ends and facing it two big awkward saddle-
bag chairs. There were pallid water-colours of some
mountainous country on the wall, and on the mantelshelf
a splendid array of wooden animals. She touched one of
them, a cow, so smooth, placid, and cow-like, that it seemed
one insulted it by picking it up. They were exquisitely
carved, in the very attitudes and colour of life.

The woman came in with a tea-pot, a cup and saucer
of fine china which did not match, and a plate of thin
bread-and-butter.

'I am sorry,' she said, in a low voice, 'there is only bread.
If I had known you were coming——'

'I am giving you a lot of trouble,' said Hervey. 'I was tired—and I happened to stop near your notice.'

'But it is no trouble at all,' the woman said. She poured out the tea as if Hervey were a guest.

'Those are lovely toys,' Hervey said, to make herself agreeable. 'If they are toys and not—not——' She stopped, unable to find a more important word to describe them.

'They were my child's toys,' the woman said. She took one of them in her hand and looked at it closely. 'This one he spoiled when he bit it. See, there are the marks.'

Hervey looked carefully, and smiled. She was afraid to ask what had become of the little boy who had left his teeth marks on the side of a yellow carved pig. As she handed it back she said: 'There are the same marks on the back of my watch. When my son was four years old he took the works out of it and threw them under his bed: it was mended, of course, but it has never gone so well since.'

'I have not seen my son since he was eight,' the woman said. She went away, leaving Hervey to finish her tea. It was very good tea, scented and pale, not the least what you would expect in this shabby house. When she had drunk it, Hervey went into the passage and looked anxiously for the woman to pay her. She came out of the kitchen.

'What do I owe you?' Hervey said diffidently. She was afraid of giving offence.

The woman said she thought sixpence, and Hervey gave it to her, with a warm smile. 'I am very grateful to you for your kindness,' she said. 'And the tea was extremely good.'

'You are welcome,' the woman said. 'With regard to the toys,' she went on, glancing at them through the door, which had been left open, 'they were carved by a Chinese servant for my child. We were living in China, I and my husband and our son. We were missionaries and my husband was a doctor. When they came to kill my husband, I took the child in my arms into the other room, but they came after us and one of them wounded me in the side. I fell down. The last thing I heard before I lost myself was the boy saying, Mother, mother, these men are hurting me. He was not there when I came to myself, and I never saw him again, and never heard anything about him. That was the end for me. I think of it every day and shall do so as long as I live. Time stood still then and has not moved since.' She stopped and looked closely at Hervey. ' I am telling you all this,' she said in a calm voice, ' because of the teeth-marks on your watch.'

She opened the door for her to go out. Hervey could not think what to say to her. She saw her sixpence held loosely in the woman's hand.

' That was terrible,' she said softly, looking at the woman.

' Yes, it is,' the woman answered. She shut the door, shutting Hervey into a world where time went on to the same hour each day, and herself out of it.

Hervey drove on. It was beginning to be dark. The sky closed round her, like the strong coil of a spring. Trees hardened into houses at the side of the car, and at last she could see only as far as the lights and these not too strong. She decided to go through London, since at night she was not sure of the way round. She was intolerably weary, but underneath it all she felt her life springing as fiercely as ever, clenched round the small white bone which is time. How long, she wondered, shall I live on this earth? Where shall I come to die, and when? She did not believe she would die at all, and a roll of drums, like gun-fire, started up in her mind, the voice of her deep life.

At Hyde Park she saw T. S. Heywood standing at the side of the road, and stopped the car. He was shocked to find that she had driven herself into Hampshire and back, when she ought to have rested all day. She was very pale. He made her turn the car round and drive to his house. She went reluctantly, wanting only to be at home. The house, too, was not his but his wife's, and the less Hervey saw nowadays of Evelyn Lamb the better she was pleased. Sometimes she hated the older woman for having patronised and bullied her when she was younger and poor, sometimes she was sorry for her; she was always ill at ease with her: she despised her instincitvely as a humbug and a snob, and feared her sharp learned mind.

T. S. took her straight to his room, on the second floor of the house, and sent for coffee. He took a flask of brandy from the pocket of a rucksack and poured a wide finger into the coffee. She spluttered over it, but drank it to please him.

He sat at the other side of his desk. She knew why he sat there rather than in one of the two easy chairs. It was because his head was big out of proportion with his short body and he looked better when his upper part only was visible above the desk. The window of the room was open, and by turning her head Hervey could see the Thames: it was at the full or at the turn, since it seemed to breathe without flowing, and the flakes of light rose and fell lightly at each breath. The air outside the room was warm.

'This room is my ivory tower,' T. S. said. 'Locked into it, I'm better off and happier, as well as saner, than you are, killing yourself to alter a society which only wants to be left alone.'

Your ivory tower, Hervey thought coldly, is provided for you by a rich wife, twelve years your senior. She was ashamed of thinking in this way about her friend under his very eyes; and said hurriedly and harshly: 'The miners don't want to be left alone.'

'They don't need your amateur help,' T. S. said rudely. 'Anyone can become a reformer or a rebel, but you would conceivably have been a writer if you hadn't tried to be so many other things. A half-witted reformer. You are wasting your energy. You can't reform cancer, but that's what you are trying to do. Cancer is growth gone wrong, the breakdown of the living structure under stress, the outbreak of a suppressed hostility. All your unemployed and unemployable miners are unwanted primitive cells left out of use by a new development; they are tumours that will certainly become malignant, and you can't believe, just because you want to believe something pleasant, that the end result will be the victory of your precious workers and a nice strong healthy body with all its organs intact. Of course society will try to adapt itself, but being an old society it is infinitely more likely to fail than to succeed: in fact it is excessively likely to deviate to chaos, revolution, war, barbarism. In any case *I* can't arrest the process, and so I keep myself to myself and use my brains as nature intended I should—to study the behaviour of forms of energy and write out the results.'

'You are doing nothing so respectable,' Hervey said, laughing at him unkindly. 'You earn your living by researching into poison gas for the manufacturers.' A living which would not pay the rent of this house, she thought.

'I haven't the slightest compunction in poisoning men out of existence,' T. S. said. 'Not more than rats. It's becoming increasingly hard to tell the two species apart; both can live anywhere, mate all the year round, eat anything. Like men, rats make war on their own kind. On the whole I prefer rats; it has not yet occurred to any of them to invent and sell poison gas, disembowel each other with explosive shells, or flog one another in prisons. I don't believe either that they will evolve to the stage of being able to invent words as disguises for their beastly cruelties. Long live the decently dumb rat! Won't you have more coffee, my dear?'

'Without brandy,' Hervey said.

'You go into hospital to-morrow?'

'Yes.'

' And zero hour Tuesday.'

' Yes,' Hervey smiled.

' Are you afraid? Don't mind telling me. How long have we been friends?—fourteen years I make it. You might as well tell me the truth; you tell so many lies.'

' I am afraid of being hurt,' Hervey said. ' Also I am so much afraid that someone there will look at me inquisitively, and notice something, that I shall take care not to think I'm afraid—it might come out.'

' My poor dear,' he said quietly. ' No, don't scowl at me, I'm not pitying you. But there's nothing I can do, and you are the only person in the world I love without greed.' He paused and added: ' By the way, I know your surgeon. Would you like to see me on Tuesday morning?'

' No,' Hervey said. ' Thanks.'

' Very well.'

' I shall be reading up till the last moment.'

He came from behind his desk, forgetting himself. ' Do you know you're much quieter these days,' he said, looking at her. ' You were lively and irrepressible—and round, rosy, and clumsy—when you lived with Philip and me before the War. What's happening to you?'

' Nicholas has happened to me,' she said.

' He's kind to you, and decent—not another Penn?' T. S. said, frowning.

' Nicholas is kind, decent, honest, overbred, and never bores me. To know him as well as I do is a liberal education. And you know, when you begin to educate a barbarian the process is painful, to the barbarian. I didn't learn anything from Penn's bullying except to cringe a little—underneath I was still sure that I knew better than anyone in the world. I was full of confidence. I could behave badly and grossly, but I was not afraid of myself.'

' And now?'

' Now I am afraid to obey my own nature. I have discovered that it is violent and undisciplined. I know now that my books were very bad, emotional in a false way, uncritical, and lying. Since I married Nicholas I have been infected by his hate of what is noisy and violent. He has better taste in living than I have. And in struggling not to offend it I have become critical of myself and my feelings and every sentence I write. And the effort is too much— it has destroyed my confidence, that irrepressible life you saw. I write better—I live more tranquilly. But I write with the utmost difficulty and struggle, and I don't feel pleasure in it now. It is the effect of the Roxbys on me!'

T. S. looked at her crimson cheeks and at her hands—they were folded round her knees, which were trembling—and felt thoroughly alarmed. He sat on the arm of her chair, and under pretence of stroking her hair, pressed his fingers against her temple and felt the pulse leaping there as though it could burst its walls. He did not invite her to stay the night in his house, because he knew it would be useless. She would not stay. He thought of offering himself to drive the rest of the way with her. He rejected that because it would embarrass her to refuse and he knew that he would be welcome this last night neither to her nor to Nicholas.

But she was growing calmer already. He felt the movement of her life becoming strong and quiet, as it rose and fell back like a spring jetting from far below the earth.

'You don't regret having married your Roxby?' he said gently.

'No,' Hervey said. After a long silence she said quietly: 'It is only that sometimes I feel trapped, and like all wild animals I fall into a panic when I feel the trap. When I think that I shall die without having been more than one of the many persons I could have been, and without having had more than one or two of the things that were waiting for me in the world, but I had no time to seek them and find.'

'That happens to all of us,' T. S. said.

Hervey nodded and smiled at him, thinking of him as a bragging, awkward boy; of his marriage, and of his passion, ridiculous in his own eyes, for Georgina Roxby. She leaned against his arm for a minute, aware of a deep intimacy with him. It was not desire, but it had the warmth of their difference of sex and their tragic likeness of nature. Both had illimitable desires; both of them had acknowledged defeat and were unable to give up fighting.

After she left him, Hervey drove through London towards the north-west—by streets known to her on more than one level of her life. Time here ran with a rapid current at the surface, but beneath it the sluggish water swept leaves, earth, dead branches with straws twined in them, against the sides of the bed; a stone rolled over and over for some distance and came to rest in the shallows, where in certain lights it caught the eye. To keep herself awake, Hervey struggled to think clearly about her life. She had meant to do this on the hill above Broughton, but somehow her life had eluded her. Why, when I long so dearly for peace, do I rebel? Why have I hours and days when I long furiously to tear down everything I have built, throw away everything I have gathered; run, run for my life? I am not at heart a rebel. This frantic longing for freedom is only the dark side of a passion for order. But I want a *new* order; I want the parts of the design to shift, and release all the trapped and maimed creatures, caught between past and future. Her mind darkened, and sank with her into the passages under the earth; she saw the walls of the earth shift and fall together, squeezing the breath and blood out of the men bowed there, as paint is squeezed from a tube. Even the bone crumbled between her fingers and was scattered like dust into the pit.

Coming to a cross-roads on the edge of London, she saw a group of men and a bus smashed against a wall. There was no excitement, as though the thing had happened earlier in the day, and they were now idle watchers. The sight of the shabby silent men bent over the wrecked engine in the night affected her strangely.   Farther on she passed a small factory.   A man on picket duty leaned against the wall under a lamp.   His gaunt patient face was sharply distinct, as though it hung on the darkness surrounding him on all sides.   She had an impulse to stop and speak to him.   But what could she say?   She went on.

In the moment when she turned from the main road into the lane a car approached going towards London.   It stopped at the side and a man got out to look at the engine.   She saw his face in the feeble light of her own car.   It was Julian Swan.   Her heart moved painfully.   She was struck, as though this were the first time she had really seen him, by the strange blankness of his face.   It was made of smooth, impenetrable planes of flesh, seeming shockingly dull, but the small full mouth looked cruel.   He is training himself to be outside human feelings, she thought.   He could now watch men being flogged without noticing that they were suffering. She was startled and saddened.

The lights of her car failed suddenly.   She had now to drive by the feel of the road, slowly, hoping that she would get home without meeting anyone.   She had reached the lucid stage of fatigue and her mind blazed with light.   The light was fed to it from a glowing crimson centre and poured out through innumerable bright passages.   All outside her was dark.   She saw the earth hanging in the darkest hour; a multitude of the living pressed forward in its streets and over its fields, each man alone in the icy darkness which has fallen on them in their journey: she saw herself as a child, and as a girl, each separate, isolated by the darkness, seeking without finding, she saw the woman looking at her child's toys, hearing his voice, the voice coming from every man at least once during his life, *Mother, mother, these men are hurting me;* she saw her own mother, indomitable and defeated, her eyes, blue and empty with staring, turned to the past.   The eyes, too, of Swan and of T. S. Heywood, turned romantically to the past, the last with despair, the other in senseless fear and hatred of the future. Some, like David Renn, pressed forward destroying without knowing what they were doing, through their blind passion for justice; increasingly aware, he too, that he was cut off and alone. As lost, isolated, and helpless, were Harben and William Ridley, living only in order to draw a profit from violence and uncertainty and the unnatural deathly needs of a world in which machines are more precious than men. They accepted life as it came, without troubling about the others, except to get the better of them as often as possible.

And I? Hervey thought. I am not even *there*, in the generation certain to pay bitterly for their silence. She held her eyelids open to watch. The frightful certainty of loneliness, the ache of separation, felt in the last hour, the sense of being thrust out to hang there alone, without even the companionship of thieves, closed round her. She thought of her home, and with deep longing wished that she were a child in the yard of her mother's house, between the hawthorn and the yellow fire of the laburnum, between the door and the path.

As she drove up to her house she saw a light in her bedroom. Nicholas was in there, preparing her bed for the night. He turned round quickly when he heard her coming in, and helped her to take off her coat and shoes. He did not reproach her for going out when she had said she would stay at home and rest. His love for her had become an anguish while he waited for her to come in. He had no idea where she had gone—in her note she said 'some distance'—and he had imagined every form of accident during the hours since he came home.

'What would you like to eat?' he asked. 'I've been into the pantry, and there is cheese, bread and butter, and honey. Let me get something for you.' He wanted to serve her.

'I'll eat them all, and drink some tea,' she said, softly and happily.

She followed him into the kitchen, which was warmer than the other room, and watched him lift the things on to a tray. While the kettle was boiling he came and stood beside her, and she leaned her head on his arm. She felt a deep happiness and peace in being with him. She abandoned herself to it, closing her eyes, and letting her body rest on his. It hurt her when he went away from her to pour the water into the teapot; she felt the sense of loss so sharply that tears came into her eyes.

'What's the matter, my love?' he said.

'You moved,' she said, turning her face aside.

'I had to make the tea,' Nicholas said, smiling. 'Come. Drink it.' He poured it out for her, and buttered a slice of bread and spread it with honey, smiling all the time. He was pleased to be doing simple, intimate things for her.

'Where have you been?' he asked.

'Quite a long way. In fact, to Hampshire. I wanted to see the place where Richard and I lived during the War.' She did not mention the name of her first husband.

'To Hampshire!' Nicholas repeated, in consternation and surprise. 'You must have been mad to make such a journey, to-day of all days.'

'I couldn't make it to-morrow,' she answered, looking at him with a slight, happy smile. She ate her bread and drank tea, leaning back in her chair with the relief of one who is at the end of her journey. There was nothing more for her to do, or trouble about. She had arranged everything, visited the past, and caught a glimpse of the future. And now that she was here, the waking dream slipped from her mind, sinking out of sight like a stone dropped into deep water; it will never be seen again except by one of those accidents which change the course of rivers and restore to the sun and man's use what was hidden in the ground. She thought only that nothing, so long as she lived, would be better than this warm silent room, with the tea at her elbow, and the assurance she felt now. I am needed and loved, she thought. A current

of warmth and kindness came to her from her husband's arm
resting lightly on hers; she was humble as if to deserve her
happiness.   Actually, she knew too much about Nicholas to
expect him to be always as easy as he was to-night.

' I hope you'll be comfortable in your room in London,'
she said.

' I shall be comfortable when I know you are all right
again,' Nicholas said, frowning.   He was anxious.   She
looked very haggard, pale, tired, much older.

' You'll look after Richard, if anything goes wrong,' she
said sleepily.

' Oh, my God, don't speak of anything going wrong,' he
said, with energy and fear.

' I am sure it won't,' she said.   ' But you will keep Richard?
I don't want '—she hesitated—' his father would ruin him,'
she finished quickly.

' Of course I'll keep him.'   He stood up, half vexed with
her for bringing in her son now.   His heart ached again
when he looked at her.   He knew that he loved her, haggard
and plain, more than he did before.

' You must go to bed, Hervey.'

She went away to her room and began to undress.   Glancing
round, she saw a drawer half open in her desk and went to
shut it.   A sheet of paper was stuck at the back, part of the
first chapter of the novel she had began to write.   She took
it out and began reading.   It struck her as dull, forced, and
commonplace.   She had written more than ten thousand
words: in a sudden impatience with it she tore the first
sheets across, and then the rest, and threw the fragments
into the fireplace.   I had better get rid of it than have it
waiting for me when I come back, she thought.

On the couch were laid, folded, ready to lay in her
case, the clothes she was taking to the home, and a list
of them she had made so that nothing should be missing
at the end.

For one moment, as she was stepping into bed, she felt

afraid. What if I never come back, she thought, and felt herself on the edge of a shameful panic. She drew back sharply, with quick scorn. The sheet, which she had been gripping between her hands, was creased, and she smoothed it carefully before lying down.

I need new linen, she thought: I must see about it at the sales in July. She closed her eyes.

Monday, May 10*th*

THE NIGHT COMETH WHEN NO MAN CAN WORK

CHAPTER XVIII

SWAN rose at six. The first moment in which he put his lame ankle to the ground was always unpleasant. Not physically— he had no pain in it—but wounding to his spirit. He had first to massage the bone between his fingers, then to set his foot cautiously on the floor and balance himself carefully until he felt the leg able to bear him. Without these precautions he was likely to fall on his knees the moment he stepped out of bed, because the ankle had stiffened during the night. The movements had become perfectly mechanical, yet he could not avert the spasm of irritation he felt while he made them, and when he was walking slowly across the room to the window to pull up the blind.

His room—he had moved to a flat in Shepherd's Market on the day he received his first quarter's salary as secretary to the Economic Council—looked out only on the angle of a wall, yet he never slept without drawing the blind over the open window. No one could possibly overlook him in this room, but he felt it more comfortable at night. In daylight he could watch the wall furtively to see that it evolved no hostile, mocking eyes.

Facing the open window, he took off his pyjamas and began the exercises he went through every day for the sake of elegance. He stooped and placed the flat of his hand on the floor, rising again and stooping twenty-eight times, one for every year of his age. He knelt down, and squatting on his heels bent backwards until his head was almost touching the floor. Squinting to the side in the long mirror he could just see his body tense and straining with the effort, from the lower ribs to the slight triangular hollow below them

187

when he breathed.   He took the sharpest pleasure and interest in the state of his body.   It was fined down and muscular; in spite of his gross appetite he had not become fatter.   He put his good fortune down to the exercises and performed them as ardently as if they were a religion.   In the sense that he was the centre of his own life they were.

In the next room his servant was laying breakfast.   It happened this morning to be a dish of which he was unusually fond, and the last trace of his bad humour vanished when he came into the room in his dressing-gown.   In the chafing dish six half kidneys, wrapped delicately in slices of bacon which had been spread with Worcester Sauce, were cooking gently; the various juices soaked into the toast on which they rested.   He waited until the precise moment when the perfection of crispness and tenderness had been reached, then switched off the heat and transferred them, sizzling quietly, to his plate.   He found the toast delicious. He kept a morsel of it to the last and put it in his mouth when he had drunk a second cup of coffee.   He felt almost too satisfied to need toast and marmalade, but after leaving the table he came back to it and ate a slice or two.   There was a hard day before him.

It was almost nine o'clock when he reached the offices of the Economic Council, but his employees, some of whom had to come from the distant suburbs, were already there. He had contrived to fill them with his own sense of the urgency and importance of their work.   Between himself and many of them had sprung the curious bond which exists between a revivalist preacher and his audience.   It was half hysteria and half the response, deep and involuntary, to an overmastering need.

He was by no means a considerate employer; his fits of temper, when he raged at them like a madman, struck terror into the weaker souls.   But no one left, except one man in the early days of the Council.   There was a scene in which the man shouted as loudly as Swan and told him he was a blackguardly bully. It was not strictly true. All Swan's outbreaks of rage were nervous; they exhausted and soothed him, and so far they had not harmed anyone. His staff actually relished them when they were over, as though they had just been through a terrifying but uplifting experience. The younger men went about for a time with dazed blank faces and eyes dilated with a peculiar excitement. They were filled with fresh zeal, and sprang quivering to their feet when he spoke to them in the course of the work.

One of these young men was in his room when he came in, placing on the desk a letter which had just come by hand. Swan took no notice of his respectful ' Good morning, sir,' except to motion him out of the way with his head. The young man flushed, half with pleasure, and went out of the room quickly. Like the other members of the staff he wore the khaki shirt of Swan's corps of volunteers. The corps had existed—in the form of a fencing club—for half a year: it became a unit of defence (defending what?) and bought khaki shirts, each man with his own money, the day after the Strike began. The fencing club, an underground room in a street off Tottenham Court Road, became a recruiting office, and each new young man as he offered himself was sent off to find and bring in six others.

Swan read his letter with a rising sense of irritation. He dared not admit to himself that its tone mortified him. It was from Gary, an unequivocal criticism of the new pamphlet. With brutal shortness, Gary advised him to tear the thing up. ' The leaders of the Trade Unions and the Labour Party are not revolutionaries, they are better politicians than yourself. It may be permissible to talk ungrammatical nonsense about civil war, a turnip-head for the fools of all classes, during the Strike itself. But don't waste your time keeping it up. There are plenty of ignorant Don Quixotes up and down the country to do that for you. It's more to the point if you'll occupy yourself preparing facts and figures on which we may press for a subsidy to forward the extraction of oil from coal. Get a letter from Mr. Harben and go with it to see a man called Heywood, in charge of the research at Stokes Chemical Works. Oil from coal is not his pigeon, but he can tell you where to find the technical facts and perhaps teach you to understand them.'

Swan felt queasy, as though he had been held up to ridicule in public. He put the letter away, and looked at the copy of his pamphlet with loathing. He did not believe it was foolish, but if it was ungrammatical he felt that it had disgraced him behind his back. A clerk came in with Evelyn Lamb's card. He played with the notion of sending her away, but she was already, sure of herself, in the doorway.

'Come in and sit down,' he said, smiling. He made no move to draw out a chair, and with a momentary hesitation she took the one nearest his desk. He continued to look at her with a smile that made her uneasy. It was welcoming and subtly impudent. She felt a faint impulse to go away at once, but her excitement overwhelmed it. She leaned towards him.

'Give me something to do, Julian.'

'What do you want?' he asked, in a gentle voice. 'There is nothing to be done here which we are not fully able to do.'

'I have been driving a car for the *Gazette*,' she broke in, not listening to him. 'Last night something happened, and I think I killed a man. It was at the corner of a country lane. I saw him a second before the car hit him. When I looked back he was lying queerly against the hedge.' She put her hand to her mouth.

'Didn't you stop?' he asked.

'Certainly not. I had pledged myself to deliver the *Gazettes* before midnight.' She looked at him with an appearance of hauteur; under it—looking behind the door where he had been himself—he guessed her hysterical fear. She did not care whether she had killed anyone or not. She was afraid for herself. He began to feel a magnanimous contempt for her, almost affection.

' Does anyone know ? '

' The car was damaged,' she said. ' They asked me when I took it in whether I had hit anything and I said No. I didn't want any delay or trouble, you understand, Julian. But they seemed to think I was not fit to go on driving, although I have driven a car for years,' she added with indignation.

Swan felt himself soothed and relaxed by her presence in his room. It was the first time she had been to see him since he had made it clear to her that he was tired of her as a mistress.

' I'm going to be very frank with you,' he said, charmingly, ' and say that I don't think you are really fit to do this sort of work—running about the country at all hours. There are plenty of younger women to do such things. My dear Evelyn, why not accept the fact that you are growing older ? '

His glance rested indulgently and ironically on her body for a moment, and moved upward slowly to her face. He looked into it with a frank intimate smile.

Evelyn looked back at him calmly, and even smiled. ' I am sorry if you have nothing for me to do,' she said, quietly, ' I thought you might be glad of help here or at your—do you call it a recruiting office ? When I remember the days of your poverty, Julian, I admire your energy and self-confidence more than I can tell you. Really, you have done wonderfully. And I hear your young men marched nobly on Saturday. How proud you must feel.'

' Young men will obey anyone who bullies them in the right way,' Swan said sincerely. Her show of spirit only made him feel kindly towards her. He realised that what would have crushed him a year ago with the sense that he had overstepped the mark, now did not touch him. He was becoming sure of himself. ' I have no respect at all for the lower middle-class mob,' he said calmly. 'They ask to be gulled and made use of—and so they are, by every politician and party. I shall make use of them myself.'

The door opened, and Hunt came in. His khaki shirt, riding breeches, and long jacket, travestied the uniform of an army officer. He had himself addressed as 'Captain Hunt,' although he had no better right to the title than any other temporary officer. He was in charge of the volunteer corps. Swan's attitude to him was more guarded and more intimate than to any other of his subordinates. He behaved like a close friend, courted him, relied on him. There was a curious tension in his feeling for the older man, as though part of his mind were on watch.

'Ah,' he said with an air of gaiety. 'My right-hand, Captain Hunt. Tim, Mrs. Heywood is much better known to you as Evelyn Lamb. You know her critical essays.' He knew that Hunt read nothing, scarcely even a newspaper. 'By the way, Evelyn, shall I find your husband at home if I go to see him this morning? Well—I can try. But do forgive me for a moment.'

He went out. Hunt stood at the desk, looked gravely at Evelyn, and said: 'I don't read any criticism except yours, Miss Lamb.'

She scarcely believed that he had heard of her until now, but she was attracted by his arrogant vitality and his big impressive body. His face had that mark of a man of violent and brutal senses, eyelids coming far down over the outer line of his eyes. His nose and mouth were long; and a dimple showed in his heavy cheeks when he smiled. Evelyn was drawn to him against her judgment: it was not always sound, and perhaps it was her breeding which warned her that Hunt was gross and ruthless. She felt a throb of excitement. She was anxious to go before Swan came back. Smiling, she said:

'You must come to dinner when this trouble is over. I suppose it will be over soon?'

'Oh, they're on the run,' Hunt said, with his engaging smile. As he held the door open for her he noticed several things—that she was no longer young, but she was dressed and cared for as very rich women are, and she was conscious of him. He was satisfied with what he saw.

He had a new ambition, a single touch of the clown in this unromantic adventurer—to know eminent persons. He had begun to feel that he would enjoy dinner-parties in their houses, comfortable weekends with them in the country. He prepared for his career in good society by having his nails manicured. So far he had made little other progress, even with Swan's unwitting help. In Evelyn's invitation he saw the first door opening to the ease he coveted.

When Swan came back neither man spoke about her. They went out together to Swan's car, and drove to Hyde Park. Swan intended to review a company of his volunteers. He drove recklessly and badly, using only his right foot. Hunt watched him without comment: he despised inefficiency in what was only a matter of learning a physical trick, and Swan's crippled foot roused in him a distaste he took pains to hide.

He despised other things in Swan, his ignorance of the grinding brutal sort of poverty, his education, his childish greed—he kept chocolate biscuits in the drawer of his desk, and ate a great quantity of them. He encouraged Swan to rely on him. At the same time he knew that without Swan he would be nothing: it was Swan's romantic force, not his, which held together the five or six hundred volunteers. He could train young men, but he could not, as Swan could, fill them with a religious enthusiasm for him. Hunt had only contempt for enthusiasm, but he understood its uses. He was prepared to use everything, the helpless virtues of young men as well as the rest, if it helped him to make his way.

The young men were drawn up in four long lines, and behind them was another, of motor cars: many of these young men drove their own cars. There were a score of shabbily-dressed men who certainly did not own cars, and a few brutalised young men, born in a slum and brought up in the streets. They stood to attention as Swan, followed at arm's length by Hunt, walked down the line. He walked slowly and stiffly, hiding his lameness; he was excited, but his face showed nothing of it: he wore consciously an air of firm severity.

Hunt was not moved or impressed by the sight of the four raggedly straight lines of men in shirts, flannel trousers and plus fours; he glanced at them sharply, with narrowed eyes, noting the rough training they would need before they deserved to be thought of even as a civilian guard. If only I'd had them in Ireland, he thought. In the second rank he saw suddenly a face he knew, a man who had been in his command with the Black and Tans. Come, that's better, he thought, surprised; I can make something of them.

Swan took a step backwards at the end of the line, and prepared to address his troops. He spoke in a grating, rather jerky voice, making stiff gestures with his arm. There were few changes of tone, and the effect was oddly monotonous, but it was the emotional monotony of a drum. It excited. The same note sounded again and again, touching the same nerve in his hearers' bodies. When at the end he raised his voice, the effect on them was like an electric current. Forbidden beforehand to make any noise, they stared at Swan with unnaturally rigid faces and the eyes of hypnotics.

' The decent people,' Swan shouted suddenly, ' have behind them the police, the military, the Tory party, and the God of battles. Let the rabble come on, let them plan their revolution, let them begin. *We are ready for them.* And I promise you this. When the Strike is over you shan't be disbanded. We'll raise the necessary money. I tell you the day is coming when we shall be needed! '

He stopped and wiped his forehead. He had been speaking

for twenty minutes. Turning to Hunt, he said: 'Give these men their orders.' He was walking towards his car when an elderly man waved to him from a cross path. Swan recognised his second cousin.

He detested his relatives, because they neglected him, and because they were wealthy and influential where he was poor, unknown, and ambitious. He was at school with this man's sons, but he had counted his few pence and they had everything for the asking. He did not forgive them for it. He would have hurried on now, but his foot prevented it. He stood still, scowling.

'Well, Julian,' said his cousin. 'Are those your *troops* you have been addressing?' By the use of this one word he managed to convey his scorn for amateur soldiers or police, and for Swan himself. His young relative's intelligence, and the spirit which had supported him in his poverty (Julian had had a very small income of his own since he was nineteen years old), were irritating in a family which for two hundred years had been distinguished for nothing worse than amiability and excellent manners. These virtues were sustained on the solid foundation of a rich coal-field. Swan's elderly cousin might therefore have been expected now to welcome him as a saviour. Not at all. Had Swan been stupid enough, he would have been helped by the fortunate side of the family to some place where he could live carefully on a moderate income. But they thought of him as incurably vulgar—he had opinions and aired them. Worse, he was anxious to make a name for himself.

'They are part of a volunteer corps I have raised,' he said shortly. He was forced to stroll forward by the side of his cousin, since a sudden dash to his car was out of the question.

'Very enterprising,' the other said, without malice. 'What is their weapon? Walking sticks, eh?'

'In *civil* life,' said Swan, 'we exist as fencing and rifle clubs. I don't think it useless,' he added, raising his voice,

' to prepare law-abiding people to defend their liberties in these days.'

'There is the army, you know,' his cousin said mildly. ' But why not archery as well ? Your grandmother was very fond of it. I believe she entered a tournament held for some charitable purpose. And do you know, Julian, I think I am the only man in the British army who has been wounded by a bow and arrow! Yes. On the North-West Frontier.'

' Here is my car,' Swan said.

He climbed into it and drove away, burning with shame. He knew that once more he had proved to his cousin—who, to be sure, was not looking for proofs—that he was ill-bred and impossible. He was not able to impress any of these people by his cleverness, which they did not value, and he had never been able to acquire the unconscious insolence they used against him without even taking the trouble to dislike him.

He stopped the car at a post office and went inside to telephone to Evelyn's husband. T. S. was at home. The Stokes Chemical Works had been closed by the withdrawal of its lorry drivers and some other outside workers. He invited Swan to come there to see him, and the young man had the experience—which did something to restore his curious self-respect—of walking past the room where he used to visit Evelyn, to visit her husband. He had never seen T. S. Heywood. He expected to dislike him.

Strangely, he did not. Perhaps because he was now in a good humour he made himself very agreeable, and exerted for his host's benefit the charm he possessed—it was rather the charm of a fine, dangerous animal when it wishes to be friendly. There was a flattery in it.

Without knowing why, T. S. was pleased with his visitor. He knew all about Swan's political labours from David Renn, but he felt that Renn—whom, by the way, he liked better than he had yet noticed—was too simple a fanatic to understand a Julian Swan. He thought he understood very well the impulse which made Swan, an ambitious and obscure young man, throw in his lot with the reactionaries. Like me, T. S. thought, he loathes the imminent destruction of what is fine and decent, for what may turn out to be only efficient.

After he had given Swan the information he needed, he said: ' Is it true that you are forming a citizen army to defend us all against revolution? '

' Yes,' said Swan, with a smile. ' Will you enlist? '

' Not I. I think you are quite wrong. If England is to be saved it won't be saved by a private army. It will be saved because the people are so modest and so decent that they will submit to anything rather than have a mess. There *will* be a mess—nothing can avert it for long. Either the next slump, or the next war, will bring us into a most unpleasant condition, with actual hunger to deal with. And then anything might happen, except a successful revolution of the poor.'

' But why risk it? Why not make sure that such a disaster couldn't happen? ' Swan said gently.

' A disaster is a disaster whatever form it takes. It will be no pleasanter for England to have people dying quietly, in an air raid, or from starvation.' He imagined that what Swan cared about was that fortunate security which, undisturbed for centuries, has made England the most civilised country in the world. ' What you should do is to preach a religion of sacrifice before it is too late. Persuade the bishops to live like simple curates and devote the treasure of their Church to good works. Persuade each wealthy family to adopt one poor family for every five thousand pounds of its income, clothe them, educate them, feed them, by going without luxuries it doesn't need. Throw open Eton to clever board-school boys. Then when the cyclone hits us, from whatever quarter it comes, we shall survive. It's the only way. Brothers in arms is a sounder basis for a nation on the verge of the storm than masters and men. You don't believe me! We shall see.'

' But I'm not uttering one word against religion,' Swan cried. ' I'm irreligious myself, who of our generation isn't? but if I were a dictator I should come to terms with the Church at once. I don't for a moment expect I should have any trouble in doing it—the Church is always on the side of authority, provided authority treats it with the usual respect. But a religion of equality—my dear fellow! No, no, I don't go along there with you.'

' Who is paying for your private army?'

' It is almost self-supporting, I assure you. All I need is the rent of the club rooms, and I know how to raise enough money for that. People make a mistake in thinking that a great deal of money is necessary to start a patriotic movement. All that is necessary is some serious danger to the country and a leader to point it out.' He laughed like a boy. ' Don't despise me for believing that I am a leader!'

He got up to go away. T. S. saw him out, and came back to his own room in a very restless state of mind. He was not working, he had spent the morning reading a monograph on a subject not his own, and this gave him a guilty conscience. He had reached the stage of obsession with his own work, when a day lost became a crime. He intended to have no life outside his work, not to look at what was going on in the world, not to think about it. In a few years' time, he thought, I shall know more about poison gas than anyone in England, then more than anyone in Europe. In the end I shall hold in my brain everything that is known about it and a little more. That little more is my secret. I shall keep it to the last, and bring it out like the youngest brother in the fairy tales to confound the lot of them. No doubt I'm going mad. In any case I ought to be working.

In his running about the room he came opposite the window and stood looking out, with an eye that saw nothing. I have no use for dictators, he thought. But if I were a dictator I should begin by gassing everyone over fifty—that would clear the world of a lot of them: then I should establish communism by bringing up every child alike, black, white, brown, yellow, all in the same nurseries, and send them to the same schools. I should teach them that monogamy is an offence against manners, that there is no life after death, and that cruelty is the only sin. Then at fifty I should gas myself and leave them to quarrel about my gospel.

Here the sun hit him a great blow in the face. He leaned forward and saw the whole river running with light, and the trees on the embankment rising on black stems into a torrent of pure glittering light, each leaf leaping and rejoicing in a living ecstasy. He struck himself on the chest. Why are you here, you miserable ball of dirt? he asked. You spoil everything by existing. Hide yourself, say to the mountains and rocks, Fall on me.

He jerked the blind down. Turning towards his table in the darkened room, he took out books, papers, a pencil, and began to work: but he was very hungry. He saw that it was after two o'clock and he went out to get food, leaving the room dark and stuffy. The servants were not used to his being at home during the day and they had forgotten him.

At this hour Swan was waiting for Georgina Roxby to take her out to lunch. She had not expected him to call on her and when he came in she was lying on the couch, reading and smoking, a slipper with a hole in it on one bare foot and the other hanging. She was not sorry to be found like this by him; she admired her feet—they were long, white, and very narrow. She smiled at him. She did not use powder, and her skin was no longer perfect; her lips were a pale bright red by nature: the bones of her face were very delicate and very strong—they were notice-able as she grew older and rather increased than took from her beauty, for those to whom form is the source of sharpest enjoyment in beauty.

Swan was more deeply in love with her than could have seemed possible in one who had never shown signs of loving anyone beside himself. He thought about her with a curious simplicity. Long ago he had made up his mind only to marry a very rich woman, and he had not forgotten this necessary step in his career, but, what was much harder for him, had decided against it. It was perhaps his first disinterested emotion since his childhood. If, like every other strong impulse he felt, it was a form of vanity, it was at least not a mean vanity. She is completely sincere and unspoiled, he thought: I shall never find anyone like her. I shall love her and be thankful I married her even though she has not a penny and I have to buy her clothes.

After their meal he drove her back to the flat in the Temple, and asked her again, for the second or third time, to marry him. 'Unless you feel,' he said, with the greatest difficulty, 'that my crippled foot makes me an impossible husband.'

'Oh my dear Julian,' she cried, 'I should never notice your foot. You think about it too much.'

'I never think about it,' he said stiffly. He saw the smile she could not suppress quickly enough, and laughed himself. 'I am a complete ass,' he said. 'I think about it every time I come into a room.'

I know you do, thought Georgina. She felt a keen pity for him, and at the same moment the least touch of contempt. A man with a physical infirmity should, she said to herself, be unconscious of it, at least to the extent of not asking to be pitied for it.

If she had been in love the thought would not have entered her head. She had enough kindness to want to turn his thoughts from it before he could be ashamed of giving himself away. Actually at this moment he would have said anything to her without shame.

' I am three years older than you are,' she told him.
' I am thirty-one.'

' You could be twenty-one,' he answered. ' You have
the look of agelessness—I think it is your cheek-bones, or
your voice. I am talking complete nonsense,' he broke off,
in despair. ' I am madly in love with you. I want to marry
you, and you force me to tell you what you look like. For
pity's sake tell me whether you are going to marry me or
not: there's nothing patient about me, I can't wait. I
don't think you would keep me waiting through vanity.
You're not vain.'

' I don't know altogether what you're doing, with your
volunteers and the rest.'

' What has that got to do with it? ' he exclaimed.

' I should want to help you if we were married,' she said
in a serious tone. ' There would be no point in it unless
I am of use.'

' I'm not marrying for the sake of my career! '

' No, for that you should marry someone with money,'
Georgina said drily. She drew down the corners of her
mouth in a smile, reckless and bitter. ' Why don't you? '
she asked.

' I told you,' Swan said, with the simplicity which was
unlike him. In another than the usual sense of the words,
he seemed beside himself now, as though he had drawn
back and allowed a younger man to take his place. He
was even shy with her, and he had the wit not to feel
ashamed of it.

Georgina felt the difference in him. She was strangely
moved by it, but her perverse memory reminded her at this
moment that less than two years ago she had offered herself
to William Gary with the persistence Swan was using for
her sake. She did not cease entreating him until he told
her he was impotent. I would have married him even then,
she said, if he had not refused me. Now she thought she
understood why he had made her suffer. It is because the

sight of love, when one feels no love, but perhaps only liking or a little pity, is very wearisome. One asks only to be rid of it, as of an intolerable burden.

'Listen—my dear Julian,' she said softly. 'I have more respect and liking for you than for any man I know. I don't feel for you the insane love you could expect from a girl ten years younger——'

'Do you feel it for some other person?' Swan interrupted her.

'No,' she said, loudly and quickly.

'Then, my beloved Gina,' he said, smiling with joy, 'there is no reason on earth why you should go on keeping me at my distance. I'll provide the insanity and all you need do is to enjoy it. We'll marry—I must be sure of you—and we shall have at first nine hundred or a thousand a year between us. That ought to be enough unless you're very extravagant. What have you to say?'

No, I don't want it, she thought quietly. She was reluctant to give him up altogether. She had no life of her own, and she knew, when she was at her most honest, that there was an indolence in her character which halted her from making any effort. She began things and dropped them. She was vain but not vain enough. Her liveliness, her eager love of life, ran away to nothing when she had no object to expend it on, and the object must be a man. She had no ambitions of her own; if she shone, it must be in order to see some man roused and admiring.

She felt convinced that she could help an ambitious man to be successful. It was the truth that she respected Swan. She respected him for just that single-minded energy and passion she lacked in herself. Her shrewd sceptical mind saw very clearly that he was vain, that he bragged about himself to the point of nauseating other people, that he was greedy. She cared very little about any of these things. He attracted her by his other qualities, chief among them his sensual restless energy. Dangerous and destructive it might be, but it roused her and made her dissatisfied and discontented with her life.

She was sitting with bent head. She was almost ready to give in to him. Suddenly, jarring both of them, the telephone bell rang on the desk. She went over to it and heard her brother's voice.

' Yes, Nicholas,' she said, ' what is it? '

' I've just taken Hervey to the nursing home,' he said, in an impatient irritable voice. She knew from it that he was anxious.

' Oh, what time is it? ' she asked.

' Almost five o'clock. What are you doing this evening, Georgie? I shall be staying in town—until Hervey is well out of this, and if you're free we could have dinner together. Don't mind leaving me out if you're already engaged.'

His voice had awakened in her the impulse they had in common—to put off a difficult decision as long as possible. Moreover, it turned her against Swan for the moment. He was everything Nicholas was not, and the very contrast between her brother's fastidious mind, which was eating up his body, and Swan's physical lusts, made Swan seem childish and almost vulgar to her. She turned her head to look at him as she answered Nicholas. ' Yes, I have this evening. Don't let us go out—come here and I'll cook a meal of some kind.'

' That was my brother,' she told Swan lightly. ' I see him very seldom since his marriage.'

Swan got up to go away. He knew that no good would come of anything he said now, and he was alienated by the look of obstinacy on her face. There was an almost furtive look in it, too, which puzzled and vexed him. As he was going out of the door he was seized by a feeling of unhappiness and disaster. He turned round and said gently:

' I am always waiting for you when you are ready for me. Don't forget that. You know you can rely on me.'

He went back to the offices of the Economic Council.

There was a great deal of work to do. He tried to put Georgina out of his thoughts and to finish it, but a hard knot of pain persisted in the back of his mind. He did not understand her. He spoke to his subordinates in a voice so unlike his own, quiet and indifferent, that they looked at him in surprise. Towards eight o'clock he ceased work, without having finished, and went away to dine.

He had an appointment after dinner, with a coal-owner (ennobled during the War—a new form of surplus profits), from whom he hoped to get a subscription for his defence corps. When he left the house of this frightened gentleman, at ten o'clock, the street was empty and almost in darkness. Half of the street-lamps were not lit, and no lights showed from any of the houses. It might have been war time. His car, which he had left a little further up the street, did not start at once. He was looking perplexedly into the engine when a man appeared in the empty street: as he drew near Swan saw that it was David Renn. We have arranged to meet only at night, he thought ironically.

Renn stopped, and asked: ' Can I help you ? '

' No, thanks,' Swan answered. He felt an explosion of anger inside himself, anger diverted from the car to the man. Looking up, he said maliciously: ' I suppose you know the Strike is finished.'

' But I don't know anything of the sort,' Renn said, smiling. ' In fact I know it's not near being finished. I'm on my way from a meeting now, and I can assure you there's not the faintest chance of the terms which have been drafted being accepted. The miners won't look at them.'

' Miners be damned,' said Swan. ' The others will accept. Messrs Pugh, Citrine, and the rest of them, whatever their names are—no one will remember them—have more sense and less spirit than your miners. You have lost your job for nothing. So have a great many other poor fools, as deluded and not half so mischievous as you are.'

' You must put them right,' the other said.

' I will too.' Swan straightened himself and came closer to Renn. His dislike of this man filled his body, which felt tense and swollen. He tried to control it, realising that there was something more than dislike of Renn at work in him. But Renn chose to laugh at him at this moment, turning away as he did it. Swan kicked him in the pit of the back, sending him with great violence against the railings of the house. In the same instant he stumbled forward, his left ankle not strong enough to balance him. Recovering, he went over to Renn and found that he was unconscious. He laid him out on his back on the pavement and loosened his collar. Then without waiting for him to come round he turned away to his car. It now started without any trouble and he drove off.

He felt quite calm, and soothed, as though he had done a necessary and worthy deed. All the resentment and bewilderment he had been enduring had gone, leaving him cool and self-confident. At the thought of Georgina he smiled to himself a little; he felt certain that all was well. She will make up her mind before long, he thought, with deep tenderness in which there was a kind of gentle, youthful triumph. He intended to be good to her.

CHAPTER XIX

In the morning Hervey woke late. She heard Nicholas moving about his room. She lay for a moment, her mind suspended in a drowsy silence, as though it were holding its breath. Then she rose, dressed, and went downstairs to prepare breakfast. Nicholas ran down to help her and she sent him off, impatient because this was not the moment when she wanted him to feel anxious about her.

After breakfast she went to the cupboard on the landing and took out two of her best sheets, the linen ones, and a good pillowcase. She made her bed up for the day when she came back. Without thinking about it, she selected the best linen she had because other eyes than her own might be the first to see it on her bed. Stretching the sheet tightly over the mattress, she looked for the H embroidered in the corner—it was one of her grandmother's sheets, bought in by her mother at the sale of Mary Hervey's things at her death. Hervey possessed two pairs; they had already outlasted those she bought herself. She smiled as she smoothed the top down. It seemed to her that she was a little girl standing in new stiff white knickers in her mother's bedroom, in front of the woman who came in to sew: with her mouth full of pins the woman mumbled: ' Now there's a bairn fit to be run over.'

In the afternoon Nicholas drove her into London to the nursing home. Closing her eyes she imagined driving until the edge of the sea came in sight, sleek, glittering; she felt the familiar nostalgic happiness of awakening in a strange place, the walls covered with foreign words, the curious look of the shops and the people; she tasted foreign food, cream wafers in the café in the *Place Gambetta* in Havre. ' Drive slowly,' she said to Nicholas. He glanced at her and she smiled.

Her happiness vanished as soon as she was inside the nursing home in Hampstead. A maid took away her suitcase, and a nurse showed her and Nicholas into the room she had engaged. It was on the ground floor, looking on to the corner of a garden. She looked round it with dismay. It was a pleasant enough room but she thought she had made a mistake to come here at all.

Looking at her watch she saw that it was nearly four o'clock. Nicholas was standing uncomfortably in the middle of the room. His only thought was to get away before he was turned out of this place given over to illness. The nurse had not left them; she was showing Hervey where to put her clothes and turning down the bed. Then she said gaily: ' I expect Mr. Roxby would like to have tea with you before he goes. I'll send it.'

' No, I had better go now,' he said, attempting to smile.

Hervey was hurt and shocked. To her bitter mortification she felt tears burning her eyelids, and turned away to hide them from the nurse. She was able to deceive herself that the woman had not seen them. Smiling politely at Nicholas, she said:

' Oh, won't you stay to have tea ? '

' Yes. Very well,' he said hastily. The nurse left them. He seized her arms and said: ' What is the matter—why are you crying ? '

' You were in such a hurry to leave me,' she muttered. She had made the effort to control herself and was able to speak calmly.

' I thought you would want me to go,' he said, overwhelmed by his clumsiness.

' No. I shall be alone when you go.'

Yet she felt a distinct relief when, after tea, he went away. Now it was he who was reluctant to leave her.

As soon as the door shut on him and she was alone, she put
her things away and laid her books on the inadequate table
beside her bed. The nurse came back and told her to get
into bed.

'What, now?' she exclaimed, before she could stifle her
surprise. She had thought of asking if she might take a
book into the garden.

'Yes, of course,' the woman laughed. 'Did you think
you were staying in a hotel?' She was a big woman, with
a sallow round face, and eyes always either dull or inquisitive.
Perhaps she had no mind except one which pried awkwardly
into the mysteries it saw slipping under her nose, birth, death,
pain. For the rest she had large capable hands which did
her work for her, lifting patients, washing, and attending to
them as to so many inanimate pieces of flesh.

She left Hervey alone to undress and get into bed. Later
she came back and did various things to her which she endured.
Inwardly she was full of resentment and self-loathing. If I
lived to be a hundred and had the withered body of a monkey,
she thought, I should not become used to being handled,
or not mind it. It seemed to her at this moment that
everything to do with the body was detestable and evil.
She submitted herself, smiled readily at the nurse's jokes,
but with an expressionless face. Not even her eyes showed
that she felt shame and disgust.

She was perfectly calm as soon as she was alone. She did
not think about the next day, nor about Nicholas. Among
the books she had brought with her was a volume of
La Chartreuse de Parme, and she sat in bed reading it,
with feelings of profound happiness and despair. She rejoiced
in Stendhal's absolute rightness and perfection, much as she
would have rejoiced if she had found herself transported
suddenly to the close of Salisbury cathedral; and despaired
because she was a clodhopper.

The matron came in while she was reading and asked her
whether she was settled and comfortable. Hervey thanked

her and waited for her to go; but the woman stayed chattering for ten minutes, and turned as she went out to say with real kindness:

'I hope you're not nervous. There's no need to be, you know.'

'I am not in the least nervous, thank you,' Hervey answered, politely and with an air of friendliness and candour.

Her face felt rigid in its false smile. She put her hand to it when the woman had gone, and rubbed it until it was rough and glowing. It seemed to her that she had before her endless time in which to feel and think. Closing the book, she tried once again to answer the question, What is wrong with my life, why have I no peace or satisfaction in it? But her thoughts eluded her, like grasping at a cloud of gnats in the sunlight. She found that she was thinking of the most trivial things: she was in the small, grimy hotel sitting-room with her first husband, who as usual was offended with her; she mixed egg and breadcrumbs on a plate for her baby; she was a child climbing recklessly the cliff from the shore at home, there were red earth stains on her knees and the roughened palms of her hands, she clung to tufts of dry grass and the steep face of the cliff reared in front of her to the reeds growing on the sky. It is no use, she thought. I shall never know why I have lived until I come to my end, and then it will be a vexation of the flesh.

The nurse brought in her supper, and afterwards she sat still until the room was dark, recalling this and that moment without regret or sadness. Then she lay down and went to sleep.

CHAPTER XX

I

Towards dusk Rachel Earlham's cat Habakkuk found the door into the upper half of the house left ajar by the tenant. He sprang up the stairs and into the attic bedroom. A skylight was open: leaping on to the washstand below it he crouched looking up at the narrow opening through which he would have to pass. Some slight sound outside the room disturbed him; he sprang upwards, flattening his body, through the skylight and on to the sloping roof. His claws slipped over the tiles.

He recovered himself at once and began to walk slowly and with enjoyment across the roof and on to the next. At the end of a short street he sprang twice his own length to the first of a welter of roofs, many of them flat, which stretched almost to the river. He felt the air growing colder. A light breeze touched his skin under the fur with a delicious shiver like an icy finger laid on it. He hastened forward, his eyes gleaming, his body alert to every change of light, the smoothness of slates, the rough harshness of concrete, the softness and resilience of the tiles.

As the air darkened it grew still colder. He moved in the shelter of a low parapet, and when his body scraped along the bricks an electric current of pure bliss ran through it. The streets below him now were narrow and piled closely against each other. The window-sills often carried plants in pots, of which the strong smell rose to his nostrils mingled with the smells of sweat, human dirt, the cooking of the last meal, and through them, only noticeable up here and to Habakkuk, the thin sharp breath of the river.

In his growing excitement he began to feel through the roof under his feet a curious movement, as though it were a heart-beat or a pulse—the pullulation of many bodies crowding together in the houses, breathing, crying, groaning, touching each other. He moved through an impalpable jungle, aware of it in every sense. His skin shivered and tingled, his muscles relaxed and drew up hard and taut, the darkness blinded him with its arrows. He had reached an ecstasy as complete as that of the mystic.

2

Before dinner William Gary went downstairs to the lowest tier of the building, where there was a swimming bath, as well as a number of large rooms in which the tenants of the flats could keep themselves fit by special baths of all kinds, pine, foam, Nauheim, and electric baths: the attendants were also able to give massage and douches, and to teach reducing exercises. The gymnasium, the fencing room, and the squash courts were on the same floor, which was the second floor below ground. The floor above was a ballroom.

Gary was concerned not to grow fat—he understood that men in his state often did—and he spent at least one hour every day in the gymnasium, and practised boxing with the instructor. To-day a series of accidents had kept him at work, and he had only time for a bath. He had learned by tortuous observations, which would have humiliated him if he had not carried them out more by the help of an instinct than with any part of his mind, that in the sweating baths it was easy to avoid the eye of the attendant. He chose one of these, took off his dressing-gown and stepped quickly into the cabinet, folding the doors over himself while the attendant bent down to the switches. Now he was safe for twenty minutes. He lay back and allowed himself to relax: the glowing bulbs were too near his hands when he stretched them out and he folded them on his body. Hurrying back, the man laid an ice-bag on his forehead and gave him another to hold against his heart before leaving him alone.

The last person he had seen that evening was George Ling, and he thought of him for a moment with a contempt in which there was no kindness. Ling was still trembling wretchedly for his person and his money. He had heard that meetings were going on between the Strike leaders and Sir Herbert Samuel and he wanted to know whether this meant that he was safe. Or did it, could it possibly, mean that the Government were coming to terms with their conquerors?

He turned pale as he put the question. In his breast-pocket he had five hundred pounds he had drawn from the bank that morning, with which he proposed when the worst came to buy his way out of the country. The old fool, thought Gary, and he explained without gentleness that the revolution was farther off to-day than it had ever been. There would be no bloodshed, the leaders were reasonable men longing to end the trouble, probably it would all be over in less than a week.

'If you are so sure,' Ling quavered, 'please keep this money for me to-night. I don't like to carry so much about with me in these times.' He handed over the notes and saw them locked into Gary's safe with a curious expression of relief, doubt, and tormented entreaty. It was all he could do not to burst into tears.

Gary's body was now bathed in sweat. Everywhere he touched it a river of water started to run over the smooth skin. He saw the man coming back to look at him. 'Had enough, sir?'

'Yes. Turn the heat off.'

The man moved the switches and prepared to leave him for a minute in the bath.

' Give me my dressing-gown here before you go.'

As soon as the man's back was turned he moved the doors carefully, snatching up his gown with one hand as he stepped out. The attendant hurried back. ' Your shower, Mr. Gary. Or would you like the hose to-night.'

' No. I'll take a cold shower. Give me some towels.'

He kept himself deliberately from thinking of anything, until dried and glowing he walked towards the lift. The slight tension in his mind relaxed without his having once acknowledged it was there. He entered his flat, and while he dressed for dinner his servant brought him a letter which he did not read, and a glass of sherry.

He was dining alone. The room was scarcely dark enough for the electric lights, but he had one lamp turned on at the far end of the room, and left the curtains drawn back. With a half turn of his head as he sat at the dining-table he could see a wide stretch of the Park, covered in a dusky amber radiance, a brown flooded with red, almost the colour of the red Hermitage in his glass. He was hungry and refreshed. He drank a cold soup and ate grilled trout, and jellied *bœuf à la mode*, followed by young asparagus.

Now his servant brought in a melon in which the tawny flesh was mixed among strawberries moistened lightly with kirsch. The fruit was icy cold. He ate it slowly, savouring the mingled yet distinct flavours of the wine, strawberries, and canteloup with a sharp pleasure. His body was warmed by the Rhone wine he had drunk, and pleasantly soothed and enlivened by the several foods with their sharp or smooth taste. He was becoming a connoisseur in food; his dinners were usually not less simple than this one, unless he had invited Louis Earlham to dine with him. Then, deferring to his friend's scruples, or what he imagined to be his friend's scruples, he ordered a plainer meal to be served. He had every hope of persuading Louis in time that delicate food and drink is not a sin against the holy revolution. When this Strike is over,

he mused, we must set to work in earnest to *educate* Louis
for the future.

The man who brought in his coffee said that Mr. Marcel
Cohen was telephoning and wanted to speak to him. 'Tell
him,' Gary said at once, 'I am engaged for the whole
evening.'

He had no reason for avoiding a conversation of a few
minutes with Cohen except a dislike which was not even
active. He was passively disgusted by him, not by anything
the older man did or said, but coldly and simply for what he
was, an intelligent and unscrupulous Jew. Gary was not
an anti-Semite—he had indeed the most profound scorn for
that sort of nasty savagery—he would have said, too, that
Thomas Harben was just as unscrupulous, as well as more
violent, gross, obtuse, and coarse in his tastes. But he saw
in Cohen what he did not see in the other, a spirit which
destroys and corrupts. There was stupidity in Harben's
crimes against his fellow-men, greed, an insensitive lust for
possession. There is nothing insensitive in the spirit and
energy of the Jew, it is almost naked fire, pure and very
sharp until it is spoiled. So much the worse for us all when
it *is* spoiled and begins to corrupt first itself and then everything it touches in order to profit from it.

Gary had a new grudge against Cohen, one more unjust
than the rest. He had heard to-day that Cohen had engaged
Nicholas Roxby to work for him as manager of the firm of
a certain antique dealer, a Jew who had died owing him
money. The thought of his friend working under Cohen's
arm, taking orders from him, perhaps—but that was less
likely!—making money for him, vexed Gary past patience.
He knew that Nicholas's own business had been doing badly;
he had known all along that certainly it would not stand the
amount of money Nicholas took out of it so that he could
give his first wife more money than she needed—he gave
her his private income and as much again out of the firm.

Gary groaned with anger when he thought of his friend's

stubborn folly. He has spoiled his whole life by it, he said. Nicholas's life seemed to him a web of mistakes: he married, too early, a young woman who turned out to be loose; he gave up his passionate wish to fly because his grandmother had brought him up to inherit Garton's and he was not able to disappoint her; in the end, and too late to save himself, he disappointed her cruelly by refusing Garton's. Now, at thirty-four, he was selling old furniture for Cohen, to earn a wretched salary—the fool, thought Gary, the fool.

He felt in his own body an agonised sickness, as though he were falling. At once he saw the long uphill road to the house of Nicholas's grandmother, darkness, and the trees clashing as he with Nicholas neared the top. We were perhaps fifteen years old, he said. We were both exhausted, muddy, wet, and Nicholas was limping: he hurt his leg when he slipped over the edge of the cliff and hung there by his arms for a moment until I gripped and pulled him back.

In his mind the road became a trench: the darkness here was different; it was almost dawn, and dawn and dark both had a sharpness that pricked his mind. His feet were heavy with mud when he tumbled into the trench after the raid and walked, swaying, thinking of sleep. He blundered into Nicholas before he saw him. Nicholas only said: 'You're back, thank heaven,' and went away. Unnoticed then, the words now made him feel the pain of love. But I have nothing, he thought. His hands jerked upwards and his mind snatched him back scarcely in time.

He sent for another bottle of the Hermitage and sat drinking it. I should go out more, he thought. Travel. Own an aeroplane and pilot. He looked sullen and angry. A deliberate satisfaction took possession of him, a monstrous exultance that remained cold the further he gave way to it. He thought of himself as a realist, a man outside common delusions. I shall fail in nothing I undertake: I am the one man in the world to whom nothing worse can happen. *I can't be defeated.*

Thomas Harben let himself into the house in Chelsea and stood a moment in the hall, waiting. He noticed a new rug on the floor, a small Persian saddle-rug, probably not expensive but in admirable taste. Lise never wasted money and never bought an inappropriate article. He put his hat and stick on the table, and bent down stiffly to examine the edges of the rug. The door of the sitting-room opened while he was in this posture, and Lise came out. ' Do you like it ? ' she said.

' Yes,' answered Harben. ' What did you pay for it ? '

' Three pounds. Is it worth as much ? I think it is.'

Harben nodded. He followed her into the sitting-room and sat down in the chair he had given her himself; it fitted his back. Her chairs were too low to allow him to sit as he liked to sit, with thighs thrust firmly down and back into the curve.

She went away for a minute to speak to the servant, then returned and stood close to him. She was wearing a black dress cut high at the neck, with long sleeves, the sort of dress he liked her to wear, simple, showing her figure to perfection. He could follow every line and curve of it under the thick dull silk. She was looking well, too, her skin glowed, the wings of her brown hair were smooth and shining.

He put his hand up and touched it and she said: ' Look. A grey hair.' That pleased him, to think she had no vanity and that she would begin now to grow old.

The dining-table was in an alcove of the room. She moved towards it and watched the woman placing the soup, a *garbure* he liked, and the bread. ' Do you like it ? ' she asked again. ' It was I who prepared it.'

After the soup they ate veal and young green peas cooked in butter. Harben chewed the meat with an almost tender satisfaction, feeling it disappear between his teeth with the mingling of firmness and smooth rich juice. He thought how fortunate it was that Lise herself enjoyed good food; it made the difference between a meal which was as serious a pleasure as anything else and an ordinary dinner. He watched her long plump arm when she stretched it near him, and the white hand with the backward-curving thumb and thick fingers. In all the years he had known her she had never worn more than two rings, another mark of her good sense. An emotion of pride filled him, that he had known at first sight she was a sensible good woman and had attached her to him.

'These peas are early,' he said. He had not noticed that she was not eating her food.

'Yes,' she said quickly, looking at him with a smile. 'I should not have bought them, but to-morrow, when you are not here, I can economise.'

She glanced at him when he was helping himself to cheese, and her eyes narrowed with a curiously cold, startled look in them. A newspaper paragraph she had read, a criticism of his shipbuilding interests, came unto her mind, and— how ludicrously just, she thought, if he were to dissolve suddenly into what he is, a map of coal-mines, furnaces, mills, guns, railways, shipyards, money. Has an artist ever painted his portrait? With the shock of revelation, she saw the geometrical figures and thick intersecting lines of a painting by a modern artist—the connection with Harben was distinct, but she did not understand it. It was not, certainly, that she had seen the very picture hanging in his wife's house when Lucy Harben opened a show of paintings there for a charity.

She smiled faintly. I shall never tell him that I bought a ticket and went; he would be angry. She was afraid of the violence she felt in him, even when she was despising him as a man of an impossibly gross coarse nature. His old strong body, pendulous fleshy nose, and long lips, filled her with repulsion when she happened to see them. She had taught herself to look at him without seeing them. She was shocked when they broke through her sight and forced themselves on her. This was never in a moment of physical intimacy. She was then too well guarded. It was in such moments as now, when she was worried. Then she lost control of her mind and saw him as if he were a man and not, oh, planes of heavy flesh and long cruel lines crossing each other like wounds or like trenches seen from the air.

She was afraid to tell him that she had been losing money. Not so many years since a woman friend had persuaded her to buy and sell a few shares without asking his advice, and she had made a little money. Even then she had not told Harben what she was doing. Now that instead of making money she had lost a great deal more than she had in the bank, she would be forced to tell him. She could have repaid it by selling some of the shares she held in various Harben interests, but she imagined he would be able to discover this.

She began her confession when the servant had brought them coffee in the sitting-room and gone. He listened to her without a change of expression, hiding surprise. So she gambled on the market, did she? He looked at her when she stopped speaking and began nervously twisting her fingers with their two rings, and his face grew dark; he was seized with distrust of her, and a bitter contempt, as though she had betrayed him.

'Why did you start such a game?' he asked.

She wondered quickly whether to try to appeal to his pity, and instantly decided against it. Looking at him boldly, she answered:

'I thought I knew more about it than I did. I was a fool.'

His mouth relaxed into the folds that did duty with him for a smile when he was really pleased or moved. If he showed his teeth he was not smiling. 'You were certainly that.'

He fell into silence again, and she waited, half confident, half filled with a sick fear.

'How much do you want to put you straight at your bank?' he said at last.

'Three hundred pounds,' she answered.

'It is enough.'

He had begun to feel complacent, as though he had found her out in a bad bargain, after all these years. In the same instant he felt the need to possess her. He followed her into her room at once: he was peremptory and abrupt—he would have seemed brutal only if he had been thinking about her. But he was thinking of nothing whatever; he brought less delicacy into this act than to eating a meal he enjoyed. It is strange, Lise thought drily, that an act which ought to rouse at least the sensation of intimacy only makes us the more strangers—a wife who is tired of her husband must feel this, and find it easy to submit. So I feel like a wife! she said, with a smile.

At the same time she felt an obscure anger against him for leaving her in doubt whether he would help her out of her trouble. It showed the monstrous nature of his egoism.

In the sitting-room she remembered the paragraph about his shipping firms. She took it out of her bag and showed it to him. '*It would be wise for the ordinary investor to realise that the statement supplied by the directors of Garton's Shipbuilding Company is of little use to him. It answers none of the questions he would like to ask about the profits, if there are any, and the losses, which certainly exist, in certain of the allied firms. It is no secret in shipping circles that the last meeting of the Board was the occasion of what would have been a scene if it had taken place in less decorous circumstances, and concerned the doubts of one of the directors about the allocation of the company's reserves.*' Lise watched his face while he read it, but gained nothing.

'What does it mean?' she asked, in a tone of indifference.

'Nothing at all,' said Harben.

He put the cutting into his notebook. What it meant to him was that there was a leakage of information about Garton's, perhaps just beginning. The reference to the scene made it certain that it had been written by some person at the meeting. He was not vexed so much as puzzled. He had no doubt he could find the leak and close it. He looked round the room and thought: Three hundred pounds. Had he told Lise about the scene at the Board meeting? No. He certainly had not. Nor would she have known the meaning of the information. Glancing at the clock he saw that it was close on ten. He asked her to give him a very little brandy, drank it slowly, and went away.

Cohen stood for a moment outside his wife's room before he knocked and went in. The doctor had finished his examination and was washing his hands vigorously in a bowl. Stooping over the bed, the nurse smoothed sheets, shook up pillows, and whispered some words in his wife's ear which brought a ghost of a smile on her lips. He went over to her and said gently:

'You feel better now, Sophie? Since you saw the doctor, eh?'

She looked up at him without speaking. Her face had sharpened during the last months, the flesh falling away from the bones, so that there were deep pits below the cheekbones. Her fine arched nose, the only beautiful feature she had, jutted like a rock below her forehead. Her eyelids, thick, white, blue-veined, came down over her eyes. She turned her head away on the pillow with a quickness unlike her. It was as though she disliked his standing there. Taken aback, he spoke to the doctor.

'If Mrs. Cohen would do as I say,' the doctor began. He had a long Jewish face, thick-lipped and melancholy. His hands, he was still wiping them, were large and immensely strong; he would say of them himself that they were more like flippers than hands. They were marvellously delicate.

Sophie Cohen opened her eyes for an instant. ' I have told you I will not allow no surgeon to lay hands on me,' she said.

The doctor looked down at her with an impassive face, his full lids half closed. His face was almost completely round, and in repose his mouth suggested a grieved smile. There was something feminine in his face and body—he could be the Goddess of Mercy.

Cohen followed him out of the room. All the lights had been on in the bedroom, and the doctor stumbled on the discreetly lighted staircase. Cohen led him into his own room.

' You won't drink anything, eh ? '

' No,' Farbman said.

' It was kind you came this evening, so late after your hours. She wouldn't let the nurse send earlier and I thought, If we don't get him here now, when she is willing, maybe to-morrow she has changed her mind again. She has this pain for two years now, sometimes bad, sometimes not so bad. Sometimes not there. Then she believes it never comes back at all. Well, what is it, Farbman ? '

He had spoken hurriedly, anxious to settle a problem which had dragged on too long. He had business to do before he went to bed. In his heart, he believed that Sophie exaggerated her pains.

' She has a growth, a large tumour. It may or may not be malignant—we can't know that until we operate, but I think it is. She refused, you heard her, to have anything done, and it is absolutely necessary. If not now, it can become malignant. You must talk to her, my dear fellow.'

' *I* talk to her ! ' Cohen exclaimed.

' You are the person most likely to influence her.'

' But an operation on the womb—she is not a young woman. It is surely difficult.'

'I did not say the growth was in her womb,' said Farbman. 'It is not. It is her right breast.'

Now why did I? Cohen thought, confused. 'She is very ill, eh!' he muttered.

He began to think at once about his son's death in the War hospital. Poor poor David, he thought; he was saying every few minutes to me, to the others, When will my mother come? She comes soon, David, I said. And she there crying and howling on her bed like an animal, afraid, she was afraid to see her son die. The son of her womb died and she was not there. How many times do I think this? How many, many, many, and my son is still dead and will never be seen by me again; other boys are walking about and feeling all he felt, but mine is nothing. His agony forced him to say: 'You remember, the boy died.'

'Yes, I know,' Farbman said.

'What makes these growths, eh? Sophie always took care of her health. I was well off before I married, and she was not hungry or sick for anything. I wouldn't ask a woman to be poor like my mother was a poor woman.'

Farbman made a curious gesture with his hands, as though he were lifting with them. 'Cancer is on the increase,' he said, in his slow, thick voice. 'You know it is always in my mind that research is on the wrong path. It is living in cities, it is the anxiety of cities, and the fear of losing hold and falling to be trampled on, it is haste, tainted air— in fact it is our whole way of life which is out of balance to-day. You could say it is civilisation itself which has begun to lose balance and is breeding tumours instead of more life.'

'But Sophie had no fears of that sort,' Cohen exclaimed.

Farbman smiled. 'You can't draw an invisible ring round fear and anxiety, as you draw it round the poor so that they remain in their slums out of your sight. If there is imbalance and fear it is everywhere at once.'

'You are talking nonsense,' Cohen said harshly. 'I have

no patience with mysticism.' He sat striking the edge of the desk with his fingers for a minute.

'No, forgive me, my friend,' he said at last. ' I have my ideas and you have yours, and you have the right to yours, you mustn't lose patience with me when I lose my temper. I have a bad temper, I know it, but there you are, a man is what he is and what his life makes him. We have both had difficult lives '—it was as though he had said, We are both Jews—' and what has made you a religious man has made me a greedy one. Yes, I say it, of myself I say it. But you were never hungry. When you were a child in Poland you were well fed at least, your father was rich, but I, I never knew what it was to feel satisfied by a meal until I was already a young man. I swore not to rest until I had power to bind and to loose, to eat when I needed food, to live decently, to clothe and educate my son.' He stopped abruptly.

'Well, you are responsible for this civilisation,' said Farbman, with his strange grieved smile. ' It is you who are undermining it, probing it to its roots in search of gold. You with your sharp analytical mind, destroying every-thing——' Even your own son, he thought. ' And while we talk,' he went on, ' your wife is lying in her bed enduring a pain which I can only alleviate—unless she will allow me to bring a surgeon to see her and agree to let him operate. You must talk to her, it's your duty.'

'Very well, I'll do my best,' Cohen said drily.

As soon as the doctor had gone, he went back to his wife's room and tried to persuade her that she must let the surgeon look at her. She refused him with a cold dry obstinacy, which impressed him painfully. It was so unlike her yield-ing hysterical ways. He thought that pain must have altered her, but when she spoke to him in her stubborn voice, so little like that of a sick woman, he felt almost angry. At the same time he was sorry for her, terribly sorry. Her old finished body under the bedclothes seemed to him sad

and repulsive. The room was too warm and smelled dry
and acrid. He had an obscure sense that he had failed in a
high duty—I have sinned towards her, he thought vaguely,
not knowing what he meant by the words.

'But, mamma,' he said quietly, 'you see I am anxious
about you. You must do like Farbman says and let them
cure you. You don't want I should worry myself into my
grave about you, do you now? Of course you don't, poor
mamma.'

His wife looked at him for an instant, with contempt
and dislike. 'Why shouldn't you worry yourself?' she said.
'It is your fault.'

The nurse frowned and motioned to him to go out of the
room. He went, feeling vexed and troubled. Even if he
had actually failed in some part of his duty towards her—
but how and when was it?—he had never failed her as she
failed David; he had richly clothed and fed her, her whole
life with him. He had not gone to other women. How
can any of it be my fault? he said to himself angrily—
she is going mad.

As soon as he was in his room again he telephoned to
his daughter at her house, and told her what the doctor
had said.

'If she won't see the surgeon, she won't,' Fanny Groelles
answered. Her voice sounded cold, it was rapid and impatient. 'She'll die, that's all—if she's such a fool as to
refuse to be cured.'

'Is that a way to speak of your mother?' Cohen was
startled into sudden anger with her.

'Very well—it's the way I speak.' Her voice rose; he
could hear in it the defiance with which she met reproof
when she was still only a little child. 'I have no patience
with mamma when she is behaving like a cry-baby—at her
age. Perhaps I'll run in to see her, but not this week, we
have too much to do this week. She won't take notice of
anything I say to her, you know, daddy. I can't stay now,

we have people to dinner—Johnny will be very cross with me if I stay up here talking to you.'

Her voice sounded in his ears for a moment after he moved away from the telephone. He was horrified by her indifference to her mother, and yet—he began to excuse her to himself—she is young (she was twenty-seven); it is right that a young woman should think first of her children and her husband and forget her father and mother. But to remember her husband vexed him. His face was darkened by the blood rising under the thick yellow skin. Johnny Groelles was a tall fair young man, a second son of one of the oldest families—one of the stupidest, thought Cohen. He could almost have forgotten that his daughter had married a Gentile if Groelles had been an intelligent man and not only one of those well-bred, handsome and reckless young men whose life consists in risking death in the air or on the ground by rushing about them at great speed because, presumably, they have nothing in their heads to detain them in any one place. Extravagant as Fanny was, she might have lived within the allowance her father made her if it had not been for her husband's debts. Cohen knew when she came to him with a tale of dressmakers' bills, or doctor's bills for the children, the odds were that at least half the sum had been spent on her husband's aeroplane or his racing car or his losses at cards. He had not even the brains to win occasionally. Time after time Cohen paid his debts for him, pretending that he believed them to be Fanny's, the cost of keeping her place in the world into which she had married—and took good care not to introduce into it him or her mother. It would have been useless for her to pretend among her new friends that she was not a Jew. She had adopted a habit of speaking about Jews as if they were the most ridiculous creatures ever born, and that she herself was one of them a superb joke.

Groelles encouraged her in this, and took his father-in-law's money without looking at it. During the past year Cohen had succeeded in having him made a director on the board of the reorganised Garton's.

He opened a drawer in his desk and took out the book into which he had entered every item her marriage cost him, beginning with the clothes, money, and linen she took with her to her new home, and ending with the latest trifle of three hundred pounds he had given her less than a week since. He saw her face as she watched him write the cheque, flushed and composed, her grey eyes almost vacant, as though she were careful to hide her thoughts from him. She had laid her thin arms round his neck with a childlike coaxing and lifted her face to him, her little bright-red lips parted in a wistful smile—he could not refuse her the money, although he knew that as soon as he had given it to her she would be off, unwilling to stay with him a minute longer than was necessary. There were three pages covered with figures in his writing. The total at the bottom of the third was a large one.

At the back of the drawer were the other things he had kept—a lace and silk fan she had when she was a little girl running off to her dancing-class; a black hair-ribbon, from the days when she wore her red hair in a plait tied at the end; a few, very few, letters from her school days—he took one from its envelope and glanced at it, but the words evoked no distinct memory of the writer—none the less he felt his heart stirring painfully as he folded it away again—it had once meant something; the photograph of a tiny self-possessed baby, holding herself upright by a chair and gazing about her imperiously, the image of the old Queen.

He loved her so much, more than anything on earth, more than himself. Nothing could make him admit, even to his heart, that she was hard, selfish, and narrow. He saw her always as fragile and even pathetic, too young to be wife and mother: when he gave her money he was giving it to his own hard youth, to console himself for having almost died of cold and hunger when he was a child, and to the only morsel of his flesh which would survive him when he was forced to go down into the earth to his fathers. He returned the small account book to the drawer and locked it.

Still thinking of her as he lit a cigar and began to walk up and down the room, he murmured: 'You know, you ought to speak kinder to mamma now she is old and sick.'

His wife's face as he had seen it on her pillows, looking at him with dislike and scorn, troubled him for less than an instant: he went on talking to Fanny, but he became confused and it seemed to him that he was also talking to himself. When she was a child he had been proud of her hardness; he encouraged her to evade her mother's whimpering and nagging reproofs. One evening when she was sent to her bedroom as a punishment he went upstairs and found her seated in the window, cheeks scarlet and lips tightly compressed. She turned on him when he came in, with unchildlike and angry words: ' I won't let anyone tell me what to do, I tell you I won't be treated as if I were a possession.' Even in those days her dislike of possessions did not touch her own. She hoarded her things, defending them with silent rage from her brother. You could say of her, even then, that she was predatory. Not that he allowed such a word to enter his mind about her—he admitted only that she never came to the house without taking something away with her, money, or a painting she coveted, or an ornament.

But why not? he said. They are mine and so they are all hers. He forgot that his wife had a share in them and in Fanny, too. It was as though he had given birth to her, as though his spirit had left him when he slept and clothed itself in the bright flesh of the young girl.

He drew the blind and looked out. Pressing his face close to the window, to avoid the reflection from the electric light, he saw at the end of the road the shadowy spaces of the Park. He was dizzy and held on to the window. An image of the world as a desert and of himself crossing it endlessly, alone, came into his mind with such cruel energy that he felt the cold of that loneliness in his belly. He dropped the blind. A look of bitter obstinacy came over his face, almost a sneer. At least he knew dust and stones for what they were, he did not pretend that they were warm and pleasant. He accepted them, and made them, whoever perished, support him.

3

After he had dined in his own house George Ling drove to his club. He took a chair as far from the window as possible and told the servant to bring him a glass of the old port and a copy of the *Gazette*. The man was only able to find an old one, of Friday. Ling sat with it in his hand, and sipped his port, and tried to compose his mind. He heard another member of the club say: ' If it goes on, there'll be trouble in the north in a few days, and then machine-guns will be used.' The man he was talking to murmured something, at which the other scoffed.

' My dear chap, who talks of shooting down a million workers? A hundred will be enough! '

Ling set his glass down on the table beside him, because his hand was trembling. Not that he objected to strikers being shot. He was afraid that if shooting started it would not end there. He had never consciously thought about a striker as a man, say a man called Brown, with a wife and four children, living in a house near the railway with a small garden which, when he was not too tired, he dug over and dropped in it seeds from Woolworth's, penny packets, the pennies filched from his tobacco money: his wife cleaned and laboured endlessly and the four children flourished in a rather hollow way on a diet of too much bread and too little of anything else. So it did not occur to Ling that there must be sound and good reason why this patient unaggressive man and woman had turned on him. He had never imagined them. His conscience was at ease. He knew that he, George Ling, had never wanted to harm anyone—it was not he who had gone on strike.

He could not, simply he could not, conceive anything wrong in a state of affairs which had resulted in his sitting in this room, his shrunken legs in their black covering crossed at the knee, the glass of port near his hand. He held that hand up and looked at it, at its thick veins, as if it were not his own. It was so clear that this hand had not and never could have driven a pick into a wall of coal that it seemed to him in an obscure way a proof of an immutable law, setting some men apart at their birth to become miners or dockers, and others to live comfortable lives, using the powers they had been fitted for by another birth and another kind altogether of infancy and youth.

He did not *see* the men who were born to be miners; each did not issue, as his own son did, from the body of a woman, open eyes seeking dimly for the light, grasp at a finger, learn the texture of thin harsh blankets, the taste of coarse food, the cold on bare flesh. They existed for him only as a vague body, as size without form, voices without words. When from this formless mass there rose a sound, like a wind heard at night, threatening, as he thought, his safety, he became afraid and fearfully helplessly angry.

His eyes fell on a paragraph in the paper he was holding on his knee: '*All ranks of the armed forces of the Crown are notified that any action they may find it necessary to take in an honest endeavour to aid the civil power will receive both now and afterwards the full support of the Government.*' It was a full moment before it became clear to his mind that this meant that the soldiers could shoot if necessary. He was half startled and half relieved. So it was come to this!

For no reason at all, except that he was soothed and half asleep and his mind wandering, he recalled the funeral six months ago of the Queen-Mother, the old Queen

Alexandra. He left his car at the other side of Trafalgar Square and walked through the slush lying after the snow, to the place which was being kept for him in Whitehall. The sky was grey and leaden and his feet cold; he was afraid he might be catching a chill. As he walked he noticed that the water below the fountain in the Square was half frozen over. A group of people were gathered outside a leather shop near the end of the Strand, listening silently to the broadcast. He heard the funeral music in the distance, sounding, it too, brittle and frozen, in the sombre air, and saw a middle-aged man leaning from a window in the Horse Guards; the expression on this man's face was such that he himself felt sad. It is the end of an era, he thought. When he was inside a warmed room and surreptitiously feeling the soles of his shoes, another man said to him: ' Y'know, Ling, this ends something; one isn't only watching the funeral of a queen who has lived a long time.' And as the coffin passed, this same man whispered to him: ' Y'know ' —he began each sentence with the same words—' I admire George; he tries to be decent.' The coffin was the smallest he had ever seen for a grown person.

His head jerked forward. He pulled himself upright in his chair, and looking up, saw his late son-in-law, Nicholas Roxby, at the other side of the room. The blood rose to his cheeks in indignation and resentment. He thought that such a scoundrel, a man whose wife had left him—for good reasons (he was not clear what these were but he supposed they had to do with morality, Nicholas must be dissolute)— ought to be made to resign from the club. It is monstrous that I should be exposed to the unpleasantness of seeing him in my own club. He rose with ostentatious energy, glared at Nicholas, who was not looking at him, and walked out of the room. To a man who stood in his way for a moment, he repeated the words: ' Monstrous, monstrous.'

He was at a loss what to do next. In his agitation he decided to take a cab and drive to his daughter's flat in

Chelsea. It was a walk of less than half an hour from his house in Grosvenor Crescent, but only at long intervals did Jenny Roxby take the trouble to visit him. He had once asked her to live with him again and take charge of his house, but she had no intention of wearying herself with the needs and fancies of a suspicious-minded old man.

Her life had already become settled; she rose late and spent the morning dressing, and after a long heavy lunch worked in a desultory way on the book she had been writing for years. It would never be written, but it provided her with an illusion. In the evening she dined, alone or with one of the two elderly gentlemen who admired her as a charming, clever, and injured woman. Eating and clothing herself were the two serious rites in her life. She had no friends of her age. Those she had at one time had fallen away from her—she was vain, indolent, and uninterested in other people, as careful as her father not to spend money on anyone except herself. Her body, which had been graceful, was full and heavy, but she was accustomed to think of herself as a beautiful woman and did not notice that she had changed. She was thirty-seven years old.

She was alone this evening: hearing her father's voice she was sorry she had not told the servant not to allow him in. She looked at him with raised eyebrows as he came into the room.

' How are you, my dear ? ' he said, nervously and effusively. ' I am afraid you didn't expect me so late as this.'

' No, I didn't.' She glanced at the clock. ' Is something the matter ? At least sit down now that you are here.'

' I feel quite ill,' Ling said, faintly. He seated himself on a chair and closed his eyes. ' This awful business will be the death of me before long.'

' Oh I am sure it will soon be over,' his daughter said indifferently, ' I don't know what it's all about ? Why should anyone strike ? But I don't feel well myself. I

sleep badly, you know. At last the doctor has given me
something that has a sedative effect, and I get a few hours'
drugged sleep.'

'You look very well and pretty,' Ling answered.

'Oh, that.' She glanced involuntarily over her shoulder
at a mirror behind the couch. 'I take care of myself, of
course.'

'God knows what's going to happen. I expect to lose
the greater part of my money through this. How can trade
and finance exist at all in a country at the mercy of the
unbridled greed of the very men who ought to be thankful
they have work to do? Tell me that.'

'Well,' Jenny said, after a brief silence. She glanced at
him with calculating sharpness. 'I hear that Nicholas
has lost all his money, I mean all the money he put into
his firm. The lawyer writes to me that I shall have less
than four hundred a year. What am I to do? It means
I shall have no holiday this year, no theatres, unless
someone takes me—nothing. I daresay he has his new
wife to thank for the mess he has made of everything—
he had better get rid of her before she ruins him. I
suppose he hasn't the courage, poor weak fool, and she has
her claws too well into him. In the meantime what am I
to do? It's terrible for me.'

Ling's manner had changed completely while she was
speaking. Forgetting that he felt ill, he sat upright on
his chair and folded his arms, as he did when he was about
to reprove his children in their youth. Beneath everything in him, below the hypocrite, the besotted moralist, and
beneath his fears, there was still some of the hardness and
shrewdness of the north-countryman. He began to suspect
her as soon as she spoke of money. Why did she want
money? She was comfortable here—he glanced round
the room and recalled the faint savoury odour coming
through the kitchen door the servant had left open when she
answered his ring. She had everything she needed, and as

much money as was suitable for a woman who had divorced her husband and lived alone.

He could not help thinking that she must be up to no good if she really could not live on four hundred a year.

He glanced at her and saw that she was yawning widely. ' It is time I went,' he said in a severe voice.

' Yes, I don't like to be kept up later than ten,' Jenny said. This was true. She turned any visitor out at that hour, to have time for the care she gave her face before going to bed.

Ling groped, with a hand shaking with mortification, for the hat and gloves he had placed under his chair— he never allowed a servant to take them from him. His suspicions of her were swept off in a wave of pity for himself, an old man, unwanted. On his way to the door he said:

' Will you come and have dinner with me next week ? '

She nodded her promise, but he knew she would make an excuse not to come. In the street he walked slowly and fearfully, looking about him for a cab. Everything has gone wrong: I don't understand anything; there are no kind-hearted people left, no security anywhere, nothing. Monstrous, it's monstrous, he said to himself: something ought to be done.

At eight o'clock Rachel Earlham had finished clearing up after her little girl's bath. She folded the child's clothes, dried the floor, which was swimming with water, and went away into her bedroom to make herself neat before hurrying downstairs to prepare Louis's supper.

She looked at her face in the glass with a childishly intent gaze. For some reason she had begun to wonder whether Louis still thought her pretty. She had never been pretty; she was beautiful in an unassuming way, small, white-skinned, with dark hair and eyes, and a soft gravity and simplicity of manner. She had been brought up strictly, taught by her mother that a Jewish maiden must be modest, silent and frugal. A Jewish maiden she remained, even when she became a socialist, married a young socialist who was not a Jew, and bore two children.

The younger child, a baby of eight months, was asleep in a cot at the foot of her parents' bed, and Rachel stooped over her for a minute, touching the child's silky skin to make sure she was not too warm. Leaning over the cot, she seemed scarcely to breathe, in her care not to disturb the sleeping child.

Satisfied, she went away. The supper was ready in half an hour but Louis did not come in until nine. He was too tired to eat. He sat with one elbow on the table propping up his head, the cup of tea he had asked for in the other hand. Without waiting for her to question him, he began to tell her that negotiations were going on. Raising his voice, he said:

' I can tell you it's all right, everything will be settled, the miners will have to be satisfied with what they can get. All sensible persons realise the need for compromise— we can't all be ruined by their obstinacy.'

' But *will* they be satisfied? ' Rachel asked gently. ' David was here this afternoon for a short time and he said——'

' If you listen to David Renn,' Louis said, with feverish energy, ' you can believe we are all traitors and cowards. He must have thought we were going to lead a revolution or some romantic nonsense. I believe he sees himself with a machine gun in Downing Street. The fool! If he knew as much about the country as I do he'd hold his tongue.'

She was thinking that until a year or two ago Renn had been his close friend, closer to him in one thing than she was. Listening to their words, she would think: Even to this day the War means more to Louis than I do. She was sad and not pleased to think he had turned David off now.

' When we were so poor,' she said, smiling a little, ' in those rooms, living near the Euston Road, David used to pretend he had had supper when he came, so that he shouldn't eat any of ours. But it was always a lie. This afternoon he admitted it.'

Louis was silent. After a minute he said in a low voice: ' It's all very fine, Rachel, but only mad fools look for a revolution in this country. The English temper is against it. Isn't it, now? Look at the faces of the English workers— do you see a fiery spark in any of them? As much as there is in your own quiet little face? I tell you, I tell that imbecile David, if some of them were really driven mad —if they listened to madmen like him, or Cook—not a soldier would disobey the order to fire on them. And do you know what would happen after that?—I'm sorry, Rachel, I'm shouting, I know, but you can't think how this maddens me. Suppose that two or three hundred men, in South Shields, perhaps, or in the Rhondda, were led by the folly of a few among them into starting what looked like revolution— you know it could easily happen at a time like this, or if things were very bad there—they would be mercilessly put down . . . it would be a massacre . . . half-armed workers against machine-guns: and then what?'

' That would be dreadful,' Rachel said. Her little body, which knew, in a memory longer than her own, what the word ' massacre ' means, felt weak. She often said: I am frightened. Crowds, noises at night, loud voices, frightened her, yet she would go, weeping sorely, into the fire for her faith.

' But socialism *is* a revolution,' she said, in her gentle voice. ' People must somehow be made willing for it.'

' Exactly what I say! ' Louis cried. ' And you can't make them willing by alarming them. Disorder, nonsense about dictators—threatening to overturn everything in a wild rush, making a mess—panics—why, it's lunacy. It gives the worst and stubbornest powers against us an opportunity —do you believe they wouldn't take it? And take steps that would make legal peaceful socialism impossible for generations? It's the danger the Party is facing, the real danger . . . not violence from outside, but folly and violence within. The wild nonsense talked by Renn and that mountebank Cook—he's an actor, that man. He's a liability to us, he ought to be got rid of, and so ought David.'

'Yes, but Louis,' began his wife. She stopped, turning crimson, and smiled. She had been going to say: You talk too much to Mrs. Harben nowadays.

'I forget what I was going to say. Oh, yes—yes, I know—it's because I'm a woman, but I know that a birth isn't possible except through the pain and the fear of death. You haven't given up believing, have you?'

'You know I shan't,' Louis exclaimed. 'But it must come slowly and peaceably, or what comes will be something else, not socialism at all. There must be no fatal attempts at violence. The negotiations that are on the way now *must* succeed. Anything can happen if the Strike drags on for another fortnight.'

'What could happen?'

'A district might get out of hand. They would call it mob violence, riot, revolution . . . you can be sure the Government would make the best use of it. It would put us back fifty years! Listening to Renn, you'd think the Conservative Party consisted of fools and scoundrels. Nothing of the sort. The few men who matter are cleverer than any one of us. Oh yes, they're clever all right.'

'Like your friend Gary,' Rachel said swiftly.

Her husband did not answer. His face was haggard still and exhausted, in spite of his excitement. She was overcome with fear and compassion when she saw him sitting silent, fearing she had hurt him, and she ran to him and put her arm round his shoulder.

'Please forgive me, Louis,' she said. 'I don't want to vex you. You ought to go to bed.'

Louis leaned against her with closed eyes. He seemed

unable to make a move. ' Yes, I'm tired,' he said. ' I can't
talk any more.' His tongue tripped up over the words as
though it were swollen.

' Come upstairs now, and sleep,' Rachel entreated him.
' I'll hold you until you are asleep. Please, Louis. Please
come.'

' Don't leave me, will you ? ' he said, not moving.

' Never, my darling, never. How could I leave you ? '
she said quietly. ' You are like my little child.'

5

Henry Smith had been waiting in Renn's sitting-room for
an hour, since ten o'clock. When Renn came in, one side
of his face was discoloured and dirty, the blood from a deep
cut dried on his temple. ' My God, what's the matter with
you ? ' Smith said.

There was a kettle on the stove, boiling water with which
he had been going to make the coffee as soon as his friend
came. He poured it into a basin, took a clean handkerchief,
and began to wash the cut. The skin down that side of
Renn's face was scraped raw and grained with dirt: he
winced, and began to tell Smith what had happened. ' I'll
murder Swan one of these days,' Smith said. Looking up
at him, Renn saw that he had crimsoned with rage; the
whites of his eyes were bloodshot. ' Don't trouble yourself,'
he said; ' he'll come to a bad end without you.'

' If I could get my hands on his neck now, though,' Smith
muttered. In the meantime his hands were moving with the
utmost gentleness over Renn's head and face. He felt the
fine bones of the skull under the hair, soft and fine like a
boy's, and his anger seized him afresh.

He controlled it with difficulty, because he saw that Renn
had had enough. Moving quickly about the room, preparing
coffee, looking—in vain—for a spoonful of rum to put into
it, he joked about the day's happenings. He had heard a story

about a certain Labour leader.   It made him roar with
laughter again as he told it.

'Yesterday evening someone came up to him in the lobby
of the House and told him he had definite information that
the South Wales miners had been hiding arms in the country
for months and were going to march on Cardiff.   And he
believed it!   He went straight back to his little house on the
West Road and buried all the spoons and forks in the garden.
After they had taken Cardiff the rebels would naturally
march on London, and by the West Road.   And this morning
his wife had to go out and dig up a couple of spoons for them
so that they could eat their breakfast eggs.   It's a fact!'

Renn listened with a subtle smile.   He was very pale.
'I'm sure it's true.   All the same, Harry, a great many
of his own followers would approve, and do the same
thing themselves in the circumstances.   It's no use pretending to ourselves that the ranks are finer and bolder
than their officers.   Any Party gets the leaders it deserves.
If things come to a crisis it is on your timid little lower
middle-class householder, afraid for his spoons, that we shall
have to rely.'

'Now you are really carrying tolerance too far,' laughed
Smith.

Renn drank his coffee gratefully, feeling its warmth flow
slowly through his body.   He had been very cold ever since
he picked himself up from the pavement and tried dizzily
to stand without holding the railings.   He was suffering
from shock, less in his body than in his mind; if you like,
in his spirit.   It seemed to him that something more important
had happened to him than being knocked out by a bully.   I
have come to another turn, he thought confusedly: I believe
in tolerance—yes, that's true—but I want justice, and
to do justice now means a revolution.   But I am not a
fighter, I couldn't kill anyone—not even Swan.   I do all my
killing with my mind.   I come beforehand, and I destroy.
The truth is that I am an anarchist.   His pointed tongue

flickered over his lips. He looked at Smith with a slight smile.

'There is something to be said for Louis Earlham, after all,' he said. 'He has as keen a horror of violence as I have, but I am certain he wouldn't trouble to bury his spoons.'

'Oh, Earlham,' said Smith. He pulled a solemn face. 'Louis is always going through some moral crisis or other.' He mimicked Earlham's sonorous voice. 'He is surrounded by precipices,' he said gravely. Then he burst out laughing.

'Louis is the kind of man who would go down to Clarkson's and order himself a crown of thorns,' Renn said, with the bitterness he felt when he thought of Louis.

'It is his fault, and the fault of the others like him, that the Party is becoming a party of workers in safe jobs,' Smith exclaimed. He jumped up and began to walk about the small room, moving his arms. When he was excited he looked more than ever like a countryman. 'Its leaders are afraid of their responsibility in a Party with the tradition and the need for a revolution. They are afraid of this Strike. They never meant it to happen, the thought of the forces they are playing with is a nightmare to them. They fear a revolution more than they fear silk breeches. They are far too decent and pliant themselves to believe that ruthlessness will be used against them when they want only to proceed peacefully. And yet the way they were treated the other night—practically kicked out of Downing Street by the butler—it should have warned them what the famous English *spirit of compromise* is worth in a crisis. This Strike ought to have taken place in 1919. If it breaks down now no general strike will ever be possible again. The Party will become ossified. You mustn't talk about a dictatorship, they say, yet that's the very thing we ought to be thinking and talking about the whole time—how the devil we can manage to have authority without tyranny. Eh? You see, that's it—it's——'

He broke off, with his mouth open, as the door opened

quickly and the girl he had taken to his room on Saturday night came in. The sight of her overwhelmed him. He was about to blab his amazement when Renn spoke.

'Why, my dear Hannah,' he said, in a voice of frank happiness and intimacy. 'I didn't know you were coming this evening.'

'It's not evening,' said Hannah gaily, 'it's the middle of the night. Look. A quarter to twelve.' She turned and looked Smith full in the face, with a warm teasing smile. 'Who is this, David?' She scarcely waited to hear the answer before she was raising herself on her toes in order to look at the bandage on Renn's head.

'Have you had an accident, my darling?' she asked in her strong clear voice. 'What has happened to you?'

Smith did not wait to hear more. He was completely at a loss and above all, angry; his strongest impulse was to blurt the truth. To avoid doing this he went away. I shall have to think this out before morning, he thought. He would have preferred talking about it to thinking, but the only person he felt moved to talk to was Hervey Russell and she was out of his reach.

As soon as he had gone Hannah put him out of her mind, but the excitement remained. She was not afraid, certain she could manage to make him hold his tongue. Her picture of herself as a young woman to whom men are bound delighted her. She felt a wave of tenderness for Renn—it was really gratitude to him for showing her to herself in this enchanting light, but it awoke in her all the most delicious emotions of love. Indeed it was love, of the fiercest and deepest kind. Self-love is not simply vanity.

'Tell me how you hurt your head, my darling. I am so sorry. Does it hurt badly?'

'Scarcely at all now,' Renn said. He told her the story. She listened to it with a slight smile, as though he were telling her something which had happened so long since that it was not necessary to take it seriously. As soon as he had finished, she exclaimed:

'But that was terrible. What a disgusting wretch the man Swan must be, I hope he will die soon. But now listen to my news, David. It is splendid, wonderful, I am so happy I can scarcely breathe. This evening Mrs. Baring—I call her that now and not Madam—invited me to have dinner with her; she took me there in her car. Oh, it is such a fine house, David—beautiful things everywhere, bowls of flowers, silk carpets, curtains from Paris, Chinese figures, and such paintings on the walls—and, ha, I have learned a trick. It is how to look at one of these new paintings. You approach it sideways, like this—look, David—you sidle— as if you were only giving it a glance, and then you stand still suddenly, struck—so! You are very quiet, you blow out your lips a little, you peer, walk backwards, then say politely, He has an admirable feeling for colour. And that's all! You are an art critic.'

With glowing cheeks, she had been acting the little scene for him, posing, lifting her arms. She struck herself lightly on the breast and said: 'Behold the new assistant-buyer for the house of Baring. I am to begin at once; soon I shall be head buyer, and then, ah, you wait. One day you will see my name in *Vogue* below the drawing of a superb coat: it will say simply Hannah Markham, as it might be Patou or Lanvin.' She laughed, looking at him with bright, half-closed eyes. 'Are you pleased?'

'Very pleased,' said Renn. This is really the finish, he said to himself, dazed. He felt nothing.

'And now we must be practical, my darling. Tell me what you are going to do?'

'Do?' Renn echoed. He looked at her with a smile. 'Forgive me, Hannah. I must be stupider than usual, I suppose my brains have run out of the hole in my head.'

She seated herself beside him and began to kiss his face and neck, slowly, stroking his body with both hands. 'Of

course you can't think about it to-night,' she said kindly.
'What an idiot I am. But all the same we must begin very
soon to find some work for you. I wonder if Mrs. Baring
knows anyone who needs a secretary. I shall ask her.'

'No,' Renn said, with energy. 'I don't want another job
of that sort.'

'Then what, my little David? what will you do?'

Rousing himself, he tried to explain to her that he was
no longer a fit person to recommend for a respectable post.
For one thing, he had no testimonial; it had been refused
by his late employer.

She had her remedy for that at once. 'You must go and
see Mr. Gary when the Strike is over. Tell him you know
you were mistaken in working for the Strike—it is all
nonsense, you know, Davy, these people are not worth
ruining yourself for. What will they do for you when you
haven't a penny? They won't even say thank-you. You
must tell him all that, and ask him to give you a letter about
your marvellous abilities. I am sure he will, if you say the
right things to him.'

'I daresay,' Renn said drily. 'But I can't do it.'

'You are too proud?'

'No.'

'Too honest—you still believe that you ought to be a
socialist even if you never have another job?'

'If you like,' Renn said. 'Don't let us discuss it now.'

Hannah had drawn away from him so that she could see
him. With a finger she traced the line of his face and lips.
'You look gentle and not strong,' she murmured. 'And you
are as stubborn as a mule. What shall I do with you?'

'Give me up,' Renn said, smiling.

'No, I shan't do that.' She felt a passionate admiration
for him, for his honest and ruthless integrity. At another
time it might only have irritated her. Now she was in a
mood to be exhilarated by any emotion. She wanted to be
caressed and praised; her feeling of tenderness for him pos-

sessed all her senses and she quivered with pleasure between his hands.

At one moment she raised herself to kiss his bandages and to whisper in his ear: 'As soon as you find another post we'll marry, shall we? and then I need never go away from you again.   Is that what you want?'

Renn wanted to believe her.

5

Towards six o'clock in the evening Sally Rigden took the children, the boy of six and the little girl, who was now a year and a half old, and walked with them as far as the kitchen which had been opened by the Strike committee. It was the first time she had been there.   She felt ashamed, thinking of it as though she were going to beg for something, for food.   It was a disgrace.   Only the terrifying fact that the Strike money Frank had given her was all but finished could drive her here.

She was a little comforted by finding in the room other women like herself, carefully dressed in their good coats, and with their children.   Many of these were older than herself. She stood beside three or four women in poorer clothes, listening to what they said.   The room was warm, she was tired after her day's work and the long walk through the streets to the kitchen; she could not be sure which of them was speaking at one time.   Their voices rose about her like the quick spatter of drops from the tap in her own kitchen, or like the hurrying footsteps in the street.   It was the same voice, quick, roughened, sharp.

'We've been hungry before and we can be hungry again, I say.'

'By Thursday I'm ashore for food.'

'What's that, what did you say?   Wh-a-at?   I mean, you ought to have seen her before she came to it as she did; eeh, she was pretty.'

The children had their meal but she pretended not to want anything. Then she walked back, carrying the little girl, with the boy keeping close to her other hand. He kept glancing at her with a lightly puzzled expression; her silence intimidated him. He knew from her face that something was wrong. When she had opened and shut the door of her own house, she felt a sharp relief. Here at least she was safe.

She moved about the kitchen, touching the yellow scrubbed wood of the table, straightening the mat, until she felt satisfied that everything was right. The baby had begun to whimper with sleep. She drew her clothes off, quieting her, and laid her in the basket to sleep downstairs until she went to bed herself. At last the little boy spoke to her. ' Why did we go to that room, mum ? '

' Because there was no supper here for you,' she answered.

She talked to him as if he were her own age; this had made him too sensitive and noticing of her. He now saw that she was uncertain herself, and he said nothing until she was pulling the blanket round him in bed. Then he said rather anxiously: ' I had plenty to eat there.'

' I hope you did,' she answered. She left him and went downstairs to wait for Frank. She had some food for him and she laid it out carefully, making the most of it. Feeling with her hand under the flattened cushion of the chair, she edged out a book in a paper cover, torn, with the picture of a woman in a black veil, and in bold print the words Tell Me Your Dreams. She turned the pages she knew almost by heart, in search of something that she could fasten to the dream she had had last night.

She believed in dreams. This one was so vivid she did not forget it. She was with other women, walking across an endless stretch of ground. They were all afraid, because they were in danger, and they were without food or homes. She had the little girl with her, grown a few years older. In some queer way she was the child, and thought as the child, while she was still herself. In their flight they came to a well; it was empty and as they stood round it the temptation seized her to throw the child into the pit, so that she would no longer have her dragging at her arms and crying for food. She felt in herself the agonised fear of the child who knew what she was thinking. The fear and the temptation slid together in her mind with the shadowy figures of the other women. She awoke shaking with terror.

There was nothing in the book even remotely like her dream. She pushed it out of sight under the chair seat as her husband came in.

Frank Rigden blinked and smiled when he came into the light of the kitchen from the darkness outside. He stooped and took off his dusty shoes and laid them between his chair and the wall, hoping she would not look at them. But they were the first things she touched when she began to clear away his supper. Carrying them into the scullery she turned them over, and there were both soles worn through and a scratch on one heel that was almost a cut. She turned with them in her hand and looked reproachfully at him.

' I'll get some leather and mend them,' he said softly.

' Nay, you'll not mend that,' his wife said. She pressed her thumb over the cut, vexed. 'With all this extra cycling you could have had a month's plain wear out of them.'

She said nothing more. She did not know why he had hurried to offer himself to the Strike committee to help; the strange thought he had of Mr. Earlham, worshipping him as you might say, was a vexation and a stumbling block to her; but she was not a woman who scolded what she did not understand. She accepted it in him as she accepted his quietness and patience and his hands on her body in the nights.

She moved about the room, preparing things for the morning. Her husband watched her, seeing now her raised arm, now the pleats of her skirt, and now a cloth on which she laid her hand. Without knowing it, he loved everything in the four rooms of their house as much as she did, feeling them almost as parts of his own body.

'Did you take th' baby with you to the kitchen or leave her with Mrs. Sanderson?' he asked. The little girl was under his special protection; he thought the mother favoured the boy and that the other child would notice it and feel disappointed.

'No, I took her,' his wife said. She stood still; her eyes dilated suddenly and she pressed her hand holding the cloth on her breast. 'Frank, whatever shall we do if the works won't take you back when the Strike's over? You know I read the notice on the gates to-day, saying everyone shall be taken back if they go *now*.'

'None of us'll go back,' said Rigden.

'No, I know—but if the job's gone—— You know, if the Strike fails. . . .'

'We shan't fail,' her husband said, with his quick, shame-faced smile. 'Mr. Earlham's given his word they'll see all us right. *Stand fast and we'll see you don't suffer by it* was what he said. He'll do the right thing by us!'

Moving now slowly towards the sleeping child, his wife answered:

'It seems as if everybody else did things, and only we have things done to us.'

Tuesday, May 11th
NO MORE TIME

CHAPTER XXI

In a strange bed Hervey slept—she who could sleep anywhere—peacefully and deeply. She awoke once, while it
was still dark, and looked round her without remembering
where she was. Then she slept again until dawn.

The night before, she had slipped from bed as soon as the
nurse left her and drawn the curtains from the window, so
that all the air to be found in a London garden could come
freely into her room. Now the light drew her slowly from
the depths of her sleep to a nearer level. She dreamed that
she was walking up the steep road in Danesacre known as
North Bank; it led from the harbour to the first house she
remembered living in with her mother. They had left it
when she was still a child. In her dream she was not a
child, but a woman, and she was naked. It was night and
she was alone between the walls of the houses, her feet
pressing the stones of this straight steep hill. She was not
afraid, and as she neared the top the houses became un-
substantial and remote: she became aware of a shadow
following her; it took dimly the form of her first husband
and certainly she recognised his voice saying: ' Poor thrawn
girl, come back again.' In her dream she wondered what
on earth the word ' thrawn ' meant. She half turned towards
him, but all the emotion she felt turned to filthy hate and
abuse, and then, as the hill, the night, and the voice lapsed
into nothing, to the deepest tenderness and pity. She awoke
in the unfamiliar room.

She did not try to sleep again, but lay watching the leaves
of a magnolia tree change colour with the changes of light.
A bird began to sing clearly and shrilly, lifting her straight

out of time into any age. This could be Chaucer's spring, she thought, seeing the air grow brighter and a petal which had been falling for more than five hundred years float at last across the grass. She felt a poignant happiness.

At seven o'clock the day nurse came in with her breakfast. She refused to eat it, but drank the tea. The nurse remonstrated with her.

' But I thought you didn't give food to people who were going to be operated on,' Hervey said.

' All that has been changed,' said the nurse. ' They discovered in the War that soldiers who had been fed beforehand did better in an operation than men who had fasted.'

But Hervey, a traditionalist in everything which touched herself, obstinately refused to eat, even when the Sister rustled in sternly to scold her. She looked at the woman with timid coldness and replied in her mother's voice, sharp and arrogant: ' Let me tell you that I don't wish to eat.' They gave her up at that, and the nurse began the last preparation of her body. Hervey endured it as she had done the other, with a stoical disgust and resentment. She felt very angry that her body, as strong and soundly built as a tree, should have been spoiled by her long neglect and hard youth. It had rallied so many times to her will that she could not forgive it for failing her.

It was now nine o'clock and the operation was at eleven. She was left alone. She was careful not to think about herself. What might be going on in the recesses of her mind, what panic or terror, she ignored with ease and vanity. Of the five books she had brought only one would do to keep her quiet and satisfied on the level at which she chose to live. She began it again at the beginning and read with a steady mind, omitting nothing. ' And as the many tribes of feathered birds, wild geese or cranes or long-necked swans, on the Asian mead by Kaystrios' stream, fly hither and thither joying in their plumage, and with loud cries settle ever onwards, and the mead resounds; even so poured forth the many tribes of warriors from ships and huts into the Skamandrian plain.' She found a strange but sharp and deep pleasure in the list of captains and ships at the end of the second book of the Iliad, and read the names over to herself, twice, slowly. This part had always bored her before.

On the piece of paper she was using as a book-mark she had written a sentence of which she had forgotten the origin. It had remained with her since she first read it, ten years before, when she was very poor, a drudge in the first house of her married life. It gave her a piercing happiness then, and she thought these the right words to remember when she came to the last. She did not need to look at them now, knowing them by heart. ' *The last peaks of the world, beyond all seas, well-springs of night and gleams of opened heaven, the garden of the Sun.*' Nothing could be more satisfying at such a time than the thought of the Sun in his strength, sauntering between groves of deep trees and over lawns, in some place so remote that the night welled between its hills.

She read on until five minutes to eleven, so sunk that she did not notice that the time was going. The nurse came in again with a pair of long woollen stockings, like the thigh stockings given to soldiers during the War. She was already clothed in a nightgown more like a penitent's sheet than anything else human.

' Oh, is it time? ' she asked.

' Yes,' the nurse smiled. ' Nervous? '

' Not yet,' Hervey said.

She looked askance at the wheeled chair waiting in the corridor, held by a grinning boy. ' Am I to get into that? ' she demanded. ' Why? I can walk perfectly well.'

She was not allowed to flout any more rules; the nurse hurried her into it and she was wheeled into a lift which rose so slowly that she was moved to say: ' I could have been up the stairs twice in this time.'

'You'll be heavier when you come down again,' the nurse said.

The operating theatre was at the end of a corridor. It was a large room into which the sun shone. To her first rapid glance it seemed to be full of people. They were all women. She saw the surgeon first, then her doctor, then a middle-aged woman who was to give her the anæsthetic: there were four or five nurses standing about.

She looked round her with intense curiosity. The room was on the third floor of the house, so that when she lay down on the table only the sky was visible through the window. It was a bright strong blue, with one wisp of cloud like the scrawled signature of the artist in the left-hand lower corner. She looked from it to the surgeon, whose large white-clad body and brown face now came between her and the light. *Last peaks of the world*, she thought, *beyond all seas, well-springs of night*. The anæsthetist had a round face, lined and sallow. She looked down at Hervey with a faint smile. 'Well, you look like a little girl,' she said.

Someone whom Hervey did not see adjusted the mask over her face. This was the moment she feared. She dreaded the choking more than anything in the world. She lay still and tried to breathe calmly.

Her doctor was close to her. Stooping a little, she took Hervey's right hand and held it in one of hers. At once Hervey thought: I must hold as hard as I can, so that they don't begin to cut before I am unconscious. She squeezed the other woman's hand.

Her sight began to fail. She saw the square of the window at a great distance, and the dim figures of the nurses. The silence round her was unbroken. Now only vague forms floated across her eyes. She lost the sensation of a hand touching hers.

With a sudden intense clarity, as though light were pouring into her mind, she thought: I must signal to the last man.

She raised her arm, holding it straight out. Did she raise it? She must have moved her arm, or her body on the table, because some person indistinct spoke to her in a quiet voice. 'Everything is all right, Mrs. Roxby.' She was now almost blind, and straining her eyes obstinately she could see only the blurred shadow of a woman near the table.

The light which had filled her mind dissolved the room.

CHAPTER XXII

RENN'S head ached, he was dizzy and stumbled when he tried to stand up. He felt dizzier when he was lying in bed and he decided, in the belief that he was unusually sensible, to sit at his table and work there. He could not walk to the Committee rooms in this state. He had brought home with him the reports he was going to turn into next day's illegal Bulletin. He pushed his table in front of him, leaning on it, against the window, and seated himself so that he could look into the street. There was nothing to look at in the room itself. To save money he had given up his second room; his landlady had brought in a camp bed, which stood close to the door in the place of a large creaking cupboard. He now kept his clothes in a suitcase under the bed and his books for the most part on the floor.

Marylebone Road seen from his window was like the entrance to a circus. The sunlight filled it with a crude light, through which women in thin gay dresses, men in shirt sleeves, sweating horses, and vehicles of all kinds moved with chaotic brilliance. He was forced to shut his window to keep out the dust and noise, not to speak of the smells of a London street on hot days. Paris smells of sewers and coffee, Berlin of cigar smoke (or did until it was *gleichgeschaltet* to smell of something less pleasant), Vienna of really good coffee, and London of petrol, oil, and gaspers.

The sun shone on him through the dusty glass and made him pleasantly warm. It accentuated the extraordinary air of fineness his face had because of its pallor and finely jutting bones. His forehead was broad and prominent; his boldly arched eyebrows were nearly colourless, as were his eyelashes and lips. His eyes were pale and very clear. In any strong light his skin seemed to become transparent, with the light coming through it from within, like a Chinese lantern lit by a candle.

He had taken off his jacket and after a time he turned round so that the sun warmed his shoulders. An army doctor had told him that the best chance of getting rid of the pain which had entrenched itself in the scars of his wounds, and attacked whenever he was tired, would be to lie for six months or a year in the sun, on the Riviera or in North Africa. He amused himself sometimes by taking an imaginary train to one or the other.

Soon after one o'clock Hannah came into his room. Her skin was always brown, like a gipsy's, and the sun made it glow: when she took her hat off and laid it on the bed he saw that her hair was pressed to her temples with drops of moisture. She scolded him for getting out of bed. She had come to look at the cut on his head and bandage it freshly. She brought a new bandage and a piece of medicated soap, and she washed the place with water from the jug standing on his washstand. She gave him a great deal of discomfort by the energy with which she went about it, but he said nothing. At one moment she saw him wince, and said cheerfully:

' I'm not any good as a nurse. It will be a lesson to you, I hope, to find some more respectable way of earning your living than one which gets you a broken head.'

' It doesn't earn me my living,' he pointed out. He had counted his money again that morning, and found that he could live on his savings for six months, provided he did not send his mother the two pounds every week. Without it she could just manage to live, and she would not complain if he told her he could not afford it any longer.

' There,' Hannah said, pleased with herself. ' You look very nice. Do you know I ran all the way from

Wigmore Street to do this for you? You can believe I love you.'

'If we were married,' said Renn, 'you could have asked for leave of absence to look after a sick husband.'

'Do you want me to live in this room?' she asked him, laughing.

'Listen to me,' Renn said. He made her sit down so that he could look at her. 'I want you to give me an honest answer to a question. Never mind whether you think it will make me unhappy, I want you to tell me the truth now. Even if I had a job as good as the one I have lost, or if I managed to get a better, would you marry me? The truth, please, my darling.'

Hannah looked at him with a serious air. 'No, I can't marry anyone yet,' she said softly. 'You know why, David. I want too much to experience everything—yes, everything—before I am old. I want to enjoy my life.'

'You mean you want to experience other men,' Renn said. 'You think that our—feeling can't remain very much longer as it is, and you won't commit yourself.'

'Feelings that can't last for ever are all the more intense,' Hannah said, smiling.

'What nonsense,' Renn said. He could not reason with her about it. 'It is time you went back to your Madam Baring.'

She came and kneeled beside his chair, and laid an arm on his knee. 'You're angry with me,' she said sadly. 'Don't you understand it, David? I love you very much, more than anyone, but how can I know now what I shall want when I am thirty? I'm only twenty-one and all my life is to come. I must be free to take what comes. I don't want to marry and perhaps have children, yet. I want to see Vienna and Paris, I want all the things the world has to give, I want to swallow the whole of life in one long gulp. Even if it disappoints me I want to taste it.' She sprang to her feet and walked half dancing towards the window. 'There!' she cried, joyously. 'You see all those hundreds of people—well, I want to be different, to live differently from any of them. Yes, David, I want everything, and I shall get it. When I am tired of experimenting I'll marry you if you still want me. But not yet.'

'Your desires are so easy that I am sure you will get what you want,' Renn said, with contempt.

'Now you are unkind,' Hannah said. Tears came into her eyes. She was hurt by his bitterness. It was foolish of him, when she loved him and they could be happy together. 'You're unfair and impossible, David.' The tears ran over her cheeks and fell on the papers on the table. She wiped them away with her brown thin hands.

Renn stood up and put his arms on her shoulders. He had to lean on her to support himself.

'You are quite right,' he said. 'I have a rotten disposition. Never mind, I'll do my best to curb it for your sake. Come, dry your face and be off, or you'll be late.'

'Then you have forgiven me and you still want me?' she asked, smiling a little.

'You can set your mind at rest,' said Renn. His mouth was dry; his tongue seemed too slow and clumsy; he spoke with difficulty.

'And I can come here this evening?' She took hold of his hand and kissed it quickly and lightly.

Renn was about to reply when he heard footsteps in the hall approaching his door. He released Hannah and sat down in his chair.

Henry Smith came in, bareheaded; his face had its usual wide upturned smile of greeting. It died when he saw Hannah. She turned to him with a dazzling smile, and a manner as seductive as she could make it.

'Now you can help me to persuade David he's not fit to go out at all to-day,' she said.

'Certainly he's not,' Smith agreed.

'Very well,' she said to Renn, 'I shall come this evening.'

' There's nothing to eat, and I don't want anything,' Renn said. ' You'd better have some dinner before you come.'

' Well, I can do that.' She looked brightly at Smith. ' But won't you give me dinner first, since David can't? ' she said, smiling, certain he would respond at once, he was only waiting to be invited.

Smith smiled back at her, looking steadily into her eyes. ' No,' he said, ' I'm sorry, but I can't go anywhere in the evening, I'm too busy.'

He had already decided. He would not give her away because he did not want to ruin his own friendship with Renn. Besides that she amused him, and he admired her spirit. She is really very good-looking, he said to himself. As she was going away he was surprised by an impulse of dislike and contempt; he would like to hustle her out roughly and see the last of her. It was as much as he could do to keep his hands off her.

He began to talk gaily to Renn. He described Earlham's speech the night before.

' He had so much to say about sacrifice that the men's faces grew longer and longer as they listened to it and at last one of them jumped up and said, "So it's all up with us, is it? "; and another chap at the back of the hall took him up and shouted, "What do you think? Oor speaker's blowing cold for fear you should blow too hot and burn yoursen." So then Master Earlham told them he had never liked the thought of a general strike, but he was doing his best to get used to it and they would hear from him later. By the way, Eccleston Square is blue with rumours about the negotiations: they're so excited that half of them don't know what they're doing, and a special delegate arrived from Peterborough by road to find out what contradictory instructions that had been sent to them might mean, supposing they meant anything at all. And they've got themselves into such a mess over the engineers and the shipbuilders they're calling them out to save further trouble.'

Someone knocked. Smith opened the door. 'Why, Nick,' he said heartily. 'Come in.'

Nicholas Roxby looked at Renn without noticing that he was bandaged. 'I came to tell you about Hervey,' he said. 'You wanted to know the result. The operation's over—it was over at half-past two—three and a half hours. I saw the surgeon. She says everything is all right, it's a success. She's still under the anæsthetic, but it's over.'

He sat down and looked round him with a sense of familiarity. This was the first time he had been in Renn's rooms, but the stained wallpaper was the colour of the canvas used on the walls of a dug-out. Even the stains were of the same colour and shape. It made him feel at ease, an irresponsible happiness seized him.

He heard Smith speaking with a lively affection about Hervey, and stirred himself to make the proper answers. But he felt a guilty sense of relief that he was sitting here with these two men, and not in Hervey's room in the nursing home, supposing he had been able to sit there now. It was something like the relief with which, towards the end of the War, he turned his back on the civilians' world and went back to one he knew better and understood. He allowed himself to relax in his chair, and the others, thinking he was tired, left him alone. Suddenly he interrupted Renn in the middle of a sentence.

'I wish you would take up in your Bulletin this question about the indomitable spirit of the workers,' he said, emphatically. 'They're no more indomitable than anyone else, and if we had the misfortune to breed a Mussolini or another Cromwell, ninety-five per cent of them would never know what had happened, or at the utmost they'd grumble and obey. As for the Trades Unions—I believe them to be the greatest power for reaction in the country. I don't mean only that they're terrified of assuming responsibility for social change. They're too anxious not to embarrass the owners of capital. They feel far closer and sharper

sympathy with them than with a working man.   They
have almost the same interests; they see alike, think alike,
and feel alike about the necessity of not having any
trouble.   Indomitable indeed!   Indomitable seat-warmers
to a man!'

'Good for you, m'dear,' Smith laughed slyly.   'But you're
too hard on them.   Some of them are decent fellows.'

'And others are bureaucrats and greedy bullies,' Renn
said in a gentle voice.   'Cook is neither the one nor the
other, by the way.'

'He looked so done the only time I saw him—that was
yesterday evening—and he was, so far as I could see, running
his own errands, that I felt like offering to run them for
him, black his shoes, anything,' Nicholas said slowly.

He had been carried away by the man; yet he wondered
how much of the world he knew would remain if men like
Cook had their way with it.   He wondered, too, why *his*
people did not come to terms in good time with the revolution
through its cautious leaders.

He kept these thoughts rigidly to himself.   He felt in his
bones the power of his own sort of people to defend themselves and their goods.   He mistrusted the strength of the
others, the hordes of the dispossessed.   He had in his bones
none of that bitterness which in a few of them had turned
to a hard faith.

CHAPTER XXIII

At six o'clock in the evening the air in the High Street was noticeable as you walked through it, because of the dust, the heat, the smell of stuffy houses, refuse of shops, dirty clothes, bodies seldom washed, too many people crammed together in an over-built space. In a few of the narrow streets and lanes to the south of the High Street a current of cool air was just beginning to flow: it came lingering from the river.

The inner room of the Strike Committee had a window which turned towards the river—that is to say, you could have seen the river from it if some hundreds of houses and factories had been demolished, as indeed from any idea of health, decency, or beauty they should have been. The air outside this window was as stagnant and close as the air in the room. Even Joe Bradford had begun to feel that he needed a night's rest. His nights during the Strike had lasted anything from two to four hours, never longer.

He was listening to a deputation of three perplexed and angry men, all steel workers, one man from each of three unions. Each union had received different and contradictory instructions from the Council. Telephone messages and a personal visit to Headquarters had not cleared it up. Now they expected Joe to tell them what to do.

'We've been marching in and out all the blurry day, Joe,' one of the men said. He smiled involuntarily. 'Ee-e, I'm sorry about it,' he said, half ready to believe that it was his fault.

'I'll send another letter,' Joe said. He saw them look at each other. He said nothing. His shrewd snouty face, the eyes almost hidden in the fleshy cheeks, was heavy and impassive. He was not going to let anyone know that he was beat by the thing, not Bradford Joe. He wrote his letter, and sent Frank Rigden off with it. 'Don't come back without you get an answer,' he said.

The deputation withdrew to the other room, and Joe settled down to work. In his mind's eye he was following Rigden through the teeming streets until he reached Eccleston Square. Here his vision failed. He had not been to Head-quarters since the first day of the Strike. He did not see Rigden pushing his bicycle through the tangle of cars and motor-cycles: he did not see him standing in a lost way in a corridor, buffeted by deputations, officials, members of interviewing, intelligence, publicity committees; sent by one man to another; told to wait; waiting. He should have been photographed as he stood there, at the angle of a wall, one hand holding his cap in his pocket, his gaunt round-shouldered body pressed closely against the wall to be out of the way: his blue eyes looked steadily at his shoes and the floor, except that once or twice he lifted them to throw a patient and bewildered glance into the face of a man hurrying past.

He stood in the same place for half an hour. Then he went back to the room. He saw the man who had read his letter talking with other men near the window. He waited again. At last the man turned and saw him. ' What d'you want?'

' An answer to th' letter,' Rigden said.

' Oh that? Just go back and tell your secretary that the proper instructions were sent to the unions concerned early this afternoon. He'll find that's all right.'

Rigden turned and went away. He had the feeling that something was wrong, but there was nothing he could do except carry the message. For the first time since last Monday he felt a prick of discouragement. At the bottom of his mind he was hurt because the man had spoken to him with so complete a lack of interest, as though the important letter he had brought, going as hard as he could, was not of importance after all. When he reached the Committee room again he was winded. He had to have a drink of water before he could walk stiffly upstairs and repeat the man's words to Joe Bradford.

Joe nodded in answer. It was now seven o'clock and he told Rigden to go home. For a minute he did not summon the deputation from the other room. He realised that he would have to take the responsibility for the muddle himself, and he was still seeking the way out when a man came into the room and came straight over to his desk. Joe looked up. 'Oh it's you, is it?' he said.

The man's name was Baker: his official grade was higher than Joe's, but they had started level. They were almost close friends. Joe admired Baker and disliked him as much as he liked him. 'Thought I'd drop in to see how you were getting on.' 'Well enough,' growled Joe: 'at any rate, it would be well enough if the ——s on the Council knew what they wanted.' The other man did not smile. He bent his heavy body—he was heavier than Joe, squat, sallow, with an overbearing manner—across the desk and said in a low voice: 'It's all but over.' 'The Strike?' 'What d'you think? The Council 'as agreed on certain terms and the miners' executive will have to fall in with them. Private and confidential to you. Nothing's settled yet, but it will be before midnight.' 'Oh, nothing's settled yet—well, we've heard that before,' Joe said, in a sarcastic voice: 'and are they the right terms, these terms of yours that aren't settled yet?'

The other man lifted himself out of the chair, which was creaking dangerously under his bulk. 'They're all right,' he said. 'And you'll see I'm right as well. Don't say I didn't tell you in good time.'

He went out, not looking at any of the other people in the room. Joe's head had begun to ache. He did not know

what to think about the information he had been given.
If Baker was mistaken it would not be the first time; but
he was often right, and he was where he could listen without
being noticed. With a sudden energy, Joe got up and went
out to the deputation. He spoke to one man.

'You,' he said. 'How many union men in your shop?'

'Eight. Out of two thousand.'

'Don't come out till to-morrow at any rate.' He spoke
to the others: 'Your lot's all right, eh? Seems you're
meant to come out now.'

'We're bound to come out if th' others do,' the first
man said.

'Have it your own way,' Joe answered shortly. 'My
advice to you is to stop where you are for another twenty-
four hours.'

He went back to his desk, his mind filled with bitter
irritating thoughts. He loathed politicians. He would
like to see hanging side by side on the railings below his
window a suave fervent wordy Parliamentarian and a fat and
genial Trades Union secretary, both of whom he detested.
I wish I had that swine Earlham here, he thought; I'd make
him take responsibility for the mess. The work he had to
do before midnight was overwhelming; he plunged into it
again, only to find himself in a moment quarrelling savagely
with the communist Grassart. Grassart asked him whether
Baker had any news. 'None to give away,' Joe answered.

'I should never be surprised,' said Grassart, 'to hear that
the T.U.C. had sold out.'

'The devil you would,' Joe snapped. 'You'd be surprised
to hear that anyone was as dishonest as your own damned silly
Party.' He was shocked by his loss of self-control, and too
stubborn to give way. But Grassart answered calmly:

'Seeing that the only preparation your precious T.U.C.
made for this Strike was to print notices, you can't blame
anyone for expecting them to make a mess of it. There
ought to have been Defence Corps, committees ready to take

over in the factories and workshops, private agreements with the co-operatives, workers' supply systems—instead of that they let the thing break on them like a thunderstorm on a lot of well-meaning hens.'

'Hold your tongue or get out,' Joe shouted.

At once he was ashamed of himself, quarrelling with the man in front of everyone. Grassart only bent his head over his corner of the table, and said nothing more. Joe went on with his work. After a time he took a letter in a blue envelope from his pocket and read it again. It came from another friend of his in Newcastle. The last sentence was: 'They say it's the police are holding the men back here, it's not the police, it's the Committee—if the Strike goes on another week, there'll be a downright mess here—you'd better come up and join in, what do you stop in London for anyway, it's a lousy place.' He folded it, thought of showing it to Grassart in sign of reconciliation, but changed his mind and put it away. A few messages began to come in from other centres. 'Pleased to report all workers here are SOLID.' 'Better heart to-day here even than last week.' 'Remains firm.' 'Success seems absolutely certain.' 'If so solid everywhere as here, victory is certain.' He felt his spirits rising. The room had grown cooler, and his head no longer ached. The unfamiliar excitement he had felt during the past week awoke again, and with it he felt confident and tireless. He looked round the room, sent away a man who was clearly done for, and settled down to work until morning if it was necessary.

At six o'clock Louis Earlham waited in the sitting-room of Gary's flat while his friend dictated a letter in the next room. He was impatient. The chair in which he had seated himself was so low that he felt uncomfortable in it. He stood up and walked about the room. It was a very large room; a wide couch ran under the window, there were some easy chairs; the rest of the furniture was old and, he guessed, of great value. The wide tall windows were partly covered with curtains in a light woven silk, the rugs old and very beautiful. A man of cultivated tastes had taken pains to provide himself with a room in which every object was perfect in itself and related politely to all the others. Earlham envied his friend this room, yet felt uneasy in it. Obeying an impulse, he walked with a little diffidence into the library next door.

He was afraid he was not wanted, but Gary smiled at him and sent his secretary away at once. ' I had just finished,' he said. ' Are you impatient? I hope you're going to dine with me, Louis.'

' No. I have too much to do this evening,' Earlham said. ' I had half an hour.' He hesitated. ' I thought you might care to know the latest news.'

' Well, sit down here,' said Gary. A servant came into the room and looked at him with that air of not looking. ' Sherry. Now, Louis, what's been decided? Do you know yet? '

' Yes,' Earlham said. ' We're going to accept the terms of the Samuel draft.'

' And press it on the miners? ' asked Gary.

Earlham stood up suddenly. He began to walk up and down the room, between the table and the bookcases.

' Don't you know that you ought to have cleaned up the mining industry after the War, before it came to a strike? You know that there are more greedy pig-headed backward owners in it than in any other. You know it's disorganised; you know that men are killed through negligence, dying with their lungs turned to stone, running ghastly risks for wages that make slaves of their women. You know that the industry will have to be reorganised from top to bottom if it is to survive. Why don't you do it? '

' Tell me one thing,' Gary said, smiling. ' Could your friend Mr. A. J. Cook reorganise the mines? '

' Probably not, but——'

'Do you yourself, Louis, believe in allowing one industry to take the law into its own hands? If the socialists were running the country could they afford to be dictated to by the miners, or the engineers or anyone else? Do you know that there is every prospect of serious trouble on the Tyne? But of course you do, and that is why—because there is a chance of something serious happening—your people are hurrying to make peace.'

For a moment Earlham did not know what to answer. 'We have been working hard for a settlement from the first day,' he said, weakly.

Gary did not look at him. He did not need to, to know that Earlham was at the end of his strength. This business has shocked him, he thought. He began to talk to him, persuasively, gently, with the affection he felt, but relentlessly pressing his advantage. His advantage was that he knew what he wanted. He knew, too, that his friendship was one thing Earlham would not give up; it was too pleasant, he had become used to it. 'I am certainly going to change the mining industry, and you, Louis, are going to help me to do it.'

'Very well,' Earlham said, 'but I must go now.'

'You won't change your mind and stay to dinner?'

'I can't, my dear fellow. I'm sorry. I'll ring you up later if there is more definite news.'

He looked at his watch when he left the flat. He had scarcely time to see Mrs. Harben before dinner, as he had promised. He decided to take a taxi to Davies Street. He had only been in her house twice before. It had not the indiscreet opulence of the flats from which he had come. A manservant showed him into the room on the right of the hall. He had been there only a few seconds when another servant came to take him upstairs to Mrs. Harben's own sitting-room. He walked up two flights of stairs, and crossed a landing on one wall of which hung a large painting by Matisse of three bulbous and naked women reclining on a glass-green mound, and four smaller friendlier Cézannes. He had never been invited into her sitting-room before. He felt pleased and nervous.

She was dressed in grey velvet open to the waist at the back; there were diamonds on her neck and shoulders and across her hair. Her full very white arms carried flat glittering bracelets. She was standing when he came in, and she came forward to greet him.

'How kind of you to come. I scarcely thought you would take any notice of my message. You must be very busy. But now please tell me what is going to happen. Ought I to go to Yorkshire to keep an eye on things there? You know that some of the Harben collieries are less than ten miles from the house.'

She always spoke, even when asking a question, as though no one were listening but herself. It was not bad manners, it was simply no manner at all. She assumed the complete equality, almost identity, of her listener with herself. Earlham had become used to this: he supposed it was an aristocratic trait and he enjoyed it. Rather, he enjoyed the fact that it did not disconcert him.

He told her what he had told Gary, only adding that he believed the miners' leaders would give way.

'I hope they will,' she said sternly. 'I should like to whip that man Cook with my own hands. And as for the Archbishop and the Churches, I feel their impudence ought to be punished in some way. How dare they interfere in the business of the State? Do you know it is monstrous. You could imagine we were living in the seventeenth century.'

Earlham was not anxious to defend the miners' leader or the Bishops from her. 'Your husband's miners are underpaid,' he said. He looked into her face as he said it, half prepared for her to turn him out.

She looked at him with the greatest kindness. 'My dear Mr. Earlham,' she said to him, 'you do not need to tell me that this age leaves much to be desired, for rich

and poor alike.   But neither, surely, do you of all men want
to improve it by pulling down everything that has taken
two hundred years to build up.   I have been into the houses
of miners, and while I should not know how to live in them,
I can assure you they are made very comfortable by the
women who do, and who would not know how to live in
mine.   One must keep a sense of proportion.   But you know,'
she went on, smiling, ' I respect your opinions.   Who knows
whether you will infect me with them before long ?   I would
do anything rather than lose your approval.   Anything except
become a socialist.   You will not ask me to do that, will
you ? '

There was an exquisite flattery for Earlham in hearing
her speak, even in jest, of respecting his opinion.   He felt
as though the couch on which he was sitting had become
more easy and proper to his back.   A gentle excitement seized
him.   There was a great deal he could teach her since she
was willing to learn; a vivid argument sprang in his mind.
But, alas, he had no time to begin it now.

Mrs. Harben rose: he knew, too, that he was expected
in Deptford.   Glancing round the room, he said to her:
' It is very peaceful here.   It makes me forget all I still
have to do to-night.'

' I am very glad,' Mrs. Harben said simply.   ' Please come
to see me when you can.   I shall enjoy talking to you.'

He took another taxi to Eccleston Square, where he hoped
to find a car or a motor-cycle going towards Deptford.   The
thought of the money he was spending made him restless and
dissatisfied with himself;   he felt that his life was becoming
disorganised.   Underneath this dissatisfaction, a secret excitement persisted when he thought of Mrs. Harben's fine
grey-clad figure and her words.   He had no idea of her age,
and he would have been surprised to hear that she had turned
fifty.   She was well cared-for.

At Headquarters he was able to pick up a small car going
to Maidstone: it dropped him near the Committee rooms at

eight o'clock. Directly he went in he was surrounded by workers eager for news. On this, the eighth evening of the Strike, a feeling of tenseness was barely covered by the other sense of being a drop in a human wave which was just lifting. It was the feeling in a company of men before an attack. Each man is vividly conscious of himself, of small things, a stain of oil on his sleeve, a chafed heel, the look of a trench in the half-light, and at the same time strangely and sharply aware of other lives pressing closely round his. The stolidity of Joe Bradford's temper was broken by little flashes of anger, irritation, excitement. When he saw Earlham come in, an hour later than he had promised to be there, he felt only a throb of anger and spite.

Earlham answered a dozen questions asked in one breath by making an informal speech. 'We're all in this together,' he said, smiling; 'it's the finest thing that has ever happened in the movement. We've only got to hold on to win!'

They came round him, one man shook his hand, someone shouted 'Good old Louis!' He saw their faces in the badly-lit room through a mist of affection. His heart yearned over these obscure willing workers, the latest of all the nameless, countless men and women who fought, starved, died, for the people. After all, they are my sort; this is where I belong, he thought, with a warm happiness. At the same moment he noticed the unpleasant stuffiness of the room. He went over to the window and began trying to open it more widely. It stuck. He tugged at it in vain. Joe Bradford came over to him, put his hands on the sash, and pretending to pull, asked in a whisper: 'Is it true that the muckers are running?'

'What do you mean?' Earlham asked. Looking at him with narrowed eyes and a sardonic smirk on his face, Joe said: 'Well, tell me this: is it a fact the miners weren't invited to the meetings with Herbert Samuel?' He said 'fact' as only a Yorkshireman can say it, like a smack on the cheek.

Earlham looked back at him with a steady gaze, detesting the cold ironic twinkle in the other man's eyes. ' It's certainly untrue,' he said. ' Nothing will be done without the full agreement of the miners.'

He had spoken more loudly than he meant. A man coming out of the other room answered him with a suddenness that gave him a violent shock. ' How d'you do, Roxby ? ' he said, trying to seem friendly.

' Surely that's not true,' Nicholas said hotly. ' I know for a fact that the Council is going to accept a compromise agreement.'

' There are quite a number of facts going the rounds now,' Earlham said, with a laugh. ' I should wait for confirmation before passing them on, if I were you.'

' I have a message for you from David Renn,' said Nicholas.

' Yes ? Where is he ? ' He looked vaguely round him.

' He's at home. He was knocked on the head yesterday evening: he'll be here to-morrow. He wants you to ring him up to-night with the latest news. Will you do that ? '

' Of course,' Earlham said. And he suddenly saw the narrow dark passage outside Renn's room with the telephone nailed to the wall at the far end of it, just outside his landlady's door, so that she could listen to every conversation her lodgers had. It was her sole luxury.

He glanced at his watch, and went out hurriedly, with a word about a non-existent meeting. He wanted to know what was going on. A desire to know minute by minute, not hours later and at secondhand, had seized him, and he went directly back to Headquarters. He found there tension sharpened by fatigue and suspense. One man to whom he spoke said that the lift had been dropping for so long now that his stomach was in his throat. Earlham stood about, talking, his ears alert for something to put an end to the torture of indecision he felt in himself. He heard a man say, in a strained voice, as though he had dust in his throat: ' It's no use talking about treachery.

What you've got to face is that every man jack of us is at war with every capitalist. And you don't win a war by giving your enemy so much ground every few months. What I want to know is, do the Trades Unions think they can get anywhere saving capitalism from all its messes by taking reduced wages? And where do they think they are getting? Tell me that.' Nonsense, thought Earlham. The sensible thing to do is to know when you're beaten and make the best of it, before you lose any more men. Working in a mine, he thought, has a curious effect on a man's mind; he begins to think there's nothing outside and above the mine except his own village.

He remembered a man in his company in France who was unearthed from the ruins of his dug-out, apparently dead. He was not dead, and for four days his battered body lay in the field-hospital where Earlham himself was being treated, while he kept up a feeble whimper like an infant's, which drove everyone near him crazy. They were all glad when he died. It must be like that in a mine, after an accident, he thought. He shuddered.

He heard a man say: 'I daresay that's true enough, but Samuel is a decent fellow: hasn't he been Governor of Palestine—he must be all right!' You can't negotiate with men like Cook and Herbert Smith, he thought: they can't see any moves ahead of their own share of the game.

At last he heard a definite statement. The Prime Minister expected to meet the Negotiating Committee that evening. And the miners' leaders had withdrawn to consider everything again. This seemed to him worth telling Gary, and he withdrew himself, to a telephone booth in the street.

He did not go back, but wandered about for a time. His thoughts, disjointed and drifting, drew him back to the War. The road was so familiar that he knew it better at night. He remembered watching Renn's face after he was wounded: he was lying against the side of the trench, waiting until dark. Renn's friend had thought he was dying because with every moment the hollows in his face deepened, as though the flesh were dissolving from the bones. He was more reasonable in those days, Earlham thought, painfully. More than anything else, men of reasonable mind are needed in the dangerous years ahead of us. He did not picture these dangers to himself very precisely, but he saw William Gary listening to him patiently and intently while he walked between the bookcases and the desk, setting out schemes which the two of them might carry out. All at once he felt that things were happening without him. He had walked farther than he meant. He turned and hurried back.

On the way he heard twelve o'clock strike. He felt very cold. He was in time to see the backs of the miners' leaders as they walked away. A queer anguish seized him as he watched them. That man (he was staring at the diminishing back of A. J. Cook) is honest, incorruptible, sincere. Calming himself, he thought, He has no ballast, he is no use at all as a leader; and perhaps he is a bit of an actor. That back— yes—he isn't so tired and dejected as that.

He asked the first man he saw for news. 'The miners have refused,' he was told. 'Then what?' 'The Strike's coming off to-morrow.' The first thought that seized him was a strange one. He wondered whether it was too late to telephone to Mrs. Harben. She had been going out to dinner; it might be she was still awake. He would risk it.

She had just come in. The strong clear note in her voice as she thanked him for the news sent a throb of pleasure and excitement through his body. When he left the place he stumbled, drunk with fatigue. A vast relief flooded his limbs. Thank God it's over, he thought; thank God. He passed his hand over his forehead. A group of men came towards him, talking in low voices, pickets from some works on their way home. He thought that one of them was Frank Rigden, and his mind gave a sudden jerk. As they passed under the lamp he saw he had been mistaken.

He remembered promising to telephone to David Renn.

No, I'm too done, he said. With thankfulness, he knew that Rachel would be waiting for him at home, waiting to hear good or bad news. She would give him a cup of something and he would go to bed, and sleep, sleep. Already as his feet carried him forward he was sleeping, his back in the curve of Rachel's body, warm, peaceful, safe.

CHAPTER XXIV

GARY had been alone for less than two minutes when his servant told him that Mr. Thomas Harben was downstairs, asking to see him. ' Let them bring him up,' Gary said.

He stood, his head bent, listening to the voice of his servant at the telephone. Life in this block of flats was too much like the nightmare of a film picture of the future—layer on layer of sound-proofed rooms separated by the long warm corridors, light glowing in them from invisible sources, lifts panelled in walnut moving between them, wires piercing the floors and walls like the nerves of a body, dining-rooms on the scale of a Grand Hotel, the waiters looking like diplomats, the gleaming floor of the ball-room, white and green glass pillars and walls of the swimming pool, enclosed, all of it, in a monstrous scaffolding of steel and concrete. Gary sickened of it in this moment of waiting while his servant and the operator downstairs in the panelled room behind the post office spoke to each other. He decided to buy a house in London, and perhaps one in Scotland.

He did not invite Harben to stay to dinner, although he knew, with that quickness he was learning, that the older man hoped to be invited. His feelings for Thomas Harben had passed through respect, diffidence, and dislike, to a complete neutrality. The man had become submerged in his possessions. It depended on what they were talking about whether Gary saw him at the moment as a score of ship-yards, or mines, or factory chimneys, or only as an entry in a banking account.

Harben had come ostensibly to speak to him about the leakage of information in Garton's.

'It could perhaps,' Gary said, 'be a secretary of mine, a man called Renn. I sacked him a week ago.'

'Ha. I told you when you took him on that he was unreliable. You'd have done better to get rid of him before.'

'If you had told me on your own knowledge,' Gary said, smiling. 'You had only Julian Swan's word for it at the time.'

'What's your dislike of Swan?'

Gary lifted his hands. 'I scarcely know,' he said quietly. 'He's overbearing—without the weight for it. Boasts. Talks nonsense about a dictatorship, as if talking about it were the road to get your way in this country. The man's a complete fool. No, not a fool, an actor.'

'He does his work,' Harben grunted. 'I didn't come to talk about him. This—thing—' he looked at the newspaper-cutting in his hand—'can be checked. Ought to be. I suggest that Garton's pays a small dividend on its ordinary shares this year.'

'From what?'

'Naturally, from the undisclosed reserve.'

'I don't agree with you,' Gary said. He felt a malicious joy in disagreeing—since he held only debenture shares in Garton's. These yielded their seven per cent. in any case, where Thomas Harben had a vast holding of ordinary shares— his own and those he bought from Mary Hervey when he took the firm from that grasping and domineering old woman. 'We should go on taking heavy account of depreciation and reserves, and pass the ordinary dividend again. It's prepos-terous to base a change of policy on a newspaper comment!'

Thomas Harben was silent. In an obscure way he was uneasy. He felt suddenly that it was important for him to assert his will against the younger man's. His face sunk into lines of grim arrogance. When he spoke he spoke in a rasping voice as if to a subordinate who was giving trouble. It vexed him that he had less than Mary Hervey's grasp on the firm, that he needed an ally. And there was something more in his mind than the cloud of anger which had risen in it; something which was almost panic.

When Gary persisted, he lost his temper. ' My experience in these things,' he shouted. His breath caught in his throat and he began to cough, his neck swelling with the effort.

' If you're going to put it on grounds of your experience,' Gary said gently, ' I give way at once. I'll support you in that sense at the board meeting.'

Harben felt no satisfaction in his victory, only a vague discomfort and uncertainty. On his way downstairs this expressed itself in another form, and when he reached the hall he asked the lift attendant to show him to the lavatory. Hurrying there, he found that he had mistaken his sensations and so departed, his bowels still full of dissatisfaction and anger.

Gary hastened his dinner because he expected Nicholas to come in time for coffee. He had asked him to stay in the flat while Hervey was in hospital, and Nicholas had refused. Gary said gently: ' I expect you to dine with me as often as you can.' ' I shall be working late,' Nicholas answered. ' Come in after dinner, then,' Gary said.

At nine o'clock Nicholas came. In the first moment Gary saw that it was a mistake to go on inviting him. Of their friendship a single bone remained, like the bone turned up in his fields by a Somme peasant. There was a lifetime of pain in it. Rather there was a double time, the one in which thoughts of doing without his friend could not have entered his mind; and this, in which he was seated with a stranger whom he had loved.

He knew this stranger too intimately. Nicholas's stubborn and rigid temper had a vein of weakness. Rather than give himself trouble, he would avoid his friend as often as he could, until the past, in which they knew one another so well that if one were asked a question the other answered, would be as meaningless as the present. He felt how reluctant Nicholas had been to come to-night: but he was not yet willing to give up.

Nicholas sat down. He looked round the room with a slight smile, and his eyebrows went up. ' You've bought a devil of a lot of things,' he said.

' You should come oftener.'

' No, this place is too much of a good thing,' Nicholas mocked. ' It's more suitable for a film star than a captain of industry; it reminds me of the time I was sent to Corps Headquarters and when I'd waited an hour in a corner a terrifying old gentleman approached me and said, " Why—why—you've—got—*mud*—on your boots." '

' Never mind that,' Gary said. ' How is Hervey? '

' She came through it all right. She was still sleeping off the anæsthetic when I rang up just now,' Nicholas said. He frowned nervously.

Noticing it, Gary changed the subject—not for the better, since they were forced to talk about the Strike. Nicholas said it would be a damned disgrace if the men were defeated. ' You and your cursed mines,' he said; ' you've had a fortune out of them and you think you'll squeeze another, if you can get out of your obligations to society and to the men who provide the coal for the miserable wages you pay them.'

' So you approve of general strikes,' Gary said, smiling.

' I know that men don't strike for nothing,' Nicholas said.

He spoke with so much vehemence that Gary was irritated. Is there any need to speak as though I were responsible for the wretched business? The tension was becoming difficult when his secretary came in to ask him if he would speak to Mr. Earlham, who had telephoned.

So that is one of his sources of information, thought Nicholas. Gary made no secret of it when he came back. ' The miners' leaders are considering whether they'll call it off.'

'That means the others have let them down.'

'Listen, Nick,' Gary said, in his slowest voice, 'what would you have felt if the Strike had gone on until the country was disorganised, the food supplies interfered with, and your wife starving in her nursing home?'

'Of course I should want someone to hang,' Nicholas retorted, 'but it would be you and Thomas Harben, not the miners.'

'Oh, you're a reasoner!' exclaimed Gary.

'My reason tells me,' said Nicholas, 'that you can't solve a major crisis by shooting or starving the victims.'

'You've been converted to the fatuous notion that enthusiasm can do away with economics. God knows what company you keep nowadays, Nick.' He spoke sadly, because he felt such a detestation of Nicholas's thoughts that it roused the other feeling in him. He felt the strange impotent anguish of a dream in which the person whom you love is injuring or mocking you and nothing you can do or say moves him from his pitiless cruelty. The violence of the feeling did not reach his mind; it was sunk below that and he felt it in the joints of his wrists and knees and in his tongue. He saw Hervey's finger-marks everywhere on his friend. Why doesn't she die, he thought.

'Let me give you some more brandy,' he said, to destroy the abstracted look on Nicholas's face. It irritated him now that he did not know what Nicholas was thinking.

Smiling, Nicholas pushed the glass across the table. When he had drunk a great deal he relaxed, the lines on his face smoothed themselves away, he looked younger and less nervous. If I had money, he thought, I should probably do nothing; I should read and stroll about the world. For the first time in their lives he felt himself able to argue Gary down: in the past it had been the other way about, Gary had said: 'Come along, time to go,' and he had obediently followed. But no, he said, strongly and suddenly, I couldn't do nothing: I want to learn, my God, how I want to learn; I've wasted half my life, and done nothing.

'What are your own notions?' he exclaimed. 'What are you trying to have in this life you've chosen? If you had told me, only four years ago, that you were going this road, I should have laughed.'

'What could I do?' Gary said mildly. 'Grow fat on my *rentes*? I can't even found a family.'

Nicholas held himself deliberately quiet, so that his face could show nothing he felt. The truth was he felt like weeping, but it was not only for Gary, it was for what both of them had lost or been cheated of.

'But you must have some idea of what you want,' he said at last. 'Not only for yourself, for the rest of us. You're not making yourself powerful for the sake of becoming richer—not if I know you, Bill.'

'Ah, but do you?' Gary said.

'Better than I know anyone.' Better, he thought, than I shall ever know anyone again.

'Well, I can talk to you,' Gary said. 'I can't talk to anyone else without a motive. I wonder how long you will care to go on listening. I should like to have authority to scour this nation from head to foot: I want to feed hungry children, tear down slums, clean the country of the foul eczema that disfigures it, give every woman security and every man his place in society. Most men are incredibly stupid and some are wicked. They don't know what is good for them. But if you can give it to them, all— except the few incorrigible rogues—will be happy. What they want, perhaps without knowing it, is to obey. They want to obey some power that they can accept with the same trust and confidence each felt when he was a child for his mother. Or for a kind nurse,' he added, with a sharp smile, as if he had remembered his own mother: from the time he could stand alone she lost no chance he gave her to humiliate him and make him ridiculous. 'They don't any of them want to think. In fact, they're not capable of it. Security and obedience. A kindly power which sees them into the world, looks after them as long as they are alive, and lets them die in comfort. What more do they want? Freedom? An east wind in the belly, Nick. Bellies were made to be filled with food and kept decently muscular. It's only when men are unhappy that they begin to talk of freedom. Even then the idea has to be put into them from above, by intellectuals who for one reason or another are discontented with their lives. Don't run away with the idea that I want to shoot your dear Labour leaders and the T.U.C. My way would be to bargain with them. Make them dispensers of food and jobs and responsible for law and order. State middlemen. Nothing like setting a servant over servants. Quartermaster-sergeants.'

' All of them rogues,' Nicholas exclaimed.

' I wouldn't tolerate bullying.'

' You've described a nation of slaves,' Nicholas said, hotly.

' What's in a name? If you could to-night ask every man in the country what he most wanted you'd be deafened by the same answer from millions. *Not to have to worry.*'

' You can't know anything about men until you give each child the same upbringing—from blankets and nurseries to schools, food, riding, dancing, swimming pools, everything alike.'

' And how will you do that?' Gary said, ironically. ' Only by the exercise of the most absolute authority. Give me the power and the authority and *I* could do it. But I should want first of all obedience. Well-trained children do as they are told.'

Nicholas sat up stiffly in his chair, rigid with excitement. ' You're talking about something which is dead,' he stammered. ' You can't treat living human beings that way. If you stop people growing freely—if you want them to be *this* man and no other, from the day they are born to the day they die—even humanity itself will decay. Man will die from the earth.'

' I'm not interested in mysticism,' Gary said coldly.

' But what you've been saying is the most perverse, poisonous mysticism I ever listened to. Are you going to be the Emperor of the World? I suppose if you find it necessary, for your own sake, for the sake of power, to have a war, you will have one. My God, have you forgotten what it was like? ' Nicholas said quietly. ' I haven't forgotten that you put a bullet through that boy's head after you'd sent for stretcher-bearers—to put him out of it. I should think we'd had enough.'

' Keep your temper, Nick,' Gary advised him. ' Some things are worse than a war. Hanging yourself at nineteen because you can't find work is worse.'

' Or joining the other pretty soldiers in your ant State. I suppose you'll have ant mothers, too, instructed to give birth to so many children, neither more nor less. Shall you expose the females if you get too many? '

' Don't be an ass,' Gary said. ' You don't think the world now is such a pleasant place for young men or mothers? '

' No,' Nicholas said. ' Nor will your Slave state be pleasant. The slaves will poison you with their slavishness; it will rise up like a foul smell from the comfortable houses you give them. The smell of their slave thoughts and feelings, their slave tastes. Don't ask me to live with my nose near it, Bill. I'll find an uninhabited island somewhere and grow my own potatoes.'

' I see I shall have either to banish you or have you shot,' laughed Gary. His hands jerked suddenly.

' May I have some more of your very good brandy,' Nicholas said, after a moment.

Gary pushed the tray across the table. ' You know, even free men can hate each other,' he said gently. ' If you take away all injustice, where can they rid themselves of their burden of hate? My way is the right way. Look after them, keep them in order—and let them fight other nations instead of you or each other.'

'What becomes of their souls?'

'Go and talk to my miners about their souls,' smiled Gary.

'Your miners are men,' Nicholas said. He relapsed into silence, his body warmed and soothed by the brandy; his mind alert, glowing with a fine flame. I shan't last, he thought, with Cohen; not my dish at all. I shall quarrel with him. Time, too, I found my place; I'm too late about it, too slow and diffident, I can't afford more mistakes. You wanted to write about the War, didn't you? Why not? Good God, how ignorant I am. Hervey said she wanted to write one book, an image of the world we live in, the young man hanging himself; the poor woman—in poverty, in a poor cold room she gave birth, the husband and her other children listening to it through the thin walls; the young boys they sent out in 1918, one was crying afterwards in fear of his pain, *Mother, mother, do come. Mother.* By-products of our civilisation, like the black damp choking men in the mines. For whose sake? A civilisation in which men are sentenced to live poor deathly lives without any of the human satisfactions. They choke quickly with the gas underground, or slowly in the air itself when their lungs petrify with dust. Should I think about it if I lived in this place, with liberty to buy all the books I wanted?

He stood up and walked across the room to look at a painting by Van Gogh. 'I have always wanted to own one picture of his,' he said. 'Only one. You can have all the rest. Did this cost very much, Bill?'

'Eight hundred pounds.'

'Is spending money your only hobby now?' Nicholas said.

'No,' Gary answered calmly. 'I fence, swim, box. I have begun to learn ju-jitsu.'

Nicholas gave a shout of laughter. He saw that Gary was vexed or wounded, but he could not control himself at once. There was something indescribably comic in the vision of his big, heavily-built friend practising ju-jitsu—his mind rocked with laughter.

'Show me,' he stuttered, making an effort to speak seriously.

Gary walked up to him swiftly and took hold of him with both hands. 'Now move,' he said softly, 'and you'll break your arm. If I knew how to break your neck I might easily do that.'

He released him at once, but stood still for a moment with his hands bent back, the fingers parted. He could seize hold of Nicholas's body again instantly. His sight darkened, and he had a curious sensation in his brain, as though his blood had become incandescent and exploded in the darkness inside his skull. The tension relaxed and he moved away. Nicholas, who had been looking at him, let his head sink forward and walked slowly to his chair.

'Do you remember that night we came back to Haze-brouck?' he said absently. 'It was dark as pitch, so quiet we felt uneasy. You wondered whether we should find that someone had let loose a new gas and choked every man on both sides.'

'Not a bad idea for next time,' Gary said. He added: 'Yes, it was quiet. I remember it very well.'

'And the next day you were sent off on a course and I had to stay and cope with that ass Jenkins.'

Gary laughed. 'By God, he was an ass. Poor little brute, too. After you left in March he ordered a pair of braces in the Old Carthusian colours to be sent out to him. He insisted on wearing them to go over the top at Ypres. I said to him, I suppose you do it so that God won't make a mistake and forget to put you with the Weekites.'

Nicholas threw himself back in his chair, smiling. The smile stayed on his lips for a minute. For just so long the relation between them was complete and perfect, as it had been in the past and would not be in the future, whatever effort either of them made, and whatever either would have given to keep things as they were for the rest of their lives.

CHAPTER XXV

HERVEY lay on her bed, propped by canvas straps into a half-sitting posture. Her head lolled: she was unconscious. She sat or lay like this for seven hours after she was carried to her room from the theatre. During part at least of this time her mind was conscious.

She was aware at first of an awful and unbearable loneliness. There are no words with which to convey this loneliness. Though it reached the point of annihilation, it did not annihilate the agonised tissue which felt it. It pressed on the marrow of the brain for centuries, which passed slowly, stripping off one and then another imperceptible covering from the marrow, so that with each century it seemed to become more sensitive to the agony it endured. There seemed at times to be a thin thread of this sentient brain marrow and again only a speck, but it *knew* its anguish. In its awful isolation changes took place in it; it seemed to grow larger and to multiply, with an inconceivable slowness and with murderous effort. It grew by dying. It died death after death in unspeakable fear. The time came when it seemed to have a double consciousness; one part of it was extended in space as though it were the bony skeleton of the firmament, so brittle that it could not endure a breath or the lightest touch of a finger; the other moved along one fragment of this skeleton, moving infinitely slowly, with a weariness for which there are not any words, not one.

This journey had been going on for so long that there could be no such alleviation as time; yet again, after age had followed age, a change began. The speck began to think. It thought of itself as a woman, and the woman discovered at last that the bony ridge over which, with pain, effort, and exhaustion, she was toiling, was a jaw-bone of the skeleton. There was no light in this universe to which she had been condemned, and from which she knew, yes, knew, there was no escape. She knew, too, that she had always been in this place, that there was nothing else, only this endless journey. And that it was meaningless. There was nothing accomplished by it, no being to whom it had any meaning at all.

The knowledge that she was living in a meaningless universe persisted through every change that took place in her. It persisted under the words in which her thoughts began slowly to clothe themselves. She had a new sense of danger, she thought she was irresistibly drawn in the darkness to the verge of a pit into which she must fall. The words 'prisons of earth' formed themselves in her brain. When at last she fell she became conscious that she had a body. For an infinity of time she had been pain, now the pain became a body, hers. She struggled along the galleries of a mine, *knowing* that the one in which she was caught would narrow gradually until she was squeezed between the walls in a last agony of bone and blood. She saw the walls heave. She began to choke for breath and it seemed that she must burst her lungs or throat in this struggle and she felt the horror of the earth crushing her. She was blotted out.

Consciousness returned to the speck of brain tissue, it became aware of its unbearable loneliness, it grew and multiplied, it became a universe of dead yet sentient bone, and a woman moving with unutterable pain towards her end in the mine. This took place for age after successive age.

Another change. The woman, in her travail, felt that curious sensation as though a shiver passed down the spine, that anguished sharpening of the senses, which comes with the perception of beauty. The universe and her body with it were dissolving into a succession of sounds, persistent rhythms as sharp and steely as knives, a glittering web which filled the whole of space. Naked and implacable, the music separated out each nerve of her body from the next; she in her own body became an anatomy of music, and the music an exquisite pain played in her and through her and through the vast womb of space, unbearable, unendurable, endured.

It was followed by a moment of peace. In this moment she lay as an infant in a cocoon of warmth, light, and darkness; she became a child, she saw a white blazing flower, the shining edge of the sea, she touched with pleasure the satin stripes of a wallpaper, her body, her mother's finger, she took a knife in her hand to kill someone, she stood in the odorous darkness formed by the branches round her of a tree of may and flew upwards until her head struck the point of heaven; she was a girl ashamed of her body, she knew lust, grief, ecstasy, she held on with bloodied fingers to a stone on which men were pressing to thrust her away; at long last she was an old woman, creeping over the earth. Here the words were simpler than they had been. *Man goeth to his long home and the mourners go about the streets.* She slept in the calm earth. As she lay there her body became the earth of Danesacre itself; it bore the delicate roots of the grass, the stones sunk in the clay, the grey foundations of the church, the old strong small houses thrust down into the cliff side between the church and the harbour; it heard the sea and the crying of gulls.

But the earth pressed the marrow forth from her bones, and it lay exposed; it felt the everlasting horror of its loneliness in a universe without meaning; it grew through ages to become a woman.

Now for the first time in its growth it became aware of time. It pondered over its thought of time, until time became the fine edge of a knife which slowly and lingeringly severed the nerve stretched tightly across it. It took an

endless time to do this, and other nerves grew alongside the
first one, stretched in the form of a crucifix, and then of a
woman.   And now the woman knew who she was as she
travelled with her burden of exhaustion and pain to a place
where she was in a room so darkened, and her sight un-
focused, that she could not see walls, floor, or ceiling.
Two men in the room with her tortured her by striking
on the same place in her head with hammers; one took
a long hatpin and made to stick it through the sore place;
she reached up her arm and broke the pin in half: he
laughed and thrust through the broken half, so that she
died.   She had to go through this so many many times, but
at last she fell away: she lay naked to all the cruelty which
had been in the world from the beginning until this moment
in which she knew herself.   She was sickened by the reality
of cruelty.   A trail of loathsome slime lay over the whole
history of man.   That speck in her brain with which alone
she was conscious was again a speck of naked pain; the
burnings, the floggings, disembowellings, flayings, piecemeal
and obscene killings of human creatures by each other,
pressed and crushed it.   She cried out against her loneliness,
and her cries were as unavailing as the cries of men have
always been.

Now her journey was no longer endlessly forward: it
seemed she must drag herself upward by a path which
turned perpetually, yet seemed turning within herself in a
descending spiral of light and agony.   Suddenly at one turn
she came face to face with her brother who had been killed
in the War; he passed her, his hands outstretched, without looking at her.   She was conscious for a fleeting second
of the room in which she was lying.   The figure of a
woman bending over something she held in her hands filled
her with terror.   Then for a moment, which might have
been a year or many years, she felt that she was suspended in
a dark red whirling flood, and she thought, This is my death.

She awoke, and saw the nurse at the far end of the room.

The room was almost dark. She kept still, unaware of the faint sound that passed her lips. The woman came towards her and bent over the bed. ' Are you awake? ' she asked.

' Time,' Hervey managed to say.

' After nine o'clock.' She went away and came back with a very small lamp, so feeble that it must have been only a night-light with a glass round it. She set this down on the table beside the bed, and went out again, leaving the door half open on to the passage. In the minute she was alone Hervey realised that she was sitting, not lying, in the bed, and was seized with sickness. Still only half conscious she thought she would be punished if she were sick in bed, and stretched her arm towards the small bowl beside the lamp.

The movement seemed to tear open her body. She whimpered and the nurse came back into the room quickly. ' There,' she said, ' I only leave you for a minute, and you haven't been sick until now.'

' I promise—not again,' Hervey said.

She was as good as her promise. The nurse stayed with her. She kept her eyes open, fixing them on the square of the doorway, which was outlined by a thread of light. The pain in her body was shocking, but it seemed to her that it was more easily bearable than the experience she had passed through. At first she held herself apart from it in fear. She clung to words. . . . *nox est perpetua una dormienda.*

But it was a lie. She had endured an endless night but it was not endless sleep. It was pain, and it meant nothing. She felt set apart by her knowledge. She could not believe she was the only person to whom the experience had happened, and supposed that she would forget it soon.

If I could sleep, she thought. Her watch was lying on the table in the circle of light thrown by the lamp; she stared at it until the face widened and swelled, and she read the figures. It was five minutes to ten. She closed her eyes and sank into a half-dozing state until the pain woke her.

At least some of this night has passed, she said to herself: until looking at her watch again she saw that it was barely ten. She lay still and endured. Again she wondered whether she was dying, but she was ashamed to ask the nurse.

Once or twice the nurse spoke to her, in a soft sing-song voice. She was Welsh. She called Hervey, 'Poor rabbit,' when a groan had forced its way from her. She told her the surgeon had forbidden them to give her morphia.

'But why?' Hervey whispered.

'She said she didn't think you ought to have it. I'm sure I'm sorry. I would give you something, I would indeed, if I could.'

'Never mind,' Hervey said.

She tried to remember her mother's first house in Danesacre, the one where she had been a child. Passing slowly from room to room, she recalled that the window of the kitchen had looked on to a yard through a wicker blind, and her mind dwelt lovingly on this blind. She had never seen one like it, it was of a sort no longer made. It seemed to her that her mother had made a grave mistake in not taking it with her to the new house. She went up to her own room in the house, and lay down on the bed near the wall. Lifting her head she could see across the upper harbour to the shipyard. A gull from the harbour passed the window, flying strongly, she saw the light through his webbed feet held far out behind him. She rose and went into the small dark room at the back which had been her brother's as an infant and a child. His bed was under the window, and he lay in it in sound heavy sleep; the hands which she had last seen stretched out in front of him were here clasped close and red within the curve of his body.

The pain wrenched her, and she opened her eyes. The nurse had seated herself near the lamp and was reading a letter that she had taken out of the pocket of her apron.

In the feeble light she peered at the words and her lips moved slightly. It was now close on eleven.

This night will never come to an end, thought Hervey. For a time she was concentrated on enduring without a sound. The minutes passed with cruel slowness. She dozed for another five minutes and the nurse pulled the blanket up over her arms. But this reminded her of the time when she was lying quietly in the earth. She was conscious of other and more sombre experiences. For the rest of the night she lay with her eyes open. She felt that she had been altered by the experience, as though some part of her had died of what it could not endure.

The light came with such slowness as she had never known light to come. She asked the nurse to draw the curtains, and sat watching the shadowy square of the window. The changes came imperceptibly, but they came, as light filtered through the greyness and touched the leaves of a tree in the garden to a living green and roused a bird to begin crying shrilly beneath the window. This sound was the first that made her know she was alive.

By now the light of the small lamp was extinguished. She could see everything in the room; the light caught the edge of a brass rail so that it gleamed as though the sun had touched it. The sun was still a short way below the outer rim of the earth. When at last it stretched upward the light changed once again: the leaves of the tree, the rail, all the things in the room, became rounder and more solid, so that they seemed to stand against a current of light whirling about them as sharply and strongly as water.

Hervey listened to the awakening sounds in the house, a door opening, footsteps, a voice somewhere that complained softly, ceased, began again. The nurse prepared her for the day. Hervey tried to smile at her, but the slightest movement of her body seemed to tear open freshly the wound which ran downwards from the navel.

' Do you know what you did when we were putting you

into bed yesterday afternoon?' the nurse said. 'You fought and struggled, we had to bring in a third nurse to help us to hold you. The Sister was afraid you would open the wound. To think you could struggle so! You kept on saying: "I must go home now, I must go home." We had as much as we could do to quiet you. My, you are strong!'

Wednesday, May 12*th*
A FAMOUS VICTORY

CHAPTER XXVI

EARLHAM believed that with the end of the Strike all the people who had taken part in it would go back to the point before the Strike started, and set out afresh. He imagined that no one, and not even himself, had learned anything from having been defeated or victorious. He believed that a leader who has made his surrender to the other side in a speech of incredible emptiness is not thereafter ashamed of it and anxious to wipe out its memory by making bold and heroic gestures against defaulters on his own side; he believed that a politician who manages to win a battle with the sublime words, ' You know my record,' will not use them again; he believed that he himself had not laid aside the last vestiges of his honesty, and that weakness, confusion, and moral blindness become strength and clear sight by simply changing their names in a report. In short, he had no idea, when he woke up on the morning of May the 12th, 1926, that another stage in a journey had been reached and passed. That even his own life, which he believed to be under his control, had been diverted on to quite different lines than the ones he supposed himself to be following with all the ardour of a high-minded crusader.

At eight o'clock that morning David Renn awoke from his first sleep—he went to bed towards five—he remembered only then that Louis had not telephoned to him the evening before. He got up, put his overcoat on over his pyjamas, and went out into the passage to the telephone. As he asked for Earlham's number he heard his landlady creeping towards the

297

door of her room to listen. She was fortunately too deaf to catch more than a word or two.

Earlham told him that the Strike was as good as over. ' Do you mean the mine-owners have offered terms which the miners are ready to accept? ' Renn asked.

' Not exactly that,' answered Earlham. ' There is a memorandum drawn up and agreed to——'

' Agreed by whom? '

' By the General Council,' Earlham said, with impatience.

' And the terms? '

Renn listened carefully. He was barefooted and the linoleum where he stood had worn through to the boards: it reminded him of the stairs leading to the attic where he slept when he was a child. The whole time Earlham was speaking, he imagined himself on these stairs and smelled the dry musty scent of the old walls and the sage and thyme his mother dried in bunches fastened to the beams. His father, for whom he had no liking, used to shut him on to this dark staircase as a punishment. Part of the child's outraged and helpless bitterness found its way out in the bitterness he felt now. Suddenly he interrupted Earlham's quietly-uttered phrases.

' But what have, actually, you got? Tell me that. You say that Samuel has no authority from the Government. Whose promises are you relying on? Who are you believing with such mildness that you accept wage cuts on the miners' behalf? Have you forgotten that the miners are locked-out? Do you mean to tell me that you have made terms before the lock-out notices are withdrawn? '

' The Council is assuming they will be withdrawn,' Earlham said.

' Assuming? assuming? Did Judas Iscariot assume that Christ would get off with a fine? '

' You don't know what you're talking about.'

' I know,' Renn said, coldly, ' that from the moment this thing started you have done nothing except wring your hands and try to settle it before they moved your cushion away and the saucer of cream. But why? That's what I don't understand yet. Why? why?'

'I suppose,' the other said, 'you'd advise waiting until the unions are starved out before making terms? To the last man and the last ha'penny—you weren't always of such bloody mind!'

Renn was exasperated by the distant voice, as though, coming from the man he had trusted and admired better than any other, it injured both of them. 'So you assumed defeat, too? Upon my word, before night, I should say before cockcrow, you will assume that the Council has played an honourable, courageous, and dignified part in breaking the Strike a few days before the other side would have been forced to make peace. I daresay that is what you were afraid of.'

'You're talking the most complete nonsense,' Earlham said. 'I can't stand here listening to it; I have far too much to do.'

He cut Renn off before he could answer. Renn stood for a moment in the passage, his feet pressing the gritty surface of the boards. He heard the woman at the other side of the door near him breathing too loudly with excitement. She has forgotten that the doors in this house of hers are full of cracks, he thought. He went back to his room, made himself coffee, and as soon as he had swallowed it he went out.

He did not go to the Committee rooms until two o'clock. And in the meantime Joe Bradford and five of the others had been at work since eight. Joe was in good spirits. He had been sent, by a friend in that town, the copy of a report from Lincoln, and he was reading under his breath the names of one union after another, some new, some old, their names the thread which bound them to men and women long dead without having seen the promise. 'And if there are any,' he read, 'I have not reported in this list, they also responded a hundred per cent.'

A man came over to him from the table (it was a small scrubbed table borrowed from a scullery, and there was still a nutmeg and a piece of string in the drawer) at which the Finance Committee sat and did its difficult work. He held out to Joe's eyes a half-sheet of paper. On it were pinned a few stamps. The sender of them had written: ' I send these towards the fund for the general Strike and if God wills it will be successful, from an unemployed builder. No more stamps to hand at present, but will send more next week.'

' That's the spirit,' Joe said. He added: ' Poor devil,' before he turned to speak to a man who had just come in. This was the engineer from yesterday's deputation. Joe stared at him reflectively.

' So you came out after all,' he said. ' How many of you did you say there was, eh ? '

' Eight,' the man said.

' That's right. Eight. And you're in Stokes Chemical Works. Is it your Strike pay you've come about ? '

' No,' the man said. ' I've come to see if there's aught I can do——' He was still speaking when Renn came into the room, and he stepped back to allow him to approach Joe's desk.

Renn bent over it, as though he were going to speak into Joe's ear, but he spoke to everyone in the room.

He told them shortly that the Strike was over. On his way he had been turning over in his mind everything Louis Earlham had said to him, and everything he had been able to learn about the meeting that morning between the Prime Minister and the leaders of the Council.

He had wanted to be quite certain that he was not making some mistake. He did not want to believe that the Council had surrendered; that in return for receiving a memorandum empty of authority they had ended the Strike without secure guarantee for all the workers who had obeyed loyally their order to strike. He did not want to believe this any more than he wanted to come here and tell the men with whom he had been working that they had been given away.

Their leaders were scrupulously generous; they had asked nothing in return.

The men came round him, and asked a few slow questions. 'Nay, I *can't* believe it,' one said.

'You'd best,' Renn answered.

'We've been twisted,' a man said, furiously. 'Don't take any notice of it, I say. If it's true they haven't made conditions, I mean if th' miners is still out and our jobs not promised us safe and secure, written down and the names to it, like it should be, if it's been done like that, I say we ought to stay out until they come to their senses.'

He had just ceased speaking as a boy who was selling Renn's Bulletin about the streets marched below the open window. This, too, was the moment he chose to shout at the top of his voice, reading from the first line of an article, the words, '*Victory in sight*.' Joe Bradford began mechanically to read through a copy of the previous day's official newspaper. He was searching in it for some warning he might have missed. But under the date of the evening before, Tuesday evening, May 11, he read only: '*No Slackening*'; '*Engineers stop to-day*'; and over the signatures of two of the leaders he read four times the words: '*Hold fast. We must see the miners through.*'

With anger, he tore the paper in half and threw it into the street. It was the top copy of a pile that had come in only that morning, to be distributed. He turned to a man and said to him:

'Here, take these t'Headquarters and throw them into the first swine's face you see.' The man took them, but Joe called him back before he reached the door. 'No, save your boot-leather, man,' he shouted. 'I said, *save* it.'

He sat back in his chair, the sweat pricking his body, and let the others talk.

It was queer what they said, as though something spoke in each man which was younger and older than the man himself, or as if the body spoke, remembering its long life of days.

'It smelled too much of the T.U.C. cut.' 'I say all out, all in together, and go back as we come out, solid.' 'I told the missus it was nobbut an argle-bargle between masters—we're *nothing*, I said.' 'We may look to ourselves after this.' 'T'hell with the lot of them, Joe, I say—I say, Joe, t'hell, are they going to see us right or aren't they, eh, d'y'know?' 'They can't blame us this time, we done what we could.'

Henry Smith came in. Hearing him at the door, every man turned sharply with the hope that he had come to tell them it was a mistake. He had imagination, and the expectance and sudden hope on their faces turned to him was too much. The young man turned very red, and sat down without speaking to them. He had come thinking to be the first with the news. He saw Renn nodding to him and his tongue was loosed.

'I see you've heard the story of the Premier and the Eight Pretty Men,' he jeered. 'I don't know were they only eight. They all marched in and they all marched out again. One of them did just mention there were a lot of men on strike would like to have their jobs back if it might graciously be allowed, and the little matter of the locked-out miners and all. The others licked their way round both boots and crawled out backwards. So I'm told. And the Prime Minister, God bless him, said he would try to make this country a better and a happier place. Damn it, he went further—he said no stone would be left unturned. The one he turned up this morning before lunch had a lot of Labour leaders and trades union secretaries clinging to the underneath. By God it had!'

'Let be, Harry,' Renn said.

'Talk of that sort's no use,' Joe said. He looked at the excited young man shrewdly, with hard eyes.

'Then you tell me what is of use,' Smith said quietly. 'If half of it's true, the miners have nothing to thank us for.'

'Thanks can be paid where they're due,' Joe said briefly. 'Th' miners aren't the only ones in this.'

He drove them all away from his desk. He still had his work to do; in no time men would be coming to him for instructions and advice, with complaints, with faith that he could get them out of the trap in which they were caught. Suddenly he remembered the eight engineers. There was not a thread of hope that the Stokes Works would take back eight union men out of that number. They had, you might say, committed suicide.

Lifting his head, he saw the man who had come to him. He was leaning against the wall a little apart from the others, his face raised, his eyes looking at God knows what: they were guarded and steady—a wall of earth rose at Joe Bradford's back, he had earth and boards below his feet; the man at whose side he had paused for a moment answered keeping his eyes on the waste land in front of him: 'Yes, sar'nt, right y'are, sar'nt.'

Joe brought his hand down on the littered desk, with a sound that made the man look at him. He looked at Joe for a minute, and half smiled. Then he went away.

But God curse them, Joe thought, they must have *known* yesterday, when they called the engineers out, that this was going to happen. Why did they do it? He had never had such thoughts as were stirring in his mind: likely he never would again.

He felt an impulse to take the engineer with him to the room where the Council deliberated. He would show the man to them, and say: '*What evil has this man done?*' His eyes, small, pale, cold, blazed. The blaze was momentary, but in it a man was consumed. When he came to himself he went on with his work.

Renn had drawn Henry Smith into the inner room. Smith had later news. 'They are saying the Government meant to seize the Union funds and arrest every man of the leaders.'

'I don't believe it,' Renn said drily.

'No, nor I. But if they'd done it, we'd been better off with them safely in jail. They could have yearned there for a peaceful settlement and shivered at the precipices surrounding them, without ruining the rest of us.' He laughed, with a sudden passion. 'I know what I'm going to do for the future. I've been working fourteen hours a day, I'll work twenty, until my throat splits. They shan't turn me out of the Party, though. E-eh, I'll be as cunning as a mole.'

His friend smiled. 'This does you credit,' he said, with quick malice. He felt better for it.

Through the open door he caught sight of a man who had just come in. He listened with an air of bewilderment. It was as though a hand wiped any expression from his face. It became blank, except for a look of extreme patience. This look was, it seemed, in the bones themselves.

The man moved slowly towards Joe's desk and stood there. The secretary looked up at him impatiently. 'Ah, it's you,' he said.

'I've got to go home and tell Sally about it, see?' Rigden said slowly. 'I thought maybe you could say if—y'know they put a notice on th'gate last week. If you went back then, you'd be taken on. Not if you didn't.' He stopped.

'Well?' Joe said.

'Y'see, I've got to tell Sally,' Frank repeated. He brought his face closer to the other man's. 'Isn't there nothing you can do for us?'

'You're not the only one.'

'Yi, I know.'

'Tell Sally I'll do the best I can.   Maybe not right away.
You go back to work in the morning and let me know what
happens—if you're turned off.'

'They meant it,' Frank said softly.

'Likely they did.'   The other man made a movement
with his arm, as if to clear his way.   'You'll have to trust
the union.'

Frank waited a moment longer.   He looked as if he had
not fully taken in what had happened.   Ducking his head,
he went out of the room without looking back.

William Gary received his news of the meeting between
the Prime Minister and the Trades Union leaders before it
was over.   His intelligence service was admirable.   At the
moment when the Prime Minister was saying quietly: '*You
know my record.   You know the object of my policy and I
think you may trust me . . .*'   William Gary turned from
his telephone and walked to the wide-open window of the
room.   It looked down into the courtyard of the flats, which
was terraced.   Three rows of young trees, like prisoners let
out for exercise, were spaced between the four towering walls
of the building.

He was faintly excited because his predictions had come
true almost to the minute.   He had felt certain for three
days that the Strike would end to-day, and he knew the
terms on which it would be brought to an end—that is,
on no terms at all.   He had never doubted that the superior
confidence of the men opposing the Labour leaders would
overpower men less used to giving orders.

At the same time he was relieved now.   A miracle was
always possible.   The leaders might have proved obstinate,
or vicious.   He took credit to himself for having known
that they would behave precisely as they did.   They are
what one would expect, he said to himself, scrupulous,
right-minded, servile to right authority.   Men who have
been lifted above their class.   He was far from thinking

that they would give him any but manageable trouble in the future.

He had imagined a world ordered down to the last screw and piece of a woman's hair-net by the intelligence of a very few men. One by one the many industries which are carried on in a modern state must be stripped of superfluous human beings and set down at a point of departure to run like young athletes against competitors from other nations. If it can be done, he thought, one should invent some scheme giving an excuse to number every man and woman in the country. It will be a beginning. He foresaw the day when it will be necessary to tell one man there is no more work for him, he must hold himself ready to do what he is told for the rest of his life, to be as little nuisance as possible; another that he must learn to fly; and another, a woman, that she must have two children, or three, or none. He was resolute that no one should starve, but no one must give any trouble, or destroy what did not belong to him.

He had a great deal to do before he could begin what he thought he could do better than anyone in the country. With impatience and anger he thought that the young trees shining in the courtyard would outlive him.

He turned from the window as his secretary told Louis Earlham he could go in, Mr. Gary expected him.

He considered Earlham with a smile, and detected, or thought he did, a new self-confidence in his looks. This awoke in him a jeering amusement. For the first time he felt a clear contempt for Earlham. It was not unkind; it was not even that he saw Louis betraying his faith or his class, men on whose pennies he had been lifted up. That was romanticism. Gary believed his own attitude to society to be the only realistic one. He believed sincerely that only anarchists and romantic fools talked of the brother-hood of man. There are men born to lead and men born to obey; all the trouble, confusion, and terror in the world springs from men's efforts to behave as if this were not so. In the moment a man of intelligence opens his eyes he can come by no other vision.

If anyone had said to him: ' You seduced Louis Earlham,' he could only have answered: ' No. I opened his eyes.'

No. What he felt at this moment was a new inhumanity towards the men who were the raw material of his plans. This man he liked was on the same step as miners, clerks, scientists, schoolmasters, and women of marriageable age.

' Well, my dear Louis,' he said, smiling, ' so the sheep have divided themselves from the goats, and the tame asses have cast out wild ones. It has happened no sooner than I expected, and it will give me the greatest pleasure to say I told you so.'

' Say it to——? '

' To those of my elderly colleagues who distrust Labour leaders.'

Earlham smiled rather palely. ' Don't trust us too far,' he replied. ' In this idiotic Strike . . . we have been working for reason to prevail. But don't—don't count on us to clear up after you for ever. If you can't put your affairs straight, we can't go on asking the workers to sacrifice themselves to pay your bills for you. . . . Your system is on trial, my dear fellow. . . . If it can be made to bear fruits of order, decency, and humanity, we shan't pull it about all our heads—no one wants a mess—we shall change it gradually. But if it can't——'

' You mean,' Gary said, laughing, ' that society is my business and educating the workers is yours. Have it your own way, Louis.'

Earlham meant nothing of the kind. He was jarred by his friend's manner. He felt an obscure loss of confidence, much like the discontent he felt when he made a weak speech in the House. He was wounded in his vanity, and in his pride, and through the hole made by this wound something more serious might have slipped away if he had

not instantly pressed his hand on it. If there is to be a
struggle of wills between us, he said, I am perfectly able
to hold my own—without raving about class war. He
rose to go.

' I told them to bring coffee in when you came,' Gary said.
' You're not in a hurry, are you ? '

' Yes. I must go. I haven't time for coffee, thanks.'

He felt irritated and uplifted when he went out. He
enjoyed Gary's coffee, it was much better than Rachel's,
but he felt glad he had not stayed to drink it.

When he reached the street he thought he had been a fool.
After all, I am in a unique position. I have made friends
with the man who will be as important as anyone in the
country. He and I stand for the two halves of the nation.
The nation is a body which walks on two legs—he stretched
his own to a longer stride—labour, and the directing mind.
Even the brain has two sides.

He was delighted with this notion of himself and William
Gary as one brain. Working in harmony we shall be the
salvation of England from the disorders that afflict other
nations. We complete each other, I keep him informed
and I learn from him. I was a damned fool not to drink
a cup of coffee. I could do with it.

He entered the Park and was walking towards the gates,
meaning to take a bus to his house. The air was soft—with
the warmth of spring. The earth at one side was thick with
tulips, now jaded. They still smelled of spring; so did
the earth itself, and even the dust. Brightness fell across the
path through the trees, and the water spouting from the
mouth of a dolphin was a jet of silver.

Earlham felt an exquisite lightness and relief. Yes,
all's well that ends well, he said to himself. A child
running down the path sent its hoop spinning against him
—he saved himself from falling over it, and this accident,
which at another time would have irritated him, made
him laugh at the startled child. Outside the gates he took

a taxi. He could afford it better now, since he was writing regularly for the *Daily Post* again, fortnightly articles for which he was paid more than his month's salary when he was on the staff of the paper.

He found Rachel in tears. This was such a rough shock to his mood that he spoke to her without kindness. 'What is the matter with you?' he asked irritably.

Renn had told her the news on the telephone less than five minutes since. Earlham was deeply vexed, seeing on her face a look he knew too well.

'He says they have made no safe conditions at all,' she said rapidly. 'The miners are still locked out, even other men may not be taken back—nothing has been won at all. The Strike has simply been stopped. Louis, is it true?' She spoke with a vehemence contradicted by her small delicate face. Her eyes blazed with reproach and anger, like those of a child, able to be angry without malice.

'Not in the sense David wants you to believe,' Louis said coldly. 'You can be sure they have got binding promises from the Government.'

'Do you know that?' Rachel insisted.

Her obstinacy angered him. 'Yes,' he said.

'But the miners are still out, *they* have not won,' Rachel said, in a dry and hurt voice. She seized his arm and shook it. 'Listen to me, listen, Louis. Surely the Strike was only begun to save them.'

'The miners' leaders are impossible,' Louis shouted. 'They could have made decent reasonable terms—they were offered decent terms. And if they choose to refuse them—is that a reason why the other unions should support them until they and the miners as well are bankrupt, and compelled to surrender? Tell me that.'

'But could it have gone on so long?' his wife murmured. 'If *we* had held out, surely *they* would have had to give in? How could things have been carried on, how could life be endurable, without the workers? You know you have always said——'

'I know that there would be an unholy mess if ignorant doctrinaire fools—I mean people like Renn—were able to influence the Labour movement. Fortunately they're not. And now,' he said ironically, 'will you let me finish my work before I go to the House? Unless you have other complaints.'

He went into the little room next their bedroom, where he did his work. There was nothing in it except his chair and the desk he had bought from a secondhand dealer. Rachel's father, who had been a carpenter until age knotted his fingers—it is surprising how many Jewish carpenters there are, and they are all socialists; Rachel took her faith from her father's lips—had covered two walls with shelves for his books.

He sat down and began his article for Cohen's paper. 'Thanks once more,' he wrote quickly, 'to the admirable spirit by which in this country both sides to a dispute are animated, the way has been opened to an honourable peace.' He was dissatisfied with the sentence and began turning it about. He was too shaken to write. He was ashamed of his spiteful anger with Rachel, and humiliated by his loss of self-control. What possessed me? he said to himself, frowning. I must still be tired.

He thought of going directly to Rachel, to ask her forgiveness, but a feeling of malice persisted. If she is unhappy, it serves her right, he thought coldly. At this moment, the telephone rang downstairs and he hurried to answer it. It was Henry Smith, speaking from Deptford. He spoke violently and abruptly.

'Yes, you, Earlham,' he said. 'I want you. Do you know that Stokes Chemical Works is refusing to take back some of its people, and offering the others less wages. What are you going to do about it, blast you?'

'It's first of all the business of the unions,' Earlham said

calmly. He despised the younger man as a blusterer. ' But
let me know the details and I'll take it up and do what I can.'

' Oh, I'll let you know,' Smith answered.

As Earlham turned from the telephone he could see Rachel
through the half-open door of the sitting-room. She was
leaning against the end of the couch, her hands folded. This
alone was remarkable, since she had always something
to do even when the baby was asleep and the little girl
sleeping after her dinner. Her face was paler than usual,
her eyes wide open: when she was unhappy her eyes
had that tragic and serious look seen in the eyes even
of young children born to old parents. Her mother was
almost fifty when Rachel, her only child, was born, and her
father fifty-eight. The day she was born Rachel's eyes
were open—she lay with them open for so long that the
women said she must be sleeping with open eyes and tried
to close the eyelids over that disconcerting look.

Earlham felt his heart aching with pity for her. He hurried
to her and took her in his arms. ' Forgive me, Rachel,' he
stammered. ' I don't know what came over me to talk to
you like that. I am a fool.'

' No, you are overworked,' she said simply.

Suddenly he was kneeling beside her, embracing her knees,
his head against her body. ' My little Rachel,' he repeated,
imploring her—but for what?

She put her hands on his head and stroked his hair, talking
to him in her gentle voice, until he felt soothed and ashamed
of his weakness. The sense of relief from a long and terrible
burden swept through him. He stood up. ' You've forgiven
me, haven't you ? ' He looked at her and noticed something
sorrowful and tired in her face. ' We'll talk to-night,' he
said eagerly. ' I'll explain everything to you.'

She smiled with a trustful and candid happiness. But
as he went upstairs to his work he felt a suspicion that
he would not convince her, and something, the least trace,
of his irritation with her returned. It disappeared when

he began to write. The feeling of relief possessed him again, and he found that he could write freely, almost gaily.

When Frank came to take his bicycle from the narrow passage leading to the Committee rooms he found both tyres flat. He decided to wheel it home, not wait here to mend it. At the moment it felt easier than to go back up the few stairs for water.

Coming out of the dark passage he felt the sunlight like a sheet of warm glass held in front of his face. He closed his eyes. The dull sense of disaster he felt turned to an active terror. If he had opened his eyes to find himself on the brink of a cliff he would have walked clean over it. He opened them on the familiar street, the shops with flies crawling behind the glass, the glare from the pavement. A child squatting in the gutter was intent on matching two torn pieces of paper.

He walked on with bent head. Words and fragmentary thoughts crossed his mind. 'Tell her.' 'One, two, three, yes, ee-e, it's a fair——' He saw the corner of the front room and the chest of drawers Sally had from her mother.

When he came in sight of the dock-gates he found a large crowd listening to a man speaking from a heap of rubbish against the wall. Nearer, he saw that the man was Grassart. He did not stay to hear him, not caring for the man's loud rasping voice, but he saw men he knew. They were like him, from the Stokes Works. They, and the rest of the crowd, were listening quietly. Perhaps they heard not only the speaker's wild flying words but the fear in their hearts.

As Frank drew level with the speaker half a dozen police-men who had been watching were joined by others. They began to clear the men off, pushing when a word was not obeyed. Frank stood still to watch. Throughout the past week the police had seemed indifferent, even friendly towards crowds listening to Strike speakers. That had changed.

A man flinging off the hand pressed on his back was seized and marched off. Men shouted. A stone struck the wall.

In a second, as it seemed to Frank, men were running towards him in twos and threes and the police were striking men on the ragged fringe of the crowd with their batons and dragging others away. He saw Grassart pulled down, his arm flung up to save his head. It was so startling, from the suddenness, that Frank himself began to run, pushing the bicycle, although he was well out of the way. He stopped at the end of the street, ashamed of running from nothing. He went on quickly. He was bewildered. His mind kept an image of a man's heavy body pushing into the crowd. They must have rare hard bodies, those chaps.

Sally was on her knees picking up the pieces of a broken plate the little girl had swept off the table. She looked up as he came in. 'You're home early,' she said at once, as if she knew.

'Yes,' he said. 'Strike's off.'

Sally stood up awkwardly, looking at him. She knew from his face. 'Is it won then?' she said slowly.

'Seems not.'

'Tell me what. Have the Government stopped it?'

Frank was washing his hands. He began to answer her question, but he was not sure what had happened. He was sure only that the Strike was over, as if it had never started: except that he had lost his job.

'I spoke to Joe,' he said.

There was a silence. He wondered what she was doing. When he turned round again, she was still standing, the pieces of the broken plate in her hand. She put them down when she noticed him and half smiled at him. 'We'll do somehow,' she said quietly.

He hung his head. He felt ashamed, as if he had done something wrong. What to do now, what, he thought. His hands seemed heavy as stones. He went and sat down by the window. His wife looked at him. She was thinking, almost without the words, that he was like the boy when he tore his new coat across. On the boy's face as he came in was the same look of helplessness and misery. Eh, but why? she thought: why must they? And for the first time it seemed to her wrong that a torn coat could fill a little boy with despair because he knew coats are hard to come by. She looked again at her husband. She wanted to speak to him and did not know what to say.

CHAPTER XXVII

Towards midday the doctor came in to look at Hervey. She was disquieted by her patient's apathy and the polite way in which Hervey listened, smiled, and said nothing. In her experience all was not well with a patient who had nothing to say about herself and did not ask questions about her operation. 'How do you feel?' she said a second time, briskly.

'Well, thank you,' Hervey answered. She did not think it worth while to add that when she moved the pain leaped in her body like a flame, licking at its walls. It would mend in time, she knew, and it seemed to her less important than the icy cold in her mind. Useless to speak of that to the other woman, even if she were able to find words for it.

She had forgotten neither the agony of her loneliness nor the knowledge forced on her of its everlasting unimportance. It stood between her and her own body. Below all that which with fear she remembered, she was aware of much else, of infinitely more, escaping her when she tried to grasp it. It was as though leaning into deep water she brushed the fin of some great fish as the creature plunged away from sight and the eye of the sun.

The one question she would have asked the doctor, if she had thought it any use, was whether a woman whose womb has been taken from her can still write books. She was convinced, having no respect for doctors, that the other woman did not know the answer, or would answer untruthfully. She held her tongue.

Later, the nurse brought in a letter, and told her joyfully that the Strike was over. Always anxious not to offend

anyone, Hervey pretended she found the news exciting.
She opened the letter when she was alone. It was from
T. S. Heywood, telling her he knew from the surgeon that
she was safely out of it.

'I won't pretend I am not very glad for myself, too.
I have no friend but you to whom I can talk openly. You
know that I love you better than any other living person,
including that vain soul, T. S. Heywood.'

She folded the letter into the copy of *La Chartreuse de
Parme* which she was forbidden to read yet.

For a moment she tried to think that Nicholas would
begin his work for Cohen at once now that the Strike was
over. When he came she must warn him not to vex
Cohen by arguing with him. It will be better to agree
at first and bring his own ways in later, when Cohen is
paying less attention to the business. She wearied of the
thought at once and let it go. She could not feel that there
was any reality at all in the project. I learned something
about reality yesterday, she thought obscurely; I ought now
to seek it everywhere.

Her mind slipped easily and comfortably into the past.
It clung to the image of her mother. At once the living
world of her childhood sprang round her, closing her between
its vivid skies and secure earth as deeply and steadily as if
she were present in it. And as though it had waited
until this moment to offer its secrets to her she saw that
everything in it, the field blazing with dog-daisies, the
hundred and ninety-nine steps to St. Mary's church on the
cliff, the hills folding in the upper harbour, the leaping curve
of the coast and the moors inland, the white burning clouds
tumbling like dolphins in the depths of the sky, all those daily
miracles with which she had lived as equals, were given to
her by her mother, through whose mind and blue staring
eyes she saw them. In everything she did in those days
she was in part obeying Sylvia Russell's hard will and jealous
masterful energy. She knew how often now her voice echoed

hers. She repeated Sylvia Russell's gestures and strove to remember particular words she used, so that as little as possible should be lost when she was no longer there to speak for herself.

All this ferment of thought was taking place below the surface of her mind, like a seed bursting and sending up its folded sheath of leaf and bud in the darkness. A heavy footstep outside her room made her start, the pain licked her with its rough tongue. She laid her hand on it lightly, saying to herself, aloud: ' *I* am the mother.'

The words had nothing to do with her pain; they were part of a scene, a morning, she remembered instantly: and smiled.

One morning when Richard was a baby, she was wheeling him home from the shops. He began to cry because he was hungry. It was after the time for his meal (in those War days one never knew how long one might have to wait in the shops). It was not more than a few minutes after, but she felt conscience-stricken, as if it were her fault, and pushed the heavy carriage as quickly as she could. Her arms ached. She felt her hat slip to one side and did not wait to put it right. Then, as they were within sight of the house, a middle-aged lady stepped in front of her and said sternly: ' You have no right to keep that baby out crying in that way. Take him home at once to your mother, and tell her not to send you out with him until he is asleep.' Hervey halted to stare at her. Her treacherous hat seized its chance to slip over one ear and she snatched it off and laid it on Richard's blanket: he stopped crying at once and tore out its solitary flower. ' *I* am the mother,' she said stiffly.

He is growing very quickly, she murmured, wondering whether they had told him she could not come yet because she had been ill and was getting better. She had asked them to tell him at once. She was afraid someone in the town would speak to him about her before he knew.

Children are so often frightened or humiliated in this way. Nothing matters if he can have a happy life, she thought. Her own life mattered less than the rest. Just as in those early years the way she lived was dictated by Richard's needs, and the time she could think of as her own was not more than an hour in the evening (when she was too tired to think of anything but sleep), so now she made no plans for the future which had not their centre in him. Often she hid from others the only irrevocable part of some plan. It was like a treaty in which the important promises and concessions are written into the secret clauses.

You could say that if her mother were the stern dictator of her unconscious life, her son, and what she demanded on his behalf from life, dictated all that part of it which was fully awake and conscious. This time with her will.

Nicholas came, and stayed with her ten minutes. She had nothing to say to him, and reproached herself for not having prepared a few remarks. He drew his chair close to the bed and told her in a low voice that he had never loved anyone as he loved her; he would take her away—to Vienna, any of the places she was longing with her heart to visit—the first day she was strong enough. You have forgotten our employer, she thought ironically. But she was pleased he had been anxious. It was no little matter that her second husband did not feel it below his dignity to worry about her when she was ill.

When he had gone, she thought she had wasted the minutes when he was with her. She had not even told him that she had been waiting for him to come. It was not true—but that was no reason for not saying it.

But a change was taking place in her. When the nurse came in she begged her to open the window widely for a moment, and since this was the first thing she had asked the nurse obeyed.

The sun was already so low that the light pierced directly through the leaves of the trees. They were as if cut in jade. Breathing on them lightly, the wind shook the branch as though it were a jet of water. Ah, thanks for that, Hervey said. It was astonishingly beautiful. Her life moved in her, so obscurely that she found herself thinking again of Danesacre and of herself as a child finding a mysterious satisfaction in a certain one of its narrow ancient streets. She felt the deep springs of her life, deeper than her days in Danesacre, but there first welling into the light of day and the clear air. Her mind sank down, down, until she was completely at peace. My dear love, she thought drowsily, but was she speaking of her husband or of the one place in the world in which she was not a stranger? Something rejoiced in her that she was still alive, able to feel pain. She had wanted to live. She insisted on living.

Death shall have nothing of me but my bones, she said to herself, with an exultance which followed her into sleep, now that she was not afraid to sleep. An exultance— unbidden but welcomed, the sudden answer of her blind patience to the challenge of fear and weakness. It answered as instinctively as a soldier, a mercenary no doubt, but an English one. She was no one, obscure, taught by pain. In identifying herself with the common earth of Danesacre she was not far out of her rights.

Also of interest

THE LOVE CHILD
by Edith Olivier
New Introduction by Hermione Lee

At thirty-two, her mother dead, Agatha Bodenham finds herself quite alone. She summons back to life the only friend she ever knew, Clarissa, the dream companion of her childhood. At first Clarissa comes by night, and then by day, gathering substance in the warmth of Agatha's obsessive love until it seems that others too can see her. See, but not touch, for Agatha has made her love child for herself. No man may approach this creature of perfect beauty, and if he does, she who summoned her can spirit her away...

Edith Olivier (1879?-1948) was one of the youngest of a clergyman's family of ten children. Despite early ambitions to become an actress, she led a conventional life within twenty miles of her childhood home, the Rectory at Wilton, Wiltshire. But she wrote five highly original novels as well as works of non-fiction, and her 'circle' included Rex Whistler (who illustrated her books), David Cecil, Siegfried Sassoon and Osbert Sitwell. *The Love Child* (1927) was her first novel, acknowledged as a minor masterpiece: a perfectly imagined fable and a moving and perceptive portrayal of unfulfilled maternal love.

"This is wonderful..." — *Cecil Beaton*

"*The Love Child* seems to me to stand in a category of its own creating...the image it leaves is that of a tranquil star" — *Anne Douglas Sedgwick*

"Flawless — the best 'first' book I have ever read...perfect" — *Sir Henry Newbolt*

"A masterpiece of its kind" — *Lord David Cecil*

THE SHUTTER OF SNOW

by Emily Holmes Coleman
New Introduction by Carmen Callil and Mary Siepmann

After the birth of her child Marthe Gail spends two months in an insane asylum with the fixed idea that she is God. Marthe, something between Ophelia, Emily Dickinson and Lucille Ball, transports us into that strange country of terror and ecstasy we call madness. In this twilit country the doctors, nurses, the other inmates and the mad vision of her insane mind are revealed with piercing insight and with immense verbal facility.

Emily Coleman (1899-1974) was born in California and, like Marthe, went mad after the birth of her son in 1924. Witty, eccentric and ebullient, she lived in Paris in the 1920s as one of the *transition* writers, close friend of Peggy Guggenheim and Djuna Barnes (who said Emily would be marvellous company slightly stunned). In the 1930s she lived in London (in the French, the Wheatsheaf, the Fitzroy), where her friends numbered Dylan Thomas, T.S. Eliot, Humphrey Jennings and George Barker. Emily Coleman wrote poetry throughout her life — and this one beautiful, poignant novel (first published in 1930), which though constantly misunderstood, has always had a passionate body of admirers — Edwin Muir, David Gascoyne and Antonia White to name a few.

"A very striking triumph of imagination and technique... The book is not only quite unique; it is also a work of genuine literary inspiration" — *Edwin Muir*

"A work which has stirred me deeply...compelling" — *Harold Nicolson*

"An extraordinary, visionary book, written out of those edges where madness and poetry meet" — *Fay Weldon*

If you would like to know more about Virago books, write to us at 41 William IV Street, London WC2N 4DB for a full catalogue.

Please send a stamped addressed envelope

VIRAGO
Advisory Group

Andrea Adam	Zoë Fairbairns
Carol Adams	Carolyn Faulder
Sally Alexander	Germaine Greer
Rosalyn Baxandall (USA)	Jane Gregory
Anita Bennett	Suzanne Lowry
Liz Calder	Jean McCrindle
Beatrix Campbell	Cathy Porter
Angela Carter	Alison Rimmer
Mary Chamberlain	Elaine Showalter (USA)
Anna Coote	Spare Rib Collective
Jane Cousins	Mary Stott
Jill Craigie	Rosalie Swedlin
Anna Davin	Margaret Walters
Rosalind Delmar	Elizabeth Wilson
Christine Downer (Australia)	Barbara Wynn

Book Tokens

Give them
the pleasure of choosing
Book Tokens can be bought
and exchanged at most
bookshops